To the captive and cruelly treated people of Syria—
especially those in Damascus—yearning to be free.

AUTHOR'S NOTE

Tehran, Iran, is one and a half hours ahead of Jerusalem and
eight and a half hours ahead of New York and Washington, D.C.

CAST OF CHARACTERS

AMERICANS

David Shirazi (aka Reza Tabrizi)—field officer, Central Intelligence
Agency

Marseille Harper—schoolteacher; childhood friend of David Shirazi

Jack Zalinsky—senior operative, Central Intelligence Agency

Eva Fischer—field officer/analyst, Central Intelligence Agency/National
Security Agency

Roger Allen—director, Central Intelligence Agency

Tom Murray—deputy director for operations, Central Intelligence
Agency

William Jackson—president of the United States

Daniel Montgomery—U.S. ambassador to Israel

Marco Torres—commander, CIA paramilitary unit

Nick Crenshaw—field agent, CIA paramilitary unit

Steve Fox—field agent, CIA paramilitary unit

Matt Mays—field agent, CIA paramilitary unit

Dr. Mohammad Shirazi—cardiologist, father of David Shirazi

Chris and Lexi Vandermark—newlyweds; college friends of Marseille
Harper

IRANIANS

Dr. Alireza Birjandi—preeminent scholar of Shia Islamic eschatology

Najjar Malik—former physicist, Atomic Energy Organization of Iran;
defected to the U.S.

Ayatollah Hamid Hosseini—Supreme Leader

Ahmed Darazi—president of Iran

Mohsen Jazini—commander, Iranian Revolutionary Guard Corps; aide
to the Twelfth Imam

Dr. Jalal Zandi—nuclear physicist

Javad Nouri—personal aide to Ayatollah Hosseini and the Twelfth
Imam

Ali Faridzadeh—minister of defense

Ibrahim Asgari—commander of VEVAK, secret police

Daryush Rashidi—CEO, Iran Telecom; aide to the Twelfth Imam

Abdol Esfahani—deputy director, Iran Telecom; aide to the Twelfth Imam

ISRAELIS

Asher Naphtali—prime minister of Israel

Levi Shimon—defense minister

Zvi Dayan—director, Mossad

Gal Rinat—field operative, Mossad

Tolik Shalev—field operative, Mossad

OTHERS

Muhammad Ibn Hasan Ibn Ali—the Twelfth Imam

Iskander Farooq—president of Pakistan

Gamal Mustafa—president of Syria

General Youssef Hamdi—air marshal, Syrian Air Force

JOEL C.
ROSENBERG

TYNDALE HOUSE PUBLISHERS, INC., CAROL STREAM, ILLINOIS

DAMASCUS
COUNT
DOWN

Visit Tyndale online at www.tyndale.com.

Visit Joel C. Rosenberg's website at www.joelrosenberg.com.

TYNDALE and Tyndale's quill logo are registered trademarks of Tyndale House Publishers, Inc.

Damascus Countdown

Designed by Dean H. Renninger

Library of Congress Cataloging-in-Publication Data

Rosenberg, Joel C., date.
  Damascus Countdown / Joel C. Rosenberg.
    pages cm
  ISBN 978-1-4143-1970-4 (hc)
1. Intelligence officers—United States—Fiction. 2. Nuclear warfare—Prevention—Fiction.
3. International relations—Fiction. 4. Middle East—Fiction. 5. Christian fiction. 6. Suspense
fiction. I. Title.
  PS3618.O832D36 2013
  813'.6—dc23   2012040475

978-1-4143-1971-1   (sc)
978-1-4143-8072-8   (International Trade Paper Edition)

Printed in the United States of America

19 18 17 16
 8   7   6   5   4   3

★ ★ ★ ★ ★

THURSDAY
MARCH 10

PREFACE

QOM, IRAN

David Shirazi glanced at his watch. He took a deep breath and tried to steady his nerves. The plan required split-second timing. There could be no changes. No surprises. Time was short. The stakes were high. And there was no backing out now. But there was one thing he had to accept: in three minutes, he'd quite possibly be dead.

David ordered his cab driver to pull up in front of the famed Jamkaran Mosque. He paid the driver but asked him to pull over and wait. He had a package to deliver, he told the man, but it would only take a moment, and he'd be right back.

David carefully scanned the crowd. He did not yet see his contact, but he had no doubt the man would show. In the meantime, it was hard not to marvel at the structure, the mammoth turquoise dome of the mosque in the center, flanked by two smaller green domes and two exquisitely painted minarets. Built on a site revered since the tenth century, when a Shia cleric of the time, Sheikh Hassan Ibn Muthlih Jamkarani, was supposedly visited by the Twelfth Imam, it had once been farmland. Now it was one of the most visited religious destinations in all of Iran.

Over the last few years, Iran's Supreme Ayatollah and president—both of whom were devout "Twelvers," passionate disciples of the so-called Islamic messiah—had funneled millions of dollars to renovate the mosque and its facilities and build beautiful new multilane highways from the mosque to Qom and Tehran. Both leaders visited regularly, and the mosque had become the subject of myriad books, television programs, and documentary films. After the recent emergence of the Twelfth Imam on the planet and the rumor that a little girl mute from birth had been healed by the Mahdi after visiting the mosque, the crowds continued to build.

David paced back and forth in front of the main gate leading into the sacred complex. He felt the satellite phone in his pocket vibrating. He knew it was the Global Operations Center. He knew his superiors at CIA headquarters in Langley, Virginia, were watching everything that was happening via a Predator drone hovering two miles or so above his head. But he didn't dare take the call. Not here. Not now. Whatever they had to say, it was too late. He didn't want to do anything that might spook the man he had come to meet. So he ignored the vibrating and glanced again at his watch. He was right on time. So where was Javad Nouri?

He watched as buses filled with Shia pilgrims pulled in, dropped off their passengers and guides, and then circled around to the main parking lot, while other buses pulled up and loaded their passengers to head home. He estimated that there were a couple hundred people milling about out front, either coming or going. There were a few uniformed police officers around, but everything seemed quiet and orderly. Nouri, a close and trusted aide to the Twelfth Imam, was a shrewd man. He had chosen well. Any disturbance here would have scores of witnesses, and David worried about what might happen to the innocent bystanders.

David felt a tap on his shoulder. He turned around, and there was Javad Nouri, surrounded by a half-dozen plainclothes bodyguards.

"Mr. Tabrizi, good to see you again," Javad Nouri said, referring to David by the only name the Iranian knew for him.

"Mr. Nouri, you as well."

"I trust you had no trouble getting here."

"Not at all," David said.

"Have you ever been here before?" Nouri asked.

It seemed like an odd question, given the moment.

"Actually, I'm ashamed to say I have not."

"Someday I will have to give you a tour."

"I would like that very much."

Nouri looked at the box in David's hands. "Is that the package we were expecting?"

"It is," David said, "but we have a problem."

"What is that?"

David glanced around. He noticed there were several more body-guards taking up positions in a perimeter around them. There was also a large white SUV waiting by the curb with a guard holding the back door open. Ahead of it was another SUV, presumably serving as the lead security car. Behind it was a third, completing the package.

"Most of the phones are damaged and unusable," David explained, handing the mangled box to the Mahdi's aide. "Something must have happened in the shipping."

Nouri cursed, and his expression darkened. "We *need* these."

"I know," David replied.

"Now what are we going to do?"

"Look, I can go back to Munich and get more. It's what I wanted to do in the first place. But—"

"But Esfahani told you not to leave."

"Well, I—"

"I know, I know. Allah help me. Esfahani is a fool. If he weren't the nephew of Mohsen Jazini, he wouldn't be involved at all."

"What do you want me to do, Mr. Nouri?" David asked. "That's all that matters, what you and the Promised One want. Please know that I will do anything to serve."

The words had just fallen from his lips when David heard brakes screech behind him. Then everything seemed to go into slow motion. The plan his team had created began to unfold, and David could only hope it went as they anticipated. He heard the crack of a sniper rifle. One of Nouri's bodyguards went down. *Crack, crack.* Two more of Nouri's men went down. Then Nouri himself took a bullet in the right shoulder. He began to stagger. Blood was everywhere. David threw himself on Nouri to protect him as the gunfire intensified and more bodyguards were hit and collapsed to the ground.

David turned to look toward the shooters. He could see rows of buses. He saw taxis. He saw people running and screaming. Then his eyes fixed on a white van driving past. The side door was open. He could see flashes of gunfire pouring out of three muzzles inside, and he knew his teammates were the ones pulling the triggers.

An Iranian police officer—a guard assigned to the mosque—pulled out his revolver and began returning fire. Two of Nouri's plainclothes agents on the periphery raised submachine guns and fired at the van as it sped away, weaving in and out of traffic and disappearing around the bend.

Now it was time for phase two, designed to slow down anyone from chasing after his men.

David anticipated the blast as a car bomb detonated just a hundred yards from them. He instinctively ducked down. He shielded his eyes and did his best to cover Nouri's body from the shards of glass and molten metal that were coming down on top of them. The air was filled with the smell of burning and panic. As the thick, black smoke began to clear a bit, David could see flames shooting from what was left of the lead car in Nouri's security package.

All around him, people were crying and bleeding and yelling for help. David now turned to Nouri. He could see the open wound in the man's upper arm, but after a fast check he didn't find any other bullet holes. He pulled out a handkerchief and applied pressure. Then he pulled off his belt and created a tourniquet to stanch the bleeding.

"Javad, look at me," David said gently. "It's going to be okay. Just keep your eyes on me. I'm going to pray for you."

Nouri flickered to life for a moment and mouthed the words *Thank you.* Then his eyes closed again, and David called out for someone to help them.

Suddenly four fighter jets roared over the mosque. They were flying incredibly fast and low, and the sound was deafening. But these were not aging Iranian F-4 Phantoms, bought by the Shah from the U.S. before the Revolution. Nor were they Russian-built MiG-29s or any other jet in the Iranian arsenal. These were gleaming new F-16s, loaded with munitions and extra fuel tanks. David knew full well President Jackson hadn't sent them. These weren't American fighters. Which could only mean one thing: the Israelis were here. Prime Minister Naphtali had really done it. He had ordered a massive preemptive strike. The war everyone in the region had feared had begun.

1

David knew one of Iran's largest nuclear facilities—the uranium enrichment plant at Fordow—was just a few miles away over the ridge, and sure enough, a split second later, he heard the deafening roar of explosions, one after another in rapid succession. He turned and saw enormous balls of fire and plumes of smoke rising into the sky and the four Israeli jets disappearing into the clouds.

But then another strike package came swooping down behind them. Four more Israeli fighters—emblazoned with the blue Star of David on their wings—descended like lightning. He assumed their mission, too, was to attack the facility down the road. But David watched in horror as one of the jets first fired an air-to-ground missile at the heart of the mosque behind him. They were sending a message to the Twelfth Imam and to all his followers. But they were about to destroy David's plan.

His instinct was to get up and run for cover, but it was too late, and he had to do everything possible to protect Javad Nouri. That was his mission. Under no circumstances could he allow Nouri to die. He absolutely had to deliver the aide back to the Mahdi wounded but alive and indebted to David. It was, he believed, the only chance to gain the Mahdi's trust and the only shred of a chance he had to be invited into the inner circle. Then again, did any of that matter now? The war he had been sent to prevent was under way. The carnage on both sides was going to be incalculable. The entire region was about to go up in flames. What was left for him to do?

Suddenly the ground convulsed as a series of explosions ripped through the complex. The minarets began to totter. People were screaming again, running in all directions as the first tower came crashing down and the second followed. David covered his head and made sure Nouri was covered too. Then, as the smoke began to clear, he turned and surveyed the carnage. Bodies were sprawled everywhere. Some were dead. Others were severely wounded. David turned Nouri over. He was covered in blood. His eyes were dilated, but he was breathing. He was still alive.

Guns drawn, three injured bodyguards soon rushed to David's side. With his help, they carefully picked up Nouri and carried him to the white SUV, severely damaged by the car bombing nearby but still intact and still running. Together, they laid Nouri down on the backseat. One security man climbed in the back with him. Another climbed into one of the middle seats. The third shut and locked the side door, then got in the front passenger seat.

"Wait, wait; you forgot these," David yelled just before the guard closed the door. He grabbed the box of satellite phones and gave them to the guard. "The Mahdi wanted these. They don't all work. But some of them do."

Then he pulled out a pen and quickly wrote his mobile number on the box. "Have the Mahdi's people call me and tell me how Javad is. And tell me if there's anything I can do for the Mahdi himself."

The guard thanked David and shook his hand vigorously. Then he shut the door, and what was left of the motorcade raced off.

David stood there alone as the ground shook again. More Israeli jets were swooping down from the heavens. They were firing more missiles and dropping more bombs on targets just over the mountains. For a moment, David couldn't move. He stared at the billows of smoke rising from the air strikes over the horizon and tried to calculate his next move.

He looked to the street, searching for the taxi he'd asked to wait. It was nowhere to be seen, but he could hardly blame the driver. People were panicked from the gunfire, the car bombing, and the air strikes. They were fleeing as rapidly as they could in every direction. David knew he had to get away as well. He couldn't afford to be caught by the police and dragged in for questioning. He had a mission. He had a plan. He had a team that was counting on him. He knew he had to stay focused, yet he grieved for those wounded around him. So he turned and rushed to the side of one severely wounded guard who was slipping into unconsciousness. Hearing sirens approaching from every direction, David took off his jacket and used it to put pressure on the man's bleeding leg. As he did, he silently prayed over the man, asking the Lord to comfort and heal him.

Ambulances began arriving on the scene. Paramedics were soon rushing to the wounded to triage them and get the most critical cases to the nearest hospitals. Amid the chaos and confusion, David saw his opportunity. He took a pistol off the wounded bodyguard and slipped it into his pocket. Then he moved to another of the downed guards. The man seemed to be staring up at the sky. His mouth was open. But when David checked for a pulse, he found none. David closed the man's eyes, then quickly lifted a spare magazine and took the guard's two-way radio.

Firefighters were now arriving to battle multiple blazes. More police officers were pulling up as well. They began to secure the crime scene and interview what few witnesses had not fled the scene quickly enough. David tried to use the commotion as cover. He was determined not to be questioned, much less exposed. But then he heard someone shouting behind him. David turned and saw an elderly cleric, blood splattered all over his robes, pointing at him.

"Talk to that man!" the cleric said to a police officer. "He was here when all the shooting started. And I think he just took something off that dead body."

The policeman looked directly at David and ordered him to stop. David didn't dare. With a surge of adrenaline, he pivoted hard and began sprinting into the blazing wreckage of the mosque. The officer shouted again for him to halt and began running after him, blowing a whistle and calling other officers to join the pursuit.

2

Everywhere David looked through the thick, black, acrid smoke, he saw a labyrinth of ruins of a once-glorious mosque and flames shooting twenty and thirty feet in the air. Racing through the maze—the heat already unbearable and his shirt almost instantly drenched in sweat—David searched frantically for daylight and fresh, cool air. He knew there was more parking on the other side of the compound. His only chance of escape was getting out of this firestorm, finding a car, and somehow hot-wiring it before he was gunned down or captured by the Iranian police.

The farther he ran into the cooking ruins, the more fearful he became of running into a cul-de-sac of sorts and finding himself surrounded, his exit route cut off by men with guns. The roar of the crackling, leaping flames was nearly deafening, and soon he could barely hear the shouts and the whistles, but he had no doubt they were hot on his heels and closing fast.

He turned right down one alley and came to a fork. He said a quick prayer and took the lane to the left. As he ran, he pulled the pistol out of his pocket and made sure it was loaded. He looked up just in time to see a gigantic pillar ahead of him crumble at its base and then collapse across his escape route. Had it happened a second later, David knew he would have been crushed. Had it happened two seconds later, he would likely have been safe, the pillar blocking his pursuers' path. As it was, he had no choice but to turn around and head back to the fork.

David raised the pistol in front of him and quickly retraced his steps. As he neared the fork, he could see two figures racing toward him through the smoke. He heard something whiz by his head, followed a split second later by the sound of a gunshot. Diving to the ground, he rolled once, took aim, and fired twice. Both men fell in succession, but David had to assume more were right behind them. He bolted down the other path, had to duck under several flaming beams, but soon found himself clearing the mosque compound and reaching the rear parking lot.

The scene before him was absolute mayhem. Anyone who had a car was in it, and they were all stuck in a massive traffic jam, trying desperately to get away from the mosque and onto the main highways back to Qom or Tehran. For the most part, the only vehicles closest to him were fire trucks and ambulances. David could see a few police cars with their flashing lights near the exit, and several uniformed officers trying to direct traffic and establish some sense of order. It all seemed futile, but he was glad the police anywhere near him at the moment were too busy to pay him any mind.

Just then David spotted two police motorcycles coming around the bend about five or six hundred yards to the south. He pulled back and crouched behind a pile of rubble, hoping the billowing smoke had obscured his movements. For now, it seemed to have. The motorcycle cops approached rapidly, then slowed and patrolled up and down the parking lot. David was certain they were looking for him, and then—as if they had just received a report on their radios—they both stopped, dismounted, drew their weapons, and ran around the far end of the compound. David grabbed the two-way radio he had lifted off the guard near the front gate. He turned it on low and put it close to his ear. As it crackled to life, he could hear someone shouting that the suspect was last seen moving along the west side of the complex. David had no idea who that might be, but it wasn't him. He was on the east side, and he seized the moment, certain the confusion on the part of the police was temporary at best.

He made a dash for the motorcycles. Neither was running, and neither officer had left his keys in the ignition. But David picked the nearest one and quickly went to work. He pulled out his pocketknife, smashed open the odometer, yanked some wires behind the dials, and clipped off a six-inch piece with one quick movement. Then he kicked the bike over and rapidly stripped the insulation off both ends of the wire. Putting away the knife, he moved to the second bike and quickly found the bundle of three colored wires coming out of the ignition. He followed those to the back of the bike until he found where they ended in a small plastic connector plugged into another set of wires. Glancing from side to side and still seeing no one near him, he unplugged the connector, took the piece of wire from the first bike in his hand, bent it into a U shape, and stuck it into both slots of the connector. He had to fiddle with it a few times to get it right, but after several tense seconds he heard the bike click on. He checked the headlight. It was shining. So he jumped on the bike and hit the ignition button on the throttle. The cycle roared to life.

At that moment, David saw the two officers coming back around the far side of the compound toward the parking lot. Stunned at first at seeing someone stealing a police motorcycle, both officers drew their weapons and began to fire. David pulled his pistol and returned fire, sending both men scrambling for cover. Then he turned and fired two shots at the toppled bike's gas tank. The second shot was a direct hit, and as soon as he saw the fuel spurting out, he fired again, creating a spark. The vapors ignited, and the tank exploded, sending pieces of the cycle flying in all directions.

David now raced toward the exit. Weaving through the snarled mass of cars and vans and buses trying to leave the mosque grounds slowed him down a bit, but he soon cleared all that and got off the local roads he feared would be clogged with cops. He found an on-ramp to Highway 7 and took it. Soon he was headed north from Qom to Tehran, on the open road and doing ninety. At the moment, almost no vehicles were on this particular stretch of road except an occasional convoy of army vehicles. Yet no one seemed to notice him or care. He had no helmet. He was certain the two officers had already radioed for backup. He fully expected a roadblock waiting for him around every bend. But right now he was alive and free and racing back to the CIA's safe house in Karaj, a city northwest of Tehran, where he had told his team to reconverge.

Just then David saw a pair of Israeli F-15E Strike Eagles streaking across the horizon ahead of him. Flying at about ten thousand feet, they banked left and made an arc around the mountains to his left. Suddenly the sky erupted in fire from antiaircraft artillery batteries hidden behind a small berm half a klick up the road. David was transfixed as he watched the Israeli jets bob and weave and roll through the triple-A fire, all the while trying feverishly to gain altitude. He cheered as one of the Strike Eagles pulled back and shot nearly straight up into the air like a space shuttle headed for the stratosphere. But as his wingman tried the same maneuver, David saw some of the tracer fire clip the tail of the second Israeli jet. Smoke began to pour out of the plane, and it was no longer climbing. In fact, David could see that one of the jet's engines was on fire. The plane began spinning wildly out of control and hurtling back toward the earth. David couldn't imagine how the Israelis were going to survive. They were only a few thousand feet off the deck and coming down fast and hard.

He watched as the canopy exploded off the top of the jet and both the pilot and his weapons officer ejected. Two parachutes deployed almost instantly, moments before the F-15 smashed to the ground in a fireball that would have been dazzling if it had not been so terrifying. David's gratitude that the pilots had ejected in time quickly evaporated as he realized what would be done to the men if they were caught by the Iranians. Without taking the time to think it through, he took the next exit ramp off Highway 7 and hightailed it to a spot in the desert just outside the Shokohie Industrial Zone, where he suspected both men would soon be landing.

David made a wide berth around the factories, warehouses, and restaurants, lest he run into any local law enforcement. He sped along a series of side streets and then went off-road. To his left, he could both see and smell the burning fuselage of the Strike Eagle, and after a few more miles, he came upon the first parachute and got off the motorcycle. He called out in English, assuring the downed Israeli that he was an American, not an Iranian, but he got no response. He called out again several times, but there was still no reply. Was this guy badly wounded from the ejection or the landing? Or was he lying low, planning an ambush when David got close?

David thought about drawing his pistol but decided against it. Instead, he raised both arms above his head and kept calling out in English. He spotted a leg sticking out from under the chute. Cautiously he approached, still shouting in English that he was an American coming in peace. By the time he finally got to the Israeli's side and pulled the chute off his face, however, it was clear that he was dead. Indeed, the body was badly burned, the face nearly unrecognizable. The pungent stench of the charred body was revolting, but David forced himself to check the man for identification or papers of any kind. He found nothing. Anything the man might have carried had been burned away.

David ran back to the bike and continued driving—more slowly this time—in search of the other parachute. It took several minutes, but he finally found it. He parked the bike near several large boulders, turned off the engine, removed the piece of wire, and put it in his pocket; then he walked carefully toward the chute, once again repeatedly calling out in English. But when he got to the chute, there was no one to be found. He looked behind several rock outcroppings but still found no one.

The satphone in David's pocket began vibrating again. This time he pulled out the phone and took the call.

"What in the world are you doing?" asked the voice at the other end.

It was a voice David knew all too well—that of Jack Zalinsky, his Agency handler.

"Trying to save the life of an Israeli fighter pilot," David replied. "You got a problem with that?"

"That's not your mission," Zalinsky said.

"You want the Iranians to capture him?" David asked. "You know what they'll do to him?"

"What do you think they'll do to you if they catch you?" Zalinsky pushed back. "What do you think the Mahdi will do when the Revolutionary Guards bring him the battered, beaten, broken, half-dead body of the CIA's most valuable undercover operative? There's already an Iranian special forces unit approaching from the south. And a helicopter just lifted off from the IRGC air base south of Qom, filled with heavily armed commandos. Now get on that bike and get out of there before you get yourself captured. That's an order."

David was about to argue, but he knew Zalinsky was right. He hung up the phone and ran back to the motorcycle and was about to hot-wire it again when he was coldcocked by someone who jumped him from behind.

His vision blurred, and he abruptly found himself on his back, staring up at a hazy figure standing over him and pointing a 9mm pistol at David's head.

"Who are you?" the man asked in perfect Farsi.

"What happened?" David asked, his vision still blurry but coming back.

"Don't move or I'll blow your head off," the man said.

As his head began to clear, David could see that the man was, in fact, the Strike Eagle pilot for whom he'd been looking.

"I'm not Iranian," he replied in English. "I'm an American. I'm here to get you out of harm's way."

The Israeli was clearly startled by hearing English, but he wasn't buying any of it.

"You're driving a police motorcycle."

"I stole it," David said. "Do I look like a cop?"

"You were carrying a police radio and a pistol specially made for the Iranian police," the Israeli retorted. "And why are you carrying a satphone?"

"Because I'm an American," David said again. "Look, we don't have much time. There's a special forces unit approaching from the south, and there's a helicopter coming up from Qom packed with Revolutionary Guards. I can get you out of here, get you to a safe house and out of the country. But we've got to move now."

"I don't believe you," said the Israeli.

"I don't care," David said. "It's true. And if we don't move now, we're both going to die a very painful, very gruesome death."

David's heart was racing. It was clear the Israeli still didn't believe him. And why should he? But they really were out of time.

"Fine," said the pilot. "Have it your way."

He pulled back the pistol's hammer and was about to fire when he instead collapsed to the ground as a gunshot rang out from somewhere to David's left. The pilot had been shot in the head, no doubt by a sniper hidden in the rocks several hundred yards to the west. That, David figured, was where he would be if the situation were reversed. He grabbed the pistol that had fallen from the Israeli's hands and ducked behind a boulder as two more shots rang out.

David heard the roar of a helicopter coming up over the ridge. As he tried to squeeze himself farther behind the boulder, he saw the chopper rise into view. His heart was pounding. His hands were shaking. He looked everywhere, but there was nowhere to hide.

The chopper stopped climbing and went into a stabilizing hover. He watched as the side door opened and one of the commandos on board fed .50-caliber rounds into the side-mounted rotary cannon. David raised his pistol and fired every shot in the magazine. None of them hit its mark. The chopper was just far enough away. Now the commando aimed the Gatling-style gun at David's head and smiled.

But then David heard a high-pitched whistle coming from the west, and as he watched, the chopper exploded and fell from the sky. David, waiting to meet his Maker, couldn't believe his eyes. What had just happened?

His question was answered when an Israeli Strike Eagle roared past and climbed for the stratosphere. He had avenged his wingman, and now he was gone. David watched the glow of the F-15E's afterburners, then forced himself back to the moment. He had no idea where the sniper team was, but he prayed they were as distracted by the missile strike and the retreating fighter jet as he was.

This was his only chance. He wasn't getting another. David scrambled to the motorcycle, hot-wired it again, then jumped on and hit the gas. The whole thing took less than ten seconds, and he was gone.

He hadn't staved off the war. He hadn't saved either Israeli airman. But miraculously, he hadn't been captured or killed either, and for right now, that was more than enough.

★ ★ ★ ★ ★

SUNDAY
MARCH 13

3

Security was airtight as Marine One landed on the South Lawn.

Sharpshooters and spotters were in position on the roof of the White House and in the Eisenhower Executive Office Building, carefully scanning for any hint of trouble. Bomb-sniffing dogs and their handlers patrolled the grounds of the eighteen-acre White House complex. Heavily armed members of CAT—the Secret Service's Counter Assault Team—took up positions while patrol cars from the Service's Uniformed Division sealed off all streets around the presidential residence, towed away any unauthorized vehicles, and completed a thorough sweep, looking for weapons, explosives, or suspicious persons anywhere within striking distance of the incoming commander in chief. So far, they had found no one and nothing out of the ordinary, but it hardly made any of them breathe easier.

It was just after midnight on a bitterly cold late-winter night. The nation's capital was covered in an icy crust of snow, and a brisk easterly wind continued driving down the already-frigid temperatures. Bundled up in a thick wool dress coat and closely flanked by his Secret Service detail, President William Jackson stepped off the gleaming green-and-white chopper and proceeded not to the Oval Office but directly and quickly to the Situation Room, where he was met by CIA director Roger Allen, his national security advisor, his chief of staff, and several senior White House aides.

"Where are we?" asked the president, handing his coat, scarf, and gloves to an aide and taking his seat at the head of the table.

"Mr. President, we are facing a critical threat to our national security," Allen said bluntly.

"Proceed."

"Mr. President, the positive progress is that the Israeli air strikes have been enormously successful. At this point, our assessment suggests they have degraded 95 percent of Iran's nuclear facilities, destroyed 75 to 80 percent of Iran's radar systems, gained effective control of Iranian airspace, and sent the regime into hiding. Most importantly, we believe the Israelis have destroyed six of Iran's nuclear warheads. The problem, Mr. President, is that two of the warheads remain intact, viable, and operative and are presently unaccounted for."

The room was silent.

"You're telling me two Iranian nukes are loose?"

"Not exactly loose, sir," Allen corrected. "Not in the sense that they are outside the control of the regime."

To the president, it was a distinction without a difference.

"But you're saying the Ayatollah and the Twelfth Imam have two working, operational, fully functional nuclear warheads, and we don't know where they are?"

"I'm afraid I am, Mr. President."

It was again quiet for a few moments, and then the president got up and began to pace the room.

"How do we know this? I mean, are we guessing, or do we have actual confirmation?"

"We have an intercept, sir." Roger Allen reached into his black leather folder and pulled out copies of the NSA's Farsi transcription and the CIA's English translation. "This is a phone call that the National Security Agency picked up from one of the satphones our man in Tehran was able to put into the mix."

"You're talking about this agent you've code-named . . . ?"

"Zephyr."

"Right—Zephyr—and this is the source you're talking about?"

"Yes, Mr. President," Allen replied. "Zephyr has been a godsend for us. Now, as you know, I wasn't convinced he could actually penetrate deep into the regime. But he has completely exceeded expectations. He's a gifted operative, and he's also had a string of remarkable luck. He's gotten these satphones into the inner circle, and they're bearing fruit."

"And this call—who's talking to whom?"

"Mr. President, it's a call between the Twelfth Imam—whom you'll see designated as TTI on the transcript—and General Mohsen Jazini, who, as you know, sir, is the commander of the Iranian Revolutionary Guard Corps."

"When did the call take place?"

"About twelve hours ago, Mr. President."

"Twelve?" Jackson said, incredulous. "Why am I just hearing about it now?"

"Well, sir, we're . . . we're doing the best we can, sir," Allen stammered, caught off guard by the intensity of the president's reaction. "As I said, the phones have been distributed by aides to the Ayatollah and the Mahdi to nearly all the members of the high command inside Iran. That's the good news, and it is good. Amazing, actually. But we're struggling with the volume of calls we're now having to process. It's skyrocketing. The Iranian leadership has taken the bait. They trust the phones, sir, but our systems are not prepared for the sheer volume of information we're getting. We're talking about several hundred phones, distributed high and low on the chain of command. In most cases, we don't know which phone has been assigned to what user. The users often don't identify themselves or each other. They're avoiding mentioning where they are as much as possible to keep operational details to a minimum. They're referring quite a bit to secure e-mails they're sending each other. That's apparently where most of the sensitive information is getting passed back and forth. All that to say, it's been an enormous challenge sorting all the incoming data."

"No, no—that's absolutely unacceptable, Roger," the president fumed. "I don't need to tell you how serious this moment is. We absolutely have to stay on top of these calls."

"Yes, sir, I understand, but—"

"But nothing," Jackson shot back. "Don't tell me the CIA and DIA and NSA and all the rest of you don't have the resources you need. I've approved every budget request you've given me—everything you've asked for. And you'd better start getting me information in real time. Am I making myself clear?"

"Yes, sir. We will, Mr. President."

Jackson's face was red, and Allen couldn't hold his angry glare for long. He looked down at the page in front of him, hoping the president would follow his lead. A moment later, the chief executive mercifully turned to the intercept as well.

TTI: I was praying, and your face came before me, Mohsen. Allah is with you, and you have news.

JAZINI: I do, my Lord. I was going to wait and bring you the news in person, but is it okay to speak on this line?

TTI: Of course. Now speak, my son.

JAZINI: Yes, my Lord. I have good news—we have two more warheads.

TTI: Nuclear?

JAZINI: Yes, two have survived the attacks.

TTI: How? Which ones?

JAZINI: The ones Tariq Khan was working on. The ones in Khorramabad.

TTI: What happened?

JAZINI: The moment Khan went missing, the head of security at the Khorramabad facility feared for the safety of the warheads. He feared Khan might be working for the Zionists. Since the warheads weren't yet attached to the missiles, he decided to move them out of his facility and hide them elsewhere. I just spoke to him. He's safe. The warheads are safe.

TTI: I thank you, Allah, for you have given us another chance to strike.

The president looked up from the transcript and stared at the CIA director.

"So where do we think they are?" he asked.

"That's the problem, Mr. President," Allen conceded. "At the moment, we have no idea."

"And they could be fired at Tel Aviv or Jerusalem at any moment, right?"

"Yes, sir," Allen said. "Or . . ."

"Or what?"

"Or, Mr. President, they could be headed here."

4

Few people on the planet knew David Shirazi's real identity.

Not a single person in the White House, State Department, or Pentagon knew. Only four people in the Central Intelligence Agency knew, and Roger Allen, the director, wasn't one of them. The truth was that David was the CIA's top NOC—nonofficial cover agent—working deep inside Iran. He was known to the president of the United States by the code name Zephyr. He was operating as a German passport–holding telecommunications specialist by the name of Reza Tabrizi, and he had penetrated deeper and faster and higher inside the Iranian government than any agent in CIA history. The question, however, was whether any of that mattered. If Zephyr succeeded, few would ever know, and he was legally prevented from ever saying so. But if he failed, the impact could be cataclysmic.

Some 6,331 miles away from the White House Situation Room, in a CIA safe house not far from Tehran, David could feel the enormous weight on him growing. He desperately wanted to deliver for his president and his country, but he also increasingly believed failure was the more likely result.

He had miraculously escaped the burning Jamkaran Mosque in Qom only to very nearly die at the hands of an Israeli fighter pilot he was trying to rescue. Now, three days later, he was back at the safe house. He was unharmed—but he worried he was being ineffective as well.

David wondered if the president or the secretary of defense or the secretary of homeland security or anyone inside the American national security establishment who was cleared to even be aware that Zephyr existed knew Washington's inside man was the youngest and least-experienced NOC the Agency had ever deployed.

Except for his age, David was in many ways the Agency's dream recruit. He was tall, athletic, and brilliant, with a near-photographic memory, multiple degrees in advanced computer science, and a near-perfect fluency in Farsi, Arabic, and German, aside from American English, his actual mother tongue. His parents had both been born and raised in Iran and had raised David with a rich cultural heritage that now helped him hide in plain sight inside their native country. His father, Dr. Mohammad Shirazi, was a renowned and highly successful cardiologist. His mother, Nasreen, had graduated in the top one percent of her class at the University of Tehran and had been offered full scholarships to study and eventually teach at almost every institution of higher learning in her country. But she turned down all the scholarships and instead took a job working as a translator for the Iranian Foreign Ministry under the Shah on various U.N. issues, rising rapidly in her division and winning a dozen commendations. Later, the Canadian Embassy recruited her to become a translator for them, a post she eagerly accepted, working her way up to the role of translator and senior advisor to several Canadian ambassadors.

When the Shah was overthrown and Ayatollah Ruhollah Khomeini came to power during the Islamic Revolution in the early, chaotic months of 1979, the Shirazis feared for what their country was becoming. They couldn't bear to see the growing bloodshed and the tyranny that was engulfing their homeland, so they fled, helping an endangered American couple escape as well. Eventually the Shirazis received asylum in the United States as political refugees, and later they achieved full citizenship. They settled in central New York and established an entirely new life.

No one in David's family—not his parents and not his two older brothers—could ever have predicted what he was doing now. Indeed, only David's father knew his youngest son worked for the Agency and was operating deep inside Iran. David had told him only recently, swearing him to secrecy.

With short-cropped jet-black hair, olive skin, and soulful brown eyes, David may not have been born in Iran, but he was straight out of central casting. He seemed to instinctually understand the culture and the rhythm of Iranian society, and it hadn't been difficult for him to appear a devout and increasingly fervent Shia Muslim, even a devotee of the Twelfth Imam. And the cover story his handlers at Langley had cooked up for him had been effective. None of his contacts or sources imagined for a moment that he was an American, much less a spook.

But no matter how well-bred or prepared David was for this mission, it had now come to a screeching halt. Israel was under attack from multiple directions, and the Israelis were fighting back with overwhelming force. David was safe, at least for the moment, but he had no idea what to do next.

He picked up his phone and dialed again. But for the thirty-sixth call in a row, no one answered. Another voice mail, another dead end. A moment later, he dialed a thirty-seventh number and waited. Again no one answered. He tried the thirty-eighth and thirty-ninth but got voice mail each time. Slamming down the phone, he continued pacing around his tiny room, seething. Indeed, it was all he could do not to throw the phone against the wall or out the window. Where were all the sources he had so carefully cultivated? Where was Daryush Rashidi, the president of Iran Telecom? Where was Abdol Esfahani, Rashidi's operations deputy and closest ally in the country? Where was Dr. Alireza Birjandi, who despite his age and blindness had been by far David's most helpful source? Why weren't they answering their phones? Why weren't they feeding him information? He hadn't even been able to reach Javad Nouri, the man he had rescued just three days before. He needed a breakthrough. He needed a miracle. He couldn't just sit around doing nothing. There had to be more he could do. But what?

Against enormous odds, David had done everything the Agency had asked of him over the past few months. He had taken enormous risks. He had gambled his own life—indeed his own soul. But what good had it really done? He hadn't been able to stop Iran from building a single nuclear warhead—they'd built nine. He hadn't sabotaged Iran's nuclear facilities to at least slow down their progress. He hadn't stopped the war from starting. Now the entire Middle East was on fire. The American economy was at risk of plunging back into a recession, as was the global economy, if the war continued. Oil prices had already shot past $325 a barrel, and gasoline back home was now $7 a gallon and certain to go higher. Israel's skies were raining rockets. Iran's skies were raining bombs. And here he was, holed up in Safe House Six just outside Tehran.

David had a first-rate CIA paramilitary unit that had come to help him. But he had no new information, no new leads, and no idea what to do or where to go next. For three days they'd been sitting around making calls and sending e-mails and text messages and making pot after pot of coffee but effectively twiddling their thumbs. David couldn't stand it any longer. They had to move. They had to take action. They needed a target. They needed a mission. But Langley wasn't giving them one, and he was out of ideas.

He was tempted to call Jack Zalinsky at Langley, but what was the point? Zalinsky was eight and a half hours behind him in Washington, D.C., which meant that while it was 8:40 in the morning here in Iran, it was only ten minutes past midnight at CIA headquarters. The only reason to call Jack at this hour would be to *provide* critical information, not to ask for any, and that knowledge set David on edge all the more.

The last seventy-two hours had been wrenching on so many levels. The images he kept seeing of the war around him were hellish, and he seemed to have no ability to affect it. If that weren't enough, just when he should have his attention laser-focused on the grave task before him, he'd had the wind knocked out of him with the news that halfway around the world his mother was now gone, having lost her battle with stomach cancer. Stuck inside war-ravaged Iran, he had missed the memorial service and the burial. His phone message and brief conversation with his father seemed pitifully small in light of his father's loss.

And then there was the completely surprising reappearance of Marseille Harper, the first and only girl he had ever truly loved. Seeing her again after all these years came with the terrible news that her father had recently committed suicide. David could not imagine Mr. Harper taking his life; it did not seem at all like the man he'd deeply respected since childhood.

David grieved for Marseille. An only child whose mother had been killed in the World Trade Center attacks on 9/11, she was now all alone in the world. That, he figured, was likely the reason she had reached out to him out of the blue after years of silence. But after a wonderful, if slightly awkward, reunion at a restaurant in Syracuse, he'd been urgently called back to Washington. Then he'd been sent to Iran. He was legally prevented from telling Marseille he worked for the CIA, of course, so he had told her his boss was sending him to Europe on an emergency business trip. He'd felt terrible lying to her, but he hadn't any other choice. He'd called her briefly from Germany, but had he called her from the road since then to comfort or encourage her, like any decent friend would do? No. Had he e-mailed or written her? No. How could he? He wasn't authorized to make personal calls or send e-mails to family and friends, and all his calls and e-mails were monitored, recorded, and scrutinized by the Agency's top officials and analysts. Did he really want Zalinsky or any of the senior management at Langley and the NSA scrutinizing his most personal communications? Hardly, and it wouldn't just be them. Eva Fischer would be in the loop as well, complicating things all the more.

Angry and confused and no longer able to stand the thought of pacing the halls of the tiny flat or staring at a laptop computer screen only to read more depressing news, David decided to get out and get some morning air. He changed into a T-shirt, sweatshirt, and shorts, then grabbed his phone and a Glock 9mm and let his team know he was going for a run. As he stepped outside, he could see dark clouds forming over the city and heard the rumble of thunder in the distance. The temperature hovered in the low fifties, and a strong wind was coming in off the Caspian Sea. David stretched his legs and scanned the area for trouble, for signs of anything amiss, but detected nothing.

He looked down the street to the right and the left, both sides lined with dilapidated high-rise tenement buildings with laundry hanging from each balcony and a forest of satellite dishes stretching as far as the eye could see. The street itself, dotted with potholes, was littered with trash, empty plastic water bottles, and blue and green and pink plastic grocery bags. Everywhere he looked, trash was piled high and

5

The governments of Turkey, Tunisia, and Morocco had just announced they were joining the Caliphate, and Indonesia's parliament was holding emergency meetings to approve joining as well. These were positive developments, to be sure, but the bitter fact remained that the war was not going as he had planned. Muhammad Ibn Hasan Ibn Ali, known to the world as the Twelfth Imam, entered a conference room off the main war room in the Revolutionary Guard Corps command center. He ordered an aide to summon Ayatollah Hamid Hosseini, President Ahmed Darazi, and Defense Minister Ali Faridzadeh without delay.

"Of course, my Lord," said the aide. "Anyone else?"

"No, just those three," said the Mahdi. "And have two armed guards posted outside this door. I do not want to be disturbed."

"Yes, Your Excellency. It shall be done as you wish."

When the aide left and shut the door, the Mahdi surveyed the room. In the center was a large, rectangular, highly polished mahogany conference table, around which were eight leather executive chairs. On the table were eight phones connected to a central switchboard in another part of the underground complex that could patch calls through to any Iranian military post or to any civilian phone inside or outside the country. The walls were wood paneled but devoid of any paintings or photographs. Instead there were two large flat-screen TV monitors, one at each end of the room, though neither of them was currently turned on, and several enormous maps on the side walls, including one of the Middle East and Persian Gulf region and another of the entire world.

Over the door were six digital clocks, displaying the current time in Tehran, al-Quds (aka Jerusalem), London, Washington, Beijing. The sixth clock—the one in the center—was set at the local time of wherever the Mahdi was at any given moment. Since he was now in the IRGC's command center ten stories underneath the largest air base in Iran's capital city, the first and sixth clocks read the same: 8:52 a.m.

Dressed in a long black robe, turban, and sandals, the Mahdi paced for a few moments. He hated being confined to a bunker. He needed fresh air. He wanted to pray in the sunshine, bowing toward Mecca. He wanted to be in Islamabad to consummate the deal he'd been cooking up with Pakistani president Iskander Farooq for the past few days. It was close. Very close. He could taste it. But he hated negotiating by e-mail, no matter how secure his aides said it was. He wanted to sit with Farooq face-to-face. He wanted to read the man's body language and make sure he was as compliant and supportive as his messages suggested.

But the Mahdi needed to step carefully. The stakes were too high for another misstep now. His team had deeply disappointed him. They were making serious mistakes. They had lost the initiative, and they didn't seem to know how to regain it. The time had come for the Mahdi to step in and reassert his authority. He had been patient long enough, and the price had been steep. Never again.

Not wanting those beneath him to see or sense his agitation, he chose to take a seat at the far end of the table, then folded his hands, closed his eyes, leaned back in the leather executive chair, and waited.

His thoughts quickly drifted to his inaugural address to the Islamic world and to the world at large, delivered in Mecca on Thursday, March 3. It was then he had made his intentions clear. "To those who would oppose us, I would simply say this," he had warned in no uncertain terms. "The Caliphate will control half the world's supply of oil and natural gas, as well as the Gulf and the shipping lanes through the Strait of Hormuz. The Caliphate will have the world's most powerful military, led by the hand of Allah. Furthermore, the Caliphate will be covered by a nuclear umbrella that will protect the people from all evil. . . . We seek only peace. We wish no harm against any nation. But make no mistake: any attack by any state on any portion of the Caliphate will unleash the fury of Allah and trigger a War of Annihilation."

But the Israelis had called his bluff.

Darazi—Iran's moron of a president—had insisted to the Mahdi's face that the Zionists would never strike first. Indeed, Darazi had claimed that the Americans would never allow it. But he was a fool. There was no other way to describe it. He'd been wrong, disastrously so, and this could not be forgotten.

Hamid Hosseini had been more cautious, hedging his bets regarding the possibility of an Israeli first strike, but it wasn't because the Ayatollah possessed any scrap of wisdom or sound judgment. The man was a coward, pure and simple. He was a sheep, not a shepherd, and his days were numbered.

Faridzadeh was a different story. Iran's defense minister had operational control not simply of Iran's military forces but all the forces of the Caliphate. At the moment, that meant primarily the men and arms of Hezbollah and Hamas, both of whom were actively engaged in the war against the Zionists. Ostensibly, Faridzadeh could also direct the militaries of Egypt, Algeria, Lebanon, Saudi Arabia, Somalia, Sudan, Yemen, and Qatar to do his bidding. All of them had joined the Caliphate in recent days. Soon, perhaps within the next forty-eight to seventy-two hours, he would oversee the forces of Syria, Jordan, and Iraq, and possibly Pakistan and Indonesia as well, should everything play out as the Mahdi expected. But was Faridzadeh capable of such enormous power?

There was a knock at the door, and then Hosseini, Darazi, and Faridzadeh entered, one after another, and bowed low to the one whom they called "the Lord of the Age." The Mahdi commanded them to take seats at the end of the table near the door. For now, he would not permit them to approach too closely. That was an honor they had to earn, and none of them yet had.

The Mahdi stared at each one of them in succession, then spoke bluntly and without emotion. "You are losing this war. This is completely unacceptable. You had eight nuclear warheads. Now you have two. You had dozens of high-speed ballistic missiles. Now you have merely a handful. You had the world trembling at the rise of a new

Persian superpower. Now it is the people of the Caliphate who are trembling and wondering—fearing—if the Zionists are going to defeat us. How do you explain this?"

A long, awkward silence ensued. The three men looked at each other and then down at the notebooks in front of them. None of them made eye contact with the Mahdi. How could they? They knew the situation was untenable.

Finally Faridzadeh cleared his throat. "Your Excellency, may I speak?"

"By all means," said the Mahdi. "You have an explanation?"

"I have a plan," the defense minister replied. "Or rather, we have a plan."

"Go on."

"We have figured out a way to slip you out of the country to meet with Farooq," Faridzadeh ventured.

"In Dubai, as we have discussed?"

"No, my Lord. Dubai is full of CIA, Mossad, MI6, the Germans—it's not worth the risk."

"But it was before?"

"The situation has changed."

"It certainly has. Where, then? Islamabad?"

"No, my Lord, we believe that is too risky. We propose a secret meeting in Kabul, preferably tomorrow—fast and quiet—and then get you right back here before anyone notices."

"Why Kabul?" the Twelfth Imam asked.

"The Americans have pulled out," Faridzadeh said. "NATO has pulled out. The West has largely given up on the place. So it's now free from infidel troops. Plus it's close—just a two-hour flight from here and barely a half hour from Farooq's palace. What's more, the ISI has a strong network in the city. And as you know, we've been putting more and more intelligence assets into Afghanistan since the Americans withdrew. We've discreetly strengthened our presence in the past few days, and we can guarantee your safety. I think we can guarantee your movements won't be detected, either, which means the trip won't get into the news unless you want it to."

"I don't."

"My point exactly, my Lord."

The room went quiet. The Mahdi studied each man closely. Hosseini was tense. Darazi was pale. Faridzadeh seemed . . . what? Confident? Self-assured? Even proud?

"Is this your plan, Ali?" the Mahdi asked.

"We worked on it together, my Lord."

"But this is your brainchild?"

"Actually, I cannot take any credit, Your Excellency—the original idea came from Mohsen," Faridzadeh said, referring to General Mohsen Jazini, commander of the Iranian Revolutionary Guard Corps. "We helped refine it, but Mohsen gave us a five-page memo outlining a detailed plan."

"When?"

"Friday morning."

"Why am I only hearing of it now?"

"We've been refining it."

"Give it to me," the Mahdi demanded.

Faridzadeh pulled a copy out of his notebook and then hesitated.

"You may bring it to me," said the Mahdi.

Faridzadeh pushed his chair back, got up, and walked the memo down to the Mahdi, bowing as he did. The Mahdi held up his hand, directing Faridzadeh to wait, and so he did, his forehead pressed to the ground. The Mahdi, meanwhile, carefully read the five-page, single-spaced document. It was not what he had expected, but he had to admit it intrigued him.

To begin with, Jazini laid out a daring strategy to secret the Twelfth Imam out of Iran and into Afghanistan without being detected, and he proposed a compelling strategy for sealing the deal with Farooq for the Pakistanis to join the Caliphate immediately and turn launch authority of their arsenal of 173 nuclear-tipped missiles—including, but not limited to, provision of all the launch codes—over to the Mahdi's control. That alone would have been enough, but that was just the first three pages.

The last two pages counterintuitively recommended *against* the Mahdi's order to attach the last two remaining nuclear warheads to medium-range ballistic missiles on Iranian soil and launch both at Israel at the same time amid a simultaneous barrage of some two hundred Hezbollah and Hamas rockets and missiles, thereby drastically reducing if not eliminating Israel's ability to identify which missiles carried the atomic payloads and thus Israel's ability to successfully shoot them down. Instead, Jazini suggested getting the warheads *off* Iranian soil—forward deploying them to Syria, transported in milk trucks or fuel trucks or something innocuous like that rather than in military convoys.

Once the warheads were on Syrian soil, Jazini wrote that they should be moved to military bases in or around Damascus to be attached to shorter-range Syrian missiles. When all was ready, ideally within the next few days, Jazini recommended the same simultaneous missile barrage from Iran, Hezbollah, and Hamas but combined with a full-fledged Syrian barrage of some twenty to thirty missiles, all aimed at Tel Aviv, Jerusalem, and Haifa.

Jazini's theory was that if the Israeli air defense systems could discriminate between Iranian missiles and Lebanese rockets, then the Patriot and Arrow systems would focus exclusively on the missiles inbound from Iran every time. The risk of having the last two nuclear warheads shot down, therefore, increased dramatically. But, he argued, in such a massive incoming missile and rocket attack from all directions, the Israelis would never suspect the atomic warheads were coming from Syria. Thus the likelihood of those warheads getting shot down would decrease dramatically under this scenario, and the chances of annihilating the Israeli Jewish population would increase.

Jazini concluded his memo by noting the critical element of the Twelfth Imam's securing full and unhindered control of the Pakistani nuclear missiles before launching the final two Iranian warheads. If this could be successfully negotiated and announced publicly, it should forestall the Americans from even considering a retaliation against Iran or any part of the Caliphate after the Mahdi wiped the Zionists off the map. Indeed, full control of the Pakistani nuclear arsenal would make the Caliphate a fast-rising superpower and the Mahdi one of the most powerful leaders on the planet, if not *the* most powerful.

"Just as Allah would have it," Jazini concluded.

The Mahdi was surprised. The memo was good—better than he had expected—and he found himself impressed with Jazini's foresight and initiative. Actually, Jazini was proving himself a far more effective tactician than Faridzadeh. It was Jazini who, several years before, had successfully overseen the program to enrich Iran's uranium to weapons-grade purity. It was Jazini who had overseen the program to make sure the warheads were successfully built and tested and attached to the Shahab-3 missiles. What's more, it was Jazini who had overseen the training and deployment of the IRGC cell that had successfully assassinated Egyptian president Abdel Ramzy in New York City. He couldn't be personally blamed for the failure to kill the American and Israeli leaders as well. At least both had been wounded. Besides, killing Ramzy had been the top priority in order to prepare the way for Egypt's joining the Caliphate, and that's exactly what had happened. Plus, the Americans had suffered another black eye, another major terrorist attack inside their homeland—and in Manhattan of all places. Oil prices had soared. Gas prices were skyrocketing. The Dow was plummeting. The American people were rattled. President Jackson looked feckless and indecisive, and Jazini deserved a great deal of credit.

Put simply, Jazini's job had been to build Iran's nuclear weapons program and make it viable while also giving Iran a terrorist network capable of striking deep inside enemy territory, and he had succeeded beyond anyone's most fervent prayers. Faridzadeh's job, on the other hand, had been to protect Iran's nuclear weapons program from sabotage and external attack, and Faridzadeh had failed disastrously.

It was Faridzadeh who had failed to stop the Israelis—or perhaps the Americans, or possibly a coordinated effort by both—from assassinating Dr. Mohammed Saddaji, ostensibly the deputy director of Iran's Atomic Energy Organization but clandestinely Iran's chief nuclear physicist running the weapons-development program. It was Faridzadeh who had failed to stop the defection to the United States of Dr. Najjar Malik, Saddaji's son-in-law and chief deputy on the weapons program. Not only was Malik now apparently cooperating with the CIA, but he was claiming on satellite television and through his wildly popular Twitter account that he had renounced Islam and converted to Christianity. And now Faridzadeh was systematically losing this war against the Zionists. Any one of these crimes would have been abominable enough, but combined they were unforgivable sins.

The Twelfth Imam had no intention of litigating any of this in front of Hosseini and Darazi. This was not a democracy. Allah forbid! Faridzadeh was not presumed innocent until proven guilty. This was no time to reprimand or demote or arrest the man. He was not, after all, merely incompetent. He was not simply a bumbler or a fool or a failure. He was a traitor to the Islamic people, a betrayer of the Caliphate. He was apostate. He was guilty of treason against Allah, and thus he was worthy only of the eternal fires of damnation.

Realizing this gave the Mahdi a great peace about what Allah required of him. Without warning, he drew a small gun from underneath his robe. Darazi's eyes went wide. Hosseini immediately recognized the pistol as his own but clearly couldn't imagine how the Mahdi had gotten hold of it. But neither of them could speak, and Faridzadeh, his forehead still bowed to the floor, had no idea what was coming.

The Mahdi aimed and pulled the trigger. The shot itself, especially in such a confined space, sounded like a cannon being fired. Guards immediately burst into the room, guns drawn, but stopped in their tracks at the grisly sight, as if unsure what to do. On the floor lay the lifeless carcass of Ali Faridzadeh, surrounded by a rapidly growing pool of crimson. In the Mahdi's hand was a pistol, which he now calmly laid on the table. No one else in the conference room was injured, though everyone in the war room was now on his feet. Sirens were going off. Security was rushing to their location from all directions.

The Mahdi, however, told all of them to go back to work, all but those necessary for removing the body and cleaning up the mess. Without saying a word to the Ayatollah or the president, the Mahdi picked up one of the phones in front of him and asked to be patched through to General Mohsen Jazini, whom he was about to name the new defense minister of the Caliphate. Then he asked to be connected to the personal line of Gamal Mustafa, the president of Syria.

6

Marseille Harper needed a few moments to herself. She needed to catch her breath and pull herself together. She stepped into the powder room in the Shirazi home, just off the kitchen by the door to the garage, to hide herself away from all the people and all the hushed conversations and all the memories this home brought flooding back.

She took several tissues from the flowered box on the vanity, dabbed away the tears, and closed her eyes. All she could see was David. She missed him so much it was like a physical ache. She longed to hear from him, to talk with him, to know at the very least that he was alive and well. It felt so strange to be here in David's house, with his father and his brothers and friends of their family, but without him around. She'd never been here without him. Why would she have been? Was she wrong to have come this time? Maybe the Shirazis were just being polite. Maybe they were wondering why in the world she was here and why she didn't leave. The very thought made her wince, and tears once again began to push their way to the surface.

Fighting her mounting doubts, she silently prayed the Lord would give her the grace to finish this trip well and get back to Portland, where she belonged. She didn't want to be a burden. She wanted to be a blessing somehow to this grieving family she loved so much.

Marseille opened her eyes and took a hard look in the mirror. She wasn't happy with what she saw. She decided she didn't like her hair down, so she reached into her small purse, took out a clip, and pulled her hair into a twist. She wished she'd worn a different outfit, like a warm sweater—this house was freezing, despite all the guests—and black slacks and more comfortable shoes. These pumps she'd chosen instead were killing her feet. She looked at her hands—no rings, short nails, clear nail polish—and realized they were shaking. She turned on the faucet until the water was good and warm but not too hot. Then she put her hands under the running water and closed her eyes again. Something about the warmth soaking into her hands seemed to give her comfort. At least for now. What she really needed was a long, hot bath.

It had been a brutal week. Gentle flurries were falling throughout most of central New York. The forecast was calling for a major lake-effect snowstorm to swoop in by dawn, but in the Shirazi home, the emotional storm had already hit hard, and Marseille Harper knew its devastating effects would be felt for a long time to come.

On Wednesday, David's mom, Nasreen, had succumbed to the stomach cancer that had appeared without warning just a few months earlier and ravaged her petite body. Her husband was devastated. Her two eldest sons were grieving too, each in his own way, though they had barely spoken to one another, at least not in Marseille's presence or in her sight. On Friday evening, the family had endured the viewing at a funeral home on Grant Boulevard—though it wasn't truly a viewing, for Dr. Shirazi didn't want his wife remembered as gaunt and nearly emaciated and had, therefore, insisted the casket be closed. David's unexplained absence had been whispered about by some who attended, a fact not lost on Dr. Shirazi and one that to Marseille seemed only to make more painful the wounds he already had to endure. Earlier this morning, at eleven o'clock sharp, they had all gathered again for the memorial service. Marseille had felt certain David's noticeable absence would be explained by someone, but it wasn't, adding an unintended but distinctly awkward feel to an already-somber mood, at least for Marseille.

That said, the service itself was well attended and beautiful. Dozens of stunning floral arrangements were on display, adorned with hundreds of yellow roses, Mrs. Shirazi's favorite. Two professional violinists from the local philharmonic orchestra, apparently longtime friends of the Shirazis, played several pieces during the service, including during a slide show that featured photographs of Nasreen as a swaddled infant being held by her parents in Tehran; Nasreen standing in front of a mosque as a young girl of about ten wearing a beautiful yellow head-scarf; Nasreen and Mohammad beaming on their wedding day; Nasreen holding her firstborn son; Nasreen and Mohammad being sworn in as American citizens at a courthouse in Buffalo, New York; Nasreen standing beside David when he was about ten or twelve years old in his Little League uniform, holding a baseball bat over his shoulder; and so many more.

Most of the pictures Marseille had never seen, of course, but some she had and some had been captured in the season of life when she had first met the Shirazis, when she herself was a young girl, and they brought back very poignant memories. The one that completely caught her off guard actually showed her family and the Shirazi fam-ily gathered together for Thanksgiving when she was about ten years old, sitting around the Shirazis' dining room table. They were all so young. None of the parents had gray hair. Neither of David's brothers had beards. David was wearing an adorable little suit and tie. Marseille was wearing a robin's-egg-blue dress with matching blue bows in her pigtails. She was sitting next to David, and just at the moment the photo had been snapped, she was sneaking a glance at him while he was making a silly face. She still remembered that very moment vividly. The photograph itself had hung, framed, on the wall of her father's den for years. The sight of it instantly made Marseille's eyes well up with tears and caused a lump to form in her throat. What a sweeter, simpler time that had been, long before the angel of death had descended upon them all—before her mother was killed in the attacks on the World Trade Center, before her father committed suicide in the woods out-side their home, before Mrs. Shirazi lost her battle with cancer, before David joined the CIA and was sent inside Iran.

As she sat in that service, she'd had to grit her teeth so as not to lose her composure. Part of her had wanted to run from the room and hide and sob. Another part of her, however, had wanted to stand up and shout the truth to everyone in the room. *David isn't here because he is serving his country! He is serving behind enemy lines in Iran. Of course he loved his mother. He loved her dearly. He would have done anything he possibly could to be in this room, but he's probably dodging a barrage of bullets or risking his life to stop the Iranians from firing their missiles. How dare you judge him! How dare you spread your gossip and lies when you don't have the foggiest notion of the truth!*

Marseille felt crushed by the pain David must be going through, unable to properly grieve his mother's death or comfort his father. But she also felt angry at the whisperers in the room who had concluded that Azad and Saeed were heroes and that David was an unworthy son who couldn't even deign to come home to his own mother's funeral. But she couldn't let her emotions get the better of her, she told herself.

No one in the room knew what she knew. In trying to learn the truth about her own father's work for the Central Intelligence Agency, she had stumbled onto the truth about who David was and what he was doing. But as much as she wanted to tell everyone—or at least tell Dr. Shirazi to ease his pain—it was not her secret to reveal. Indeed, David's life likely depended precisely on no one else knowing what he was doing, especially his own family, and the last thing she intended to do was put him in any more danger than he already was.

KARAJ, IRAN

The brisk winter air on David's face was refreshing. The pounding of the cracked pavement under his feet was a good change of pace. But nothing could lift the weight from his shoulders, and though his recent "successes" were now legendary within the Agency, he struggled to see that he had achieved anything of real substance or lasting significance thus far. People were dying. The Mideast was in flames. That wasn't success. That was failure.

That's not how Langley saw it, of course. To the suits on the seventh floor of the CIA headquarters, David's most important accomplishment had been tracking down Dr. Alireza Birjandi and developing him into an effective source. The aging scholar, professor, and bestselling author was also the world's leading expert on Shia eschatology, widely described in the Iranian media as a spiritual mentor and senior advisor to several of the top leaders in the Iranian regime, including Ayatollah Hamid Hosseini and President Ahmed Darazi. Birjandi spoke to these leaders by phone on a regular basis. He dined with them. Occasionally they shared the state's most prized secrets with him. They trusted him. Indeed, the elites in Iran revered Birjandi. Little did they know how intensely Birjandi had come to repudiate their theology and eschatology. Nor did they know Birjandi had a direct pipeline to the Americans. It was from Birjandi that David had learned about Iran's eight operational warheads and that the regime had already tested one in a previously undisclosed underground facility near the city of Hamadan. And it was Birjandi who had pointed David to Dr. Najjar Malik, the highest-ranking nuclear scientist in the country.

David had not only tracked down Malik but had persuaded him to defect and gotten him safely out of the country. With Malik's help, David had hunted down Tariq Khan—nephew of A. Q. Khan, the father of Pakistan's nuclear weapons program. Tariq, a top Pakistani nuclear scientist in his own right, had been helping the Iranians build the Bomb. At enormous risk to his own life, David had captured Tariq, forced out of him the precise location of all eight of the regime's operational nuclear warheads, gotten that information back to Langley, and then secreted the scientist out of Iran and off to Gitmo for further interrogation.

But so what? Khan was no longer talking, and David hadn't had any success in tracking down Jalal Zandi, Khan's partner in crime and now effectively the highest-ranking nuclear scientist still alive in Iran.

And where was Dr. Birjandi now? Why wasn't he answering any of David's calls? And it wasn't just Birjandi. Over the past several days, David had called every source, every contact, every person he knew in Iran. What did they know? What were they hearing? Where was the Mahdi? Where were Hosseini and Darazi? What were their plans? What were their strategies? David desperately needed answers, but no one was answering.

In the fog of war, so much was hazy and confusing. But at least two things were certain: the rocket and missile strikes against Israel were relentless and devastating, and the Israeli air strikes on Iranian targets kept coming, wave after wave.

Hamas had already fired hundreds of Qassam rockets at Ashkelon, Sderot, and Beersheva, endangering the lives of nearly half a million Israelis living in cities and towns along the southern border with Gaza. They were also firing dozens of longer-range Grad rockets at Ashdod and Tel Aviv.

At the same time, Hezbollah forces in southern Lebanon had already fired thousands of Katyusha rockets at Haifa, Karmiel, Kiryat Shmona, and Tiberias, threatening the nearly one million Israelis living along the northern borders with Lebanon and Syria.

For reasons beyond David's comprehension, the Syrians hadn't fully joined the war yet. They hadn't fired rockets or missiles except for those first three. They weren't engaging their air force or even using their antiaircraft systems, despite long-standing defensive treaties between Damascus and Tehran. They still could join the war at any moment, of course, and David, along with every operative and analyst at Langley, fully expected them to do so. What made that prospect particularly worrisome was Syria's stockpiles of chemical and biological weapons. But for the moment, the Syrians were lying dormant. It made no sense, but for now it made the most dangerous strategic threat to the Jewish State the Shahab-class missiles coming out of Iran. True, the Iranians had already fired hundreds of them and weren't believed to have many left. But every time one of them was fired, the question was, what kind of warhead was it carrying—nuclear, chemical, biological, or conventional? It was a crapshoot every time, and it was driving deep fear into the hearts of the Israeli people.

The Israelis, for their part, kept launching fighter jets and their own missiles against Iranian targets. As far as David knew, Israel had at least succeeded in taking out Iran's nukes, but this was still all-out war on both sides, and it wasn't clear to anyone how it was going to end. There didn't seem to be any part of Iran that was out of the Israelis' reach, though the city of Karaj, at least, where this safe house was located, had not yet been hit.

Nevertheless, most other strategic Iranian cities had been, and the near-nonstop bombings and missile strikes were taking an emotional toll on people. Most of the power for Tehran and other major cities had been knocked out. Nearly every Iranian TV and radio station was off the air. The Internet was down. Key government buildings, especially in the capital, were now flaming heaps of wreckage. The Ministry of Defense was a smoldering crater, as was the Ministry of Intelligence, the headquarters for VEVAK. Every real or suspected significant nuclear facility in Iran had been hit multiple times, and while the Israelis had clearly taken great pains to minimize civilian casualties, there had certainly been collateral damage. Thousands upon thousands of Iranians were dead and dying. David didn't know the number, but he was sure whatever it was, it was climbing by the hour.

Most of his contacts, David had to assume, either were working feverishly to obey the orders of the Mahdi and Iran's top generals to strike back at the Israelis or were huddled with their families in basements and bunkers. Those without satellite phones might not be reachable for the duration of the war, however long it took. But even the ones with satphones—the insiders—weren't answering. Why not? Wasn't that the point of having the satphones—so that such key men could be reached at all times regardless of the circumstances? Were they really too busy, David wondered, or was it something else? Were they avoiding him? Was he under suspicion after the near-assassination of Javad Nouri? Were they under orders not to speak to him anymore? He was burning to know the answer. He was desperate to find a lead. But for the moment, he was stuck.

WASHINGTON, D.C.

Roger Allen stepped out of the West Wing, got into the bulletproof black SUV waiting for him, and ordered they head back immediately to CIA headquarters in Langley, Virginia, roughly a twenty-minute drive at this time of night with no traffic. He was furious, and someone was going to hear about it. No sooner had they pulled out of the White House gates than Allen picked up his phone and speed-dialed his deputy director for operations, who picked up on the first ring.

"Tom Murray," said the voice at the other end.

"Tom, it's Roger. I'm on the way back."

"How'd it go?"

"How do you think? The president is fit to be tied. He wants to know why he's not getting hard intel in real time, especially from these satphone intercepts."

"What did you tell him?"

"What could I tell him? I told him of course we'd do a better job. But frankly I'm as angry as he is. Why are the translations and analyses going so slow?"

"It's the same as we discussed before you left," Murray replied. "The calls are a treasure trove. But we're getting more than we expected, faster than we expected, and we've got every man on the project we possibly can."

"Every man, maybe," the director said. "But not every woman."

There was a pause. "Sir, let's not go there," Murray said.

"We don't have a choice," Allen replied.

"You're talking about Eva Fischer?" Murray asked.

"Of course I'm talking about Eva. Frankly it was idiotic for Zalinsky to lock her up in the first place, and it's time to stop this nonsense, release her, and get her back to work."

"Sir, Agent Fischer co-opted a multimillion-dollar intelligence plat-form. She did it without authorization. And why? To save the life of a friend."

"No, Tom, to save the life of an agent," the director shot back. "For crying out loud, she saved the life of Zephyr, who by your own admis-sion is our most effective agent inside Iran, the guy who single-handedly identified the location of the warheads. Come on now, you're telling me you don't think Jack overreacted?"

"Jack did exactly what I would have done."

"Really? Lock up one of our best Farsi speakers and best analysts in the middle of a war with Iran, and for what? For saving our best asset inside the regime?"

"Sir, she compromised our ability to track one of the very nuclear warheads inside Iran that we now can't find—one that could be headed toward the United States."

"Enough, Tom," Allen said. "I want Fischer released immediately, with a full exoneration and a $50,000 bonus as compensation."

"Sir, I don't think—"

"That not a suggestion, Tom. It's an order. I want Agent Fischer released, apologized to, fully reinstated, compensated, and sitting in my office by the time I get back. You've got sixteen minutes. I suggest you get cracking."

7

What had struck Marseille most about the memorial service was how clearly beloved Mrs. Shirazi had been throughout the Syracuse community. She hadn't known that David's mom had, for more than two decades, been a loyal volunteer for the American Red Cross or that she'd been a tireless—and apparently quite effective—fund-raiser for the pediatric heart center at Upstate Medical, the hospital where Dr. Shirazi worked. So many of the friends she had made in both places came to show their respects, as did several families whose lives had been touched or whose children had been saved as a result of this dear woman's efforts. Most touching to Marseille was watching several of Mrs. Shirazi's closest friends read tributes, some of them successfully fighting back tears, some less so.

None of it, Marseille was certain, had provided the closure the family really needed. To make matters worse, Mrs. Shirazi's burial would have to wait until sometime in April or early May, since the ground at the cemetery was presently covered with too much snow and was far too cold and hard to dig a grave, all of which meant the family's raw wounds would be subjected to even more pain in another few weeks when they essentially had to do this all over again.

When the service was over, Dr. Shirazi had invited everyone back to his home. Indeed, he had insisted upon hosting three days of mourning for family and friends. This, it turned out, was an Islamic tradition, which Marseille found curious, since Dr. Shirazi was not a religious man, and neither were his wife or their sons. The Shirazis had long since abandoned Islam, but Marseille sensed that this ritual was far more about tradition than religion. This was about Dr. Shirazi operating on autopilot, doing what he had seen his parents do, and their parents before them, not trying to invent a new family tradition at a time like this. So she had followed everyone else over to the Shirazi house and offered to help serve food and run out for more ice and help in any other way she could. When she wasn't needed, she just sat in the back of the living room and kept quiet, observing the people coming and going, and praying a lot, sometimes with her eyes open and sometimes with them closed.

She observed that this was not really dissimilar from the tradition of her Jewish friends in Portland who sat shivah for seven days following the death of a loved one. There was something simple, even sweet, about sitting in a family's living room, saying little or nothing, but just being near them, with them, around them while they grieved for their loved one and she grieved with them. Marseille found herself wishing it was a tradition her family had practiced after the death of her mother. It would have been good, Marseille thought, for her father to sit with friends for seven days and let himself cry and weep and mourn properly. She had been only fifteen then, but she was pretty sure her father had never mourned properly. He had certainly never been able to heal from the gaping wound in his heart. Losing a spouse was obviously different from losing a parent. But maybe sitting shivah—or whatever they called it in Islam—was a good thing to do in either case.

"Loved ones and relatives are to observe a three-day mourning period," read one website on Islamic death rituals that Marseille had looked up on her iPhone after the service. "Mourning is observed in Islam by increased devotion, receiving visitors and condolences, and avoiding decorative clothing and jewelry."

Marseille hadn't wanted to sit around and "observe" everyone's mourning, however. That's why she'd offered to help as much as possible. She'd taken special care to make sure Dr. Shirazi had a fresh cup of Persian tea by his side at all times, with a little drop of honey stirred in, just the way he liked it. She'd helped set out and arrange the food people brought. She'd refilled buckets of ice and made pot after pot of coffee and tea. When she'd noticed that neither of the Shirazi sons were doing it, she had emptied the trash can under the sink in the kitchen, replaced it with a new Hefty bag, and taken the overflowing bag out to the can in the garage. She'd answered phone calls and taken messages when the Shirazi family members were busy. She'd washed dishes as needed and made sure there were enough forks and spoons and napkins available. Perhaps most importantly—or at least most usefully—she had continually refilled the Kleenex canisters strategically positioned all around the first floor.

All the while, however, she tried to keep a low profile, acting more like the hired help than a friend of the family. She wanted to show her love to the Shirazis, but she didn't want to presume to be part of the family. Nor did she want others to perceive her as acting like one. She didn't want any of the real friends of the family asking who she was or why she was there, in large part because she had no idea how to answer such questions. Who was she to these people, really? Why was she there? She couldn't just come out and say the truth. She wasn't even entirely sure what the truth was. Was she doing this for the purest of motives, out of genuine, sincere love for the family? Or was she doing it for David, though he probably had no idea she was even there?

She could see the enormous pain in this family, and not just because of Mrs. Shirazi's passing. These relationships were broken. The boys were estranged from one another. Worse, they seemed estranged from their father as well. There were clearly deep tensions just under the surface, and there were moments she feared those pains might explode into the open. She prayed throughout the day that they wouldn't and that no one else would notice.

For some families, tragedies brought them together and helped heal old wounds. This didn't appear to be one of those families. What the Shirazis needed most, Marseille began to see, was the same thing her father had needed most but never found. Not ancient traditions or a house full of family and friends or a piping-hot cup of Persian tea. What they needed was the healing touch of God's Son, Jesus. They desperately needed Christ's love, his comfort, the "peace of God, which surpasses all understanding," that he had promised to all who followed him. She wanted them to know the love and mercy and healing she had found after her mother was killed in the Trade Center attacks. She wanted them to know the amazing truth of God's great love.

But now didn't seem the time to say anything, and again, who was she? Why should they listen to her? Yes, Christ had poured into her heart an everlasting, transforming love she hadn't known existed. He had adopted her into his family and truly healed the wounds in her soul. She desperately wanted this family to know the Jesus she knew. But "there is an appointed time for everything," she recalled from Scripture. "And there is a time for every event under heaven. . . . A time to weep and a time to laugh; a time to mourn and a time to dance. . . . A time to be silent and a time to speak." Tonight, she knew, was a time to be silent, and so she was.

Marseille glanced at her watch. It was now well past midnight. This very long day was finally winding down. She stepped into the kitchen and took a look around. Most of the guests who had come to mourn with the Shirazi family had gone or were in the process of saying good-bye. Dr. Shirazi hugged the last few to leave and then headed upstairs without a word. He had to be exhausted. But Marseille felt a twinge of disappointment that he wouldn't take a moment and say good-bye to her as well.

She quietly began helping Azad wrap and put away the mounds of food that people had brought over. A few moments later, Saeed stepped into the kitchen but continued out to the back deck without a word, fixated on his BlackBerry and raising not a finger to help. Marseille tried not to let it bother her. She was exhausted after such an emotional day. She needed a good night's rest and some time to herself before packing up and finally flying back to Portland late the following evening. But as tired as she was, she couldn't quite bear to leave. Not yet. So she began wiping down tables and then rinsing dishes and loading them into the dishwasher.

There was something special about being back in this house. She loved how it looked, how it smelled, how it felt to be here. She smiled, remembering the love and affection the Shirazi parents had for each other. They held hands. They took long walks together. They doted on one another, and they seemed to genuinely enjoy each other. Marseille suspected they would have been deeply in love anywhere on the planet, regardless of the circumstances, for they were, at heart, classic romantics. The kind of love they'd had for each other—the kind they seemed uniquely wired for—was at once special and magical and deeply mysterious, and Marseille found herself wondering if David was wired for that kind of love as well.

Fond memories notwithstanding, she had never really expected to be standing here again after so many years. Not after how she had treated David. Yet here she was, alone with David's family, trying to love them and comfort them in their loss, while David was somewhere far away. Life had a funny way of working out, she told herself as she rooted around on her hands and knees under the kitchen sink, looking for some dishwasher detergent.

She wondered if she would ever see David again. Surely she would, right? God hadn't brought her all this way to reconnect with his family only to lose him all over again, possibly forever, had he? The very thought made Marseille wince. She again offered a silent prayer for David, for safety and for his speedy return. She'd been foolish to wait so long to reach out to him. He'd been so warm and encouraging when they'd met, glad to see her again after so many years. Perhaps her fears had been misplaced. Perhaps David was still her friend. Perhaps he could be more than just a friend.

She wondered where he was at that very moment. What was he doing? Whom was he with?

KARAJ, IRAN

David felt his phone vibrate, signaling an incoming message. He checked it as he kept jogging and found that it was actually a Twitter post from Najjar Malik. Where was Najjar, he wondered. And why hadn't the FBI found him yet? The man had been Iran's top nuclear scientist and the CIA's top prize, and now he was gone? How was that possible? Who was the moron who had let Najjar escape?

Then again, though he couldn't admit it to anyone on his team, David wasn't entirely disappointed it had happened. Najjar was a transformed man. He had not only had a vision of Christ in Iran but now had the courage to tell the world about it. Najjar was fast becoming the modern-day apostle Paul of Iran, and David found himself intrigued by every tweet the man sent. And he was not alone. Najjar's Twitter following was surging exponentially, and he was using all the sudden interest to urge his countrymen to turn away from Islam and turn to Jesus. He was linking to sites exposing the evils of the Iranian regime and warning about the dangers of the Caliphate and the Twelfth Imam, whom Najjar openly and unapologetically called a "false messiah."

Najjar's latest messages contained a link and the comment "Mustafa is evil, but make no mistake—the Mahdi is behind this savagery. But God will not be mocked. Judgment on Iran and Syria is coming."

Intrigued, David clicked on the link as he rounded a corner and headed up Abu Bakr Street. The page that loaded was from the website of the *Daily Star*, a Beirut-based newspaper. The headline read, "Syrian Girl Found Mutilated."

The horrifying story began: "A young woman was found beheaded and mutilated, and the crimes were reportedly committed by Syrian security agents. According to reports, the eighteen-year-old woman's brother was arrested and killed earlier this month. When their mother was brought by security forces to pick up his body, which showed bruises, burns, and gunshots, she found her daughter's body as well. The family said the girl had been decapitated, her arms cut off, and skin removed. After the burial last weekend, women held a protest . . ."

David stopped reading.

God will not be mocked. Judgment on Iran and Syria is coming.

David could only hope Najjar was right. Syrian president Gamal Mustafa was arguably the most bloodthirsty tyrant in the Middle East, and that was saying something. David wasn't entirely sure how close Mustafa and the Mahdi were. It was odd that the Syrians weren't yet engaged in the war with Israel, but he had little doubt they would be soon. These dictators needed to be toppled. Their people needed to be liberated. But it was going to take an act of God, David realized. For clearly the U.S. government was no longer in the business of regime change.

David's phone rang. His pulse quickened. Perhaps it was Birjandi or Rashidi. But then, to his surprise, he found himself wishing most that it was Marseille. And yet how could it be? She didn't know this number, and he knew Langley wouldn't let an unauthorized call from the States come through to his phone anyway. Unless, perhaps, it was his dad.

David read the caller ID. His heart sank. It wasn't any of his contacts calling him back with a new lead, or Marseille or his father. It was Zalinsky at Langley. He took a break from his run to catch his breath and answer the call.

"Hey."

"Hey—are we secure?" his handler asked.

"Absolutely. What have you got?" David wondered if his voice betrayed the level of anxiety he now felt.

"We've intercepted a call from the Iranian high command," Zalinsky began. "It's not good."

"What?" David pressed. "What is it?"

Zalinsky paused. He seemed to be steeling himself for the conversation to come. David scanned the street around him. There were few people out and no one who looked suspicious. He looked behind him but saw no one following. Taking a deep breath, he braced himself for whatever was coming next.

"The Israelis missed two of the warheads," Zalinsky said finally. "They seem to have gotten the rest, but they've missed two. How, I don't know. But they're out there somewhere, and we don't know where. And that's why I'm calling. The president is directing you to find both warheads fast and help us take them out before it's too late."

8

"We have a missile launch," shouted the IDF watch commander. *"Missile in the air—no, make that two Shahab-3s—just launched out of Tabriz."*

Five stories beneath the heavily fortified Israel Defense Forces head-quarters in Tel Aviv, in a high-tech war room whose walls were lined with large-screen plasma computer screens and TV monitors, Defense Minister Levi Shimon looked up from a sheaf of briefing papers and scanned for the correct images. When he found them—stunning satellite images from the Ofek-9 spy satellite in geosynchronous orbit six hundred kilometers over northern Iran—his stomach tightened.

"Estimated targets?" he demanded.

"Looks like Haifa and Jerusalem, sir, but we'll know more in a minute."

Levi Shimon didn't have a minute.

His country was being pummeled. Hundreds of Hezbollah rockets were being fired out of south Lebanon every hour. Dozens more rockets were being fired by Hamas out of Gaza. Israel's missile defense systems were cutting down 75 to 80 percent of the incoming, but the sheer volume of rockets made it impossible to stop them all. Most of the inbounds had no targeting systems. But some of the more advanced rockets did. The problem was, the IDF commanders had no way to determine which were which.

Schools were being hit. Apartment buildings and hospitals were being hit as well. Synagogues and shopping centers were being decimated, along with power stations and cell towers. Millions of Israelis had been forced into bomb shelters. All flights into and out of Ben Gurion International Airport had been canceled. Nearly a third of the country was suffering blackouts. No lights. No heat. No TV. No computers. No power whatsoever. More than three-quarters of the country had no mobile phone coverage. Worse, the death toll was spiraling. Over the past three days, nearly five hundred Israeli citizens had been killed. The casualties of the past twenty-four hours had been the worst—triple the rate of days one and two of the war. The number of injured was ten times that. Israeli hospitals were at their breaking point, and there was no end in sight.

But the rockets were the least of Shimon's worries. They were deadly but not decisive. What Shimon feared most were the advanced ballistic missiles that Iran and Syria possessed, the kinds with highly sophisticated guidance systems and warheads that would be horrifying enough with conventional payloads but could be apocalyptic if they were NBC—nuclear, biological, or chemical. Damascus, oddly, had fired only three missiles so far—and conventional ones at that—in the first hour of the fight on Thursday. After the IDF's Arrow system had shot all of them down, Syrian missiles had suddenly and inexplicably stopped coming. Iran, however, was firing five or six of their most advanced Shahab-3 missiles every hour. By the grace of God, the IDF was taking out almost all of these, but those that did penetrate Israel's state-of-the-art missile defense systems were devastating. Fortunately none of them—so far—carried unconventional warheads. None of them were weapons of mass destruction. But they were still causing the most damage, Shimon knew, and wasn't it only a matter of time until one of them created an extinction-level event?

KARAJ, IRAN

David hung up the phone with Zalinsky and started walking again, his mind reeling. How could the Israelis have missed two of the warheads? Where were they now? And how in the world was he supposed to track down either of them, much less both? He had no leads and couldn't get a single one of his contacts to even take his call.

He had hoped for a longer run, but it was time to get back, brief his men, and come up with a plan. Maybe they'd have an idea. He hoped so because at the moment, he had no idea where to start.

As best he could tell, he was about three miles from the safe house. He began jogging back, taking a right down a side street. He spotted a little corner market a few blocks up and decided to sprint. When he reached the bodega, he slowed his pace, then entered the shop and bought a bottle of water and a banana. He wolfed down the fruit and discarded the peel before leaving the store, then chugged half the bottle of water. He pulled out his satellite phone and once again dialed Dr. Birjandi.

Nothing. Again he tried Rashidi, then Esfahani, and again he came up empty. This particularly infuriated him, since these were the two who had insisted David take enormous risks to find, buy, and smuggle into Iran several hundred of these satphones for the Mahdi and his key men so they could be reached at all times. Rashidi and Esfahani were both members of the Group of 313, the Twelfth Imam's most elite warriors, operatives, and advisors. They were personally responsible for overseeing the creation and smooth functioning of the Mahdi's own private communications system both here in Iran and in whatever foreign countries he traveled to. And now neither of them were answering their satphones.

In desperation, David decided to try calling Esfahani's secretary at Iran Telecom. Mina wasn't exactly in the Mahdi's inner circle. Though she was smart and sweet and highly effective at her job, Esfahani practically treated the woman like a slave. He cursed at her and threw things at her and made her life miserable, though she never complained and still worked hard and professionally every day. Then again, she wasn't likely to be at work today with Israeli bombs falling all throughout Tehran. David scrolled through his contacts list and realized he no longer had her home number. He called her work number anyway, on the off chance that she had her work calls forwarded to her home number. But even as he dialed and hit Send, he realized how stupid that was. Most of the mobile phone system in the country was down, and what were the chances that Esfahani had given Mina, of all people, a satphone? Sure enough, the call went to voice mail. David didn't bother to leave a message. What was the point?

David shoved the phone in his pocket and started jogging again, heading for the safe house. He had taken only a few steps when the phone rang. He stopped, pulled out the phone, and was surprised to see Mina's name on the caller ID.

"Hello? Mina? Is that you?"

"Yes, it's me," Mina said. "Is this Reza? Reza Tabrizi? Are you okay?"

"Yes, it's Reza, and I'm safe, thank you, Mina," he said. "And you? How are you and your mother?"

"Praise Allah, we are okay," she replied, though her voice was trembling. "We've been living in the basement of our apartment. I just came upstairs to get some more food and water, and the satphone rang. But when I picked up, you'd already hung up."

"Abdol gave you a satphone?"

"In case he needed me to help him."

"Are you helping him?"

"A little, here and there," Mina said. "But no, not much."

"Where is he now?" David asked. "I'm trying to find him and Mr. Rashidi."

"I don't know where Mr. Rashidi is. Mr. Esfahani has been trying to find him too."

"Okay, but where is Abdol? It's urgent, Mina. I must talk to him."

"I just spoke to him about twenty minutes ago," she replied. "He's heading to Qom."

"Qom?" David asked. "Why Qom? The Israelis are bombing the daylights out of the nuclear sites and military bases there."

"That's why he went."

"I don't understand."

"His parents live in Qom," Mina said. "Near one of the bases. His mother is terrified of all the bombing. She wants to leave, but his father, as you know, is a big mullah there. He won't leave the seminary. He says leaving would show a lack of faith in Allah."

"So why's Abdol going?"

"To get them out of there before they are killed."

David suddenly realized his best chance—maybe his only chance—to reconnect with Esfahani, or anyone inside the Mahdi's Group of 313, was in Qom.

"Mina, I need an address," he said, his mind already made up.

"For what?"

"For Abdol's parents."

"No, Mr. Tabrizi, please, you cannot go," Mina said.

"I have to."

"But why? It's a suicide mission."

"No, it's not. It's to help a friend."

There was a long silence.

"Mina? Are you still there?"

"Yes," she said softly.

"Please, I cannot let Abdol go alone," David insisted, trying to come up with a plausible-sounding rationale for what clearly seemed to Mina an act of insanity. "Abdol's life is too valuable to the Mahdi to let him die in Qom. I must help him get his parents to safety and then get him to safety as well. The fate of this war may very well depend upon it."

It was silent again for a few moments, and then Mina relented and gave him the address.

TEL AVIV, ISRAEL

"Haifa is a confirmed target," the IDF watch commander said urgently. *"I repeat, Haifa is a confirmed target."*

"And the second target?" Shimon pressed. "You're sure it's Jerusalem?"

"No," the watch commander said.

"Then where's it headed?" Shimon demanded, moving quickly to the watch commander's side to get a closer view of the images on the laptop.

"The computer says the second target is Dimona, sir—and now three more Shahabs have been fired and are heading toward Dimona as well."

"No—you can't be . . . Are you positive?"

"Computer puts it at a 97 percent confidence level, sir."

Shimon felt physically ill. This couldn't be happening. Dimona was a desert town, not even a city. Thirty-some kilometers south of Beersheva, it certainly wasn't a major population center. Only about 33,000 Israelis lived there—nothing like the three and a half million who lived in and around metropolitan Tel Aviv. But Dimona had something Tel Aviv didn't—Israel's only nuclear power plant. The Iranians were gunning for Dimona, and if they hit it with ballistic missiles as powerful as the Shahab . . .

Shimon grabbed the orange phone on the console in front of him, chose a secure line, and hit number one on the speed dial.

"Get me the prime minister."

HAMADAN, IRAN

Dr. Alireza Birjandi was startled by loud knocking on his front door.

He wasn't expecting anyone. How could he be? He heard neither the sounds of cars on the streets nor the laughter of children in yards. He had, however, been woken up repeatedly by the sounds of fighter jets roaring overhead. He had heard explosions, one after another, and had felt the ground shake. The Israelis were here. They had bombed the nuclear facilities in the mountains just a few miles away. They had returned multiple times to make certain the job was finished. And from what he had heard on TV, before the networks were knocked off the air, a full-scale war of rockets and missiles had erupted.

Who, then, would be crazy enough to be pounding at his door?

The knocking grew louder and more insistent, but Birjandi would not be rushed. Now eighty-three, the internationally renowned theologian and scholar of Shia Islamic eschatology was in remarkably good health—aside from being blind—but he was growing slower in his old age and increasingly felt it every year. Groaning at the aches and pains in his knees and ankles and back and hips, he laboriously forced himself up from his recliner and, feeling for his cane and grabbing its handle tightly, slowly padded to the door as the knocking intensified still more.

"Dr. Birjandi? Dr. Birjandi? Are you okay?"

Birjandi smiled to himself as he reached the door and began to undo all the locks. He knew that voice and loved it dearly.

"Ali!" he said warmly as he finally got the door open. "What a joy! But what are you doing here, my son? Do you want to get yourself killed?"

"It's not just me," Ali replied. "Ibrahim is with me too. We wanted to make sure you were safe."

"Yes, I am safe. The Lord's grace is sufficient. He is my Shepherd; what more could I want? Now, come in, come in, boys. What a joy to have you here."

Ali and Ibrahim, two young men in their early twenties, entered Dr. Birjandi's small bungalow, gave him a hug, and kissed their mentor on both cheeks. They sat down on low, cushioned chairs, their regular seats during their beloved study sessions. Each of them gave Birjandi a quick update on how they and their families were doing—all safe, so far as they knew—but they also shared their deep and growing fears for the future of their country.

"We could not wait for Wednesday," Ali explained, referring to their usual meeting time. "We have a million questions, and you are the only one we know who has the answers. I hope it is okay that we came. With the phone lines down, we had no way of giving you advance notice."

"Yes, yes, of course it is okay," Dr. Birjandi assured them. "Are the others all right?"

"They are safe, praise God," Ali said. "But they couldn't come on such short notice."

"Well, I am honored that you both have come," Birjandi said. "We have been through much in the past two months, but it was all a prelude to this moment. I have told you from the beginning: our Lord, in his great and unfathomable sovereignty, called you to himself for such a time as this. He has chosen each of you to know him and to make him known. The question is, are you ready to serve the Lord your God with all your heart and soul and mind and strength and to love your neighbors enough to tell them the truth, no matter what it may cost you?"

"We are," they insisted. "But we are scared."

"I understand," Birjandi assured them. "But you needn't be. Come, let us start on our knees with prayer."

9

"All that to say, Mr. Prime Minister, it is time to stop this madness. It is time to accept President Jackson's call for a cease-fire and end all hostilities with Iran, Hezbollah, and Hamas—now, within the hour."

This meeting wasn't going as planned. Sitting in a thick leather chair in his personal library, Prime Minister Asher Naphtali had listened carefully to the long-winded case being made by Daniel T. Montgomery, the American ambassador to Israel. But he wasn't buying a word of it, and he was losing patience. What's more, he was still in tremendous pain from the burns he had suffered in the Iranian terrorist attack at the Waldorf in New York, and soon it would be time for his nurses to change his bandages.

"Dan, you and I have known each other a long time," Naphtali said. "Yet with all due respect, I've sat here for the last half hour and listened to you lecture me about how my country is endangering the security of the Middle East and threatening the economy of the world by embarking on—in your words—'a reckless military adventure.'"

"They are the president's words, not my own, I assure you," Montgomery replied.

"Nevertheless, now the president is warning me to stop defending my country from the threat of a second Holocaust, and that is completely unacceptable," Naphtali countered. "We are under attack from a country that has built and tested nuclear weapons and has continually threatened to wipe my people off the face of the planet. At any moment, we could discover that one of the warheads that successfully penetrates our defenses is nuclear, chemical, or biological. At the same time, we're under attack from Gaza by rockets and mortars fired by Hamas and Islamic Jihad. We're under attack from the north by rockets and missiles fired by Hezbollah. The only sliver of good news, if you can really call it that, is that the Syrians have not unleashed the totality of their missile force—yet. For the life of me, I cannot figure out why. Apparently Gamal Mustafa is more concerned at the moment with killing his own people than killing us Jews. Yet I have no doubt the Syrians will strike soon and very likely with devastating effect. So where is the president of the United States, ostensibly our most trusted ally? He is warning us—Israel, the only real democracy in the entire Middle East—to stop defending ourselves or risk, what? A U.N. Security Council resolution condemning us? Then what? Economic sanctions on my country? Sanctions enforced by the American Navy and Air Force? A cessation of U.S. military aid? What exactly is the president saying here?"

"Believe me, Mr. Prime Minister, President Jackson does not want it to go that far."

"But you're certainly suggesting that if I don't accept the president's conditions, Israel is facing scenarios along these lines, correct?"

"I'm not here to deal in hypotheticals."

"They're not hypotheticals," Naphtali said flatly. "The State of Israel will not accept the president's terms. The Jewish people will not lay down our arms in the face of threatened annihilation, and furthermore, we won't be intimidated into surrender by our most important ally."

Ambassador Montgomery shifted uncomfortably in his seat. "You are putting the president in a very awkward position," he explained.

At this, Naphtali laughed out loud. "Really? Are you kidding me?" Then he sighed and said, "I have to tell you, my friend, I don't see it that way. And frankly the American people don't see it that way either. The new CBS/*New York Times* poll shows 73 percent of your country siding with us, not Iran. The NBC/*Wall Street Journal* poll finds 69 percent of the American people saying the White House should do more to support us, while the new ABC/*Washington Post* poll out yesterday shows your president's approval rating down nine points in three days, almost entirely because he's not perceived as doing enough to stand with his most trusted ally in the Middle East."

Montgomery began to protest, but Naphtali raised a hand to cut him off.

"No, no—look, Dan, I'm not interested in engaging in a Lincoln-Douglas debate on this. The facts speak for themselves. The American people—along with the vast majority of Congress—understand the magnitude of the threat we faced before the war. And they understand what we face now. They know how patient we were for the international community to act decisively to neutralize the Iranian nuclear threat. They know the president didn't do enough. They know the U.N. didn't do enough, that NATO didn't do enough. They believe President Jackson badly miscalculated vis-à-vis Iran. He vowed never to let the mullahs get the Bomb, but they did. The president vowed to have our back, but now a lot of people believe he has turned his back on us."

"Is that how you see it?" the ambassador asked.

"I'm saying that's how a whole lot of Americans see it," Naphtali replied, sidestepping the direct question. "The American people overwhelmingly support our right and our responsibility to protect our people from this apocalyptic, genocidal death cult that runs Iran. The president's resistance to standing with us, to keeping his word, is costing him politically. It's costing his party. The favorable rating for the Democratic Party is down sharply. Jewish giving to the party is down sharply. We read your papers. We see what's happening. But look, the domestic politics of this battle inside your country are not my concern, and I'm not looking for a public dustup with President Jackson. To the contrary, we both need each other right now."

"What are you suggesting?" the ambassador asked.

Naphtali didn't hesitate. "Tell the president to change his tune—*today.* Tell him to back me and the State of Israel publicly, wholeheartedly, and without reservation. And then give us the tools to finish this job."

Naphtali paused to let his words sink in, but right then a military aide rushed into the room, cleared his throat, and handed the prime minister a phone.

"I'm sorry to interrupt, sir. But you've got Defense Minister Shimon on line two, and it's urgent."

HAMADAN, IRAN

Birjandi felt a lump form in his throat.

How he loved these two young men. He was amazed at how much and how quickly they had changed. Three months earlier, each of them had been a devout Shiite. Each of them came from a deeply religious family. Their parents were Twelvers, religious zealots fiercely committed to the Twelfth Imam and the establishment of the Caliphate.

Yet both men had been watching Iranian Christian evangelists on satellite television. Both had begun reading the New Testament on the sly in hopes of refuting it. And both of them had had dreams and visions of Jesus. Within a few short weeks, each had become absolutely convinced that Jesus—not Muhammad and certainly not the Mahdi—was the Savior of mankind and Lord of the universe. Each of them secretly had, therefore, become a follower of Jesus, and the Lord had directed them to Birjandi.

For the last nine weeks, Birjandi had met secretly with them for four to five hours every Wednesday to teach them the Holy Scriptures, starting with the Gospel according to John. He had taught them how to carefully observe, properly interpret, and faithfully apply every single verse they found in the Bible. He had answered their many questions—hundreds upon hundreds of them—and he had challenged them again and again to spend time in prayer. "We serve a prayer-hearing and a prayer-answering God, a wonder-working God!" he loved to say. "And answered prayer is one of the ways we experience him."

"So where do you want to begin?" Birjandi now asked them after they had thanked their Father in heaven and committed their time in the Word to him.

Ali didn't miss a beat. "With the prophets," he said. "We want to understand the prophecies of the Scriptures. We want to know if the Bible speaks to the future of Iran. Does the Lord give us any clues as to what will happen to us? And if so, does it tell us what is going to happen with this war, how it will play out?"

"You want to know if the Israelis are going to win or if the mullahs will?" Birjandi asked.

"Yes."

The old man leaned back in his chair and clasped his hands. He seemed to ruminate over their request, but not for long.

"Very well, gentlemen, the time has come for us to search out together some of the mysteries of the ancient prophets," he said softly. "Understand that they did not speak about future events in *all* countries at *all* times, but they certainly spoke to the future of *some* countries in the last days of history before the return of Jesus Christ, and they most certainly spoke of the future of Iran. Now let's put on some tea, and we will begin."

JERUSALEM, ISRAEL

Prime Minister Naphtali grabbed the phone and took the line off hold.

He was now on a secure line with Defense Minister Levi Shimon in the IDF war room deep below Tel Aviv.

"Levi, it's me. What is it? I'm in a meeting with Monty."

"Mr. Prime Minister, we have five Shahab-3 inbound from Iran. One is headed for Haifa, but four appear headed for Dimona."

Naphtali was stunned. "You're sure?"

"That's what the computer track says."

"How long to impact?"

"Three minutes, maybe less."

"Can you shoot them down?"

"We're trying—but it's going to be close."

TIBERIAS, ISRAEL

Lexi Vandermark kept tossing and turning. She didn't want to disturb her husband, Chris, but nor did she have any idea how he could actually sleep at a moment like this. She finally lay on her back, nestled her body next to his, and stared up at the unmoving ceiling fan.

The fan wasn't moving because the hotel had no electricity. They had no electricity because a missile from Lebanon—or several, actually—had taken out the power station nearby. But Lexi refused to think about the war. She refused to look out the windows at the burning buildings in Tiberias and all the zigzagging contrails in the sky above the Sea of Galilee, some from the Israeli fighter jets that screamed by every few minutes, heading north, and some left behind by the rockets and missiles coming in from Lebanon and from Iran, heading south and west.

She closed her eyes tightly and dialed back a few days to when all was quiet and peaceful, and she and Chris were enjoying the honeymoon they had always dreamed of. Ever since they had landed at Ben Gurion International Airport, Chris had been teasing her that she'd packed too much. But she knew he didn't really mind lugging around her two suitcases in addition to his own. It made him happy to make her happy, and she hoped he planned to spend his life doing it.

They had loved seeing Jaffa and the beaches of Tel Aviv and working their way up the coast to see the ruins at Caesarea and the church on top of Mount Carmel. Chris had been especially intrigued with Megiddo, where Lexi knew the Bible foretold a great battle—the battle of Armageddon—would one day take place. But coming to Galilee—especially by Chris's side—had by far been her favorite part of the trip.

As they'd checked in to the Leonardo Plaza Hotel, with a great view of the calm and gentle sea behind them, Lexi had sat on a plum-colored sofa in the lobby watching her new husband with shining eyes. Chris was all she had ever dreamed of. He was handsome, especially in his cargo shorts and gray T-shirt, but he was also hilarious, adventurous, and brilliant. Best of all, Chris loved God more than her, and that was exactly the type of man she wanted to spend the rest of her life with. How had she gotten so lucky? It was God's gift to her, and she hoped she'd never get over the amazement of it all.

And now they were not only in the Holy Land but looking out over the water upon which Jesus had walked, upon which Peter had fished. She and Chris had spent months planning every detail of this once-in-a-lifetime journey. They'd read dozens of books and commentaries and novels about events that happened on or around the Sea of Galilee. One of Lexi's friends from church had made them matching personalized journals with biblical maps and many key Scriptures accompanying them, and they'd devoured it all. There were spaces for them to write their thoughts and paste in snapshots and brochures, and both journals were already full.

They had begun on the north shore, in Capernaum, where Jesus had established his base camp for a ministry of teaching, healing, and discipleship. Then they'd gone to the museum that housed the "Jesus Boat"—a fishing boat dating back to the first century that was just like the kind the Messiah and his disciples used. Lexi had loved holding Chris's hand as together they had watched a movie about the boat and learned about its discovery.

Slowly but surely now her eyelids were beginning to get heavy. The more she savored the sweet memories they were making, the more peaceful she felt; and the more peaceful she became, the more she let herself drift away, just for a little while, a catnap to take the edge off, and then . . .

At first she thought it was a dream or a nightmare, but suddenly Lexi realized the air-raid sirens were going off again. She was terrified. Rockets and missiles were inbound, and Lexi had no idea how many or where they would strike. Shot through with adrenaline, she jumped out of bed and shook Chris, shouting at him to get up and run with her to the bomb shelter. Though she tried to rush him, it took Chris a moment to get his bearings. Groggy and half-conscious, he wasn't listening, wasn't responding.

"Honey, sweetheart, we have to move," she shouted. *"We have to go now!"*

They'd spent most of the last three days in the hotel's bomb shelter. The war they'd never believed would really happen was happening indeed. The rocket barrage coming from southern Lebanon the first night had been so bad, they'd remained awake for nearly twenty-four hours as they heard one rocket after another hitting the seaside town of Tiberias and felt the ground shaking almost continuously from the impact. Then, to their surprise and relief, there had been a lull for the past several hours. Desperate for some sleep in a real bed, Chris had insisted they go back upstairs to their room on the ninth floor, with its king-size bed and gorgeous panoramic view. The hotel staff had begged them not to do it, but as Lexi was feeling increasingly claustrophobic herself, she had agreed. Now she realized they had both been terribly foolish.

The air-raid sirens were screaming at them to move, and she could hear people racing through the halls and yelling for others to get moving. For the first time she realized she and Chris were not the only ones who had taken advantage of the quiet to try to get a bit of sleep and some fresh air. Lexi grabbed her watch, her Bible, and her purse and dragged Chris from bed. He grabbed his glasses and a bottle of water off the nightstand and followed her out the door. They raced down the darkened hallway, but even before they got to the stairwell, they could hear the explosions, one after another.

And they were getting closer.

PALMACHIM AIR FORCE BASE, ISRAEL

Real fear was palpable in the IAF's battle management center near Tel Aviv, code-named Citron Tree. Too much was happening too fast.

The Israeli Air Force's premier missile defense command was now tracking inbound rockets and missiles from the north, south, and east, but nothing terrified them more than the possibility of a direct hit on the port city of Haifa and on their country's nuclear power plant at Dimona. The only system that could stop these particular missiles was the U.S.-funded, Israeli-designed Arrow defense system. But hitting all five missiles simultaneously with 100 percent accuracy and fewer than three minutes to spare was going to push the limits of everything they'd trained for.

The watch commander wiped his brow, knowing there was no margin for error. He and two of his senior deputies were fixated on wall-mounted flat-screen monitors displaying incoming telemetry from all five missiles being tracked by the Green Pine fire-control radar system.

High-speed supercomputers updated the precise location and trajectory of the missiles in real time and issued five separate defense plans. The commander scanned the recommendations, approved them, and immediately barked orders that they be followed, locking in the target solutions and setting into motion a sequence of events that would either save or seal the fate of the nation.

TIBERIAS, ISRAEL

Chris and Lexi raced down nine flights of stairs. They were breathless by the time they reached the bomb shelter in the hotel's basement. But to their horror they found it closed and locked.

TEL AVIV, ISRAEL

Fire-control orders were instantly relayed via secure fiber-optic lines to four different missile batteries. Two were in the north—just south of Haifa—and two were in the south, just north of Beersheva. Within moments, five two-stage hypersonic Arrow missiles exploded out of their casings and streaked into the eastern sky, one after another. Seconds later, a dozen Patriot missiles shot skyward as well, trailing the Arrows to provide a second layer of defense in case any of the first-tier interceptors should fail.

Levi Shimon stared at the monitors on the IDF war room walls. He watched as radar systems tracked the Israeli missiles lifting off and speeding toward their targets. He watched, but he could not breathe. The stakes were too high, the cost of failure simply unimaginable.

TIBERIAS, ISRAEL

Lexi could hear rockets detonating up and down the street above them. There was not another living soul in sight. Breathless and panting, she and Chris pounded on the door, screaming for someone to let them in while she silently pleaded with God for mercy.

They were trapped. They had no place else to go. They couldn't go outside. They dared not go back upstairs. So they pounded all the harder.

JERUSALEM, ISRAEL

"Quickly, come with me," Naphtali said, motioning the ambassador to follow him out of the library and down the hall to the prime minister's secure communications center, not unlike the Situation Room at the White House. "Up there—look—screens one and two."

The ambassador, flanked by several of the PM's senior aides, scanned both screens and tried to make sense of what he was seeing. The first monitor showed a digitized computer image of the upward trajectory of the Shahab missiles, lifting off from silos in northwestern Iran and arcing over Syria and Jordan. The second screen showed the downward trajectory of the Shahabs descending toward Haifa and Dimona with terrifying speed, combined with the trajectory of the Arrows and Patriots racing upward to intercept their prey.

"Mr. Ambassador," Naphtali said, now far more formal than he had been earlier, "let me be crystal clear: if any of those Iranian missiles are carrying nuclear, chemical, or biological warheads, you'll have the honor of being my guest as I order the Israeli missile force to turn Iran into glass."

10

Chris kept banging, but Lexi was too exhausted and frightened. She had all but given up hope when the door opened. A hand reached out and grabbed her, pulling her into the shadows with Chris right behind. Someone sat them down in a dark corner of the bomb shelter. It was hot and stuffy inside, and Lexi began to perspire. But she was grateful to the Lord for answering her prayers and grateful, too, that she was not alone. She squeezed her husband's hand and tried to calm her breathing and not think about the panic surging within her.

TEL AVIV, ISRAEL

Shimon and his commanders watched as the Shahab inbound for Haifa hit its apogee about ninety miles over Damascus. They watched as it began its white-hot descent. They watched as the Arrow sizzled skyward at blinding speed and closed the gap for the kill.

"Thirteen seconds to impact," said a young military aide to Shimon's right, a tremor in his voice.

Shimon turned away. He couldn't look any longer. He'd been present for all the early Arrow tests. Most had gone well. Almost all of the Arrows had hit their targets over the past few days. But now he couldn't watch.

"Ten seconds."

He was getting too old for this. And Shimon knew something most of the men in the war room didn't know. These state-of-the-art anti-ballistic missiles were far more expensive than the IDF let on. Publicly, it was said the Arrow cost $3 million each. Actually, with all of the R & D costs included, they were coming in at more than $10 million each.

"Eight seconds."

Even with American assistance, Israel could only afford a limited number. And the Arrows in the air right now, Shimon knew, were the last in their arsenal for the northern command.

JERUSALEM, ISRAEL

"Seven seconds . . . six . . . five . . ."

Prime Minister Naphtali listened to the audio feed from the war room as he and Ambassador Montgomery watched the computer screens. The computers indicated the intercept of the missile inbound for Haifa would happen first, followed in close succession by the intercept of the missiles aiming for Dimona.

"Three . . . two . . . one . . . impact!" said the young aide.

But there was no impact.

TIBERIAS, ISRAEL

Unable to see while her eyes adjusted to the near-complete darkness, Lexi fought to gain control of her emotions. Though safe for the moment, she couldn't let herself think about what still could be ahead. She was terrified of losing Chris. They'd been married for only a week. She worried for her parents. She hadn't been able to e-mail or call them. What were they thinking? She couldn't imagine.

In the darkness, Chris asked her to pray with him, but she couldn't. She was too scared. She knew he was right. She knew she needed to turn to the Lord for comfort at this moment, but something in her rebelled. She wasn't just scared. She was also angry with God. How could he have let this happen? Why didn't he want her to be happy?

She'd waited so long to finally be married, to finally have a husband and a honeymoon—here in the Holy Land, no less. Why in the world would God ruin it now?

To fear and anger, Lexi now added guilt and embarrassment. This was not the way a Christian should think, she knew. And she was mortified by the prospect of Chris knowing she was going through such a crisis of faith. But she didn't know what to do or what to say. She had to think about something else, anything else but this war and where it might lead. And inexplicably she found her thoughts shifting to Marseille Harper.

Her best friend since college, Marseille was the woman who had led her to Christ and had been the maid of honor at her wedding. Lexi closed her eyes and could see Marseille helping her with her makeup and hair before the ceremony. She could see Marseille dancing with Chris's brother, Peter—the best man—at the reception, and she remembered wishing Marseille showed even a flicker of interest in her brother-in-law, who Lexi was certain was a perfect match, but to no avail. She could feel Marseille giving her a hug as they said good-bye at the reception hall just before Chris and Lexi were driven off in that gleaming silver Bentley to a bed-and-breakfast for their wedding night before leaving for Israel the next day.

And then a thought Lexi would have preferred to stay forgotten popped into her mind. It was Marseille who had asked whether it was really such a good idea to go on a tour of Israel right now. Lexi could still hear herself scoffing at her best friend and telling her not to be such a worrywart. What Lexi wouldn't give now to have really listened, to have gone to the south of France or to Santorini or another one of the Greek isles, as Marseille had gently suggested.

But suddenly Lexi was pulled back to her current, grisly reality by the shrill voice of an older woman shoving a gas mask into her hands and telling her to put it on right away. Lexi did the best she could in the beam of the woman's flashlight. Chris, she noticed, had his mask on, but as he helped her put hers on, she began to panic. She couldn't think. She couldn't breathe. This thing was suffocating her, and her heart began to race out of control.

TEL AVIV, ISRAEL

No impact? How was that possible? Had the Arrow actually missed its mark?

Shimon could see the red line of the computer track, designating the flight of the Shahab, crossing the blue line, which designated the trajectory of the Arrow interceptor. How could that be? What had gone wrong? He tried to contemplate the horror facing the 600,000 souls living in and around Haifa.

But before he or anyone else in the war room could say anything, he saw two green lines—each designating a Patriot missile—converging on the red line.

JERUSALEM, ISRAEL

Naphtali's stomach tightened as he pounded his fist on the console beside him. Nineteen miles above Damascus, the first Patriot had sliced past the Shahab, missing the Iranian death machine by less than twenty yards. But just moments later, the second Patriot clipped one of the Shahab's tail fins and exploded upon impact. The fireball could be seen throughout all of northern Israel and was being broadcast live on Israel's Channel 2 by a camera crew on "missile watch" on the Golan Heights.

TEL AVIV, ISRAEL

Cheers erupted in the IDF war room, and Shimon imagined the same thing must be happening in the prime minister's communications center in Jerusalem. But what neither Naphtali nor Shimon nor any of their aides realized was that while the body of the incoming Shahab had vaporized upon impact, the warhead itself had not been destroyed but was simply knocked off course. Too small to be picked up by radar, the warhead hurtled downward without a guidance system and without warning. There were no more Israeli missiles in the air to stop it, and even if there had been, there was no more time.

Descending faster than the speed of sound, the warhead spiraled wildly over the Golan Heights and crossed over the Jordan River and the Sea of Galilee, heading for Tiberias, on a crash course for the city's tallest hotel—the Leonardo Plaza.

TIBERIAS, ISRAEL

The sound of the explosion above them was deafening beyond belief.

Lexi instinctively covered her ears with her hands and curled up in a fetal position, pressing hard into her husband's side. But that was only the beginning, as a series of additional explosions, each as horrifying as the first, was set into motion. Everyone in the bomb shelter was screaming. The ground beneath them shook violently. So did the walls and the ceiling. But after a few moments, everything grew quiet, including the guests and the hotel staff crammed so closely together.

For Lexi, it was too quiet. Something was wrong. She could sense it. Something evil was coming. She was soaked with sweat. She couldn't breathe in the gas mask. Her claustrophobia was kicking in. Everything in her wanted to jump up and bolt for the door. With or without Chris, she had to get out of this hellhole, out of this tomb. It was too hot. Too humid. Too cramped. She needed fresh air. She needed to run. She tried to pray but couldn't. She tried to remind herself of Bible verses she had memorized, but in her rising panic her mind went blank. She was gasping for air and hyperventilating in the process. Unable to take it anymore, she sat up, pulled away from Chris, ripped off her gas mask, and sucked in as much air as she possibly could.

She wasn't thinking about whether the air was contaminated with lethally toxic chemical or biological fumes from the Iranian missile strike, and she wouldn't have cared if she were. She couldn't wear that thing for a single second more. She couldn't imagine how Chris or the other tourists or any of the Israelis could keep those blasted things on. But no sooner had she ripped off the gas mask and felt free than she saw

Chris jumping up to help her—maybe even force her—to put her mask back on. Then she heard the groaning of the concrete and steel and rebar above her. Her eyes went wide. So did Chris's. She tried to say something, but her mouth was dry. No words would form. She knew what was coming, but she couldn't warn anyone. And even if she had, what good would it have done? They had nowhere to go and no time to run.

Chris continued to try desperately to convince her to put her mask back on, but she adamantly refused. Then came the roar she had feared most—the entire twelve-story hotel above them was beginning to implode.

JERUSALEM, ISRAEL

Naphtali watched as one by one the Israeli Arrows found their marks.

In rapid succession, four Iranian ballistic missiles were successfully intercepted. They exploded in stunning fireballs that lit up the skies over the Hashemite Kingdom's historic capital. In the prime minister's communications center, all eyes were glued to the monitors, and Naphtali knew that in homes all throughout Israel that still had power, families were huddled around television sets in their bomb shelters. They watched the live images and the video replays. They began to cheer and cry and laugh and breathe again. None of them yet knew about the tragedy in Tiberias. They were simply desperate for some good news, and now they had some.

A visibly relieved and smiling American ambassador tore himself away from staring at all the video screens and scanned the digital clocks on the wall. It was now 7:32 a.m. in Jerusalem, 9:02 a.m. in Tehran, and 12:32 a.m. at the White House. Then he turned to Naphtali and stretched out his hand.

"Congratulations, Mr. Prime Minister. I think it's fair to say on behalf of my government that while we regret and oppose this war and want you to bring it to an immediate end, we are certainly glad to see you and your team successfully defending your people, especially using technology we helped sponsor and develop. Hopefully we can ratchet this thing down very quickly and get back to talking peace."

Naphtali took a deep breath and ran his hands through his hair. Then he took the ambassador's hand and shook it firmly. "Dan, nothing would please me more than to bring this war to an immediate end. I'm not going to surrender in the face of genocide, but please tell the president if he can find a way to shut the Iranians down, I would be very grateful."

"I will certainly convey that to the president, along with the rest of our conversation."

"Thank you. It is always a pleasure to spend time with the American ambassador," Naphtali said.

But just as the prime minister was about to show the ambassador out, his military aide cut him off. "It's the defense minister again."

Naphtali took the phone. "Levi, what's wrong?"

"Sir, we have a problem."

"Why? What is it?"

"One of the Arrows missed."

"What are you talking about? I just saw—"

"No, sir. We still have an Iranian Shahab-3 ballistic missile inbound for Dimona."

"But we just watched on the monitors. I thought we got them all."

"I did too, but apparently we missed one."

"What about the Patriots?"

"They've missed as well. We're about to launch another Arrow, but it's the last one on the launcher."

"How is that possible?"

"We've had too many incoming missiles. My men are scrambling to load more missiles, but they're not miracle workers. It takes time."

"How much time?" the prime minister demanded.

"More than we have."

Shahab means "meteor" in Farsi.

True to its name, the final, unscathed Shahab-3 blazed across the morning sky like a shooting star at seven times the speed of sound, leaving a trail of flame and smoke in its wake. Having reached its apogee over the northern deserts of Saudi Arabia, the last of the Iranian death machines now began its sizzling descent toward Dimona, hell-bent on genocide. Three Israeli interceptors had already missed it, and all that stood in its way now was one last Arrow, locked and loaded but still awaiting an order from Tel Aviv.

"Fire, fire, fire!" shouted the commander, sweat pouring off his brow as he was told there was a technical glitch preventing the launch. Cursing violently, the commander picked up a phone and opened a direct line to the engineers on site, but no sooner had the call gone through than the glitch was finally resolved.

Finally the Arrow exploded into a vertical hot launch and tore into the eastern sunrise. Moments later, the missile jettisoned its solid propellant booster, began a secondary burn, and accelerated toward max speed. But precious time had been wasted on the ground. The Arrow soon hit Mach 9, or nearly two miles a second, as its onboard computers received continual updates on the Iranian missile's velocity and trajectory from the command center near Tel Aviv. Combining this data with its own infrared sensors and active radars, the Arrow's computers calculated and recalculated the optimum point of intercept, adjusting its thrusters and control fins to get it to that precise point. But would it be enough?

JERUSALEM, ISRAEL

"Ten seconds to impact!" came the voice of the war room commander over the speakerphone in the communications center.

Naphtali, flanked by the American ambassador, who couldn't leave now, turned back to the video screen, which included a live shot on CNN International from the roof of the King David Hotel in Jerusalem and another live shot on Al Jazeera from the roof of the Four Seasons Hotel in Amman. Neither were clear or sharp images. Indeed, all that could really be seen was the flaming tail of the Shahab on its downward trajectory and the upward trajectory of the Arrow. But however poor the quality, rarely had live television captured such compelling images of a potential catastrophe of this magnitude.

TEL AVIV, ISRAEL

"Eight seconds to impact."

Shimon held his breath. His eyes kept darting from the monitors providing him classified tracking of the two missiles' telemetry and the live TV images being watched by all of Israel and all of the Muslim world, if not the rest of the world as well.

"Seven seconds . . . six . . ."

The Arrow was certainly gaining, but how could it be fast enough?

"Five . . . four . . ."

Suddenly Shimon realized that for some reason the watch commander was no longer counting down the time until the Arrow's impact with the Shahab. Rather, he was counting down the time until the Shahab's potential impact with the nuclear reactor at Dimona. And just then, the red and blue lines crossed.

The Arrow had missed.

11

David was running back to the safe house when a silver sedan raced up beside him and screeched to a halt. Startled, he instinctively reached for his pistol before he saw Marco Torres behind the wheel.

"Get in," Torres shouted.

Not quite thirty years old, Torres was a former Marine sniper who had dazzled his superiors during two tours of duty in Afghanistan and was now the commander of the CIA paramilitary team assigned to assist David deep inside Iran.

"What's going on?" David asked, catching his breath while walking over to the open driver's-side window.

"The Iranians just hit Dimona."

David could hardly believe what he was hearing, but the look on Torres's face said it all—this was as real as it was serious. He got in the car, and Torres hit the accelerator.

Two minutes later, they were back at the safe house, where the rest of the team was watching the latest coverage on satellite television.

"What do we know so far?" David asked, setting his phone and pistol on a coffee table as he pulled off his sweatshirt and used it to dry his face and neck.

"Not much," said Nick Crenshaw, a former Navy SEAL on Torres's team. "Details are sketchy. The Israelis aren't saying anything, and their military censor has clamped down on any reports or even pictures leaving the country. Sky News out of London is saying a Shahab missile hit the sixty-foot dome over the reactor, but that's all we've got."

"The Israelis couldn't shoot it down?"

"It sounds like they tried but failed," said Crenshaw, hunched over a laptop and scanning for the latest headlines. "Agence France-Presse is quoting eyewitnesses in Amman saying the Israelis intercepted several Iranian missiles but missed another, and the AP has a high-ranking American source saying that's the one that hit the Dimona facility dead on."

"Who's the source?"

"Unnamed."

"Radiation?"

"No word yet, but it's got to be horrific."

"Casualties?"

"Again, nothing yet."

David was pacing the living room.

"What are you thinking?" Torres asked.

David didn't answer right away. He was trying to consider all the angles.

"Everything depends on how bad it is," he said finally. "I mean, Dimona is out in the desert—way out in the Negev—far away from most population centers. There's a decent-size city that's grown up around the facility, but I read a few weeks ago that they evacuated all nonessential personnel for just such an eventuality. Now, if it was really a direct hit, that could set off secondary explosions that could rip apart the reactor and possibly the cooling towers. That, in turn, could release radioactive clouds in any direction—toward Beersheva for certain, but also toward Eilat to the south, Cairo to the southwest, or to Tel Aviv and Ashdod to the northwest. Or Jerusalem and even Amman or Damascus to the north. A lot depends on the winds, of course, but whole cities could be in danger. And then the question is, what does Israel do to retaliate?"

"Could they go nuclear themselves, against Iran?" Torres asked.

"They might," David replied. "They really might."

There was a long and sober pause as everyone in the room processed the implications of what David was saying.

"So what would that mean for us?" one of the guys finally asked.

And there was another long pause.

"I don't know," David admitted. "But I have more bad news."

"What's that?" Torres asked.

"Zalinsky just called from Langley," David said. "It seems they intercepted a call from the Iranian high command. Somehow—and I don't know how—the Iranians still have two more nuclear warheads. At the moment, no one knows where they are, but Washington has two fears. The first is that both of the warheads are being attached right now to Iran's remaining Shahab missiles, about to be fired at Israel. The second is that only one of the warheads is going to be fired at Israel, and the other is being shipped to South America, to be transported up to Mexico and smuggled into Arizona or Texas and detonated in any of three hundred American cities."

A deathly quiet came over the room.

"Our new mission—and this comes straight from the top—is to find both of those warheads and destroy them before they leave Iran," David explained. "The good news: we're authorized to use any force necessary to accomplish our mission. The bad news: we have no leads, no sources, and very little time. So here's the plan: we're going to Qom." He quickly explained why.

"Sir, with all due respect, that's crazy," Torres said. "The Israelis have attacked the Fordow nuclear site just outside Qom over and over again. From what I hear, a radioactive cloud is building over the city. People are hiding in their homes. The government isn't telling them what to do. No one in his right mind would—"

"I get it, Marco; you're not for it," David replied, cutting him off. "But this isn't a discussion. This is our new mission. We've been wasting away around here for the last three days, and it's getting us nowhere. No, the ante has just been raised, and we need to get into this fight. So get your gear, and let's move."

LANGLEY, VIRGINIA

Deputy Director Tom Murray buttoned his brown corduroy sport coat and straightened his maroon cloth tie. He checked to make sure he didn't have any crumbs on his blue oxford shirt or his khaki trousers and prepared to swallow a mouthful of humble pie. Then he boarded the elevator and headed down into the bowels of the building. A moment later, he stepped off the elevator, three floors below street level, showed his ID badge, signed in, and asked to be taken to Eva Fischer's cell.

He was surprised by how quiet it was down there. But then, of course, there weren't likely to be more than a handful of people being held at the moment, and most of them were probably asleep. One armed guard turned on the fluorescent overhead lights while another pushed a button, electronically opening the door to Detention Wing Two. Murray was led down a long, freshly mopped hallway until they reached the designated cell. He heard a series of electronic locks releasing; then the door opened, and he cleared his throat.

"Good morning, Agent Fischer. Sorry to wake you, but it's time to get you out of here. Come on, grab your things, and let's go upstairs where we can talk."

SYRACUSE, NEW YORK

"Well, I think that's everything," Marseille said, turning the dishwasher on after she had finished tidying up the kitchen. "Guess I'm going to call it a night."

Azad had just come in from the garage after taking out the last of the garbage. He washed his hands in the kitchen sink and thanked Marseille for her help. "I don't know how we would have made it through the last few days without you, Marseille," he said with genuine warmth she'd rarely seen from either of the older Shirazi boys. "You remind me a little of Nora—tireless and full of hospitality. I wish you two could have met."

Nora was Azad's wife, who had missed the funeral because she was home in Philly, still bedridden after giving birth to their first child. From Azad, this was high praise, Marseille knew, and she was grateful.

"Well, Nora and I are becoming good e-mail and Facebook pals. I look forward to meeting her someday as well. How are she and little Peter doing?"

"Pretty well—thanks for asking," Azad replied. "I mean, she feels guilty not being here, but Peter is certainly keeping her hands full."

"I'm sure she's going to make a great mom."

"She will," Azad said, his voice catching. "She's a lot like my mother. They certainly were the glue that held this family together." He exhaled and added, "I was really stressed about coming up here and not having Nora at my side to help. I really didn't know what I was going to do. You can see Saeed is no help. Part of me is surprised he came at all. I mean, he has barely talked to anyone. He's only said a few sentences to Dad. He's . . . well . . . whatever. Let's just say I'm really grateful you showed up."

Marseille smiled. "Well, I hope it was helpful at the margins."

Saeed came in from the back deck, finished his work on his BlackBerry, and headed upstairs, presumably to bed, without saying a word.

"Good night to you, too," Azad said sarcastically after Saeed was gone.

Marseille smiled again but said nothing. The two of them stood in the kitchen together for a few more moments, neither quite sure what to say next. This wasn't the time or place to talk to Azad about spiritual things, Marseille knew. But she wondered, if it were a few hours earlier and they weren't so exhausted, how that conversation might have gone. And that made her think of David again. She wondered where he was spiritually and whether she'd ever get the chance to talk to him about Jesus.

"It's been good to see you again, Marseille," Azad said at last. "It was a surprise when you showed up, but you know . . . a good surprise. I'm just sorry my pathetic excuse for a brother couldn't be here to say thank you too."

"Which one?" Marseille joshed.

Fortunately Azad smiled.

"Either of them," he whispered. "But I meant David."

"I know," Marseille whispered back. "It's okay."

"No, actually it's not okay," Azad protested. "I mean, how could he not come home for his own mother's funeral? How could he not even call or write or anything? I want to wring his neck."

"I'm sure he has his reasons," Marseille offered.

"Reasons? What reasons could he . . . I mean, even Saeed came back."

"I know, but I'm just praying David is okay," said Marseille. "You never know. Maybe he's ill. Maybe he's in the hospital. He's not the kind of son who has a track record of not loving or respecting his mom, right?"

Azad looked quizzically at Marseille. "You still like him, don't you?" he finally asked.

Marseille immediately blushed. "What? Why—what are you talking about?" she stammered.

"I'll take that as a yes," Azad said. "Even though he didn't bother to come."

Marseille thought about that before responding. "You know, Azad, I try to believe the best of people. I know David has a good heart. I know he loved your mom. I know he loves your dad. If he could have been here, he would have been. Wild horses couldn't have kept him away. Which means that something's wrong, and to tell you the truth, I'm worried about him. Maybe you should be too."

At that, Azad winced. "Maybe you're right."

"Maybe I am," Marseille said in a whisper.

"Listen," Azad said, "I know my dad will want to say good-bye to you. You're flying back to Portland tomorrow, right?"

"Actually, later today."

"The blizzard passed?"

"Enough to open the airport, at least."

"Well, we're going to miss you. But let me go upstairs and get Dad. He'll feel terrible if he doesn't give you a proper thank-you."

"Okay." Marseille really did want to see David's father one more time, no matter how tired she felt.

"Actually, you know what would be really helpful?" Azad added just before he went upstairs. "That is, if you can stay a little bit longer. I know it's late, but . . ."

"Sure, what do you need?" Marseille asked.

"I really hate to ask this, but we've been overwhelmed the past few days with condolence calls from family and friends—I'm sure you can imagine. Anyway, if you could just compile a quick list of those callers and maybe a summary of their messages, that would be a big help. Then Dad can eventually try to call them all back. It should only take a few minutes; do you mind?"

Marseille shrugged. "Sure."

Azad gave her the phone number and passcode for their voice mail system. Then he thanked her and headed upstairs to find his father.

It was, in some ways, an odd request, and she felt a bit like she was spying on the family, but tired though she was, she did want to help them in any way she could, and if this was what they needed, then that was fine with her. She dried her hands, picked up the cordless phone, found a pad of paper and a ballpoint pen, and sat down at the kitchen table. She dialed, punched in the passcode, and began listening through the dozens of messages, taking careful notes of each, including the date and time they called.

Beep . . .

"Hello, Mohammad. Oh, my goodness—I'm so sad to hear your news. This is Rita McCourt, your old neighbor. Remember Larry and me? Oh, dear, I wish we could do something. Please call us. It's Thursday night. We're in Liverpool now, but we'd love to come by and see you. We're free tomorrow and all this weekend. Anything you need. Just know you're all in our thoughts. Will there be visiting hours? And when is the funeral? Larry and I would like to come to both. Okay, thanks—call us."

Marseille felt bad for these folks. She didn't know them, but the woman sounded sincere and obviously cared for the Shirazi family a great deal. Now Marseille wished Azad had given her this job sooner so she could have called these people back and made sure they got to the memorial service.

Beep . . .

"Dr. Shirazi? Hi, this is Linda—Linda Petrillo—the secretary at your old practice. Marge was just telling me that Nasreen is sick. Is that true? I can't believe I hadn't heard. Is she going to be okay? Are you okay? Do you need anything? I'd love to cook you a meal and bring it by. Please let me know if that would be okay. And have Nasreen call me. Here's my number . . ."

Ouch. The poor woman didn't even know Mrs. Shirazi had passed. *Beep* . . .

"I can't believe I didn't get to say good-bye to Nasreen. This is Farah—her cousin Farah, you know, in Houston. I got an e-mail from Iryana in San Jose. She just heard the news too. Please call me back. It's Friday morning. I hear the memorial service is going to be tomorrow. I so wish I could get there, but I don't think I can make arrangements so quickly for my kids. But, oh, Mohammad, I am so, so sorry. I knew she was sick, but I had no idea she was so close to the end. Please get back to me as soon as you can. Best way to get me is probably on my cell. The number is . . ."

Marseille carefully wrote down the number and then, as she did with all the others, hit 9 to save the message and went on to the next. But when the next person began to speak, she heard a voice that gave her chills. It was David.

"Dad . . . oh, Lord . . . Dad, I just heard the news about Mom. I just got your e-mails and Nora's. I can't . . . I can't believe Mom is really gone, and I'm so sorry that I'm not there. I can't believe I'm so far away, and where I am and doing what I'm doing. . . . I just want to be there with you, you know, to give you a hug and cry with you. I just . . . I don't know what to say, and I don't want to say it to a machine. You can't call me back, of course, but I'll try you again as soon as I possibly can. I don't know when that will be yet. I'm not really supposed to make personal calls, but I'm sure they'll make an exception. Of course they will. But anyway . . . Look, I'm safe. . . . It's hard, but I'm safe, so hopefully you'll get this and know that I'm thinking about you and praying so much for you and Azad and Saeed. I'm so sorry, Dad, that I won't be able to be there for the funeral. Please forgive me, and know that if there was any way I could be there, I absolutely would. And I hope you'll be able to withstand all the people who think I'm a terrible son for not being there. I'm sure you'll hear some awful comments about me. Just knowing that you understand and that you want me to do my job makes me feel a little better, but I still feel sick not being there. . . . Guess I'd better go, but . . . I can't believe she's really gone. I pray that you're okay and that you know I love you and that I loved Mom. Like I said, I'll call again if I can. I love you, Dad. Bye."

Marseille sat as still as a stone for several minutes, then hit 2 to replay the message and listened to David's voice again. It was coming from so far away. She was flooded with a sudden longing to see David again, to sit next to him and get to know the man he had become. But as she listened to the message a second time, she heard something that puzzled her. David was grieved, yet he seemed to have a confidence that he hadn't hurt his father and that indeed his father somehow understood his need to be away. He talked about being safe. That was a relief to her, but why would David's father think he was in danger? And why did David say what he did about his father understanding? Did David's father know what she knew? Did he know David worked for the CIA and was at that very moment inside Iran? How could he? Had David told him? Marseille's heart raced. She hoped that was the case. She wanted Dr. Shirazi to know the truth and to be as proud of David as she was. She would love to be able to talk openly to Dr. Shirazi about his son. Maybe he knew more than she did. Maybe she could learn more about what David was doing and when he might be coming home.

Marseille was careful to save David's message, but even though she had forty-three more messages to listen to, she knew she had to get this one to Dr. Shirazi right away. But how? It didn't seem quite appropriate to go upstairs and knock on the man's bedroom door. But she so wanted to tell him the good news.

And then, before she could make a decision of how best to proceed, Marseille began to weep. She did her best to stay quiet. She didn't want to wake up Saeed or draw any attention to herself. She wasn't even entirely sure why she was crying, but she couldn't stop. It wasn't sorrow, she told herself. It was mostly relief. But there was more to it, she knew.

She couldn't think clearly. Something inside her had just broken loose, a dam of sorts bottling up complicated emotions long suppressed. She was embarrassed, crying here in the Shirazis' kitchen. She was mortified by the possibility that Azad might find her like this. She didn't want to have to explain herself. She didn't even really know what she was feeling or why.

She reached for some paper napkins lying on the center of the table, wiped her eyes, and tried to take a few deep breaths and regain control.

12

Gamal Mustafa took the call without hesitation.

It was the fifth time he had spoken to his chief of military intelligence in the last six hours, but Mustafa wasn't angry or impatient. He had made it crystal clear to the Mukhabarat that he wanted every scrap, every update, every morsel of news he could get his hands on—even rumors—and his men were delivering.

"What do you have for me?" the Syrian president asked, stepping out onto the veranda of his third-floor office and surveying the sprawling capital city before him.

The intel chief didn't bury the lead. "The Iranians have hit Dimona," he said as professionally as he could, but Mustafa immediately picked up the barely concealed excitement in his tone.

"You're sure about this?"

"Yes, Your Excellency."

"How do you know?"

"All the Arab TV networks are reporting it—and the Western networks too. But we have other confirmation as well."

"You've heard from our man?"

"Yes, Your Excellency. He is hesitant—and rightly so—to transmit too much, lest the Zionists intercept the transmissions. But we received two short bursts, minutes apart, just moments ago. I am calling you first with the news."

"What did he say?"

"He can see the reactor from his apartment—there's a huge fire, lots of smoke. It can be seen for miles."

"Is there a mushroom cloud?"

"He didn't say."

"Radiation?"

"He's picking up some, yes, but no details yet. The moment I have more, I will let you know."

"You know what this means, don't you?"

"Is it time?"

"I don't see how we can wait any longer. Are your men ready?"

"They are."

"And the missile forces?"

"Everyone and everything is in place."

"All the targeting information is uploaded?"

"Yes, Your Excellency—the Zionists won't know what hit them. Just give us the word."

"Very good," Mustafa said as the call of the muezzin began to ring out across the ancient city from every minaret he could see. "Put everyone on standby. I'll be back to you soon. But there is someone I must talk to first."

TEHRAN, IRAN

Ahmed Darazi was in shock. He hadn't suspected for a second that the Mahdi was angry with Faridzadeh. Nor had it ever crossed his mind that the Mahdi would kill the man without warning. How were they supposed to prosecute the war now? How exactly were they supposed to win the war against the Little Satan, much less the larger battle—the more important battle—against the Great Satan, without Faridzadeh at the helm? General Mohsen Jazini was a fine and able man, to be sure, but he wasn't ready to be the defense minister of the entire Caliphate. He didn't possess the strategic foresight and genius of Faridzadeh.

And why was the Mahdi sending Jazini to Damascus? That made no sense. Syria wasn't even engaged in the war, at least not yet. Then another terrifying idea entered Darazi's heart. Could the Mahdi read his thoughts? If so, Darazi realized, he was a dead man.

Trying desperately to wipe such heretical notions away, Darazi began quietly reciting several suras from the Qur'an, hoping to keep his thoughts occupied and to jam any ability the Mahdi might have to replay the last few moments. The Twelfth Imam brushed by him without a word. Hosseini followed, so Darazi did as well.

Darazi noticed that even two and a half hours after the murder—he didn't know what else to call it—blood was still splattered over the Mahdi's robes and face, but the Mahdi himself didn't seem to notice or care. Rather, he walked into a meeting room to take the call with the Syrian president, which had just come in, and motioned Hosseini and Darazi to take their seats nearby and listen in on extension lines.

"Gamal, is that you?"

"Yes, my Lord. Thank you so very much for taking time out of your busy and glorious day to speak with your humble servant."

"You know what I'm going to ask, then?"

"I suspect I do," said Mustafa, his voice trembling ever so slightly.

"You have an answer for me?"

"Yes, my Lord. Please forgive the delay. Not all of our Cabinet members were in the country, and it has taken us several days to get everyone back to Damascus, where we could meet and discuss this very important matter."

"And?"

"And we are unanimous in our decision. We humbly request that you allow the Syrian Arab Republic to join the Caliphate, to make you our Supreme Leader, and to transfer all control of our weapons and our resources—human and financial—to your care and good stewardship."

"It is about time, Gamal," said the Mahdi. "I will be honest with you: I was losing patience with your foot-dragging and pathetic incompetence."

"Again, my Lord, please forgive me and my Cabinet. I take full responsibility. But I wanted the decision to be unanimous."

"Nonsense, Gamal," the Mahdi snorted, blood rising through his neck and face. "You wanted evidence that we were going to win, that we were really going to annihilate the Zionists as I have promised. And only now, minutes after hearing that we successfully hit and destroyed the Zionists' nuclear facilities in Dimona, do you want to join the winning side."

"We have never questioned your destiny or your power, my Lord," Mustafa protested. "As you know full well, Your Excellency, when the war started, I immediately ordered our missiles to be fired at the Zionists, until you personally called and asked me to stop—an order I immediately obeyed."

"I didn't want you involved in my War of Annihilation unless or until you had joined the Caliphate."

"We are ready to do so, my Lord. And we have all our missiles fueled and targeted and ready to fire at the enemy. Give me the command, and we will join the war this very hour, even if a few days late."

"No," said the Mahdi.

It was quiet for a moment.

"I beg your pardon, my Lord," said Mustafa. "I'm not sure that I heard you correctly."

"You did, and I said no. Of course I will accept you into the Caliphate. But I don't want you firing your weapons at the Zionists. Not yet."

"But we are ready, my Lord—and more importantly, we are eager to join the fight. I have been eager for days. It's just that—"

"Yes, yes, I know—you wanted it to be unanimous."

"Well, you see, I—"

"Silence, Gamal," said the Mahdi. "You have already tested my patience beyond its healthy limits. Now *you* will be patient and do what I say or suffer the judgment of the damned. You are not to fire upon the Zionists until I say so. Instead, you are to continue slaughtering the infidels among your people. Indeed, I want you to accelerate your operations. Kill the Christians, the Jews, and any so-called Muslims you find who won't bow to me. Find them all. In every city. In every province. Show them no mercy. I know you have begun because you heard I had given similar orders here in Iran and throughout the Caliphate. And because you have already begun the slaughter, you have bought yourself precious time you would not otherwise have. But now I want to hear reports that the blood of the infidels is flowing thick and fast through every Syrian street. And not just rebels. I'm not simply talking about you killing your political enemies. You've killed enough of those—and turned the world against you in the process. No, I want you to unleash your fury on the real infidels, the ones who will defy me as Lord of the Age. Do you understand what I am saying to you?"

"Yes, my Lord, I believe I do."

"You had better. And if you do this and do this well—if you are faithful in this small thing—I may put you in charge of something more. But not until then. Do I make myself clear?"

"Yes, my Lord; you can count on me."

"Perhaps," said the Mahdi. "We shall see. Now, there is one other thing."

"Yes, of course—whatever you want."

"Some special friends of mine are on the way. You will receive more details later. Treat them as you would treat me. Make sure they have everything they need. *Everything.* And remember this—I am watching you, Gamal, and your very soul hangs in the balance."

QOM, IRAN

Torres drove. David sat in the front passenger seat with his window down and the wind whipping through his hair as they raced south along Route 7, winding through the mountains, headed for Iran's most religious city. The rest of the team sat in the back of the stolen van, cleaning their weapons and readying themselves for whatever was to come. For the most part the roads were clear of civilian traffic, but there were a lot of military convoys about, especially those moving fuel and food.

As they exited Route 7—the Tehran-Qom Freeway—onto Highway 71 and approached the outer suburbs of Qom near Behesht-e-Masomeh, they could actually begin to smell the war. David winced. It was an odor he would never get used to—the smell of burning flesh and burning jet fuel.

A moment later, they came around a large mountain peak and over a ridge, and they could see the enormous columns of smoke and the fires raging. They were still about ten kilometers from the city center, but they suddenly felt the ground shaking and heard a massive explosion off to their right. A split second later the ground shook again, though another mountain blocked their ability to see exactly what was happening. As they kept racing forward, however, they soon broke out into a valley, and that's when they saw a group of Israeli F-16s roar overhead. David counted four jets—no, six—and soon the Israelis began dropping their ordnance. But now the sky erupted with the sound of anti-aircraft artilleries as well. The Iranians were shooting back.

"Step on it, Torres," David ordered, "and everyone stay sharp."

It was tempting to watch the battle in the skies. The planes and ordnance were mesmerizing, to be sure. But David didn't want Torres and his men distracted. There was little chance of getting hit by an Israeli air-to-ground missile or a bunker-buster bomb. Those were being fired at the Fordow uranium enrichment plant located on the northern edge of Qom. What really worried David was the possibility of running into a military checkpoint and having to explain who they were and why they wanted to enter the war zone. David had his official papers identifying him as Reza Tabrizi, a subcontractor for Iran Telecom. Torres and his men all had false papers identifying them as members of Reza's technical team. But David prayed they wouldn't have to use any of them. No Iran Telecom employee in his right mind would be working today, certainly not without a hazmat suit and portable oxygen supply. David and his team had neither, but they were going in anyway.

"Look there," Crenshaw shouted from the backseat. "Two o'clock high."

David couldn't help but turn his eyes to the right, and as he did, he felt his stomach tighten. An Israeli fighter jet was trailing smoke and rapidly losing altitude.

"He's hit," Torres said.

"Say a prayer, gentlemen," David agreed. "Looks like one of the good guys is about to go down."

It was painful to watch but impossible to look away. The Israeli pilot was valiantly trying to regain control of his plane, but even to the untrained eye it was obvious what was going to happen next. Less than a minute later, they lost sight of the F-16 behind another ridge, but they could feel and hear it hit the ground in a massive explosion, and soon they could smell it as well.

CAPE MAY, NEW JERSEY

Najjar Malik couldn't sleep—again.

He missed Sheyda, his beloved wife. He missed his daughter. He even missed his mother-in-law. He wondered where they were. Was the CIA taking good care of them? Were they safe?

Najjar rolled out of bed and went down to the kitchen of the enormous and gorgeous beachfront home in which he'd been staying nearly since he'd escaped from CIA custody the week before. It was owned by a friend of one of the producers at the Persian television network that had broadcast Najjar's now-world-famous interview explaining to his fellow Iranians why he had converted to Christianity and defected to the United States. He'd been given use of the home free of charge, for as long as he needed, on two conditions: that he not use the telephone in the house (only the untraceable cell phone the producer had given him), and that he not do anything that would alert the authorities to his presence in that particular house. Najjar had promised not to implicate the producer or his friend, and he was a man of his word. But there were moments like this when he wondered whether it was time to go to the Cape May police station and turn himself in. He wasn't a criminal, and he didn't want to be a fugitive. He had told the CIA everything he knew. He had turned over all his computer files and answered all their questions, a hundred times over. Now he just wanted to be with his family and to study the Bible with them, pray with them, and continue to communicate with the people of Iran—and Muslims around the world—telling them the good news of the one true Savior.

He went to pour himself a glass of milk but realized he had used up the last of it at dinner. He would have to go out when the sun came up and get some more. Indeed, a shopping run would do him good, as there were a number of staples he was running low on. Najjar grabbed an icy-cold Coke out of the fridge instead and went into the study, where he sat at the computer and caught up on the news.

He clicked on the BBC Persian website and was stunned by the headline: "Israeli Nuclear Reactor at Dimona Hit by Missiles." He quickly scanned the coverage, but it was sketchy at best. No specifics yet on the death toll and no official reaction from the Israeli government, but a widespread evacuation of the area around Dimona was under way, and Najjar feared Prime Minister Naphtali might now be seriously contemplating going nuclear against Tehran. He grabbed his mobile phone and tweeted a quick note about the attack along with a link to the BBC article, but he decided against adding any of his own commentary.

Sifting through other websites, he was in search of more details about Dimona and the rest of the war between Israel and Iran when to his surprise he found himself diverted by news out of Damascus. One headline in particular caught his eye: "Massacre in Syria: Hundreds Killed." He clicked on the link. The article, written by a *Time* magazine reporter in a dispatch filed in English, described the latest "horrific massacre" in a string of attacks carried out by Syrian security forces. More than three hundred people had been killed, and over a thousand more were injured.

Najjar shuddered as he continued reading about how the Syrian president appeared to be specifically targeting Christians, Jews, and other minority groups in the Islamic nation. Meanwhile, the United Nations seemed obsessed with passing resolutions condemning the Israelis for responding to the attacks of madmen instead of doing anything to condemn—much less stop—Gamal Mustafa from systematically slaughtering thousands upon thousands of innocent men, women, and children.

There was nothing he could do about it, Najjar knew, besides informing the world and staying in prayer. But for some reason the story made him miss Sheyda and their child all the more, and he got down on his knees and pleaded with God to reunite them soon.

13

"Let's go, let's go. We're almost there," David insisted as they entered the city limits and raced through the ghost town that Qom now was.

As instructed, Torres pushed the pedal to the metal. And why not? There were no cops. There was no traffic. There were no pedestrians and seemingly no activity of any kind. The streets were empty. The sidewalks were empty. Not a single child could be found on the playgrounds. Not a single shopper browsed in the stores. It was surreal.

David had been to Qom just a few days earlier—on Thursday, in fact—to meet Javad Nouri. He had met the aide to the Mahdi at the Jamkaran Mosque, in a suburb of Qom. On that day, as on every day, the city had been wall-to-wall people, and the streets had been clogged with every kind of car and truck and cab and motorcycle imaginable. Now everyone—all of it—was gone. The entire population had gone into hiding or had fled the city completely, probably fearing the possibility that one of the Israeli missiles would be nuclear and kill everything within a fifty-mile radius. David had never seen anything like it, and the entire bizarre situation gave him the creeps.

However, when they reached the entrance to Haqqani Street, where Abdol Esfahani's parents lived, everything changed again. Normally there would be nothing particularly noteworthy about Haqqani Street. Like many neighborhoods in this part of Qom, it was lined on both sides with cherry trees not yet in bloom bracketing small, two-story, single-family homes, typically owned in this neighborhood by Shia clerics and seminary professors and some of Iran's more prestigious intelligentsia.

The homes had well-manicured lawns with gorgeous rosebushes out front and varying arrays of tulips and forsythias and chrysanthemums. But this was not a normal day.

To David's surprise, the street was clogged with people looking and pointing and covering their mouths in shock. Torres slowed the car, and David peered down the street. Once again he could smell jet fuel and smoke, sharper and more pungent than any other place he had been. Smoke was billowing from a house halfway down the street. Flames were shooting twenty or thirty feet in the air. And suddenly he realized what had happened. The Israeli fighter jet they had seen falling from the sky had crashed here. And now, amid the wailing and shrieking of neighbors and onlookers and their children, David heard sirens approaching in the distance.

"Stop the car," he ordered and jumped out once Torres had pulled over. "I'm going to find Esfahani. The rest of you find a place to park on the next street. Then fan out into the crowd in a way that allows you to see his parents' house from all sides. Be discreet, and don't talk to anyone. None of your Farsi is near good enough."

Before Torres could object to the plan, David was sprinting, checking house numbers on both sides of the street until through the thick, black, billowing smoke he could make out the number 119 just two doors down from the house that had been demolished by the burning fuselage of the F-16. He was making his way around the crowd when a secondary explosion from the plane erupted to his left, sending him flying through the air and smashing onto the gravel street. Flames were now shooting a good forty or fifty feet into the air. Molten metal from the plane and burning embers from the house were landing everywhere and starting new fires.

David pulled himself back up and wiped the soot from his face. He wondered whether the Israeli jet had more ordnance on board, bombs or Sidewinder missiles that were now cooking in the flames and preparing to blow and take out the entire neighborhood. And it was then that he saw the roof of the Esfahani home ablaze.

Bolting for the front door, he started shouting for the Esfahanis and pounding as loudly as he could on the door, but it was clear no one could hear him. He could barely hear himself. He tried the handle, but the door was locked. He tried kicking it in but to no avail. He looked around. There was no one near him. The crowds that had come to gawk were now screaming and running away. But the sirens were getting closer, and David did not want to be around when the police or the army arrived. He had done nothing illegal, necessarily—nothing obvious or immediate, anyway—but he still didn't want to be interviewed or interrogated or slowed down in any way. But he absolutely had to find Abdol Esfahani, if he was really there. Or had he come and gone already? Had he already gotten his parents out and left for a safer place? After all this, was David too late?

Determined to get into the house and find out for sure one way or another, he worked his way around to the side of the house, peering through windows but seeing no one. When he got to the back door, he was fully prepared to pull out his Glock 9mm and blow through the lock. There was no one watching, and few would care even if they were. Any observers would likely assume he was a member of the secret police. But to David's surprise, the door was not only unlocked; it was open.

With the top of the house now completely ablaze, David calculated he had only a few minutes before the entire roof collapsed into the second floor, trapping and burning alive anyone who might be up there. So without hesitation he rushed into the ground floor, scanning for any movement, any signs of life.

"Abdol! Abdol Esfahani!" David yelled. *"Are you here? Is anyone here?"*

The house was rapidly filling with smoke, making it extremely difficult not only to breathe but to see.

"Hello! Is anyone here?" he yelled again.

With no sign of anyone in the kitchen, the dining room, the living room, or the first-floor bathroom, David raced up the first few stairs, continuing to shout at the top of his lungs, when suddenly, to his shock, he found himself staring up into the bleary, bloodshot, and terror-filled eyes of Abdol Esfahani. Over his shoulder he carried an older woman, clothed in a brown chador, who looked at least eighty years old, if not older.

"Reza?" Esfahani asked, stunned.

"Yes, it's me, Abdol. I came to help you save your parents," David replied.

Esfahani just stood there, paralyzed, trying to make sense of this. "How did you—?"

"No, not now," David shouted as another explosion erupted nearby. "Is that your mother?"

"Yes, yes."

"Then let's go, get her outside. This place is going to blow any second."

"But my father is upstairs too."

"Just go," David shouted. "Get your mother out. I'll go for your father."

Esfahani started choking violently.

"Go, go—don't wait," David shouted, and Esfahani finally began moving. "Take her out the back, and get her as far away from the house as you can. Is she breathing?"

"I'm not sure," Esfahani admitted as he came rushing down the stairs.

"I'll be there in a moment," David said. "Now run, and don't stop."

When he saw that Esfahani was listening and doing what he told him, David scrambled up to the second floor, dropped to his knees, and pulled part of his shirt over his nose and mouth, trying to find some decent air. But breathing was not his main problem. In his haste to get Esfahani and the man's mother out of the house, David had neglected to find out which room the father was in. He could hear the fire roaring above him. Ashes and pieces of burning lumber were already falling from the ceiling, which was clearly about to give way at any time. David crawled down the hall and peered into the first bedroom. He couldn't see a thing, so he sucked in a big gulp of air, jumped to his feet, and began feeling his way across the bed and along the floor only to find no one there. He moved to the hall, dropped to his stomach, and again took several short breaths.

"*Mr. Esfahani!*" David shouted at the top of his lungs. "*Can you hear me? Where are you? Hello?*"

The house began to rumble and shake. Burning sheetrock was now falling from the walls, and behind him a ceiling light fixture fizzled and popped and then crashed to the floor. He took another few breaths, then jumped to his feet and headed to a second bedroom, where again he felt his way through the smoke-filled darkness for what he now presumed was the unconscious if not lifeless body of an eightysomething-year-old man. But he was nowhere to be found in this room either.

David made it back to the hallway and dropped to his stomach. He put his head as low to the floor as he possibly could, but there was almost no good air left. He began choking. His eyes were watering. The heat was unbearable. His clothing was soaked with sweat. But he started crawling forward, groping with his hands in the darkness as he held his breath and prayed for mercy and God's favor.

Suddenly he hit a door, a closed wooden door. He cautiously reached up and felt for the knob with the back of his hand. He found it and winced, as it was blazing hot. He pulled the end of his long-sleeved shirt over his hand and, using that as a sort of oven mitt, turned the knob and fell into what felt like a porcelain-tiled bathroom. He worked his way across the floor and found the bathtub, and there, within it, he found Esfahani's father. The man was unconscious and covered in wet towels, Abdol's apparent effort to keep him as safe as possible until he got back. But Abdol was not coming back. No one was coming up those stairs. And if David didn't get out of this house soon, he was never getting out.

His air supply was nearly depleted. His lungs were burning. His temples pounded. Sweat poured down his body. But he kept telling himself that as desperately as he needed to inhale, if he did so, he would pass out and die a grisly, fiery death moments later. David willed himself to his feet, pulled the towels off the man, heaved him out of the tub, and slumped him over his shoulder. And then the blazing ceiling collapsed on top of them.

SYRACUSE, NEW YORK

Dr. Mohammad Shirazi came down the creaky stairs and padded into the living room in his pajamas, bathrobe, and slippers. He looked around the first floor and, seeing no one, shrugged. Not wanting to trudge all the way back up to his room yet, he lowered himself slowly into his recliner beside the embers of a dying fire. Then he drew from his bathrobe pocket his favorite pipe and some rum-and-maple tobacco, lit up, and soon was leaning back and puffing away, hoping to decompress in the first few minutes he had truly had to himself since his wife's death.

It had been such a long day, and it felt good, even at this late hour, to get off his feet and just savor the quiet. He was grateful for all the people who had come to the service. It had been a beautiful one at that, one that truly honored Nasreen for the remarkable wife and mother and friend she had been. She would have liked it, he thought, though she wouldn't have admitted it. Rather, she would have complained he was making too much of a fuss.

He was surprised that David had not called, but he didn't begrudge that. He was proud of his son, off fighting the mullahs of Iran and trying to take down the Mahdi, that wretched beast. Indeed, the only thing that had made this week bearable was the knowledge that his youngest son was fighting the good fight. He was sticking it to the regime in Tehran, and his father couldn't have been more proud. He just wished he could actually say that to David—even say it face-to-face.

Dr. Shirazi studied the pipe in his hands and enjoyed the sweet aroma of the smoke. Then he put it back in his mouth and looked at the rows of photographs on the side table near the window and around at all the special decorating touches his wife had added to the room over the years. He smiled at the memories and the faces in the frames, thankful for a very happy marriage. What a history they'd had together. What adventures. But neither he nor Nasreen had ever dreamed that their youngest son would be on an adventure such as this. *What would she have said?* he wondered. But he knew. He knew all too well, and in a way, there was a part of him that was glad she did not know. She would have been horrified to learn that David was back in the nation they had turned their backs on long, long ago. She had never wanted to go back, and neither had he—not that they could have, of course. They were both wanted criminals in Tehran.

Dr. Shirazi shuddered to think of the darkness surrounding David.

He hoped with every fiber in his being that his boy was safe. In his heart, he knew David was making a difference, and he felt a sense of honor he had never before felt about any of his sons—that his family might be a part of bringing justice to an unjust place, of bringing redemption for millions of people trapped under an evil leadership. For a moment, he considered turning on the television to see the latest news out of the Middle East, wondering if his heart and his imagination could handle what he'd see. *Not yet,* he thought. He'd check a few headlines later. Perhaps it was best to take the news in small doses.

Just then he heard the toilet in the first-floor bathroom flush. Then he heard the door open and the creak of floorboards behind him. He set down his pipe and turned his head to see Marseille Harper standing there, a yellow notebook in hand.

"Oh, Marseille, I was afraid you had left," he said. "Indeed, I was sure of it. But I'm so glad you're still here. I came down specifically to see you."

14

This was longer than the "quick discussion" Murray had expected. It was more of a negotiation, actually, and when it was over, he had what Director Allen wanted: a document signed by Eva Fischer absolving the Central Intelligence Agency of all culpability in unfairly detaining her and denying her access to even a phone call, not to mention a lawyer.

Eva, in turn, got what she wanted:

- a $100,000 settlement—twice what Allen had initially offered;
- a letter signed by Murray apologizing for "unfair treatment" of her; and
- a transfer to the National Security Agency in Fort Meade, Maryland, where she would be promoted to senior Iran analyst.

On this last point, Murray had resisted, but Eva had made it clear she wanted no part of working under Jack Zalinsky's supervision. For her, this was nonnegotiable. Given the fact that the Middle East was in a hot war, she told Murray, she wasn't inclined to leave government service altogether. But she wanted to work directly for the NSA, translating intercepts of Iranian satellite phone calls and providing analysis of the most important transcripts. In that capacity, she would be willing to interface with the CIA and, when needed, talk to Zalinsky—though she made it clear she preferred to work through Murray—but she wasn't going to work directly for Zalinsky, she didn't want to see him, and the less she could hear his voice, or even his name, the better.

In the end, Murray capitulated to every demand. He was under orders from the director of Central Intelligence to get this deal done, and fast. So he swallowed his pride and signed on the dotted line, and it was finished.

CAPE MAY, NEW JERSEY

Another grisly story out of Syria caught Najjar's attention. On the website of the German magazine *Der Spiegel,* he found an article headlined "Inside the Syrian Death Zone," detailing the brutality of the Mustafa regime.

The article described the horrific scene as Syrian government agents picked off pedestrians with sniper rifles during a busy shopping time. People doing nothing more dangerous than trying to buy a loaf of bread were being shot down in the street. Hundreds of thousands of people in Homs, Syria's third-largest city, were essentially being held hostage, afraid to leave their homes for fear of becoming targets.

Tears filled Najjar's eyes as he read. He knew of the evils committed by his own government in Tehran. He had seen such sadism, such unspeakable horrors in his own country. But the press in Iran never reported the crimes of Iran's neighbors and allies. Overcome by gratitude that he and his family had escaped such barbarism and were safe and free, but also overcome with grief for those still trapped as slaves of evil regimes, he fell to his knees and began to pray.

"How long, O Lord?" he cried. "How long until you bring justice to such wicked men? How long until you liberate such dear, innocent children? How long until you reveal Jesus to all of them, rich and poor, young and old, men and women, powerful and powerless? How long, O Lord? How long?"

SYRACUSE, NEW YORK

Mohammad Shirazi started to get up, but Marseille insisted that he remain seated, and finally he acquiesced.

"May I sit with you for a moment?" she asked.

"Of course, dear," he said. "Please sit right over there."

He pointed to the slightly worn blue-and-red plaid couch directly across from his recliner, and she nodded and sat down. It was a couch Nasreen had picked. He had never been a fan of the pattern, but he had learned long ago not to interfere in matters of interior design. Shaking his head, he looked up from the couch at Marseille and noticed that her eyes were puffy and a bit bloodshot.

"What a lovely thing, to have a member of the Harper family in this home again," he said. "You are a sweet girl, Marseille. You always have been, ever since your dear mother bore you. Nasreen and I fell in love with you the moment we saw you at the hospital. And now look at you; you've been an unexpected angel in our time of sorrow. I cannot thank you enough."

They were silent for a time, and then he said, "Your mother would have been very proud of you, Marseille. I know your father was."

"Thanks, Dr. Shirazi," she replied. "I hope you're right."

"I know I am," he said. "You forget I knew them a long, long time."

"How could I forget?" Marseille asked, smiling somewhat wistfully. "You and Mrs. Shirazi were their best friends in this world. Look, I didn't want to bother you. I didn't expect to stay this long. I just wanted to say again how sorry I am for your loss. You two had one of the most special and, dare I say, magical marriages I've ever personally had the privilege to witness. I hope someday I'll have a marriage like that."

She suddenly looked embarrassed for saying it, but he was glad she had. He and Nasreen had always wanted to see David and Marseille get married and raise a family together. To him, it was their destiny. They were just taking their own sweet time to realize it. "I have no doubt you will," he said gently.

She blushed and looked at the embers growing cold in the fireplace. "I cannot imagine what it must be like to lose someone so dear."

Dr. Shirazi saw the tears immediately well up in her eyes. He knew what she meant, but he couldn't let the moment pass.

"Sure you do, my dear," he replied. "Twice."

Marseille just nodded, unable to speak, her bottom lip quivering and a tear streaking down her cheek. After a few moments, she regathered herself. "Dr. Shirazi, is this an okay time to talk together? I don't want to bother you, but there are just a few things before I leave."

"Marseille, please, you are certainly no bother. We have never had enough lovely young ladies in this house. Our sons have not spent enough time at home. My beautiful Nasreen had to fill this place with loveliness all on her own. Happily, she had no trouble doing that. But you are a breath of fresh air to me. And you are practically family. Please, what is on your mind?"

"Well," she began, dabbing her eyes with a tissue scrunched up in her hand, "for starters, Azad asked me to listen to all the messages on your voice mail and make a list of the people who have called to express their care and sympathy for you and the family. There were dozens of voice mails to go through. It was actually amazing. You are both so dearly loved."

"That is all Nasreen. She had a way with people."

"It's both of you," Marseille replied. "There were some very nice calls. I saved them all so you can listen when you have time. But did you want to look at this list? Or I could read through it for you. I'm not sure what Azad meant for me to do with it."

"Oh, I'm not sure I can go over it now. But that is very kind. If you just set the list here next to me, I'll look over it later. I suppose eventually I'll start calling people back, maybe in a few days, when I'm left all alone in the quietness of this house. I'll need to talk to someone!"

Marseille smiled warmly at him, and he was grateful. She had a pleasant, calming way about her, and he wished she weren't leaving. She was like the daughter they'd never had but always wanted, and he wished she didn't live so far away.

"Dr. Shirazi, there was another call I wanted to tell you about."

"Of course," he said. "From whom?"

"Well, I have to admit, I rather felt like I was doing something wrong, listening to messages meant for you. But again, it was Azad who insisted that it would be helpful, and I—"

"Oh, Marseille, I'm so grateful. For everything I'm grateful. I don't know what we would have done without you. Nora is usually the one who keeps things working around here. Well, Nora and Nasreen. But like I said, you were an angel sent from God to us just when we needed you most."

"Thank you, Dr. Shirazi. That's very kind."

"So who called that has you so . . . I don't know . . . so 'sensitive,' if that's the right word?"

Marseille said nothing. He looked into her eyes, filling once again with tears, and suddenly he knew. "Oh, goodness," he said. "It was David, wasn't it?"

She nodded.

He sat up immediately and leaned forward. "Is he okay?"

"Yes, yes," she told him. "It's a beautiful message, meant just for you, of course, and not for me. But I admit, I cried when I heard it. He's safe. He wanted you to know that. And he loves you. And he feels terrible not to have been here for you and for his mom and for the memorial service."

"Would you play it for me?" he asked, putting the pipe back in his mouth, the aromatic smoke curling around his head.

Marseille looked surprised. "Are you sure?"

"Yes, let's listen to it together."

So they did, then sat in silence for several minutes.

"He's a good boy," Dr. Shirazi said finally.

Marseille nodded.

"I'm not angry with him," he continued. "His business—his work—it made it impossible for him to return to the United States. I know how deeply he loves his family, and I know he feels guilty. But he shouldn't. I am a very proud papa, and I can't wait to tell him when he gets home."

Marseille nodded, but there was something in her eyes that struck him as strange. What was it? Surprise? Curiosity? No, it was different from that. She seemed . . . *knowing*. It was a strange word to use in the circumstances, and yet, oddly enough, it fit.

"Proud of him for being a businessman, hard at work in Europe?" she asked quietly.

Why was she asking that? he wondered. *And why was she asking that way?*

"I'd be proud of him whatever he was doing," he replied.

She seemed to shrug a little.

"I have no doubt you would love him no matter what," she said at last. "But your standards were always very high, Dr. Shirazi. Somehow I don't think you'd be proud of any old thing David was doing."

"Perhaps," he said, drawing on his pipe some more. "What are you trying to say, Marseille?"

She waited for a few moments, looking deeply into his eyes.

"I think you . . ." And then she stopped herself.

"You think I what?" he asked.

She looked away, down at the floor, and then back in his eyes. "I think you know where David really is and what he's really doing," she said. "I think that's why you're proud, and I know you can't say it. But then again, neither can I."

His eyes widened. "What are you saying?" he asked again, wondering if he was hearing her right.

"I'm saying I know."

"You know?"

She nodded.

"He told you?"

"No," she said. "He told me he was a businessman going to Europe, and of course I believed him. But I found out."

"How?"

"I'm sworn to secrecy too, Dr. Shirazi. So I need to be careful about what I say. And you must understand that David doesn't know that I know. But I do."

"But I don't understand. I—"

"I realize that, and I'm sorry," said Marseille. "It's just that . . . how can I put this?" She looked into the fireplace, searching for the right words. "The thing is, Dr. Shirazi . . . well, the thing is that I recently found out my father didn't work for the State Department."

"He didn't?" Dr. Shirazi asked, genuinely perplexed and wondering what that had to do with David.

"Well, officially he did," she clarified, "but in reality he didn't."

"Then who did he work for?"

"He was a NOC, Dr. Shirazi."

"A what?"

"A nonofficial cover operative."

"A NOC?"

"Right."

"I'm sorry, but I don't understand."

"Sir, my father wasn't really a political officer for the State Department. That was just his cover. In reality, he was a spy for the Central Intelligence Agency," Marseille said bluntly.

"No, that's not possible," Dr. Shirazi insisted. "I knew him. We were the best of friends. He would have told me such a thing."

"He never told me, either. But after he died, I was taking care of his papers, and I stumbled upon a safe in the back of his bedroom closet. When I finally got it open, I was stunned. Flabbergasted, really."

"Why? What was in it?"

"Pay stubs from the CIA. The ID he used to get into Langley. A file of correspondence between him and a man named Jack Zalinsky, all on CIA stationery. I found other correspondence, too, between him and a man named Tom Murray. Do you know who he is?"

Dr. Shirazi slowly shook his head.

"He is now the CIA deputy director for operations," Marseille explained. "I even found a letter of commendation from the CIA, praising my father for his work inside Iran during the Revolution. And part of that work was helping get you and Nasreen out of the country and saving my mother's life when she was having a miscarriage."

"She told you about that?"

"No," Marseille said. "Neither of them did. I didn't find out until my father died. I found all the medical records and a bunch of journal entries. I've learned a lot about my family in the last few months, things I never imagined before." She paused for a moment, then added, "In the last few days, I've learned a lot about David, too, things I never knew either. Maybe that's why I've come to love David so much, Dr. Shirazi. Because I loved my father so much. I couldn't have been more proud of my dad, and I miss him so much it hurts. And, well . . . maybe that's why it hurts so much to think about David. It turns out they were an awful lot alike."

Dr. Shirazi was too stunned to speak. But she was right. She knew. And she not only knew about David; she knew things he didn't know about his own dearest friend. His eyes began to fill with tears. He reached for her hand, and she came over and gave him a hug as they both started to cry.

"It's nice to be able to share a secret with an old friend," she whispered.

He held her closer and nodded. "It is indeed."

15

Torres and Crenshaw saw the roof collapse. They saw flames licking out of every second-floor window. They had seen Esfahani run out the back door with his mother, and now, from their vantage point in a neighbor's backyard, several houses south of the plane crash, they could see Esfahani giving his mother mouth-to-mouth resuscitation. But they did not see David emerging from the inferno.

Glancing nervously at his watch, Torres could see that it had already been more than three and a half minutes—almost four—since David had gone into the house. He couldn't wait any longer. This was not the mission. They were here to stop nuclear warheads, not rescue elderly Iranians from burning buildings. He sprinted for the back door, shouting for Crenshaw to follow but radioing the other men to head back to the car and get it running.

The entire bathroom ceiling had collapsed on top of them.

Everything that could burn was burning. Ironically, though, with Mr. Esfahani on his back so David could save his life, the elderly man had actually saved David's by protecting him from the immediate impact of the falling timbers and the flames. Even so, he had to move fast, or they were both going to die.

Still holding his breath, his lungs screaming and about to burst, David pushed up with his forearms and got to his knees. Though he couldn't see through the smoke, he cleared away some of the debris in front of him and was able to pull himself to his feet. Then, knowing he was mere moments away from blacking out, David again heaved the old man onto his back and pushed his way into the hall. He bolted down the stairs and got to the living room just as Torres and Crenshaw reached him. He couldn't have been more stunned to see their faces, and he had never felt more grateful. They moved to take Mr. Esfahani, but David shook his head. Gasping for air, he hoisted the old man again and ran out the back door, with Torres and Crenshaw close on his heels as the entire building began to rock and sway. They were no more than ten or twelve yards away when the second floor collapsed into the first and the entire home was consumed by flames.

David didn't look back. He kept running until he reached Esfahani, then gently set the man's father down on the grass, not far from a fire engine that had just pulled up. Emergency crews raced to their side, dousing the old man with water and then giving him CPR. Another crew worked on the man's wife.

Five minutes went by. Then ten minutes, fifteen. After twenty minutes, the EMT chief stopped his work and told his colleagues to stop as well. He looked up, then rose and walked over to Abdol Esfahani, who stood covered in soot and drenched with sweat but emotionless.

"These were your parents?" the man asked.

Esfahani nodded.

"I'm so sorry. We did the best we could."

Esfahani nodded again but still showed little emotion. He didn't cry. He didn't tear up. He stood stone-faced until the medic and his team stepped away.

"I need to go," he said, glancing at his watch.

"No, it's okay," David said. "We'll stay with you. I'm so sorry, Abdol. I only wish we'd gotten here sooner."

"I have to be in Damascus," Esfahani replied as though he hadn't heard a word David said.

"Damascus? Why?" David asked.

"It's for the Mahdi," he said. "I can't say more. I'm just supposed to go there. But I don't have any . . . I guess I can . . . well . . ."

He was becoming incoherent.

"Look, Abdol, you can't go anywhere right now," David said. "You need to stay here. You need to finish this."

"No. They're dead," Esfahani shot back. "I can't bring them back. I'm alone now, and I must do what I can to serve Imam al-Mahdi. This is my calling. I cannot disappoint him."

"What does he want you to do?" David asked.

Esfahani looked into his eyes, then around at David's men. "Who are they?"

"Part of my technical team."

Esfahani shook his head. "I've never seen these men."

"You never met my entire team."

"I thought I had."

"You hadn't, but never mind," David said, trying to change the subject. "I trust them. You can too."

"It doesn't matter," said Esfahani, still shaking his head. "Rashidi swore me to secrecy."

"Even from me?"

"Well, I don't know, but I . . . I have to go."

"Can I go with you?" David asked, determined not to let this man out of his sight without extracting actionable intelligence from him. "I can help you. What do you need?"

"No, I sent a crew ahead this morning," Esfahani said, patting his pockets as if in search of his car keys. "I have to join them. It's very important. I'm sorry."

David grabbed him by the arm and pulled him close. "But, Abdol, my friend, I came here to help you," he said. "This is my war too, you know. I want to help. That's why I haven't fled the country. I have Persian blood. You know me. I want to serve the Mahdi. I want to know what he knows and make a difference in this country. Tell me—how can I help? What can I do?"

Esfahani looked into David's eyes for a moment. His were dull, lifeless, drained of all color and emotion. He pulled away and started walking toward the street. "I cannot help you, Reza. Call Mina. Have her find Mr. Rashidi. Maybe he can help you. But I cannot."

And then he broke into a sprint, disappeared around a corner, and was gone.

David stood there for a moment, looking at the burning homes before him, looking at the two dead bodies at his feet, and not believing that Esfahani had just left.

"What just happened there?" he asked, as much to himself as to his team.

"I have no idea, boss," Torres replied. "Do you want us to stop him?"

"And do what?"

"I don't know," Torres said. "Maybe we grab him, take him back to Karaj, interrogate him, and find out what the Mahdi has him doing."

"No, no, we can't do that," David said.

"Why not?" Crenshaw asked. "You said it yourself—he's our only lead."

"Then we have to find another one, and fast," said David. "Come on. This was a complete waste of time."

"Where are we going?" asked Torres.

"Back to the safe house," David replied, "before we get caught."

HAMADAN, IRAN

Ali was a desperate man. Well, perhaps *desperate* was not the right word, but he was a young man in a hurry. He wanted to save his country. He wanted to make a difference. He wanted to know everything Dr. Birjandi knew and how to articulate it with the same power and authority and clarity so that it would have the same impact. But how could he ever catch up?

He never ceased to be amazed by how many books Dr. Birjandi had. Every room of the house—except the kitchen—was lined with bookshelves, and every shelf was jam-packed with the most interesting books on theology and eschatology and history and poetry, and it went on and on and on. There were stacks of books in piles everywhere—on the couches and on chairs and in the corners of every room. And it wasn't just books. There were magazines and journals and more things to read than any human being could possibly handle, even if he could see. And Birjandi could not.

It was Birjandi's late wife, Souri, who had read it all to him, Ali had recently learned from Ibrahim, who'd had the temerity to actually ask the old man why he had so many books he couldn't read. According to Ibrahim, Souri had been fluent in five languages. She had memorized the entire Qur'an. And when they got married fresh out of high school, Souri had helped her husband memorize the entire Qur'an as well. When he went to seminary, Souri had helped him every step of the way. She had read his textbooks to him. He had dictated his homework to her. She had typed all his papers. She had even walked him to class. And apparently, so the story went, when he graduated from seminary, he was actually first in his class. And then they started writing books together, including his doctoral thesis, which was eventually published in 1978 as his first book, *The Imams of History and the Coming of the Messiah*.

Ali wanted to put a memory stick in the man's head and download everything he knew. But how?

Dr. Birjandi stirred a bit of honey into yet another cup of hot tea Ali had just placed in his hands. Then he returned the spoon to Ali and carefully took a sip.

"Ah, excellent, my son—just like Souri used to make it."

Ali laughed. The man said the same thing every single time Ali made him a cup of tea, and he had already said it three times today. Nevertheless, Ali thanked his mentor and poured a cup each for Ibrahim and himself. Then he checked his phone and noticed a new Twitter message from Dr. Najjar Malik. "Dr. Malik just sent another tweet— actually two."

"What do they say?" Ibrahim asked.

"The first reads, 'Anyone notice spike in Syria killings? Not normal brutality. Something new. Pray 4 God 2 remove Mustafa from power b4 more innocents die.'"

"He seems really worked up about Syria in the last few days, doesn't he?" Ibrahim asked.

"Yeah, he does," Ali agreed. "He's always been so focused on Iran. It's out of character."

"Maybe God is speaking through him," Dr. Birjandi said.

"To tell us what?" Ibrahim asked.

"I don't know yet, but we should ask the Lord to show us great and mighty things we do not know," Birjandi replied.

Ali and Ibrahim agreed and made a note in their journals to start really praying for the people of Syria. Then Ali read them Najjar's second tweet.

"He writes, 'More Muslims turning 2 Christ today than any other time in history. I did, and he's changing my life. R U ready? Call on Jesus!'"

"He's so bold," Ibrahim said. "I can't believe they haven't caught him yet. Is it because he's in America that he speaks so bravely?"

"No," Ali quickly disagreed. "He's bold because he has given up everything he has for Jesus. He doesn't have any more fear. He used to be trapped in a prison of lies. Now he knows the truth."

"I agree," Birjandi said. "And look how much impact you can make when you speak the truth in love and from your heart."

"Almost nine hundred thousand people are following Dr. Malik on Twitter," Ibrahim said. "It's too bad most people don't have any electricity and can't watch TV right now. I hear the satellite networks keep replaying Najjar's interviews explaining how he became a follower of Jesus. Until my phone stopped working, I was getting text messages from people all over Iran who saw part or all of the interviews before the Israelis shut down the power."

"Do you think it was really the Israelis?" asked Ali. "How do we know Hosseini and Darazi didn't order the power shut down so people couldn't see Najjar's interviews?"

"Well, either way, his message is getting out. People all over the country are openly debating what he's done and what he's saying. Some are furious at him. Some are intrigued. But they all seem to be retweeting, don't they?"

Now the two young men took their places on floor cushions as Birjandi prepared to teach them. Ali couldn't wait to hear what his mentor had to say.

"Each of us was raised not simply as a good and faithful Muslim but as a devout and fervent Shiite," Birjandi began. "What's more, we were raised as Twelvers. We believed we were living in the last days. We believed the messiah was coming soon. We believed there were signs all around us indicating that the end of human history as we had known it was at hand, that a new kingdom was coming, and with it was coming judgment for the infidels and peace and prosperity for the believers. And we were right—correct?"

"Absolutely," Ali said.

"Now, of course, when we were lost, we believed that the Twelfth Imam was our messiah. We believed the Mahdi was not only coming to save us and redeem us and rule over us and the whole world but that Jesus would be coming too, as the Mahdi's lieutenant, as his deputy. But, my sons, we were deceived. We believed a lie. In our ignorance, we did not even think for a moment—for a single second—that what we had been taught might be false, that it might have been fed to us to corrupt us, to beguile us, to lure us away from the true path. Yet God took pity on us. In his loving-kindness and mercy, God chose us, reached out to us, decided to open our eyes and enlighten us and reveal to us the truth—that Jesus is King of kings and Lord of lords and that the Mahdi is a thief and a liar. Amazingly, we're not alone. Najjar is right. God is waking up Muslims all over Iran and all over the Middle East and North Africa and across Central Asia and even in Indonesia. There is a great spiritual awakening under way right now. Millions of Muslims are renouncing Islam and choosing to follow the true King, Jesus Christ!"

The young men heartily agreed.

"Now, it's important to realize that while Shia Islam has an eschatology—an End Times theology—so does Christianity. But while Islam's eschatology, sadly, is built on the lies and the false teachings of men, make no mistake, gentlemen, the Bible is the truth—the very Word of God. The Bible is not shy about describing itself as a supernatural book. Yes, it was written down on tablets and parchments and scrolls of various kinds across the span of several thousand years by a wide variety of men, including shepherds, kings, warriors, fishermen, and prophets. But though the Scriptures were written down by men, they were not written by men. On the contrary, the Bible states clearly

16

The watch commander of the prime minister's communications center got off the phone with the IDF war room in Tel Aviv. Asher Naphtali was hoping for an update from Dimona, but this was bad news on a different front.

"Sir, we have a report that a hotel in Tiberias has collapsed," the commander told the prime minister. "Emergency crews and hazmat teams are on the scene. At this point, they have no indications of radiation or other weapons of mass destruction. But fires are raging out of control."

"What happened?"

"Witnesses are saying the hotel was hit either by a missile or possibly by debris from a missile that was intercepted over the Golan."

"How many casualties?"

"Too early to say, sir. But I'll let you know the moment we hear anything."

"And Dimona?"

"No specifics yet, sir," the commander said. "As you directed, the area has been cordoned off for a twenty-five-mile radius. Hazmat teams are assembling now and preparing to go in. I suspect we'll know more in the next half hour or so."

"Do we have any visual evidence of the damage yet?"

"No, sir, not yet."

"Have we sent in a drone?"

"No, sir—not until we have a clearer sense of the radioactivity levels."

"Are we certain there was a nuclear explosion?"

"We have no reports of a mushroom cloud per se, but beyond that I don't have any more information. I've opened a line to the IDF commander in the forward position. I can put you on with him if you'd like."

"No, that's fine," the prime minister said. "Let him do his work. Just keep me posted."

"Yes, sir."

Naphtali turned to Ambassador Montgomery. He thanked the American for coming to meet with him but said he now needed to turn his full attention to the ongoing rocket attacks. Still, he had a message for the White House he wanted Montgomery to deliver.

"Tell the president I'm going on television within the hour to update the Israeli people on where we are in the course of this war," the prime minister said calmly. "Tell him the enemies of Israel are going to pay dearly for what they have done. And make it clear that I am not going to ratchet this war down. To the contrary, I'm going to expand it. As of this moment, I am ordering a full ground invasion of Lebanon and Gaza and a massive new wave of air strikes into Iran. Simultaneously, I've sent a message through the British ambassador in Damascus to President Mustafa, warning the Syrians not to even think of joining this war. And so help me God, if any nation or terror group uses weapons of mass destruction against the State of Israel, they are going to trigger a level of retaliation the world has never seen."

Ambassador Montgomery's face was ashen. But he nodded, shook the prime minister's hand, and thanked him for the courtesy of his time. Then he was led by a security detail out of the residence and to his waiting motorcade for the quick drive back to the newly completed American consulate in the Jerusalem neighborhood of Arnona.

When he was gone, Naphtali speed-dialed his defense minister. "Levi, he's gone," he said calmly. "But I made our position clear. Now start the music. It's time."

★ ★ ★ ★ ★

HAMADAN, IRAN

Dr. Birjandi leaned back in his chair, closed his eyes, and without notes began directing his students to key Scripture passages from memory.

"Turn to Isaiah chapter 46," he said.

Ibrahim found the passage first. "What verse?" he asked.

"Nine and ten," Birjandi said.

"Here it is," Ibrahim said, stroking his beard. "Speaking through the prophet Isaiah, the Lord said, 'I am God, and there is no other; I am God, and there is none like me. I make known the end from the beginning, from ancient times, what is still to come.'"

"Good," the old man said. "Now turn to Jeremiah 33:3."

This time Ali got there first. He cleared his throat and read it softly. "'Call to Me and I will answer you, and I will tell you great and mighty things, which you do not know.'"

"Very good," Birjandi said. "Now I want you to always keep this truth in mind: the prophecies we find in the Bible are intercepts from the mind of the all-seeing, all-knowing God. They tell us God's secrets. They tell us 'great and mighty things' that we do not know about the future. And often—not always, but often—Bible prophecies are storm warnings about the future. They warn us of wars or natural disasters or other catastrophic events that God has decided he is going to allow to happen or cause to happen. But he is not telling us these things to frighten us. He is telling us in order to prepare us, so we are not surprised and so we can be ready to take bold, courageous action in service to him when the time comes."

"But what about Iran?" Ali asked. "You said the Bible tells us about the future of our country, right?"

Birjandi nodded. "There are two critically important prophecies about the future of Iran in the last days. The first is found in Jeremiah 49:35-39."

Ibrahim found the passage and began to read it. "'Thus says the Lord of hosts, "Behold, I am going to break the bow of Elam, the finest of their might. I will bring upon Elam the four winds from the four ends of heaven, and will scatter them to all these winds; and there will be no nation to which the outcasts of Elam will not go. So I will shatter Elam before their enemies and before those who seek their lives; and I will bring calamity upon them, even My fierce anger," declares the Lord, "and I will send out the sword after them until I have consumed them. Then I will set My throne in Elam and destroy out of it king and princes," declares the Lord. "But it will come about in the last days that I will restore the fortunes of Elam," declares the Lord.'"

"Elam is Iran?" Ali asked.

"Yes," said Birjandi, still leaning back, eyes still closed. "Elam is one of the ancient names of Iran, just like Persia. The passage tells us that in the last days, God will scatter the people of Iran all over the earth. For many centuries, this seemed impossible because we Persians are such a proud and nationalistic people. But as incredible as it was, this prophecy actually began to come to pass in 1979. In that year, for the first time in history, our people were scattered all over the globe. When the Shah's regime fell and Ayatollah Khomeini came to power, Iran went into upheaval. Many were overjoyed, myself included. We were deceived. Our eyes were blinded. But many others understood the evil Khomeini represented. They understood Islam was not the answer and jihad was not the way, which is why many fled Iran as soon as they could. Guess how many Iranians now live outside our country."

"Half a million?" Ibrahim guessed.

"No, higher," Birjandi said.

"A million?" Ali asked.

"Higher."

"Two million," Ali ventured.

"There are now about five million Iranians scattered all over the world," Birjandi said. "Such a thing has never happened before in the entire history of the Persian people. But it started happening in 1979, and it's still happening today."

"My uncle left Tehran in 1979. He took his whole family; they went to Canada," Ibrahim said. "My father still curses him today. Says he's a coward, an enemy of the Revolution, and no longer his brother. I wasn't even born yet. But that was it. He made his decision, and he and his whole family were dead to us. We weren't allowed to ever mention his name. I did once and my father beat me with a cane."

"I'm so sorry," said Dr. Birjandi, sitting up and leaning forward. "But you're not alone. The Revolution divided many families. But at least you know what I'm saying is true."

"Yes, I guess I do."

"Well, that's just the beginning of the prophecy," the old man continued. "The Lord says he is going to 'break' the current structure of Iran. Do you see that in the text? And the Lord goes on to say that he will 'shatter' Iran 'before their enemies.' He says he will bring his 'fierce anger' against the leaders of Iran and says, 'I will send out the sword after them until I have consumed them.' In verse 38, the Lord then says he will specifically 'destroy' Iran's 'king and princes.' Now, what does all this tell us?"

"That we're doomed," Ali said.

"Why do you say that?" Birjandi asked.

"What do you mean?" Ali replied. "God says he's going to destroy us. He's going to shatter us. He's going to break us. Sounds to me like he's going to unleash his vengeance upon us and let the Israelis utterly annihilate us, just like the Ayatollah has been threatening to annihilate them."

"In that case, young man, you're not reading the text carefully enough," Birjandi said. "What does verse 39 say?"

Ibrahim took that one. "It says that God will 'restore the fortunes of Elam.'"

"Exactly," Birjandi said. "What does that mean?"

The two young men were stumped and silent.

"Hello? Are you boys still there?"

"Yes, sir, we're still here," Ibrahim said.

"Then when does it mean?"

"We don't know."

"Really? Why not?"

"Well, it seems contradictory. Is God going to destroy us or bless us?"

"Could it be a little bit of both?" the old man asked. "Look, gentlemen, the truth is that God loves the people of Iran. He has a beautiful future planned for us. He promises to bless us in the last days. But before he can bless us, he has to purify us. Which means he is going to judge our political leaders and our religious leaders and our military leaders. He's going to break them and shatter them and consume them. Not all the people, but the leaders. See how he specifically refers to the 'king and princes'? The Lord is talking here about judging the leadership of the country. Not the people. Quite the contrary. The Lord says he is going to restore our fortunes and move his throne here—right here, in Iran."

Ali and Ibrahim were silent, poring over the text and trying to grasp the magnitude of its importance.

"Can you imagine?" Birjandi asked.

"Are you saying that after God judges our leaders and military, he's going to allow the people of Iran to become politically free and economically prosperous?" Ali asked.

"That's one interpretation, and I would certainly love to believe that. However, I lean more toward the interpretation that God specifically means he will bless the people of Iran spiritually. I believe he is going to pour out his love and forgiveness and his Holy Spirit on the people of Iran. He's going to open their hearts and their eyes and help them to see clearly that Jesus Christ is the only Savior and Lord in this world. And when he says he's going to move his throne here, I believe that means he is going to make Iran a sending country—a base camp, as it were—from which thousands, perhaps tens of thousands, of Iranian followers of Christ will fan out throughout the Middle East and around the world, preaching the gospel, making disciples, planting churches, and advancing the Kingdom of Christ. Iran is not doomed, my dear ones. Iran is on the verge of one of the greatest spiritual awakenings in the history of mankind. We are about to begin exporting the Jesus Revolution, not the Islamic Revolution. I know it looks very dark now, but the Truth is about to dawn on the Persian people."

SYRACUSE, NEW YORK

It was almost two thirty in the morning.

Marseille Harper was exhausted, physically and emotionally spent, and as she pulled her Ford Focus rental car into the driveway of her friend's childhood home in Fayetteville, a quaint and upscale suburb of Syracuse, she couldn't wait to tiptoe downstairs to the guest bedroom, slip into her nightgown, crawl into bed, and pull the covers over her head. She didn't want to see anyone else. She didn't want to talk to anyone else. She just wanted to hide away from the pain all around her and ask the Lord to hold her while she cried herself to sleep.

As grateful as she was for the time she had just spent with Dr. Shirazi, she was deeply worried for him. He was actually doing better than she had expected for the moment, but that was on the outside. What was really happening inside? He didn't know the Lord. He didn't know what the new day would hold, much less what was waiting for him in eternity. She wondered if he would ever be able to recover from the immense grief of losing his wife of more than thirty years. And she feared what news of David's death might do to Dr. Shirazi if it came in the next few hours or days, as she increasingly expected it would. She dreaded the prospect of attending yet another funeral for yet another dear, close, personal family friend. But she was beginning to steel herself for just such a prospect.

David was a CIA agent operating deep inside Iran in the midst of a cataclysmic war, the worst in modern Middle Eastern history. She didn't know exactly where in Iran he was, of course, or exactly what he was doing, but did that really matter at this point? Every minute of every hour could bring a death sentence. He was in God's hands, of course, and that, she believed, was the safest place to be. But who was to say that the Lord wouldn't allow David to die? She was praying for his safety, but she knew all too well that sometimes God said no.

Knowing the truth about David was a burden that fell heavily upon Marseille's shoulders. She was grateful that Dr. Shirazi knew too. It created a solidarity between them. But it didn't change the fact that she might never see David again, and that was a truth she wasn't certain she could bear.

After so many years, so much distance, so much silence, she had finally reached out to David Shirazi and asked to see him again. To her shock, he'd said yes, and she'd loved every second in his presence. He wasn't a boy anymore. He had truly grown into a man.

Of course, being with David was impossible. He wasn't a believer, as far as she knew. She could never join her life with someone who hadn't given his heart to Christ. Still, there was no denying how she felt. She couldn't describe how good, how safe she had felt when he'd embraced her after their too-brief visit. She could still feel his warm breath on her cheek, and it made her shiver. She couldn't say such things to his father, of course. Still, she wanted to tell someone. But whom? Her mother was gone. Her father was gone. Lexi was far away. She didn't have anyone to confide in, and even if she did, she had given her word not to say anything about David's real work, which made knowing all the more painful.

17

HAMADAN, IRAN

"You said there was another prophecy about Iran," Ali noted.

"There is," Dr. Birjandi said. "Turn in the Old Testament to the book of Ezekiel, chapters 38 and 39."

Birjandi then proceeded to walk them through a series of prophecies he said was widely known as the War of Gog and Magog. They revealed an apocalyptic showdown against Israel and the Jewish people that would be led by a nation called Magog. "There are quite a few clues that make it clear the nation referred to as Magog is modern-day Russia," Birjandi said, "including the writings of Flavius Josephus, a Roman historian. But what's critical for us to understand is Ezekiel 38:5. What is the first country mentioned that will form an alliance against Israel?"

"Persia," Ibrahim said.

"Exactly," Birjandi confirmed. "The ancient prophecies speak of a Russian-Iranian alliance sometime in the future. To many scholars, this has seemed very odd, given that for most of the last several thousand years, the Russians and we Iranians have never had such an alliance. Indeed, the leaders of these countries have hated each other. Until 1943, the Russians occupied parts of northern Iran. Under Khomeini, we prayed for Allah to bring judgment upon the heathen, godless, atheist Communists in the Kremlin. But then what happened? We suffered through eight years of the war with Iraq. We had lots of oil money but desperately needed new weapons. The Soviet Union imploded, and the Russians suddenly had lots of weapons but desperately needed money.

131

Sure enough, in the mid nineties, Iran started buying weapons from Moscow. When Vladimir Putin came to power in 2000, we started buying even more weapons. When Hosseini and Darazi rose to power, we hired the Russians to help us build our first nuclear power plant and other nuclear facilities. They sold us nuclear materials and trained our nuclear scientists. Today, as you well know, we've developed military, diplomatic, and economic ties between our two countries, just as Ezekiel 38 suggests will happen."

Birjandi explained that the prophecies indicated that this Russian-Iranian alliance would also draw more nations. Ancient Cush, he said, was modern Sudan. Put was modern Libya and Algeria. Gomer was modern-day Turkey, and Beth-togarmah he described as a group of other countries in the Caucasus and Central Asia, all with Muslim majorities or strong Muslim minorities, that would come together under Russian leadership intending to attack Israel and plunder the Jewish people.

"Now, look at 38:16," the aging scholar said. "When does God say this war is going to happen?"

Ali read the verse. "'It shall come about in the last days that I will bring you against My land.'"

"Precisely," Birjandi said. "So this is clearly an End Times prophecy. It's future-oriented, not something that has already happened."

"So who wins this apocalyptic Russian-Iranian war with Israel?" asked Ibrahim.

"Short version?" Birjandi said. "Not us."

ISRAELI-LEBANESE BORDER

Without preamble, the Israeli Air Force launched a massive new air campaign against Hezbollah positions in southern Lebanon. The first wave of fighter jets targeted Hezbollah command centers, communications facilities, missile pads, rocket launchers, arms depots, and Lebanese military bases. The next wave took out bridges over the Litani River, roads, tunnels, and other transportation infrastructure, all designed to cut off—or at least hobble—resupply efforts from the north.

Hundreds of Merkava Mark IV battle tanks—the most advanced in the IDF arsenal—soon began crossing the border into Lebanon, clearing mines and laying down withering fire against stunned Hezbollah forces, who for days had been told by their commanders that the Zionists were too cowardly to attack them. Racing across the frontier, backed up by artillery units and a massive deployment of Israeli reserve infantrymen, the Israelis gained ground faster than expected, demolishing any home, farm, factory, or mosque where rocket launchers or arms were being used or stored.

Simultaneously, Israeli tanks, armored personnel carriers, and special forces units punched into Gaza as well, initially encountering fierce resistance but responding with overwhelming force that soon crushed the front lines of the Hamas and Islamic Jihad fighters and caused them to scatter and regroup deeper in Gaza City.

Levi Shimon provided the prime minister with fresh updates over a secure e-mail system every fifteen minutes, but Naphtali's initial questions were not so much about the progress being made in Lebanon and Gaza but about whether there was any sign that Syria was getting into this fight. Thus far, the answer was no. Yet the prime minister and Shimon still couldn't understand why.

The Syrians had signed pacts with the Iranians and with Hezbollah. They were legally and morally obligated to fight. And Shimon had no illusions about just how lethal the Syrian threat was. Damascus had long ago embarked on an aggressive program to develop and stockpile large amounts of chemical weapons such as sarin gas, VX, and mustard gas. The Mossad had identified at least five facilities in Syria that were producing these deadly chemicals and had solid evidence that the Russians had helped the Syrians become fully capable of launching such weapons against Israel by aircraft, missiles, and artillery shells.

Yet something was holding the Syrians back. Yes, Naphtali and Shimon had sent Mustafa warnings through numerous intermediaries, not just the British ambassador. They had also passed word through the king of Jordan, through the U.N. secretary-general, and through the French foreign minister. Yet the silence was unnatural. Syrian missiles were not being unleashed on Israel thus far. Nor were Syrian tanks or artillery units engaging IDF forces on high alert in the Golan Heights. Something was wrong. Mustafa and the Syrian high command were up to something. Prime Minister Naphtali sensed it. It was why he kept asking questions. But Shimon had no answers, and as he opened his third pack of cigarettes since midnight, his mind raced to figure out the mystery before his country was blindsided by an evil they didn't see coming.

HAMADAN, IRAN

"The War of Gog and Magog will be unlike any other war in human history," Birjandi told his students. "No nation will come to Israel's defense. Not the U.S., not the U.N., not NATO—nobody. But Israel will not be alone. Ezekiel tells us that the God of Israel will go to war on behalf of the children of Israel and against her enemies, with devastating results."

Birjandi directed them to consider verses 18 through 20 of Ezekiel 38. "What does the text say will happen to the enemies of Israel?"

Ali took a moment to read the passage. "It looks like there will be a huge earthquake," he said.

"Correct," Birjandi affirmed. "'All the men who are on the face of the earth will shake at My presence,' the Lord says. The epicenter of the earthquake will be in Israel, but its shock waves will be felt around the world. What else?"

Ibrahim read, "'I will call for a sword against him on all My mountains. . . . Every man's sword will be against his brother.'"

"Right," said Birjandi. "In other words, in the ensuing chaos, the enemy forces arrayed against Israel will begin fighting one another. The war will begin all right, but Russian, Iranian, and other Muslim forces will be firing at one another, not at the Jews. Now look at verse 22."

Ibrahim continued reading. "'With pestilence and with blood I will enter into judgment with him; and I will rain on him and on his troops, and on the many peoples who are with him, a torrential rain, with hailstones, fire and brimstone.'"

"Here the Lord talks of the judgment he will bring against Gog, the

Russian dictator, and his allies. This will be the most terrifying sequence of events in human history to date. On the heels of a supernatural global earthquake that will undoubtedly take many lives will come a cascading series of other catastrophes. Pandemic diseases, for example, will sweep through the troops of the Russian coalition. And the attackers will face other judgments such as have rarely been seen since the cataclysmic showdown in Egypt between Moses and Pharaoh. Devastating hailstorms will hit these enemy forces and their supporters. So, too, will apocalyptic firestorms that will call to mind the terrible judgment of Sodom and Gomorrah. The Scriptures indicate that the firestorms will be geographically widespread and exceptionally deadly."

Birjandi took a sip of tea as he let the implications of the words sink in.

"Think about it, gentlemen. This suggests that targets throughout Russia and the former Soviet Union, and perhaps throughout some of Russia's allies, will be supernaturally struck on this day of judgment and partially consumed. These could be limited to nuclear missile silos, military bases, radar installations, defense ministries, intelligence headquarters, and other government buildings of various kinds. But other targets could very well include religious centers, such as mosques, madrassas, Islamic schools and universities, and other facilities where hatred against Jews and Christians is preached and where calls for the destruction of Israel are sounded. We don't know for certain because the text does not say. So we need to be very careful not to overreach in our interpretation. But I think however it plays out, it's fair to say we would have to expect extensive material damage during these supernatural attacks, and it's possible—not definite, but very possible—that many civilians will be at severe risk."

Ali and Ibrahim were taking notes as fast as they could. But Birjandi was not finished.

"Now, look at Ezekiel 39:12," he continued. "It tells us that the devastation will be so immense that it will take seven full months for Israel to bury all the bodies of the enemies in her midst, to say nothing of the dead and wounded back in the coalition countries. What's worse, verses 17 and 18 indicate that the process of burial would actually take much longer except that scores of bodies will be devoured by carnivorous birds and beasts that will be drawn to the carnage like moths to a flame. This is going to be a horrible, gruesome time. But this is what is coming. A terrible judgment is coming against Russia, against Iran, and against our allies. And perhaps what is most sobering of all is that some of Ezekiel's prophecies have already come true."

SYRACUSE, NEW YORK

Marseille turned off the lights of the Ford and shut off the engine but didn't get out and go into the house just yet. She had been thinking about David, but now, despite how tired she was, she found herself thinking about the enemy David was fighting against—the Twelfth Imam. Who was this monster that was wreaking havoc throughout the Middle East? Who was this fiend that was trying to kill her best friends, that was trying to kill all the Jews in Israel, that was trying to build a global kingdom he could rule with an iron fist? Could he be stopped? How? And by whom?

For some time now, Marseille had been seriously mulling over the possibility that the Mahdi was, in fact, the Antichrist that the Bible said would rise and rule in the last days. She had, therefore, been carefully studying the Scriptures to truly understand the prophecies about the Antichrist from both the Old and New Testaments. She had read dozens of news stories about the Mahdi, his mysterious background, and his murderous objectives. At first, she felt there must be a connection between the two. But in the past forty-eight hours or so, she had become less sure that the Mahdi, however horrible, was really the final, satanically driven tyrant of which the prophets and apostles wrote. Wasn't the Antichrist supposed to conquer Israel and rule the world? Why, then, was the Mahdi losing this war to the Jews?

She shook off the thought and put the keys in her purse. It was too late for such thoughts, and she had other matters to be concerned with. She pulled out her iPhone. She had been texting and e-mailing Lexi for days but hadn't heard anything back yet. The last e-mail she had was from several days before the war had actually begun.

Marseille wondered where her friend was and prayed for her and Chris's safety. She wiped moisture from her eyes, then checked the rearview mirror to make sure she wasn't too much of a wreck. She needed a shower and a cup of tea, but that would have to wait. For now, she just needed to close her eyes and let all the cares of the world melt away, at least for the next few hours.

She made herself get out of the car and quietly closed and locked the doors behind her. Lexi's parents—Richard and Sharon Walsh—had been through enough the past few days, and the last thing she wanted to do was wake them up. Still, as she walked up the driveway to the front door, she found herself glad that she had opted to stay with the Walshes rather than go back to the Sheraton on the university campus. Lexi's parents had strongly discouraged their daughter and new son-in-law from taking their honeymoon in Israel. Now they were beside themselves with fear. They were watching cable news nonstop as the hailstorm of rockets and missiles kept hitting the Holy Land hour after hour. Whenever she'd been able to spend time with them, Marseille had done her best to comfort Lexi's parents, though her efforts hadn't seemed to do much good. She had prayed with them and for them, but they were not believers and didn't care much for Lexi's interest in spiritual things. Marseille just hoped they were getting a decent night's sleep, at least.

She carefully opened the front door and let herself in. But to her shock the house wasn't dark and quiet. Lexi's parents weren't asleep. Her father was pacing the kitchen with a phone to his ear. Her mother was weeping, crouched in front of the television in the family room, while images of a roaring fire filled the screen.

"Have you heard the news?" Mr. Walsh asked as Marseille entered the kitchen.

"No, why? What's happening?" Marseille said.

Lexi's father pointed to the television set, and Marseille gasped as she read the text scrolling across the bottom of the screen: "CNN BREAKING NEWS—Israeli hotel in Tiberias destroyed by missile strike. . . . 46 confirmed dead, say local police. . . . 93 injured . . . Frantic search under way to find more survivors."

18

David and the team arrived back at the safe house exhausted and discouraged, David most of all. He had led his team into some extreme risks, and what had they gotten for it? Nothing. They were no closer to finding out where the warheads were, and time was running out.

He badly needed a shower, but the apartment had only two, and both were already being used. Pacing his tiny room in the safe house—a room with one small window looking out into an alley and covered with rusty metal bars that obscured what little view there was anyway—he pulled out his satphone and began dialing again, trying to reach someone, anyone who might give him a lead.

When Daryush Rashidi's line picked up, David's pulse quickened, but almost immediately his call was transferred to voice mail. He left a message, using his Iranian alias.

"Mr. Rashidi, hi again; it's Reza Tabrizi," he began. "Just trying again to reach you and make sure you're okay. Please call me as soon as you get this. I'm guessing you heard about Abdol's parents. We did everything we could. I'm so sorry. But look, I'd really love to help in any way I can. I don't know what I can do, but I'll do anything I can to help build the Holy One's kingdom on earth. I offered to go with Abdol, but he said he had all the help he needed. Is there something I can do for you? Anything? Thanks. Talk to you soon."

Frustrated but determined not to give up, David called the leader of the Munich Digital Systems technical team to see how they were doing. He knew the team was holed up in the basement of the German Embassy in Tehran, but again he got voice mail.

"Dietrich, hey, it's Reza again," he began. "Are you guys okay? I can't seem to reach anybody. Please call me back."

David continued working his way through his list of Iranian contacts. He was still not connecting with anyone, and his growing anger was palpable. When he came across Dr. Birjandi's name again, however, he hesitated. Few people had been more helpful to him personally or professionally. But was he pushing his luck? Maybe the old man wasn't answering for a reason. Maybe there was a problem. Maybe Birjandi was compromised or in danger. Was it a mistake to call him again?

Still, it was Rashidi and Esfahani—men close to the Iranian high command and the Twelfth Imam—who had introduced him to Birjandi in the first place. It was they who had encouraged him to meet the aging scholar. Indeed, it was Esfahani who had personally given David Birjandi's home phone number and address. Esfahani had urged the two to meet, and why? To encourage David's professed interest in the Mahdi. To deepen David's interest in building the Caliphate. To recruit David to join the Twelfth Imam's army. David's cover, therefore, was solid. On the face of it, he didn't have anything to fear from calling or visiting or meeting with Dr. Birjandi. And the old man himself could not have been more warm or encouraging every time the two had spoken. Why then was he not answering David's calls?

HAMADAN, IRAN

Dr. Birjandi suggested they break for a while to prepare a meal. But his young students were by no means finished with their questions.

"You're absolutely certain this War of Gog and Magog has never happened before?" they pressed.

"Yes," he replied directly.

"So you're certain these are End Times prophecies?"

"What does the text say?" he asked. "It says this will happen in the 'last days.'"

"Do you think this will come to pass soon?"

"I don't know," Birjandi conceded. "But what's intriguing to me is that as you examine the text carefully, you'll see at least three prerequisites before the prophecy may fully come to pass."

"What are they?" Ali asked.

"First," Birjandi explained, "Israel must be reborn as a country. Second, Israel must be 'living securely' in the land. And third, Israel must be prosperous. Let's consider these in reverse order." He paused for a moment, then inquired, "Do you feel Israel is prosperous?"

"Yes, of course," Ibrahim said.

"Why?"

"Well, it's certainly better off economically than any of its immediate neighbors."

"That's true," Birjandi said. "Israel as a nation is wealthier than Jordan, Syria, or Lebanon, and its economic growth rate is far better than Egypt's. In fact, the Israeli economy is consistently growing at 4 or 5 percent a year—faster than any of the major industrialized countries of the West, including the United States. And did you know that the Israelis have in recent years discovered massive amounts of natural gas offshore? There is even growing speculation that there may be enough to make Israel not only energy independent but a net exporter of natural gas, mostly to Europe. And which European country would be harmed most if Israel began selling massive amounts of natural gas?"

"Russia," Ali said.

"Exactly, but why?" Birjandi pressed.

"Because right now they're the major supplier of gas to Europe, and the Kremlin is getting filthy rich as a result."

"Correct again. Now let us consider Israel's security. Obviously at the moment, the Israelis cannot be described as living securely in the land. But what if they win this war? What if they destroy all of Iran's nuclear warheads and decimate most of our offensive military capabilities and shame the Twelfth Imam? What if they pulverize Hamas and Hezbollah, too? Wouldn't that suddenly make them more secure than at any time since 1948?"

They agreed that it would.

"But you know what's most remarkable of all?" Birjandi asked them. "So many skeptics say that the events of Ezekiel 38 and 39 will never take place, but the fact is that Ezekiel 36 and 37 have already come to pass."

JERUSALEM, ISRAEL

"Mr. Prime Minister, I have an update on Dimona," the defense minister told Naphtali over a secure line.

"Go ahead. I'm listening."

"First, the missile that hit the reactor was not carrying a nuclear warhead."

"Thank God," Naphtali said as he paced the floor of his communications center.

"Agreed," Shimon said. "Second, we are picking up significant amounts of radioactivity—but less than we had initially expected or feared."

"Good," said the prime minister. "Then I want to go to Dimona."

"What?"

"I want to see it for myself."

"Absolutely not," the defense minister retorted. "The situation is far too volatile."

"But you just told me the radioactivity is far less than expected."

"You didn't let me finish," Shimon said. "Yes, it's less than expected, but that's because we knew the facility was a high-priority target. I ordered the reactor shut down ten days ago. We quietly removed as much of the nuclear fuel and waste as we possibly could."

Naphtali was stunned. "Why wasn't I informed of this?"

"Because I was afraid someone in the Cabinet—or one of your aides—might leak the story. That would have indicated we were getting ready to strike."

"And you were right," Naphtali said. "And now I want to go and assess the damage."

"Mr. Prime Minister, this is . . . No, it's not possible. The reactor building has been severely damaged. It's completely ablaze at the moment. We can't send in fire crews because we don't want to expose them to the radioactivity that has been released—which, yes, is less than we feared, but it's still incredibly dangerous. Several of the other facilities nearby are on fire as well. We've cordoned off the entire area. We're in the process of evacuating the residents we hadn't already resettled over the past few weeks. We're going to air-drop fire-retardant chemicals on the whole complex like it's a forest fire. That's the safest bet at this point. But there are still missiles and rockets in the air. And the last thing the Shin Bet or the IDF wants is for you to be outside, in a chopper or on the ground."

"The Israeli people need to see me in command."

"Then go back on television," Shimon insisted. "Give them an update. Reassure them. But don't put yourself at risk. Can you imagine the propaganda coup Tehran would have if they killed you, even accidentally?"

"I don't like being cooped up in my office," Naphtali said, suddenly craving a cigarette though he hadn't smoked in nearly two years. "Talk to me about Damascus. Why hasn't Gamal launched his rocket force against us?"

"Who says he still won't?"

"I'm just wondering why he hasn't."

"I still don't have any answers, sir. It's gnawing at me as well. It doesn't make sense. But thank God the Syrians haven't engaged yet. I think it would push our missile defense systems beyond their limits."

"Do you think Tehran is holding Mustafa back?" Naphtali asked.

"They must be. There's no other explanation. But as for why, I don't know yet. But listen, we've got a new development. Something's cooking."

"Good or bad?"

"I can't say. Not yet. I need another fifteen minutes or so and then I'll be ready to brief you."

"Is it good or bad, Shimon?" the wearied prime minister pressed.

"Fifteen minutes, sir. I'll let you know then."

KARAJ, IRAN

David decided against trying Birjandi again. Something didn't feel quite right, though he wasn't sure what. He made a few more calls to others on his list but still got nothing. He scrolled through his contacts one more time, looking for any other source to try. He was about to give up and find some ointment for the minor burns he'd suffered in Qom when he came back across the name Javad Nouri. He had the man's private mobile number. He'd ignored it for the last few days. Was it worth trying now? Or was it too risky? He still feared Javad—or those around him—suspected him of being involved in some way in his attempted assassination. But maybe that was a mistake. Maybe the plan had actually worked like it was supposed to. Was that possible? Had David's moves to save Javad's life actually had the effect of clearing him of any suspicion? Had their gamble worked, or had it set him up for arrest and certain execution? David knew he had put the call off too long. There was only one way to find out. He took a deep breath and dialed Javad's number. To his shock, the call connected.

"Hello?" said a weak and scratchy voice at the other end.

"Is this Javad?" David asked, stunned that he had actually gotten through.

"Yes?"

"Javad Nouri?" David confirmed.

"Yes, yes. Who is this?"

"Hey, Javad, it's Reza Tabrizi. I'm just calling to check in and see if you're okay. I still feel terrible about what happened on Thursday."

"Oh, Reza, hello," Nouri replied, clearly in some pain and out of breath. "How kind . . . of you to call, my friend."

"I'm sorry I haven't been able to call sooner, Javad. How are you feeling? Are they taking good care of you?"

"Yes, well, I'm . . . I'm not good. But then again, I'm not dead . . . and for that I have you to thank. You saved my life. May Allah reward you many times over."

"No, no, it was my honor. But really, are they giving you proper treatment?"

"Yes, of course," Nouri said. "I'm at Tehran University Medical Center."

"One of the best," said David.

"Yes . . . the best," Nouri agreed, still struggling to finish full sentences without wheezing. "The Mahdi gave them strict orders to . . . take good care . . . of me. He even . . ."

"Yes?"

"He even came to . . ."

"To what?"

". . . to visit me."

The man's discomfort was palpable, and David could see he wasn't going to be able to ask Nouri anything of substance. For now all he wanted to do was get off this call and keep working through his list. He didn't have time to chitchat.

"That is wonderful," David said. "I'm glad you're in good hands, and I have no doubt you will recover quickly and be back to full health soon. And again, I'm very sorry about the condition of those satellite phones, how damaged they were. I should have gone back to Germany or to Dubai and picked them up myself. But I—"

"It's not . . . your fault, Reza," Nouri said, interrupting him. "You did the best you could. . . . Some things are out of our hands."

"Well, I still feel terrible," David said. "All I wanted to do was help."

"I know," Nouri said. "And you have. Listen . . . my nurse is telling me I must go."

"Of course, I understand," said David, glad to be moving on.

In another context, he would have to laugh. After days of trying, the one person he'd managed to reach was a senior aide to the Twelfth Imam who was lying in a hospital in the center of a city raining with bombs and missiles, a city that might very well soon be annihilated by the Israelis. He hung up even more discouraged and slumped to his knees, bowing his forehead to the ground.

"Lord, please help me," he pleaded. "I don't know what to do. Nothing I'm doing is working. This can't be your will for me. Help me, Father. People are counting on me. Millions of lives are in the balance. But I can't do this on my own. I need your wisdom. Show me what to do. Please, Father, in Jesus' name. Amen."

David remained kneeling for several minutes. Waiting. Listening. Hoping. But nothing happened. He wasn't sure what he'd expected, but the room was silent save the low hum of the fluorescent ceiling lamp.

He thought of Najjar Malik. The man had been a Twelver, and then Jesus had appeared to him in the mountains of Hamadan. Jesus had appeared to his wife, Sheyda, and to his mother-in-law. David had heard the man share his story on several television interviews. He knew God was speaking clearly and directly to Najjar Malik. Why wasn't Jesus speaking clearly and directly to him, in this room, right now?

Come to think of it, Dr. Birjandi had heard from Christ clearly and directly as well. So had his young disciples, some of whom had been radical Shia mullahs and sons of mullahs just a few months earlier. They'd all had dreams and visions of Christ. Why not David? He couldn't think of a better time than now.

But it didn't happen. What did that mean? Was God mad at him? What should he be doing differently? He remained on his knees for another few minutes, but still nothing happened.

David knew he didn't have the luxury of hesitation. Too much was on the line. He wasn't mad at God, and he hoped God wasn't mad at him. But he was lost. He was confused. And then he remembered something Dr. Birjandi had once told him: "When you aren't sure what to do, do what you are sure of." It hadn't made much sense at the time, but it actually seemed to make sense now. *Don't look for a new strategy. Don't get creative. Don't lean on your own understanding, but trust in the Lord with all your heart. Do what you've been taught. Be true to your training.* Which meant what? In this particular circumstance, what did that mean?

David sat up and looked at his phone, and he suddenly knew. He needed to talk to Dr. Birjandi. If he couldn't reach him on the phone, then he'd have to take the team to the man's home in Hamadan. One way or another, he had to connect with Birjandi—and fast.

19

Birjandi was moved by the intensity of his students' questions. These young men were so hungry to understand the future of their country and the world. They were so eager to study the prophecies and be ready for the second coming of Jesus Christ. But they had so much to learn.

"Gentlemen, Ezekiel 36 and 37 are among the least likely prophecies in all of Scripture to have actually been fulfilled," he said, sitting up in his chair and wishing he could look them in the eye. "These chapters indicate that in the last days, Israel will be reborn as a country, the Jews will return to the Holy Land after centuries in exile, the ancient ruins in Israel will be rebuilt, the deserts will bloom again, Israel will experience a spiritual awakening, and the renewed nation will develop an 'exceedingly great army.' Against all expectation, this began to happen in the early 1900s. It came to fruition on May 14, 1948, and it continues to come true to this day. Your parents and grandparents were furious about this. Ayatollah Khomeini was enraged by the prophetic rebirth of Israel, as have been his successors. They cannot even bring themselves to say the word *Israelis*. They call the Jews *Zionists*. The Arabs are not happy either, of course, and they've fought war after war since '48 to throw the Jews into the sea or annihilate them forever. But as difficult and as painful as it has been for many in this region, the fact is the rebirth of Israel is an act of God. It is the fulfillment of ancient biblical prophecies given to us by Ezekiel himself. It is ironclad proof that we are living in the last days. And given the fact that the prophecies of Ezekiel 36 and 37 have come to pass in our own time, isn't it remotely possible that the prophecies of Ezekiel 38 and 39 could come true in our lifetime as well?"

Just then, Birjandi heard a buzzing. He sensed Ali fishing in his pocket for his phone, and then the young man said, "It's another Twitter message in Farsi from Najjar Malik. 'Breaking: Iranian missile just hit Israeli nuke reactor. Rumors growing of possible Israeli nuclear strike on Iran. Pray and turn to Christ.'"

The men's tones grew far more sober. They began to discuss what this news could mean for their country and their families, none of whom were yet followers of Christ. What should they do? Where should they go? How could they reach them? Were Israeli jets—or Jericho missiles— already on their way?

Birjandi's phone rang, but he didn't get up. It rang several times more, but still he ignored it. He had no interest in answering anyone's call at the moment. There were serious things to discuss, he told himself, but he had not factored in the curiosity of his guests.

"Shouldn't you get that?" Ali asked.

"Not right now," Birjandi replied. "It's not important."

"But how do you know unless you answer? Maybe it's about this possible Israeli nuclear strike."

"Let your hearts not be troubled," Birjandi assured them.

But the men weren't buying it. "How are you even getting a phone call? Most of the phones—except for Ali's—aren't getting any reception. How come yours does?"

The phone rang again.

"Come now, let's not be distracted," Birjandi said.

But the men wouldn't let it go. They desperately wanted contact with the outside world. Birjandi desperately did not.

"It's not a mobile phone," the old man finally explained.

"What is it, then?"

"It's a satellite phone."

That seemed to intrigue them. "I've heard that the Mahdi's inner circle all have new satphones," Ali said. "Rumor has it they're German."

"Don't believe everything you hear," Birjandi warned them.

The phone continued ringing. The young men became quiet,

waiting to see if he was going to answer this time or not. Birjandi didn't want to. He feared it was going to be Hosseini or Darazi, and he didn't have any interest in talking to either of them. But then he remembered it could be David and wondered why he hadn't thought of that before.

"Okay, hand it to me, Ibrahim," he said finally. "It's on the kitchen table."

SYRACUSE, NEW YORK

Marseille returned from the powder room to the family room and took her place again on the couch beside Mrs. Walsh. She handed the griev-ing woman a fresh box of tissues and put her arm around her, but Mrs. Walsh would not be consoled.

There was still no hard news, despite all the calls Lexi's father was making. Officials at the U.S. Embassy in Tel Aviv said they did not yet have confirmation of any Americans injured or killed in the collapse of the hotel in Tiberias, though they promised to call or text back if they received any news about the Walshes' daughter and new son-in-law. The State Department in Washington was no help. It was, of course, the middle of the night on the East Coast; the international crisis hotline was supposed to be working, but all the lines were jammed because of the war in the Middle East. None of the hospitals in Tiberias or the Galilee region seemed to have any information yet. And unfortunately, the cable news networks were giving little attention to the attack in Tiberias since the Iranian strike on the Israeli nuclear reactor in Dimona was dominating all the coverage.

Marseille had suggested they turn off the television and try to get some sleep until more information was available, but neither of the Walshes would even consider the notion. She had made a pot of tea, but Mrs. Walsh wouldn't drink anything. And then it dawned on Marseille that she had an inside source. She gently patted Mrs. Walsh on the back, excused herself, and stepped away from the television into the dining room, which was a little quieter. There she pulled out her cell phone and dialed.

"Hello. You have reached the headquarters of the Central Intelligence Agency. Our working hours are 8 a.m. to 5 p.m., Monday through Friday. If you know the extension of the person you're trying to reach, press 1. If you know the name of the person you're trying to reach, press 2, then type in the last name, followed by the first name. If—"

Marseille pressed 2, then entered *Murray, Thomas.* A moment later, to her surprise, she was talking to the executive assistant to the deputy director for operations.

"Hi, Ellen, this is Marseille Harper. I'm sorry to call so late at night, but I have an urgent favor I need to ask of Mr. Murray."

KARAJ, IRAN

"Hello?"

"Oh, thank God!" David said at the sound of the old man's voice, stunned that he had actually, finally gotten through to him. "How are you? Are you okay?"

"I'm sorry; who's this?" Birjandi asked, his voice tinged with suspicion.

"Dr. Birjandi, it's me, Reza Tabrizi—David Shirazi—who do you think?"

"Oh, yes—how good to hear your voice, my friend!"

"And yours as well. How are you? Are you okay?"

"Yes, yes, of course."

"The war hasn't affected you?"

"It's affected all of us, I'm afraid," Birjandi replied. "But I'm fine. Thank you for asking."

"Do you have enough food?"

"Oh yes."

"What about power?"

"From the Lord, yes. From the electric company, no. But I have gas to cook with, so we're making tea."

David tensed. "*We* who?"

"Two from my little discipleship group," Birjandi explained. "You recall, you met them the last time you were here."

"Right," David said. "But I'm surprised you're meeting now, under these circumstances."

"Me too," Birjandi said. "They just showed up a short while ago. They wanted to study the Scriptures, so we're having a Bible study. There's not much else to do, but what could be more important? Indeed, I wish you were with us."

"So do I," David said. "So you're really safe? You're okay? You have everything you need?"

"The Lord is my Shepherd, David. I shall not want."

"I'm so glad. I've been trying to reach you for days. Why haven't you been answering your phone?"

Birjandi apologized for not answering, though he didn't really offer an explanation. Rather, he asked about David and how he was doing.

"I'm safe," David replied. "I'm well. How does the song go? 'I get by with a little help from my friends.'"

Birjandi didn't say a word, and David figured he probably wasn't much of a Beatles fan anyway.

"Anyway, listen," he continued, "there's so much I want to talk to you about. I have a lot of questions. But there's a specific reason I've been trying so hard to get ahold of you, Dr. Birjandi. Can I start with that?"

"Yes, certainly, my son. Whatever you need."

"Dr. Birjandi, we have a serious problem, and we need your help."

"Yes, I've heard."

"Really? What do you know?"

"That the Iranians have hit the Dimona reactor, and that the prime minister is considering nuclear retaliatory strikes."

David's heart raced. "I thought you had no electricity."

"I don't," Birjandi said.

"Then you don't have radio or television?"

"No."

"Did you hear this from Hosseini or Darazi? What else did they say?"

"No, no," Birjandi said. "I haven't spoken to either of them. Nor do

I want to. One of the young men here has a mobile phone that works. He's getting Twitter messages from the West. From Najjar Malik, actually. That's how we heard. But from your reaction, apparently it's true."

"Dimona was hit, yes."

"And are the Israelis going to fire nuclear weapons at us?"

"I don't know, Dr. Birjandi. I really don't."

"But it's possible."

"Yes, I'm afraid it is."

"Just possible? Or probable?"

David hesitated. He didn't want to worry his friend or the man's students. But Birjandi had always shot straight with him. David figured the man deserved the same. "Honestly, I think it depends in large part on how much damage was done to the reactor at Dimona. If the reactor was severely damaged and a radioactive cloud begins to spread across the State of Israel, that would put thousands of lives at risk, maybe millions. There are a lot of variables. But if I were a betting man . . ."

David paused, but Birjandi got it.

"It's that bad?" the old man asked.

"Yeah, it is."

"If the Israelis fired nuclear missiles, they would certainly hit Tehran, right?"

"That I don't know."

"Bushehr?"

"Probably."

"Natanz?"

"Probably."

"Qom?"

"Maybe."

"Hamadan?"

"Almost certainly," David conceded.

There was a long silence at the other end of the line. Finally David had to shift gears. "Listen, Dr. Birjandi, that's not all. There's another problem too. And it's on this that I really need your help."

"Yes, of course. What is it? How can I help?"

LANGLEY, VIRGINIA

Murray was on the line with the CIA station chief in Islamabad when his office intercom buzzed three times. That was his secretary's signal that he had an important incoming call.

"Yes?"

"Mr. Murray, I'm sorry to bother you, but I thought you'd want to know Miss Harper has just called. She's on line three. What do you want me to tell her?"

"Marseille Harper?" Murray asked, incredulous.

"Yes, sir."

"It's 3 a.m. Is she crazy?"

"Her best friend is in Israel and is staying at the hotel in Tiberias that collapsed. Her friend's parents can't get through to the embassy or the State Department to get any confirmation on whether their daughter and son-in-law are alive or dead. She said she took a chance that you were not only up but in the office, and she wondered if you could take a moment and talk to her."

"No, I can't," Murray said. "I'm on the line with . . . I'm in the middle of . . . If I take this call now, I . . . Forget it. Never mind. Tell her I can't come to the phone. But get all the information you need on her friends, get a number where you can call her back, and then get on the horn with our station chief in Tel Aviv and see what they know."

KARAJ, IRAN

David explained the situation with the two missing Iranian warheads and the fear in Washington that one could be headed toward Israel and the other toward the U.S. homeland. He didn't say how the CIA had learned of the warheads, but he did press Birjandi for intel.

"I haven't heard anything about them."

"Then I need you to call the Ayatollah."

"What on earth for?"

"I need you to ask Hosseini for a meeting with the Twelfth Imam."

"Absolutely not," said the old man. "That's out of the question."

"Dr. Birjandi, look, I know it's a lot to ask. But our only hope of finding those warheads is finding the Mahdi. He's the only person we can be sure of who knows precisely where the warheads are. Maybe Hosseini knows, and maybe he doesn't. Maybe Darazi knows; maybe not. But we can be certain the Mahdi knows where they are and is personally directing the strategy to use them against us and Israel. We need to find him, Dr. Birjandi. We need to know what he's thinking, what he's saying, what he's doing. And right now you're the only person who can reach out to him, ask for a meeting, and get one. The Mahdi has already indicated he wants to meet with you. You've been stalling. But you need to say yes, and you need to do it right now."

"My friend, you are a good young man, and you are doing good work," Birjandi replied, "but you're asking something I cannot deliver."

"With all due respect, *my friend*, you can; you're just choosing not to," David pushed back. "But you're perfect for this. They love you. They trust you. They believe you're one of them. You can find out where the warheads are and what cities they'll be used to attack, and you can call me on your satellite phone once you find out."

"No; you're not listening—that is out of the question."

"But why?" David pressed. "Don't you see how high the stakes are?"

"Of course I do," Birjandi replied. "But I am not to see the Twelfth Imam under any circumstances. Don't you understand?"

"No, honestly, I don't. You're the perfect mole. You've been summoned into the inner sanctum. And now you can say yes. You're the answer to a lot of prayers, Dr. Birjandi. God has raised you up and prepared you for this very moment. Don't you see?"

Birjandi's exasperation was becoming evident in his voice. "Please listen carefully. Let me say it as clearly as I can. The Twelfth Imam claims to be the messiah, the Lord of the Age, right?"

"Right."

"But he's not the true Messiah, is he?"

"No."

"So that makes him a false messiah, true?"

"True."

"Okay, so we're agreed. The Twelfth Imam is not just a false prophet. He's not simply a false teacher. He is a false messiah. He may be possessed by Satan himself. His closest lieutenants—Ayatollah Hosseini and President Darazi—are evil men as well, deeply influenced by satanic powers. I don't think they have always been, but I suspect they are now. And what do the Holy Scriptures tell us? In Matthew 24, the Lord Jesus made it very clear. 'If anyone says to you, "Behold, here is the Messiah," or "There He is," do not believe him. For false messiahs and false prophets will arise and will show great signs and wonders, so as to mislead, if possible, even the elect. Behold, I have told you in advance. So if they say to you, "Behold, He is in the wilderness," do not go out, or, "Behold, He is in the inner rooms," do not believe them.' Now you may not understand any of this because you refuse to take the lost condition of your soul seriously. But I gave my life to the Lord Jesus because he gave his life for me. And if he tells me not to go out to meet with false messiahs, then I am going to obey him—no matter how much it costs me or how much it displeases you."

There was a long pause.

Then David said, "Well, Dr. Birjandi, I respect you a great deal. I really do. I disagree with you in this case, but I have the utmost respect for you, even love for you because of how much you have cared for my soul."

"I want what is best for you, my son."

"I know, and that's why I need to tell you something."

"What is that?"

"Well, it's true that for most of my life, I refused to even think much about my soul, much less take care of it. But I want you to know, those days are gone."

"What do you mean?" Birjandi asked. "What are you saying?"

"I'm saying the main reason I've been trying to get ahold of you for the past few days is not because of the war," David explained. "The main reason is because the other night I got on my knees and repented of my sins and asked Jesus to save me."

At that, Birjandi's tone changed entirely. He laughed with evident joy, so loudly that David wondered what the man's students must be thinking of this strange phone call they were probably overhearing.

"That is the best news I have heard in a long time, my friend. I'm so happy for you! Everything will be okay for you now. No matter what happens, nothing can separate you from the love of Christ! Bless you, my young friend! Now please, tell me everything. Tell me how it happened."

And David did, grateful for Birjandi's joy and excitement at his decision but hoping in the end he could still persuade his friend to say yes and arrange a meeting with the Mahdi.

It didn't happen.

20

Hanna Nazeer was only twelve years old, but he had been looking forward to this moment since the age of seven. He could still remember the cold winter night five years before when he had knelt beside his bed with his mother and father and prayed to receive Jesus Christ as his Savior and Lord.

Hanna was not from a Muslim background. His parents were Orthodox Christians, as were all four of his grandparents before them, and all eight of his great-grandparents before them, and so forth going back at least two centuries. Still, Hanna insisted to his family and friends that he had not placed his faith in Christ simply because of his Christian heritage but rather because he truly believed. And now, to demonstrate that faith, he wanted to be baptized, just like the Lord Jesus was, just like Saint Paul was—indeed, perhaps in the very place where Saint Paul was baptized.

Hanna and his parents and his two younger sisters walked briskly through Bab Sharqi, the Eastern Gate, and soon arrived at the Chapel of Saint Ananias at the end of Straight Street in the Old City. They were a few minutes early, but there was already a small crowd. Amazed as he counted at least sixty people who had come for the ceremony, Hanna held his father's big, calloused hand with his own left hand and held one of his sister's small, smooth, dainty hands with his right as they squeezed through the mass of bodies to find the priest making final preparations at the front of the cavern-like stone sanctuary.

"Ah, finally, you are here," exclaimed the priest. "Welcome, welcome. You have attracted a bit of attention here, Brother Hanna, haven't you?"

Feeling shy amid all the attention and a bit warm and even claustrophobic with so many people crammed into so small a space, Hanna smiled awkwardly and looked down at the freshly swept stone floor. He hadn't anticipated any of this. He'd never really thought about what would happen or how. All he knew was that he wanted to be baptized, and where better than the church built directly over the ancient home where Ananias was used by God to heal Saint Paul from the blindness he'd received upon seeing Jesus on the road to Damascus—the same house where Ananias had befriended and encouraged the Pharisee-turned-persecutor who would go on to be the greatest of the apostles?

HAMADAN, IRAN

"Do you realize, my friend, that you have now been adopted into God's family?" Birjandi asked.

"Yes—it's amazing," David replied.

Birjandi hoped his young friend's disappointment over his own lack of cooperation on intelligence matters would be mitigated by his enthusiasm over David's decision to receive Christ. "But do you truly realize that you have been adopted by God himself?" Birjandi pressed. "That all your sins have been forgiven? Do you realize this?"

"I'm trying to, Dr. Birjandi," David replied. "It's still all so new to me."

"I will pray for you, my son," Birjandi said. "That's all I can do for you now. I wish it were more. But this is my pledge—to pray without ceasing for you at this critical hour."

David thanked him, and then the line went dead.

"That was a marvelous phone call!" Birjandi told the young men when he had hung up the satellite phone. "A dear friend has given his life to Christ."

"Yes, we gathered as much," Ali replied, smiling. "That's so exciting, and we want to hear all the details. But first, we're wondering: why was he trying to get you to go see the Mahdi?"

"That I cannot say, my friends," Birjandi demurred.

"Why not?"

"I'm afraid that's just between him and me."

"But who is this friend, and what's his interest in your going to see the Mahdi?" Ali asked. "Given your side of the conversation, he must have been quite adamant."

"That is not for you to know," Birjandi replied. "I don't want you to speculate, and I would ask you not to repeat to anyone what you've just heard."

Birjandi realized his cryptic answers were only making his disciples more curious, so he tried to get the conversation back on track. "Let us continue our study of the prophecies," he said. "Open your Bibles to the book of Revelation. There is something I want to show you."

"Wait a minute, wait a minute," Ibrahim said. "I respect you enormously, Dr. Birjandi. We both do. You know that. And we respect your privacy in certain matters, to be sure. So we won't ask you any more about this friend who certainly seems to be working with—or for—a foreign government. A government that might be able to bring down the Mahdi and this evil regime that is leading our country to destruction. A government that perhaps the Lord wants to prophetically use to set into motion the liberation of the Persian people. Nevertheless, we won't ask you about him, as incredibly eager as we are to understand how he might be able to help us. But still, I need you to clarify what you told this friend about meeting with the Twelfth Imam. You said he is a false messiah, correct?"

"Yes."

"But the Mahdi is a man, a human being, flesh and blood, correct?"

"Yes, of course."

"He's not God."

"No."

"He's a person, like you and me?"

"I suppose. In a manner of speaking. Why?"

"If you have access to him, shouldn't you try to share the gospel with him? Shouldn't you try to save him?"

"I cannot save anyone, my son. Only God can do that."

"Yes, of course, but you know what I mean. Isn't Muhammad Ibn

Hasan Ibn Ali a soul worth sharing the Good News of Christ's love and mercy and forgiveness with?"

"The man may be possessed by Lucifer himself," Birjandi said.

"Maybe so," said Ibrahim. "But didn't Jesus cast demons out of lost souls and thereby win them to himself?"

"Of course."

"And haven't you been saying that Jesus chose us to share the gospel and to have authority in the spiritual battle to set people free from demonic oppression all over Iran? Shouldn't you be doing the same?"

Ibrahim was younger than Ali, but he was also brilliant, the son of a highly esteemed Shia cleric in Qom. He had memorized most of the Qur'an by the age of nine. He was sharp and inquisitive and fearless about his newfound faith, but he was also impulsive and had a tendency to speak too much and to act without having fully thought everything through. If Birjandi gave him permission, Ibrahim would rush into the most esteemed seminaries in all of Qom and make the case for Christ powerfully and effectively with the best of the religious leaders of his day, even if that meant going to prison, which it would, and even if that meant being tortured and executed, which it might. With enough time and the proper training, Ibrahim was going to make a gifted leader of men, a powerful ambassador for the Lord Jesus Christ. But this was not yet the time, and Ibrahim was not yet ready.

The teacher and the student had clashed over this many times in recent weeks. Ibrahim argued that the hour was late and the need was enormous. Why, then, was Birjandi holding him back? Birjandi counseled patience, that Ibrahim's time would come, that the Lord would open a significant door for him—and for the others as well—and that the Lord would do great and mighty things through each of them.

But the conversion of Najjar Malik, Birjandi now realized, had upset the apple cart. Najjar had been a believer for only a matter of days, and now he was reaching millions with the dramatic story of his conversion. The young men sitting before him, meanwhile, had been saved for half a year already. They certainly knew the Word far better than Najjar, but how many people had they shared Christ with so far? A few dozen, at most.

Maybe Ibrahim was right. Maybe it was time to set these men free to preach and teach and make disciples without reservation. Both of them knew the cost, and both of them were ready to give their lives for the One who had given his life for them. Maybe it was also time to set a powerful example for them . . . but not with the Mahdi. That was a bridge too far, Birjandi told himself. Being bold for Jesus was one thing. Being disobedient was quite another, and he would not cross the line.

Birjandi suddenly realized he had been quiet for several minutes, contemplating his answer longer than he had planned. "Your heart for the lost is admirable, Ibrahim," he began. "I commend you for it, and heaven forbid that I should stifle or smother it. That is certainly not my intention. Perhaps it is time for you to stand up publicly for Jesus, the way our brother Najjar has done with such power and with such effect. Perhaps it is my time too. I have been your teacher for these six months, but you are teaching me something today, and for this I am grateful. But listen to me, both of you. Please hear my heart. As ready as I am to die for my Jesus, I cannot disobey his clear teaching. You heard me repeat on the phone the passage from Matthew 24. The Lord told his followers not to pursue false messiahs, not to seek them out, not to visit them or spend time with them."

To Birjandi's surprise, this answer seemed to satisfy Ibrahim, but it also stirred up new questions in Ali, who until now had sat back and listened.

"Dr. Birjandi, would you say you are really still part of the Mahdi's inner circle?"

"No, not the Mahdi's."

"But perhaps Hosseini's and Darazi's?"

"Perhaps."

"You wouldn't describe them as false messiahs, would you?"

"No, I suppose not."

"So isn't it possible that they are still reachable, still redeemable— theoretically, at least?"

The old man took a moment to contemplate that. "Yes, theoretically."

Apparently satisfied by that answer, Ali took the next step. "Then may I ask you a sensitive question?"

"What, you haven't already?" Birjandi smiled.

"Dr. Birjandi, in your time with the Ayatollah and the president, have you ever actually told them you believe in Jesus?"

There was a long, pregnant pause. "No, Ali," the scholar admitted. "I have not."

"May I ask you why not?"

"Have you told your father, Ali?" Birjandi countered, knowing full well Ali's father was an F-4 fighter pilot and the commander of a tactical air wing in the Iranian Air Force, stationed in Bushehr.

"No," Ali said, shaking his head.

"May I ask you why not?"

"Well, at the moment, I'm not even sure he's alive."

"I know, and I'm praying for his life and his soul," Birjandi said. "But until now, knowing war was coming, why did you not share the gospel with him? Please know, my son, that I'm not blaming you or criticizing you. I'm simply asking, as you have asked me."

Ali was silent for a moment. "My father is a Twelver, as I was," he said at last. "He is fully devoted to the Mahdi and this regime, and he hates Christians and Jews with a vengeance. If I told him I had renounced Islam and become a follower of Jesus, my father would kill me—literally kill me."

Birjandi reached out and put his hand on the young man's shoulder. "And yet, doesn't Jesus tell us that unless we're willing to pick up our crosses daily and follow him no matter what the cost, we're not worthy of him?"

"Yes," Ali said quietly.

"And didn't the apostle Paul say, 'For to me, to live is Christ and to die is gain'?"

"Yes."

"Paul wasn't afraid to die. Indeed, he was looking forward to being in the presence of Jesus, to worshiping his King and Savior. So Paul preached without fear. And so should we. The fear of death should have no part in our thinking."

"You're saying we should share the gospel even if it means certain death for us?"

"Each of us must move as the Holy Spirit guides us," Birjandi replied. "Our job is to say what he wants us to say, when he wants us to say it. The words and the timing must be the Lord's, but yes, we must be faithful to share the gospel with anyone and everyone the Lord opens the door for us to reach."

There was another long pause.

"You're right," Ali said. "I've been counting the cost, and I have to confess before both of you, my dearest friends, that I've been struggling. But the past few days I've been praying and fasting in agony, begging the Lord to save my father and the rest of my family, to give me another chance to share the Good News with each of them. And if you will pray for me for strength, then I will be faithful to the task, come what may."

Birjandi and Ibrahim promised to pray for Ali and his family. But Ali was not finished.

"With all due respect, Dr. Birjandi, the question really comes back to you," he said gently. "Maybe the Mahdi is unreachable or unwinnable for Christ. I don't know. I'm not the scholar. You are. But isn't it time for you to share the gospel with Ayatollah Hosseini and with President Darazi? Isn't it time to tell them that you've renounced Islam and become a fully devoted follower of Jesus Christ? You're in the inner circle. You can reach them. We can't. Najjar can't. No one else can. Perhaps the Lord has given you this open door not to spend time with the Mahdi but to spend time with Hosseini and Darazi. Isn't it possible that he has raised you up for such a time as this?"

DAMASCUS, SYRIA

"Is everyone here—all your family and friends?" the priest asked.

Hanna's father turned and scanned the faces, recognizing most and beaming at them all. "Yes, I think this is all of us."

"Wonderful! Let us begin."

But no sooner had the words fallen from his lips than Hanna heard the unmistakable sound of gunfire, followed by bloodcurdling screams. Hanna instinctively turned to see where the noise was coming from but suddenly felt his father pulling him and his mother and his sisters to the floor. Bodies were falling everywhere. The gunfire didn't stop. It came in short, quick bursts. Again and again and again.

Hanna tried to scream as he saw more people cut down, row upon row, but he couldn't make a sound. He could hear bullets whizzing over his head and heard them drilling into the stone wall behind him. Terrified, he turned to his mother, desperate to hold her, to cling to her for comfort and protection, but as he did, his heart stopped. His mother's eyes were open, but they were glassy and lifeless. Hanna looked down and saw a pool of crimson growing beneath her.

"No, no!" he screamed, and the gunfire ceased, almost on cue.

Hanna turned and saw three men in long, black leather coats and thick black boots—but no hats, no masks—stepping over bodies to enter the little church. Two of them carried automatic rifles, like the kind he had seen on television, their barrels hot and smoking. But the third carried a small black pistol. He walked slowly and paused to kick each person with his boot. If they flinched, if they were alive, he aimed the pistol and pumped a bullet into their skull.

He went one by one, killing them all, until he stopped at Hanna's father. Hanna knew he should look away, but he was paralyzed with fear. He knew he should close his eyes, but he couldn't believe this was happening. And then it did happen. The man put not one bullet but two into the back of his father's head and then turned the pistol on little Hanna.

21

David took a long, hot shower. Then he toweled off, put on some clean clothes, and—inspired by his conversation with Birjandi—took ten minutes to read the first three chapters of the Gospel of Matthew. He desperately wanted to read more. He had a hunger for God's Word that he'd never experienced before. It finally made sense to him, and he wanted to lock himself away and read through the entire New Testament, even if it took all night. But he couldn't. Not now. His team was waiting for him, and he had to do his job.

He stepped into the living room to check on his team. Torres and Crenshaw were hunched over computers, returning e-mails and scanning headlines while the two other members of their team, Steve Fox and Matt Mays, were cleaning an MP5 machine gun and a Glock 9mm pistol, respectively.

"How's it going?" he asked.

"We're okay, boss," Torres said. "How 'bout you?"

"Better than I deserve," David replied, deeply relieved that he had been able to tell Birjandi about his decision to trust Christ and deeply encouraged by Birjandi's reaction.

"Does that mean you've got a lead?" Torres asked, brightening.

"No, it doesn't," David admitted.

"No one's answering?" Mays asked.

"Not so far," David replied. "I did reach Javad Nouri and Dr. Birjandi, but don't get too excited. Javad sounds horrible, and Birjandi doesn't know anything new. He's got no new leads. And he absolutely refuses to reach out to Hosseini and Darazi."

"Why?"

"Says it's against his convictions."

"Bringing down a nuclear-armed tyrant is against his convictions?"

"Normally, no—but going to visit false messiahs is," David explained. "But what can I say? The guy is the real deal. He believes what he believes. He's not going to be moved one way or the other. Period. End of story."

"Maybe we should pay him a visit," Fox suggested. "You know, a little one-on-one, a little personal persuasion."

"Steve, I'm telling you, he's not persuadable. We need to find another source."

"Where?"

"I don't know. How about you guys? Any progress?"

"Nothing," Torres said. "We've tried every source, every operative, every foreigner we know in the country. They either aren't answering their phones, or they don't know squat."

"Have you talked to Langley? Are the drones picking up anything? Are we getting any good intercepts?"

"All the satellites and drones are pretty much tied up doing bomb damage assessments," Torres said. "They're not trolling for two missing nukes. Not at the moment, at least. Zalinsky assures me he'll redirect assets to us if we pick up a lead. But not if we're just spitting in the wind."

Then David had an idea. He couldn't take this anymore. All this sitting around, waiting around, making calls, sending text messages was getting them nowhere. They needed a target. They needed to make something happen.

HAMADAN, IRAN

"Ali, my son, I'm not afraid of being arrested or tortured or dying for my Savior," Birjandi replied gently. "The only thing I fear is doing anything to displease the Lord. Now, you're right—I do have a special opening with our nation's leaders. For years they have invited me for meals or even for weekend retreats. I go when I can, and we chat, and I mostly listen to all that they want to say. But believe me, I have wanted to explain the gospel to them each time. I long to do so. I hate what these men are doing to our country, but I love them as Christ loves them, and I want them to repent. I want them to know the joy and the peace that I have found. I tell you boys in all honesty, I pray and fast for these men for hours and days at a time before I go to meet them. I lay prostrate before the Lord and seek his will before I go. I plead for wisdom and discernment and courage. But each time the Lord has told me to be quiet, to say nothing, to trust him alone, and to listen."

"But why?" Ibrahim asked. "That doesn't make sense. Why would Jesus tell you not to share the gospel? Doesn't he command us at the end of Mark's account to go and 'preach the gospel to all creation'? Doesn't he command us at the end of Matthew's account to go and 'make disciples of all the nations'?"

"Yes, he does," Birjandi said. "And to be honest, I don't know why the Lord has covered my mouth each time. It has bothered me. I have come home wondering if I had failed him by being disobedient. But then I remember the life of Paul, how the Holy Spirit forbade him to preach in Asia in Acts 16:6 and in Bithynia in verse 7."

Both young men quickly found the passage.

"Now, why would the Holy Spirit forbid Paul from preaching the gospel?" Birjandi asked. "Twice in two verses the Lord prevented Paul and his team from going where they thought they should go and saying what they thought they should say. Why?"

It was quiet for a few moments; then Ibrahim spoke up. "To obey is better than sacrifice," he said.

"Yes. Why?" Birjandi pressed.

"Well, Jesus also said, 'Why do you call Me, "Lord, Lord," and do not do what I say?' I guess it's always more important to do what Jesus says on a tactical, moment-to-moment basis, than to just do whatever you want, even if it seems like the right thing to do."

"Very good, Ibrahim." Birjandi smiled. "You are truly becoming a disciple of our Lord. Yes, we are to tell everyone the gospel. Unless the Lord tells you for whatever reason to keep your mouth shut. He knows better than we do. His thoughts are higher than our thoughts. We should also err on the side of boldness, I believe. But if the Lord says to be quiet, then we must obey. But now I ask you boys to pray for me. Maybe the Lord will open a door to share the Good News with the Ayatollah and the president and be able to avoid meeting with the Mahdi. Nothing is impossible with God. Amen?"

"Amen," they replied.

"Good. Now, let us get back to our study."

FORT MEADE, MARYLAND

Eva Fischer glanced at her watch. It was 4:17 in the morning. She had been awake for only a few hours, and she was still trying to make sense of the stunning turn of events. She had gone to sleep in a basement cell in the CIA detention center in Langley. Now she was staring out the rear window of a black Lincoln Town Car driving through Maryland, exiting Route 295, and driving past a large green sign marked *NSA Employees Only.*

She was still fuming over her "discussions" with Tom Murray, though she didn't hold him personally responsible. All that had happened in the last few days had been Zalinsky's fault, not Murray's. It was probably too much to expect that Zalinsky would be seriously reprimanded, much less fired, for what he had put her through, but a girl could dream, couldn't she?

But Eva didn't really want to waste her time thinking about Zalinsky. Her thoughts turned instead to David Shirazi, aka Reza Tabrizi. She had helped craft his cover story. She had been with him on his first trip inside Iran. She wasn't technically David's handler—that was Zalinsky's role—but she had been one of David's closest allies. It was she who had supplied him with much of the research he needed in the field. It was she who had secured the satphones he'd needed and personally brought them to him in Munich. It was she who typically maintained direct communication with him, she whom he had turned to when he needed a Predator drone to save his life. True, she had hesitated at the time, but in the end she had done what she thought was right, and she'd do it again.

It had almost cost her job. It could have put her in prison for several years. She was glad to have been exonerated and compensated, but the whole experience had left a bitter taste in her mouth. She had answered all of Murray's questions. She had signed all the documents. She had, in the process, cleared the CIA of all wrongdoing. But she was not going back to Langley. That was out of the question. Still, she couldn't abandon David now. His life was in extreme danger. He needed her now more than ever.

She asked her driver to turn up the heat a bit, which he did. Soon they were clearing through a guard station and a 100 percent ID check and entering the grounds of the sprawling National Security Agency campus, less than an hour north of Washington, D.C., and about half an hour southwest of Baltimore.

It was a dark and moonless night, bitterly cold, with a howling easterly wind. A fresh blanket of snow lay on thousands of cars still parked in the 18,000-car parking lot, and Eva realized these people had not gone home, probably in several days. Nearly every light in every building was on. The Middle East was in a full-blown war, and Eva was encouraged to see the NSA humming with activity.

Three men were waiting for her at a side entrance. As the Lincoln came to a stop, one of them opened her door and shook her hand.

"Eva, hi. I'm Warren McNulty, chief of staff for General Mulholland. Welcome to the Puzzle Palace."

"Good to meet you, Warren. Sorry to keep you up so late."

"Believe me, we've been here and awake the last few days," McNulty replied, helping her out of the car. "Never a dull moment, I'm afraid."

He introduced her to the two armed guards at his side. One was assigned to him full-time. The other, he explained, would be assigned to her whenever she was inside NSA headquarters.

"Expecting trouble?" she asked.

"Wartime protocol," he explained. "Come on, let's get you inside, where it's warm."

McNulty—who Eva guessed was in his midforties and likely a former Marine, well built, in good shape, with a closely cropped haircut and piercing blue eyes—handed her a temporary badge and a hot cup of coffee and gave her a quick briefing on security protocols as they stepped on an elevator.

"General Mulholland will want to see you when he gets in around six," he said, pushing the button for the top floor. "I've cleared out an office just down the hall from his, right next to mine. It's nothing fancy, of course. We didn't have much heads-up that you were coming. But it's clean and quiet and secure, and I don't have to tell you what a high priority we've given your work."

"Thanks; that's very kind," Eva said, taking her first sip of coffee and finding herself surprised that it was a Starbucks dark roast with a hint of hazelnut creamer, just the way she liked it. Someone had done his homework.

A moment later, they passed through two more security checks—one getting off the elevator, the other as they approached the suite of offices of the NSA director, General Brad Mulholland, and his senior staff—before arriving at Eva's new office.

McNulty was right—it was nothing fancy. Indeed, Eva half suspected it had been a supply closet an hour earlier. It was small and cramped, and it had no window. But there was a desk with a lamp and a computer workstation, a phone, and a stack of files at least three feet high. Eva opened the top file. It was a transcript of an as-of-yet-untranslated Farsi satphone call, intercepted less than an hour earlier.

"All of these are untranslated?" she asked in disbelief.

"I'm afraid so."

"Don't you have other Farsi translators?"

"Five—though one is in the hospital with a burst appendix, so four, really."

"Are they here, in the building?"

"Of course," McNulty said. "Downstairs. Their names and extension numbers are all on that sheet by the phone."

"Why aren't they working on these?"

"Because they're working on stacks even higher than this."

"You're kidding me," said Eva, feeling completely overwhelmed.

"Wish I were," McNulty said. "Listen. I'll tell you what I told them. There's no way you'll be able to translate all of this word for word, type it up, proof it, and transmit it to Langley, much less do that with all the other intercepts that are coming in hour by hour. So at this point the general is asking that you simply start scanning these as fast as you can. Make notes in English on any that stand out. If something is hot, call me or one of my deputies. Again, names and numbers are on that sheet. You've got to triage this stuff. Top priority is anything that refers to the warheads, anything that references a possible strike on the U.S. or Israel or any other regional target, and anything that comes from the troika at the top—the Mahdi, the Ayatollah, or President Darazi. Got it?"

Eva took a deep breath and another sip of coffee and found herself wishing—at least for a moment—that she was back in her cell in the detention center at Langley, sleeping soundly and relieved from such an enormous burden. "Got it."

"Good," McNulty said. "You hungry? Can I get you something from the commissary? They're open round the clock this week."

"No thanks. I'm fine for now."

"Okay. I'll check in with you in a few hours. But call me if you strike oil."

"Will do." She sighed, then sat down, picked up the first transcript, and got to work, already overwhelmed by how much she had to do and how little time she had to do it.

22

David speed-dialed Zalinsky, who picked up immediately.

"Please tell me you've got something, anything," Zalinsky said.

"Only a hunch, but I need your permission to move on it," said David.

"What is it?"

"A little while ago, I actually got through to Javad Nouri," David explained. "He's weak but definitely recovering. I couldn't get much out of him over the phone, but he said something curious."

"Like what?"

"He said the Twelfth Imam had come to visit him in the hospital."

"Why?"

"He didn't say, and I didn't ask. At the moment, it didn't seem relevant."

"But now it does?"

"Now I'm wondering why the Mahdi would have taken such a risk," David said. "Why would he leave whatever bunker the Iranian military has him in to visit the hospital of a junior aide, a body man—a secretary, really?"

"Unless Nouri is a more senior guy than we thought," said Zalinsky.

"Exactly," David said. "The Twelfth Imam doesn't strike me as the kind of guy to drop by with a box of chocolates and a vase of flowers and a get-well card. They were talking about something. Nouri knows something that the Mahdi needed to talk about in person."

"Like the location of the warheads?" Zalinsky asked.

"I don't know," David conceded. "Maybe they didn't discuss the location but did discuss the possible targets. Or maybe something else entirely. Whatever it was, it wasn't a courtesy call. It was important, and it was timely. Do we have any intercepts from Nouri's satphone?"

"Let me check."

David could hear his handler typing.

"We're horribly backed up on translating the intercepts," Zalinsky explained as he searched his files. "But the NSA is at least providing me an hourly tally of the number of calls made to or from specific frequencies—that is, specific phones—that we know have been given to specific people. Obviously we know the phone you're using and the one Dr. Birjandi is using. And unless they've changed, we know the phones the Mahdi, Hosseini, Darazi, and Nouri are using, based on the calls we've intercepted from them so far. Let's see, looking at the tally for the last three days, Nouri has only made one outbound call, lasting about six minutes. He's only received six calls—three of which were from you. Two of the others lasted thirty seconds or less, but one lasted nineteen minutes."

"Do we have transcriptions of the two longest calls?" David asked.

"No, not yet."

"Can you ask Eva to make those a top priority?"

Zalinsky hesitated.

"What's wrong?" David asked.

"You can ask her yourself," Zalinsky said.

"Why? Isn't she right there with you?"

"No."

"Why not? Where is she?"

"Never mind," Zalinsky said. "I'll explain later. It'll take too long to do it now. I'll get the message to her, and we'll prioritize those two calls."

Something didn't sound right to David, but he didn't have time to probe. He had a case to make, and he had to make it fast. "Listen, I know this is a long shot. I admit it," he began.

"Just say it," Zalinsky insisted.

"We need to grab Nouri."

"Who's *we*?"

"Marco Torres, his team, and me."

"You want to kidnap Javad Nouri?" Zalinsky asked, the tone of his voice not exactly indicative of confidence in David's recommendation.

"Immediately."

"Why?"

"What do you mean *why*?" David asked. "To interrogate him, to find out everything he knows."

"Whoa, whoa, wait a minute here, Zephyr," Zalinsky replied. "Let's not go crazy. Let's get those calls translated. Let's see what they say. Let's see if he makes any other calls. And then we'll go from there."

"Jack, come on—we don't have time to wait," David said, putting all of his cards on the table. "Right now we have no leads, no clues, no trail to follow."

"What about Birjandi?"

"I talked to him. He's got nothing."

"Tell him to go meet with the Mahdi."

"You don't think I tried that?"

"And?"

"He won't do it."

"Why not?"

"What does it matter?" David asked. "He just won't."

"Can't you push him, persuade him?"

"Believe me, I tried. It's not going to happen."

"What about your other sources?" Zalinsky pressed.

"Jack, you're not listening to me," David said. "I've got nothing. No one is answering their phones. Maybe they're all in bomb shelters and they're not getting satellite reception. Maybe they don't want to talk to me. Maybe they've been told not to talk to me. Maybe they're dead. I have no idea. All I know is Abdol Esfahani is going to Damascus. I don't know why. Birjandi is refusing to go see the Mahdi. And now we've got the location of an apparently senior advisor to the Twelfth Imam. We know where he is. We know that he's just spoken to the Mahdi. We know he's in a relatively unsecure facility. I'm telling you we can do this,

Jack. We can grab him. We can shake him down. And we can make him spill his guts. That much I know. But time's a-wastin'."

"And if you're caught?" Zalinsky countered.

"I won't get caught."

"But if you do, the Iranians will shut down the satphone intercepts immediately."

"And do what?" David asked. "The Israelis have taken down almost all of Iran's phone network, at least temporarily. Without the satphones, the Twelfth Imam wouldn't be able to talk to most of his inner circle."

"It's too big a risk."

"Compared to what? Look, we've got a narrow window here, and it's rapidly closing. We know the nukes are out there. We don't know where they are. We suspect at least one is going to be fired at the Israelis. The other may be coming to the States, to New York or Washington or L.A. But the president told us to find them, to stop them, using whatever means necessary. I've looked at all our options, Jack, and I'm telling you, this isn't just our best play. It's our only play. It's this or nothing."

There was a long pause, so long David wondered if he had lost his connection to Langley. But finally Zalinsky spoke.

"Where exactly is Javad Nouri right now, right this minute?"

"Tehran University Medical Center."

"How long will it take you to get there?"

"Assuming we don't get hit by an Israeli cruise missile or stopped at a checkpoint and arrested for espionage?" David asked.

"Funny."

"Less than an hour," David assured him.

"Then do it," Zalinsky said. "And don't get caught."

"Right," said David. "And I'd be grateful for those transcripts from Nouri's calls—and a Predator drone if you can spare one."

"I'll do my best," Zalinsky replied. "Good luck."

"Thanks."

David hung up and quickly stepped out of the office, where he found Torres and his men assembled in the living room.

"Saddle up, gentlemen. We have a target."

★ ★ ★ ★ ★

TEHRAN, IRAN

Ahmed Darazi stepped into the war room, thick with smoke and tension, looking for the Twelfth Imam, but he was not there. Darazi checked in several of the anterooms but did not find him there either. The Ayatollah had not seen where he went, nor had the top generals, fixated as they were on prosecuting the latest missile onslaught against the Jews. A corporal, however, told Darazi he had overheard the Mahdi say he wanted some fresh air. In disbelief, Darazi and his personal security detail boarded the elevator and departed the underground bunker.

Ten stories up, they disembarked from the elevator and scoured the first floor of the Mehrabad Air Base headquarters, heavily guarded by armed military police. But the Twelfth Imam was nowhere to be seen, inside or out. Darazi boarded another elevator and took it three stories up, and there on the roof he found the Lord of the Age, bowing toward Mecca and finishing his prayers.

The scene around them was surreal. As far as the eye could see, hangars and buildings were on fire. Row upon row of fighter jets were ablaze. Most of the administrative and maintenance buildings were raging infernos. All the runways had been bombed, making it impossible to take off or land. The base—long the home of Iran's Western Area Command and the 11th and 14th Tactical Fighter Squadrons—lay in ruins. The thundering sound of aircraft taking off and landing had been replaced by the wailing sirens of fire trucks and ambulances streaming in from all directions.

The civilian side of the airfield, on the other hand, was relatively unscathed. The Imam Khomeini Airport was Iran's largest and most heavily trafficked international commercial facility, and the Israelis had chosen not to hit it directly. The Iranian Revolutionary Guard Corps, obviously military, was headquartered there, but their bunkers and command center were actually secretly located under the main commercial terminal to cover it, essentially, with thousands of human shields—ordinary citizens and foreign nationals transiting to and from the airport built for Iran's capital city.

Darazi was stunned. No one had briefed him on how much damage had been done by the Israelis to this prize of the Iranian Air Force. There were no news reports to watch. Even if the Iranian TV networks were operating—and they weren't—the military censor would never have cleared images of such devastation at such a major airport. Darazi's information had all come from planning meetings with the Mahdi, and he wondered why he of all people wasn't being briefed on this.

As Darazi looked out over the smoldering wreckage, his knees grew weak. He began to gag on the thick, black, acrid smoke and the stench of burning human flesh laced with jet fuel, and he knew this was not safe. The Jews would return, he knew. Wave after wave of attacks were coming, hour after hour, day after day, and he desperately wanted to get the Mahdi indoors, back downstairs into the safety and security of the war room bunker. But he didn't dare violate the sanctity of the Twelfth Imam's communication with Allah. So he immediately fell to his knees and began praying as well. Only when he could hear the Mahdi was finished did Darazi open his eyes. Then, still bowing, he addressed his leader and pleaded for mercy.

"You may speak," said the Mahdi, now on his feet and motioning the president to rise too.

"I've communicated with General Jazini via secure e-mail, Your Excellency," he said, rising quickly.

"Good," said the Mahdi. "How long until General Jazini is on site?"

"Very shortly. I will brief you the moment he gets there."

"Fine—make sure all the arrangements we discussed are in place."

"Of course, Your Excellency. Everything is set. You can count on me and my men. Now, is there anything else I can do for you?"

"Yes, there is," the Mahdi said. "Contact our ambassador in Vienna. Have him release a statement that Iran and the Caliphate are withdrawing from the NPT."

"The nuclear nonproliferation treaty?" Darazi asked.

"Is there another?" the Mahdi responded in disgust.

"No, no, of course not," Darazi said, bowing once again and feeling foolish. "I will do it immediately, Your Excellency. Anything else?"

"Have you heard from Firouz and Jamshad?" he asked.

The Twelfth Imam was referring to Firouz Nouri, the head of an Iranian Revolutionary Guard Corps terrorist cell, and one of his deputies, Jamshad Zarif. The two were part of the cell that was responsible for the assassination of Egyptian president Abdel Ramzy and the attempted assassination of American president Jackson and Israeli prime minister Naphtali at the Waldorf-Astoria Hotel in New York a week before.

"Yes, my Lord," Darazi replied. "We got them successfully out of the States to Venezuela, where they holed up in our embassy in Caracas. Last night they flew to Frankfurt, where they are awaiting further instructions."

"They are traveling under new identities?"

"Yes, my Lord, as you instructed."

"Very good. Tell them to get to Damascus as soon as possible and await my orders. I have an important assignment for them there."

"But, my Lord, no one is flying into or out of Damascus because of the war."

"Did I say anything about having them fly to Damascus?" the Mahdi retorted, his voice dripping with disdain for the Iranian president. "Tell them to fly to Cyprus. Tell them to look up a man named Dimitrious Makris. He's a ship captain in the port of Limassol. From there, they should take a boat to Beirut. Makris will take care of everything. When they get to Beirut, they should make contact with a man named Youssef, who is in charge of security at the airport. Youssef is Hezbollah. He will provide them with a car, and they will drive to Damascus as quickly as they can. Tell them not to delay. I need them there in forty-eight hours. Is that clear?"

"Yes, my Lord. Anything else?"

"Just do those things and do them well," said the Mahdi.

"Of course, Your Excellency," Darazi said. "But may I ask a question?"

"If you must."

"When will we launch the last two warheads at the Zionists, my Lord? When will we finally have sweet vengeance upon those apes and pigs?"

"One step at a time," the Mahdi replied. "You must be patient. I have everything under control. Allah has a plan and a purpose, and it cannot be thwarted. We want the Jews to think they have the upper hand, but we are luring them into a false sense of security. And when they least expect it, we will finish them off once and for all. Just you wait, Ahmed. You will see it with your very eyes—and soon."

LANGLEY, VIRGINIA

Zalinsky picked up the phone and dialed Tom Murray's extension. He briefed the deputy director for operations on David's call and his plan. Then he asked for Murray to relay the translation request to Eva. And he requested permission to retask a Predator drone over Tehran University Medical Center.

JERUSALEM, ISRAEL

"Mr. Prime Minister, Defense Minister Shimon is on hold."

"Put him through," Naphtali said. He was sitting in his office, poring over dispatches from each element of the ongoing war. When the secure connection was made, he asked for the latest update.

"Six deaths in Dimona so far," Shimon said, "but none from radiation. They're all due to the fires. Several dozen injuries, too. But the hazmat teams are in. The fire-suppression efforts are going better. I think we're going to be able to contain the damage, but it's too soon to say more than that."

"What about Tiberias?"

"The hotel is a disaster. It's not just the collapse of the building. It's the fire and smoke. The rescue crews can hear tapping coming from the bomb shelters in the basement, but they can't control the fires, and until they do, they can't get to the people. The death toll is climbing. I should receive updated numbers soon."

"Please, Levi, as soon as you can get them. The Foreign Ministry is screaming for details and a statement from me, but I don't want to put out anything official until we know more."

"I know, and we're working on it."

"Okay, what's next?"

"Good news and bad," said Shimon. "Which do you want first?"

"The bad."

"I just talked to Roger Allen at Langley. He says they've got credible evidence that we've destroyed six of the eight warheads but missed two."

"How does he know?"

"He wouldn't say."

"But they're sure?"

"All he said was the evidence was 'serious' and 'credible' and they're throwing everything they have at hunting down these two warheads and destroying them."

"What's the chance that it's just disinformation?"

"Unlikely. I know Roger. He wouldn't tell us this unless he was worried. I'm not entirely sure he was even authorized to tell us this. But he clearly wanted us to know. And he can't think that's going to make us back down from the fight or accept a cease-fire."

"True."

"Anyway, we're using every asset we can to hunt for the warheads as well, and I'll keep you posted. But there's more."

"What?"

"Well, for starters, our ground forces are encountering severe resistance in southern Lebanon. Hezbollah is using a new kind of Russian antitank missile. We haven't seen it before, so we weren't expecting it. We're taking heavy casualties. And we just lost two F-15s—one from triple-A fire over Sidon, the other because of mechanical troubles over the Med. But Hezbollah and the Iranians are taking credit for both."

"When's the good news?"

"Not yet," Shimon said. "Our ground offensive in Gaza isn't off to a strong start. There are a whole host of reasons. It's house-to-house combat right now, sometimes man-to-man. Booby traps. Land mines. Real ugly stuff. I'll get you a more detailed report soon. But the bottom line is we're taking heavier losses than we would have expected and it's going slower than we'd hoped. Hamas and Islamic Jihad are still firing rockets into the south at pretty near the same rate. But obviously we expect that to diminish once our forces gain the upper hand and we can begin clearing more territory of the launchers and the jihadis operating them."

"And the Syrians?" the prime minister asked.

"Still nothing," Shimon reported.

"Is that the good news?"

"No, this is. We think we can take out Darazi, eliminate some of their leadership."

"Tell me."

"Our agents inside Tehran have been noticing an unexpected increase in helicopter activity near the Imam Khomeini Mosque in Tehran. When they looked more closely, they noticed an odd level of security around the mosque, especially in the plaza out front, where the helicopters are arriving and departing."

"Okay . . ." Naphtali indicated that Shimon should get to the point.

"Political VIPs have been known to worship there from time to time. But with the war under way, you wouldn't expect any VIP activity there, and certainly not this much. They've actually erected a tent out front to obscure those getting on and off the choppers from viewers outside the grounds. What's also strange is that there is new, high-tech microwave relay equipment installed on the roofs of the office buildings that are connected to the mosque. Just went up in the past twenty-four hours. But officially the mosque is closed. They're not holding prayer services. The general public is pretty much staying indoors. There are hardly any vehicles on the streets, besides ambulances, fire trucks, various military vehicles, and some police cars."

"You think Iranian political officials are going there to worship during the war."

"No, sir," Shimon said. "We think the military high command could be preparing to use the mosque as an operations center."

"I thought they were operating out of the bunker at the airport."

"We've decimated most of that military base. But we haven't actually tried to hit the bunker."

"Why not?"

"First, it's located underneath and to the side of the main passenger terminal. Our IAF commanders say there would be too many civilians killed if we bombed it. Second, the Iranians think we don't know about that bunker. We believe the main IRGC op center is six or eight stories underground. We're not entirely sure we could destroy it with a bunker-buster if we tried. But we've got a drone monitoring the site, hoping the Iranians will make a mistake and give a clear and direct shot at one of their top people, maybe even the Mahdi."

"Then if the op center is still up and running, what's the deal with this mosque you're talking about?" Naphtali asked.

"Sir, we think the Iranians may be setting up an alternate facility, a new or separate command center. By definition, the mosque is a religious site. It's in a residential neighborhood. It's not close to any military buildings or other major government buildings. Thus this particular mosque isn't likely to be watched by satellites or by spies. They probably think it won't be noticed by Western intelligence agencies, and even if it is noticed by us or others, they expect that we'll hesitate before attacking a mosque. Honestly, sir, they were pretty close to being right. We just got lucky to even pick up on the activity going on there."

"And why do you think Darazi is there?" Naphtali pressed.

"We don't think he's been there yet, but we do think he's coming," Shimon said. "One of our men photographed Darazi's chief of staff and head of security strolling the grounds a few hours ago."

"You think they were advancing the site?"

"Zvi does, yes," said Shimon, referring to Zvi Dayan, the Mossad director. "I'm ambivalent so far. Not enough information. But it's certainly got my attention."

"Now it's got mine, Levi. But tell me this: if Darazi arrives, is he likely to have Hosseini and the Mahdi with him?"

"I don't know. That would be nice, wouldn't it?"

"One-stop shopping? Sure," said the PM. "Okay, what do you need?"

"The Mossad wants to put snipers in place and position a dedicated drone overhead to take out Darazi, if they spot him, and others, if they're there too."

"Shouldn't every drone we have be looking for the nukes?"

"I know. I thought that myself at first. But if we could actually take out Darazi or others in the high command . . ."

23

David and his team were approaching the outskirts of the Iranian capital. For much of the drive from Karaj, they had sketched out a detailed plan of attack and tried to imagine everything that could possibly go wrong and how they would handle each scenario. David knew they really could have used another few hours. He also knew they'd have been far better off attempting this in the dead of night. But they didn't have the time to wait. He knew that Torres and his men were consummate professionals. If this could be done at all—and it was a big *if*, to be sure—these guys would not let him down.

David's satphone rang. That had to be Zalinsky, and he was late. David glanced at his watch. It was 3:14 p.m. in Tehran and 6:44 in the morning back in Washington. They would be at the hospital in less than fifteen minutes. He put on his Bluetooth and took the call hands-free even though Torres was driving.

"Jack, where've you been?" David said. "We're almost there."

"Actually, it's Agent Fischer. Sorry to disappoint."

"Oh, Eva—no, not disappointed, just surprised," David said.

"How are you?" she asked.

"A little stressed."

"Guess that makes sense."

"How about you?"

"A little stressed," she mimicked. "It's been a long night. I'll fill you in later. But listen, I just finished translating Javad Nouri's calls, and I wanted to try to get you before you headed in. Tom briefed me on what you're about to do."

"You think it's crazy?"

"It *is* crazy," said Eva. "I just hope it works."

"Me too," David said. "So what did you find?"

"The only call Javad made, the six-minute one, was to his mother in Mashhad," Eva explained. "It was pretty straightforward, just explaining what happened to him and that the doctors say he's going to be fine. That call was last night, and his mother said she and Javad's father would call back after work tonight."

"Okay, how about the nineteen-minute call he received?" David pressed. "Please tell me it was from the Mahdi."

"No, sorry," said Eva. "It was actually from Darazi."

"President Darazi?"

"Yes."

"Really? Why? What did they say?"

"Hold your horses; I'm getting to that," Eva said. "The call occurred just after nine o'clock this morning, local time. Darazi says the Mahdi asked him to check in on Javad to see if the doctors have cleared him to come back to work. Javad says he needs a couple more days, at a minimum. And get this. Darazi says, 'No, that won't do. The Mahdi says this will be over in a couple more days. We need you now.'"

"He said 'a couple more days'?" David asked.

"That's verbatim," Eva confirmed.

"What else?"

"Javad says he would like nothing more, but his doctors are being pretty firm. Darazi says the Mahdi doesn't care what the doctors say; he wants him at his side for this 'final operation,' quote, unquote. He says they're going to transfer him sometime this afternoon and bring his doctors with him."

"Did Darazi say when *exactly* the transport would happen?"

"No."

"Did he say where they're going to move Javad to?"

"Not exactly, but Javad indicates he doesn't think the road to the airport is secure. He's hearing reports that the bombing of the airport has been relentless. Darazi confirms this but says they're not bringing him to the airport bunker. Javad then asks if it's the Qaleh, up in the mountains, because he still thinks that's not secure either. Darazi says no. That was destroyed by an Israeli missile strike. He says they've set up a new war room. It's very impressive, state-of-the-art, and unlikely to be noticed by the Israelis since it's, as he put it, 'hiding in plain sight.' Javad asked for details. Darazi said he'd know soon enough. And that's pretty much the gist of it."

"That took nineteen minutes?"

"Well, no, Javad gave him an update on his medical situation. He's got a pretty nasty wound in his right shoulder where the bullet passed through. They've got him on a bunch of antibiotics, and they're hoping he won't develop an infection."

"Anything else?"

"You want me to e-mail you the transcript?"

"No, we're almost there."

"That's pretty much everything," Eva said. "Oh, well, this was interesting."

"What?"

"As they finish the call, Javad asks Darazi how he thinks the war is going. Darazi says they've been hit harder than he'd expected, but that he has, quote, 'full faith in Imam al-Mahdi and in those two aces up his sleeve.'"

"Two aces? You're sure?" David pressed.

"That's what he said," Eva confirmed. "Two aces."

"So he knows about the warheads."

"Apparently so. Looks like your instincts were right. Who knew?"

"Very funny," David replied, about to fire back with a wisecrack when another call started coming in. "Look, I gotta go. But good work, Eva. Let me know when you work your way through more of those intercepts."

"Will do. Take care of yourself."

"You too—bye." And David disconnected.

Torres turned off Azadi Road onto North Kargar Boulevard. Traffic was nonexistent. The streets of Tehran were practically abandoned, and they were making great time.

"Heads up," said Torres. "We're two minutes out."

David nodded and checked his watch—it was now 3:28 p.m. The rest of the team loaded magazines into their MP5 machine guns and screwed silencers onto their automatic pistols. David did the same, careful not to let anything he was doing be seen from outside the van. Then he took the incoming call. It was Zalinsky.

"Put me on speaker," Zalinsky ordered.

David complied.

"Can you all hear me?" Zalinsky asked.

"We can," David said.

"Good. Listen, I'm in the Global Ops Center. I've got Tom at my side. Roger is on his way."

"Hey, Zephyr." It was Murray's voice. "Good luck today."

"Thank you, sir. I appreciate that."

"You guys are the main event right now," Zalinsky said. "Even the president has been alerted to this operation. We've retasked a satellite, and we're currently tracking your van driving north on Kargar. We've been watching the hospital from a Predator. Tom is e-mailing a layout of the campus to each of your phones along with schematics of building two. We've also hacked into the hospital's mainframe. They've actually got Javad registered under his own name. He's in building two on the fifth floor, room 503."

"Great," Torres said. "What's the security setup there?"

"Nothing special out front," Zalinsky said. "There's a security post when you first enter the parking lot. Just one guy. No big deal. Rent-a-cop. Unlikely to be armed. There are two security guards at the front door of building two. We zoomed in on them. They're heavily armed. Machine guns, sidearms, radios. Thermal imaging shows four more just like them in the lobby."

"Is that normal?" David asked.

"I doubt it," Zalinsky said. "We're guessing security has been beefed up because of their special guest."

"He's getting more 'special' and intriguing every minute."

"True," Zalinsky said. "Obviously we want you to steer clear of the lobby. There's an exit door on the south side. We're not sure if it's locked from the outside. But that leads into a maintenance area. From there, you should split up. There's a stairwell on the left, just inside the doors. To the right, you have to go about halfway around the building, but there's another stairwell there."

"Any of that guarded?" Torres asked.

"Not on the ground floor," Zalinsky explained. "But once you guys get to the fifth floor, you'll definitely have company."

"How many?"

"Thermal imaging shows armed guards at each of the stairwell doors. Two more by the elevators. Two more outside Javad's room."

"Security cameras?"

"We don't know, but you'll have to assume so."

"Dogs?"

"Not that we've seen."

"Plainclothes officers?"

"Can't say for certain."

"Any free safeties or roving teams?"

"Not that we can tell," Zalinsky said. "But I wouldn't rule it out. And look, it's crowded up there. There are a lot of war wounded coming into the hospital. Plus they're doing a blood drive this afternoon, and they're actually getting a decent turnout, despite the fact that so few people are out on the roads. Not sure how people are hearing about it, but they're there. So be alert. Every floor is jammed. They've got stretchers in the hallways, too. All leaves have been canceled. Doctors and nurses are being ordered in from everywhere. They've got a lot of staff on duty. It's going to be a mess. This would be a lot better at night."

"I agree, but I don't see how we can wait," David said.

"No, neither do I," said Zalinsky. "You guys all set?"

"I guess," David said, "though I just talked to Eva."

"She told you Darazi is sending people to get Javad this afternoon?"

"Right. Should we be worried?"

"Let's hope not. It's still fairly early over there, right?"

"Just after three thirty."

"Well, let's just hope for the best," Zalinsky said. "But we'll definitely keep an eye out for unwelcome guests."

It wasn't much of an answer, but what else could they do? They needed more men and more firepower to do this right. But they simply didn't have the luxury of either.

Torres turned off the main boulevard onto a side street, then pulled the van over to the curb and came to a stop. David began to assess their surroundings as he plotted each move. They were on the perimeter of the hospital grounds. He could see the guard station by the parking lot. He couldn't see building two from this vantage point, but he could see building three, the oncology department. The team checked the maps Murray had sent and calibrated their watches.

It was 3:32 p.m. local time.

TABRIZ, IRAN

It had been too dangerous to travel by plane or even by helicopter, and anyway the runways were now unusable, so there would have been nowhere to land. So General Mohsen Jazini arrived at the Second Tactical Air Base, about fifteen kilometers northwest of the Iranian city of Tabriz, in the back of a Red Crescent ambulance, his security detail having decided such cover was the safest—if not the only—way to get the new head of the Caliphate's army to the base from Tehran without attracting attention or another Israeli missile strike. Fortunately their plan had worked, and the general, two of his deputies, and three body-guards (including the driver) arrived without incident. But even from a distance, seeing the thick, black columns of smoke rising into the after-noon sky, Jazini could scarcely take in how much damage the Israelis had done to the air base. Seeing it up close and personal was horrifying.

As he'd been briefed back in Tehran, every runway here in Tabriz was now pockmarked with enormous craters, the result of devastatingly accurate Israeli air strikes. Nearly all the F-5E and MiG-29 fighter jets on the tarmacs were ablaze, as were most of the helicopters, transport planes, and civilian airliners that shared the airfield. All but one of the hangars, and all of the administrative buildings, had been taken out by air strikes. Even the control tower had been hit. Some of the strikes had occurred as recently as that very morning. Firefighters and their equipment had come from all over the area, but it was immediately clear to Jazini that they were having little success controlling the raging infernos. Ambulances, too, were converging on the base from every direction, but the destruction was severe, and Jazini had to assume the death toll was already high and still mounting rapidly.

Once they cleared a security checkpoint on the outer edge of the field, the general directed the driver of the ambulance to a small, one-story, nondescript concrete building on the eastern edge of the airfield. It hadn't been fired upon and thus hadn't been damaged in any way. After all, it didn't look like a strategic target from the air or even up close. Rather, it looked like a two-vehicle garage that might hold maintenance equipment like tow trucks or perhaps lawn-care equipment like a few large commercial mowers.

When they arrived and parked near one of the garage doors, a member of the detail jumped out, walked over to the door, found an electronic keypad, and punched in a ten-digit code. Jazini could see the bodyguard then look up at a small security camera mounted on the overhang of the roof. A moment later, one of the doors opened, and two armed men greeted them and waved them in.

Jazini and all of his team except the driver quickly exited the ambulance and entered the small concrete structure. The driver then sped off and parked the ambulance with the rest of the emergency vehicles, in the unlikely but still remotely possible chance that the scene was being monitored by spy satellites.

"General Jazini, what an honor," said the ranking officer on site, saluting once the guests were safely inside and the door was closed and locked behind them. "I'm Colonel Sharif. Welcome to our humble abode."

Jazini, dressed not in his military uniform but in black slacks and a white button-down dress shirt, did not return the salute. "Colonel, I'm not here for you or for any chitchat," said the highly decorated commander of the Iranian Revolutionary Guard Corps, who at the age of fifty-nine was still quite fit and trim, though his once-jet-black hair was now graying at the temples and his beard was beginning to show more salt than pepper. "I'm here to see Dr. Zandi without delay. Where is he?"

"Yes, sir," said Sharif. "He's three floors below us. I can take you there now."

"Lead on," Jazini said as he and his entourage followed the colonel onto a lift that descended rather slowly but eventually opened up into a cavernous, warehouse-like facility, much larger than could be imagined given the far smaller outbuilding on the surface.

To his left, the general could see nearly a dozen technicians in white lab coats huddled around a large steel table bearing one of the two remaining warheads. It looked like they were doing open-heart surgery on the weapon of mass destruction. To his right, Jazini saw a large wooden crate atop a similar steel table, surrounded by four IRGC commandos holding automatic weapons. He assumed the crate held the second of the remaining warheads, but he was about to find out for sure.

Approaching him down the center of the facility was a somewhat-youthful-looking man about five feet six inches tall, balding, clean shaven, and wearing round spectacles. He, too, wore a white lab coat with various ID badges dangling from a thin chain around his neck. He wasn't smiling. Rather, he looked anxious and a bit gaunt, as though he had not been eating well—or at all—over the past few days or even the past week or two. He had two security officers at his side, armed with pistols, not machine guns. The three men made their way across what appeared to be a freshly mopped floor, then stopped about a yard and a half from the general and his security detail.

"You must be Jalal Zandi," Jazini said, taking immediate control of the conversation.

"I am your humble servant, General Jazini," replied Zandi, forty-seven, neither offering his hand nor looking the general in the eye but looking down at the floor instead. "It is an honor to finally meet you."

Jazini stepped forward, put his hand on Dr. Zandi's shoulder, and turned to the security men around him.

"Take good care of this man, gentlemen," Jazini said with a laugh. "I can't tell you how much the Zionists would love to get their hands on him. It's your job not to let that happen."

When the men nodded in agreement, Jazini turned to Zandi and looked him in the eye.

"Are you being taken care of?" he asked. "Are they getting you everything you need?"

"Yes, yes, of course," Zandi said, his hand trembling slightly. "Everything is fine."

"How long have you been here?"

"The warheads have been here since Thursday morning, just before the air strikes started. I got here yesterday."

"Ambulance?" the general asked.

"Pardon?"

"Did you come in an ambulance?" Jazini repeated.

"No, in a fire truck," Zandi replied.

"Have you slept much?"

"A little," said Zandi. "But mostly we've been making adjustments to the warheads. One is finished and ready for transport. The other should be ready within the hour."

Jazini nodded and checked his watch. "Very well. We will leave precisely at five."

"I don't understand," said Zandi. "Leave where?"

"To the missile complex."

"But I thought my team and I were going to attach these warheads to missiles here, at this facility. Didn't you bring the missiles with you?"

"No," said Jazini. "It's too dangerous to do anything more here. I'm taking you and the warheads with me."

"And the crew, of course."

"Negative. You'll have another crew waiting for you at the next location."

Zandi blanched.

"Is there a problem, Dr. Zandi?" the general asked.

"Uh, no, sir; it's just that . . ."

"Just that what?" Jazini pressed.

"Well, sir, I just prefer . . ."

"Prefer what?"

"Having my team with me, sir," Zandi finally explained. "We work well together. I trust them."

"Well, I don't, Dr. Zandi," the general shot back. "I believe one of

194 ★ DAMASCUS COUNTDOWN

them leaked the location of our other six warheads. One of them is a mole. And when I find out which one, I am going to gouge out his eyes, one by one, and cut out his tongue. And then I'll decide what his real punishment will be."

"Yes, sir."

"Good. Make sure the second warhead is ready for transport no later than 5 p.m.," Jazini ordered. "But don't tell anyone that they're not going with us. That will just be our little secret. Understood?"

"Yes, sir," Zandi said quietly. "I am your humble servant."

"Good. Now carry on."

And with that, Jazini turned on his heel and walked to a small office in the back of the facility to finalize his own plans and make sure every detail was in place.

24

Sitting in the front passenger seat of the van, David slipped on his headset, consisting of an earphone and small microphone, then clipped the wireless receiver to his belt. He switched on the power and made sure he was on the right frequency.

"Check, check, check—we all good?"

"Reading you five by five," said the others.

Satisfied, David grabbed an extra magazine for his MP5, double-checked his pistol and its silencer, and loaded his flak jacket with additional ammo but didn't put it on. Rather, he put it on the floor in front of him and covered it with a blanket.

"Everyone all set?" he asked.

He got a thumbs-up from everyone as they all hid their weapons and gear and got their minds into the zone for the mission ahead.

"Good. Look sharp," David said. "Let's do this thing."

David gave Torres clearance to drive up to the guard box and into the parking lot of the hospital while keeping his eyes peeled for any signs of danger. His pulse quickened, but he tried to steady his breathing by saying a prayer for himself and his team—for safety, to be sure, but also for wisdom and success. A moment later they were at the guard station. Torres rolled down the window.

"May I help you?" the guard asked, peering into the van from behind a pair of sunglasses.

"We're here to give blood," David said in flawless Farsi, leaning

195

toward the open window to make eye contact with the guard. "We're scheduled for a 3:45 appointment."

"Okay, pull through and turn right," said the guard. "But you'd better move smartly. I'm pretty sure the blood drive ends at four."

"Thanks; will do," David said.

Torres followed the man's directions, and they all breathed a sigh of relief. One hurdle crossed.

"Home Plate, can you hear us?" David asked when Torres had put his window back up.

"Roger that, Zephyr," Zalinsky replied. "And we see you moving through lot B to the far side."

"Roger that," David said, then turned to his team and gave them the one-minute warning, alerting each man to uncover his gear, put on his flak jacket, and get ready to move. He, too, finalized his preparations and then opened the glove compartment and pulled out black ski masks, which he quickly handed out.

Forty-five seconds later, Torres backed into a parking space and scanned the grounds for anyone who might see them exit the vehicle. Several doctors were approaching along a nearby sidewalk, but they were engrossed in conversation and didn't seem to be paying much attention to their surroundings. David instructed his men to wait for the group to pass, and the delay proved fortuitous as Torres noticed that the exit door they were about to head to didn't have a handle on the outside. He asked one of the men in the back of the van to reach under his seat, open the compartment containing the spare tire, and pull out the iron crowbar typically used for prying off hubcaps when changing a flat. That, he said, was their new key into the building.

David did a final scan. There were still cars coming in and out of the parking lot, an occasional ambulance driving by, and a few people walking by distant buildings. He glanced at each member of his team, checking their focus, their steadiness. Aside from David himself, the youngest member of their team was Matt Mays, the twenty-eight-year-old former Marine lieutenant who would serve as their driver and lookout, staying in the van and idling until they returned with their prize. Steve Fox, thirty-one and a former Navy SEAL, held the crowbar and was ready to "key in" to the building. Nick Crenshaw, thirty-three years old and another former SEAL, sat next to Fox, poised to move.

Figuring things were about as good as they were going to get, David gave the order to go. He opened his door and exited the vehicle, careful to hide his MP5 machine gun under a folded blanket. Behind him, the side doors of the van swung open simultaneously, and the others did the same. On the other side of the vehicle, Torres stepped out of the driver's-side door and was handed his gear—also wrapped in a blanket. Mays then got behind the wheel and shut all the doors.

Fox moved the fastest and used the crowbar to open the back exit in a single fluid motion. Crenshaw followed close behind, while David and Torres brought up the rear. Inside, they fortunately found no one in their way, so the four men donned their ski masks and broke into their respective teams. David and Fox moved left, heading up the closest stairwell as quickly and quietly as they could. Torres and Crenshaw moved to the right, headed for the opposite stairwell.

As planned, David took the lead up the stairs, with Fox providing cover at his six. When they got halfway between the fourth and fifth floors, they stopped, crouched down, and strained to listen for any signs of trouble. David clipped a shoulder strap on his MP5 and swung it over onto his back, then pulled out his silencer-equipped pistol and flicked off the safety. Fox followed suit as they reached the fifth floor.

"Alpha One to Bravo One," David whispered. "Do you read?"

"Five by five, Alpha One," came Torres's reply.

"You in position?"

"Sixty seconds," Torres said.

"Roger that."

David reached back, and on cue Fox handed him a fiber-optic camera snake. David switched it on, crept up to the fifth-floor stairwell door, and slowly slid it underneath, careful not to make a sound. Fox moved up as well and held the palm-size monitor so both of them could see it. As Zalinsky had promised, the hall was hopping with incoming injured patients and all manner of medical personnel. What was strange, however, was that as David rotated the snake, he could find no sign of anyone guarding this exit. Perplexed and anxious, he continued scanning the hall for any sign of an armed guard on this side of the floor but found none.

"Bravo One to Alpha One, we're in position," Torres radioed. "We've scanned the hall. Our guard is in position. We can see two more in front of Javad's room."

"Roger that, Bravo One," David whispered. "But we can't find our guard."

"Say again?"

"Repeat, our guard is not in position. We don't know where he is. Home Plate, do you have eyes on our guard?"

"Negative, Alpha One, but we'll keep looking."

David tensed. He had no intention of bursting through this door and getting shot in the back because he hadn't done his homework. They had to find this guard—and fast. In the meantime, David pulled a small black box out of his pocket and magnetically attached it to the exit door. Then he erected a small antenna connected to the box and turned on the power switch to let the unit warm up.

FORT MEADE, MARYLAND

Eva Fischer had just found a lengthy and intriguing phone call between the Twelfth Imam and Pakistani president Iskander Farooq and was beginning to translate it into English when the pager on her desk started going off. Eva grabbed the pager and checked the incoming code; when she saw it read 911, her heart skipped a beat. She had asked the NSA Ops Center to alert her if Javad Nouri made or received any phone calls over the course of the next hour and to allow her to listen in on the call in real time by dialing a secure, dedicated extension.

Jumping to her feet, she grabbed her phone and hit 6203. Instantly she was patched through to the live feed and was stunned to hear Ahmed Darazi's voice in midsentence.

". . . any longer, so he ordered them to come get you now," the Iranian president was saying.

"That's very kind of him," Nouri replied. "I'll ask the nurses to pack my bag and pull together some of my medications. How soon until they arrive?"

"They're already on their way," Darazi said. "They should be there any moment."

"Great. And you'll both meet me there?" Nouri asked.

"In a few hours, *inshallah*, once I finish up my work here," Darazi said. "I can't say for certain when he'll come over, but he is anxious to talk to you and get your answers to his questions."

"I'm ready," Nouri replied.

"Good. Now remember, my team will take care of everything," Darazi assured him. "So just relax, and I'll see you soon."

With that, the two men said good-bye and hung up.

A panic-induced jolt of adrenaline spread instantly through Eva's system. She hung up the phone, then picked up again and speed-dialed Tom Murray at the Global Operations Center.

"Tom, it's Eva," she said the moment he answered. "We have a huge problem."

LANGLEY, VIRGINIA

Murray and Zalinsky and the rest of the Global Operations Center listened on speakerphone as Eva Fischer relayed to them the essence of the call she had just listened to. Zalinsky quickly scanned the enormous flat-screen monitors on the wall in front of them. One displayed live images from the Predator drone hovering several miles above the hospital. Another displayed the thermal imaging feed from the Predator. Yet another screen carried the live feed from the KH-12 spy satellite now in geosynchronous orbit over Tehran, and it was this one that caught Zalinsky's eye.

"Screen three—zoom that out a bit," Zalinsky ordered the watch commander.

A split second later, everyone in the room saw what Zalinsky had seen. A three-vehicle motorcade—what appeared to be an ambulance sandwiched between two SUVs—was approaching the hospital grounds from the east. They were out of time.

"Alpha One, this is Bravo One, awaiting your command," Torres said.

"Bravo One, hold your position," David replied. "Do not move—I repeat, do *not* move—until I find this other guard."

"With all due respect, sir, we can't wait," Torres pushed back. "We cannot hold this position much longer. Not secure. We need to move now."

"You got your targets marked, Bravo One. We don't. We hold until I can get—"

But Zalinsky cut in before David could finish his thought. "Alpha One, this is Home Plate; do you read?"

"Roger that, Home Plate," David said, shifting gears. "Go ahead."

"You're about to get company, son. We've just intercepted a call to the target. He was told his ride is on the way. Now we're tracking a three-vehicle convoy about to enter the perimeter. Bravo One is right. You need to move now and move fast."

"Negative, Home Plate. We need to find and mark our target. Then we'll move."

An argument was brewing. But before it could escalate, David heard footsteps in the stairwell. Someone was coming down from the sixth floor. David pulled the snake out of the hallway and back to himself, then turned just in time to see an armed Revolutionary Guard Corps officer coming down the stairs. Their eyes met at the same moment. Clearly stunned by the sight of two masked men, the officer raised his AK-47 to fire, but David raised his pistol faster and double-tapped the man to his forehead.

David knew silencers weren't truly silent. They were really sound suppressors, but even the top-of-the-line model on David's pistol couldn't completely eliminate the sound of a 9mm pistol being fired at close range, especially inside a concrete stairwell. David's two shots, muffled though they were, echoed up and down the building. And nothing could silence the sound of an Iranian man collapsing to the floor, falling down half a flight of stairs, and smashing against the wall. His own heart racing, David didn't waste time checking the officer's pulse. There was no question he was dead. But he and Fox would be too if they didn't move fast.

"Go, go, go," David shouted into his microphone as he sprang forward. *"We found the guard and took him out. Now moving into the hallway—go, go, go!"*

David flipped the switch on the little black box, instantly jamming all communications on the floor and thus neutralizing mobile phones, landlines, and security cameras. Then he pulled open the door and turned left with Fox, his wingman, a few yards behind him. He moved hard and fast, weaving through the crowded hallway and occasionally pushing aside those startled doctors, nurses, and visitors who wouldn't or couldn't get out of his way fast enough.

The building was a large rectangle, and as he came around the first corner, he saw a guard none of their recon had identified. The guard was clearly stunned and terrified, but he reacted quickly. He opened fire with his AK-47, spraying bullets everywhere, felling a nurse who happened to get caught in the line of fire. She was dead before she hit the floor, and everyone else in the hallway was now screaming.

In the pandemonium, David dove into a room on the right. Fox dove into a room on the left. But it was Fox who recovered fastest. A moment later, he popped his head out of the doorway and returned fire. Unfortunately his shots went high. The guard was not running toward them. He was now flattened on the ground on his stomach and unleashed a burst of fire at Fox's head. David feared for his colleague's life, certain he was going to see Fox's head explode. But the SEAL's reflexes were lightning quick; he pulled back into the room and out of harm's way just in time.

David seized the moment. He pivoted out from his doorway and fired three shots. At least one hit its mark. The guard shrieked in pain as David moved in and fired two more shots into him, ending his screams.

"Alpha Two, clear—let's go," he shouted, then holstered the pistol and grabbed the MP5 off his back.

He came around the corner and found Torres and Crenshaw in an intense firefight. Three guards were down, writhing and bleeding. But at least two that David could see were returning fire. He unleashed two short bursts and felled one of them. The second—apparently stunned by hearing gunfire behind him—dropped to the floor and was about to fire when Fox roared past David and pumped two bullets into the man's forehead. Suddenly the guns went silent, though people everywhere were shouting and screaming and running for the exits.

David was less than ten yards from Javad Nouri's room and was about to make a break for it when he heard Torres's voice in his headset.

"Alpha One, hold, hold," Torres yelled. *"There's another guard out here somewhere. Do you see him?"*

Both David and Fox scanned the hallway from side to side. Neither saw the guard, and they were about to begin clearing rooms one by one. But now it was Zalinsky's voice in their ears.

"Alpha One, the final guard is in the target's room," he said. "I repeat, he's in the target's room."

For a moment, David froze. If he'd darted in there as planned, he would have been killed instantly. Fox would have been too, if he'd stayed at his side. He was grateful for his team's presence of mind to keep a careful count of the bad guys. But then another thought flashed through David's mind. What if the guard had orders to kill Nouri should anything like this ever happen? He had to do something quickly, but what?

David flattened himself against one wall, aiming his MP5 at the door to Nouri's room. Fox, meanwhile, flattened himself against the opposite wall, aiming his MP5 the other direction, lest they be ambushed from behind. That was, after all, increasingly likely. They were jamming communications on this floor, but what about the others? All this gunfire could certainly be heard throughout the building. IRGC backups had to be on the way, and the transport team could be here any second.

"Home Plate, can you jam communications throughout the whole building?" David asked.

"Already done," Zalinsky said. "But you've got reinforcements coming up the elevators and up your stairwell. You need to get your target and get out of there—*now*."

Just then, the elevator doors opened down the hall. David turned, but Torres and Crenshaw were on it. They opened fire and dropped three Revolutionary Guards before they even knew what had happened. More screams and sobbing erupted amid the renewed gunfire. David decided to use the cacophony to make his move. He reached into his flak jacket, pulled out an M84 stun grenade, yanked the pin, tossed it into room 503, and shouted, *"Fire in the hole!"*

A blinding flash and deafening roar consumed Nouri's room. While his colleagues watched his back, David moved immediately. He raced for Nouri's door, crouched down, and pivoted inside, his MP5 leading the way. Through the lingering smoke, he spotted the guard in the corner. Instinctively David squeezed the trigger once, paused a split second, then fired again. The man crumpled in a bloody heap, having never even gotten off a shot.

25

"Room secure," David shouted, then turned his attention to Javad Nouri.

The man was terrified and balled up in a fetal position, hands over his ears, which were dripping with blood. David felt little sympathy for this man who was trying to help unleash genocide on the Israelis and perhaps on the United States as well. He began pulling tubes and IV lines and various wires out of and off of Nouri's body, causing the Iranian to shriek in pain. Then he pulled a syringe from his pocket, flicked off the plastic tip, tapped it to clear out any remaining bubbles, and jammed the needle into Nouri's neck. The serum took only seconds to activate, and Nouri's body went limp almost immediately. Not taking any chances, David quickly cuffed Nouri's hands and feet and put a strip of duct tape over his mouth, grateful for all the tools Torres and his team had brought with them from the States. He also checked the closet and looked through several drawers and found Nouri's satphone and wallet, which he stuffed into his pockets.

"Target secure and acquired," David said into his microphone, his heart and mind racing. "Alpha One ready for extraction on your signal, Bravo One."

"Roger that—Bravo One, clear," said Torres, his MP5 trained on the elevators for any new reinforcements.

"Bravo Two, clear," said Crenshaw, hunkered down at the nearest stairwell and maintaining their escape route.

"Alpha Two, clear," Fox said last, now repositioned farther up the hallway to watch David's back and keep an eye on the stairwell they'd come up.

"Okay, let's move," Torres said.

David reengaged the safety on his MP5, grabbed a radio out of the hands of the dead guard in the corner, and then proceeded to hoist Nouri and sling him over his shoulder. He made his way out of room 503 quickly and turned left, past trembling doctors, nurses, and patients, up to Crenshaw, who moved into the stairwell to take the lead. Torres pulled back to secure the stairwell door and ordered Fox to hightail it to his position. David tossed the IRGC soldier's radio to Torres so he could monitor the latest traffic, and sixteen seconds later, in a tight formation, they were making their way down five flights of stairs.

"We've got a problem," said Torres, listening to the radio chatter. "The IRGC commander hasn't been able to call out for reinforcements, but he's ordering his men to take up sniper positions aiming at every ground floor exit."

Crenshaw cursed, but David kept his cool.

"Bravo Three, you safe?" he asked, making contact with Mays in the parking lot.

"I'm good," said Matty. "They're evacuating the building. There are hundreds of people pouring out. A lot of them are heading to their cars, so they haven't picked up on me yet."

"Can you see the snipers?"

"No—there's too many people."

"Can you move the van to the door and give us some cover?"

"I can try," Mays said. "But they may start shooting for the tires, or worse."

"Actually, you've got a new problem," said Zalinsky.

"What's that?" David asked as they passed the third floor and headed down to the second.

"We've got a helicopter inbound from the south."

"An air ambulance?" David asked, though he knew that was too much to hope for.

"'Fraid not—we're monitoring police radio traffic," Zalinsky said. "It's part of a SWAT team."

"How did they get the word out?"

"I don't know, but if one helicopter's coming, you can bet more will be coming soon if we don't get you out of there fast."

David and his team hit the ground floor. They entered the maintenance area and, to their shock, found themselves surrounded by about a dozen hospital staff members, janitors, and mechanics trying to evacuate the building. The staff was just as shocked to see them, and David, thinking quickly, seized their fear and used it to his advantage. He ordered them all to stop immediately and to be quiet. Then he assured them that no one would be hurt so long as they formed a human barricade around the team and got them to their van.

"We're all going out on the count of three," David told the hospital workers. "If you run, you die."

Terrified, all of them agreed to the plan, and Mays and Zalinsky heard everything over the radio.

"Bravo Three, move into position," David said.

"Bravo Three, on the move," Mays replied.

"Home Plate, we need a diversion," David said.

"Like what?" Zalinsky asked.

"Where's the closet police car?"

"One just pulled up. It'll be about thirty yards to your left when you come out that back exit."

"How many officers?"

"Two."

"Armed?"

"One has a shotgun; the other is brandishing a pistol," Zalinsky said.

"Can you take it out?"

"With what?"

"A Hellfire," David said.

And all went quiet.

LANGLEY, VIRGINIA

All eyes in the Global Operations Center were on Zalinsky. They had all been there a few days earlier when Zephyr had asked Eva Fischer to launch a Hellfire missile to save his life. They had all, therefore, seen the price Agent Fischer had paid for saying yes. True, Eva had been released. True, she was now working for the NSA. But none of them knew the details, and now they were once again at a moment of truth.

Zalinsky looked to Murray.

"It's your call, Jack," Murray said. "It's your op."

TEHRAN, IRAN

"Home Plate?" David asked.

But there was still radio silence from Langley.

"Home Plate, I need an answer fast, before we come out this door."

David couldn't believe this. He was doing everything Zalinsky had told him to do, and now his own mentor wasn't giving him the cover he needed to make this op a success. How badly did the Agency want Javad Nouri to live and divulge information about the warheads and anything else he knew?

Then again, how much did Langley want David and his team to live through the next five minutes?

Mays knew they had only a matter of seconds to succeed and survive . . . or fail and die. Taking matters into his own hands, he pulled the van out of the parking lot, carefully weaving through the throng of people emerging from the hospital. Then, rather than return past the guard station, he took a right on a service road and was able to double back around the entire building. It took a few moments, but soon he had nearly come full circle, which meant he was coming up behind the two officers crouching behind their police cruiser, guns drawn, waiting for David and his team to emerge from the building and get shot down like Bonnie and Clyde. Mays slowed to a halt, trying one more time to assess the situation.

Craning his neck, Mays turned and looked behind him. For the moment, at least, he saw no more policemen or IRGC officers. But he could hear the faint sound of sirens approaching in the distance. He looked to the left, then to the right. He saw no other armed men, and the crowd ahead of him was beginning to thin as one of the policemen shouted at them to move away from the building quickly and find cover.

"Alpha One, this is Bravo Three—you ready to come out?"

"Hold radio traffic, Bravo Three," David responded. "We're waiting for Home Plate."

But Zalinsky still wasn't saying anything.

"We're out of time," Mays said. "I can already hear the sirens of more police approaching. We need to get you out of there now. I'm going in."

Mays lowered his window, picked up the pistol from the seat beside him, and clicked off the safety. Then he aimed the van for the police cruiser and hit the gas.

The van accelerated instantly and plowed directly into the car. The sound of the violent crash—metal upon metal and glass shattering—stunned everyone within earshot on the hospital grounds. One of the officers was killed on impact while the other dove out of the way. But he was out in the open now. Mays slammed on the brakes, threw the van into park, then pointed his pistol out the window and fired three shots, killing him instantly. Then he jammed the van back into drive and raced to the back door of the hospital.

"Alpha One, targets neutralized," Mays shouted over the radio. *"I'm in position outside the exit. All clear, at least for now. Let's go!"*

David wasn't quite sure what had just happened, but he trusted Mays implicitly. If the man said it was time to move, it was time to move. He ordered the door opened and everyone to start moving. The hospital staff—more terrified than ever now—immediately complied.

Within seconds they were out in the fresh air again. David told everyone to surround the van, and they did, while Crenshaw pulled the side door of the van open and helped David put Javad Nouri inside. Then David jumped into the front passenger seat while the rest of the team climbed into the back and Mays laid on the horn. Everyone surrounding the van fled, and Mays hit the gas and peeled away just as gunfire erupted behind them, blowing out the rear window and sending glass flying everywhere.

LANGLEY, VIRGINIA

Zalinsky was stunned. He was watching the entire scene unfold from the satellite feed but couldn't believe his eyes. Nor could Murray or anyone else in the Global Ops Center. Zalinsky's hesitation had put the entire mission at risk, and it still could, he realized.

True, David had his man. Javad Nouri had been visited in the hospital by the Twelfth Imam and seemed to be one of his most senior advisors. If anyone besides the Mahdi knew the full plan of where the warheads were and how they were going to be used, it could very well be Nouri. But as he watched Mays speeding away from the hospital, he knew he had only a matter of seconds to protect Zephyr and his team from certain death—death from the sky.

TEHRAN, IRAN

"We've got a chopper at four o'clock, low and coming in fast," shouted Crenshaw, who was hunched down in the backseat and trying to get his MP5 into position.

Mays was gaining speed, but it wasn't helping. He couldn't possibly outrun a police helicopter, which meant the sniper on board was getting dangerously close. Crenshaw opened fire. A moment later, Fox and Torres were leaning out of their respective windows and firing at the chopper as well.

"We hit them," Crenshaw shouted. *"They're backing off."*

For now, the team's return fire seemed to have worked. But it was only a temporary fix. David and the others soon watched as the chopper sped ahead, looped around, and then accelerated. It was coming right for them. The sniper was beginning to lean out from the right-hand side and was preparing to fire.

Mays told everyone to hold on, then slammed on the brakes and took a hard left turn. Again, the maneuver worked. The chopper sailed right past them. But they couldn't outfox this guy for long, David knew. They needed to find cover, but even then, what good would that do? If they went underground, the pilot would alert every police officer in the city. They would soon be surrounded, and David didn't dare contemplate their fate in the hands of the Twelfth Imam, especially since they were in possession of one of his advisors.

David craned his neck, hoping to reacquire the helicopter and help Mays plot an evasive route. A moment later, he saw the glint of the rotors in the afternoon sun. The pilot was banking around from the east, about to make another dead run at them. The problem was that Mays had pulled onto a major highway. It was mostly clear. Because of the war, few Tehran residents were on the streets, and Mays was now driving at more than two hundred kilometers an hour. But there were no more side streets. There were no more alleys. There were no more overpasses. This was it. They were out in the open, and the chopper was dead ahead. David could see the sniper getting into position again and aiming his rifle directly for Mays—or for him. Did it really matter which? They were all going to die in the next three seconds, and all their hopes for stopping the Mahdi from launching his last two nuclear warheads would die with them. And there was nothing they could do about it.

Then David saw a streak of light out of the corner of his eye, coming in from the right and moving fast. It took a split second to register what was happening, and then David realized Zalinsky had just said yes. Slicing across the sky was a Hellfire missile, and sure enough, an instant later he watched the helicopter ahead of him explode into an enormous fireball, the pilot and the sniper having never seen the missile coming. Fire and smoke and twisted scraps of molten metal came raining down from the sky. But Mays never slowed, and David didn't want him to. They still had to get out of this city to one of the three hotels in the suburbs that they had preselected as possible rendezvous points, and then they had to wake Nouri up and get him talking before it was too late.

26

"Asher, it's Levi. I need to speak with you immediately," Defense Minister Shimon said when the PM came on the line.

"Of course, Levi; what is it?"

"No, not over the phone. I need to meet with you in person—you and Zvi," Shimon said, referring to Mossad chief Zvi Dayan.

"Then come," Naphtali said. "Is it about Dimona?"

"No."

"Then what?" Naphtali insisted.

The defense minister hesitated for a moment before saying, "It's about the Twelfth Imam. That's all I can say."

"Then come quickly," the PM said. "And be safe."

"Thank you, sir. We'll do our best."

TABRIZ, IRAN

General Mohsen Jazini stood in the shadows in the corner of the garage, lighting up a Cuban cigar and watching the proceedings with great interest. Jazini said nothing, but Jalal Zandi had no doubt the general was monitoring his every move. Zandi could have done without the open flame as they were topping off the gas tanks of both ambulances and loading in the two large wooden crates, one into the back of each vehicle. The warheads he was not worried about. Those could not be set off without the proper codes. But he couldn't help imagining himself dying in a petrol-induced fireball because the commander of the Caliphate couldn't control his nicotine fix for five more minutes.

They didn't die. By five o'clock on the nose, the fuel tanks were full. The warheads were safely loaded. Eight more heavily armed Revolutionary Guards had arrived in the past hour, detailed to this mission from a nearby base. Two IRGC counterassault team members climbed in the back of each ambulance to babysit the warheads. Two more Guards took the front seats, one to drive and the other to navigate. All that was left was for Jazini and Zandi to climb into the trail car—a brand-new charcoal-gray Toyota Sequoia, which Jazini's men had commandeered from the widow of the base commander, who had been killed in the recent air strikes—along with their driver and Jazini's security detail. By 5:10 p.m., they were on the road.

"So," Zandi asked, "where exactly are we headed with these things?"

He assumed the missile bases either in Kerman or in Rasht but was stunned when he heard the answer actually come out of Jazini's mouth.

"Damascus."

FORT MEADE, MARYLAND

Supplying satellite phones to the upper echelons of the Iranian political and military leadership had seemed like a masterstroke at first. Now it seemed to Eva Fischer like a millstone tied around her neck.

With Eva's help, David had personally smuggled dozens of satphones built by the Thuraya corporation, located in Dubai, into Iran—and the Agency had managed to send in scores more. Thuraya's system was comprised of forty-eight LEO, or low earth orbit, satellites operating at an altitude of about 1,400 kilometers—roughly 870 miles above the earth. The company also operated four more satellites at all times as backup units. The satellites transmitted calls to one another in the frequency band of 22.55 gigahertz and 23.55 gigahertz, while the Thuraya phones themselves used L-band transponders, allowing callers on the ground to talk to one another using frequencies in the band of 1616 to 1626.5 megahertz. Each phone Eva had supplied to David to give to the Mahdi and his associates operated on a specific, designated, and trackable frequency on one of 240 separate channels, allowing the NSA to intercept the calls off the satellites in real time without installing a bug that could be detected by Iranian counterintelligence and without the intercepts being detectable by the Thuraya corporation.

The problem was, the plan was working too well. Now that much of Iran's power grid was down because of the Israeli air strikes—and now that much of Iran's mobile phone system had been knocked out as well—the Mahdi and his top commanders were no longer using landlines or mobile phones. Rather, they were using the satphones almost exclusively. That meant nearly every call they made was being recorded and transcribed by the National Security Agency.

In theory, that was a godsend, allowing the NSA and then the CIA to listen to every call and thus tap into a good deal of the discussion under way within America's most dangerous enemy. In reality, however, the U.S. intelligence system was being severely overloaded, and it was creating the risk that incredibly valuable material would be lost.

It wasn't just the sheer magnitude of material that was coming in that made their lives so difficult, however; it was that the NSA and CIA Farsi translators—of which there were only a dozen—often didn't know who was talking to whom. Hundreds of calls were being made each hour. Thousands upon thousands of calls were being made each day. Some of the calls were between high-ranking officials. But most were between colonels and majors or between lieutenants and sergeants or between bodyguards and drivers or between advance men and pilots, and so forth. Much of what was said was too cryptic or too brief to be properly understood.

Moreover, the translators often had no idea where the calls were being physically placed from or where they were being physically received. If, for example, a caller said he was going to be sending a truck loaded with more Scud-C missiles to the recipient of the call, it was often unclear where that shipment was going to come from and where it was going. It was, therefore, not actionable intelligence. It was not information that could be used to any real or serious effect to destroy that shipment of arms. Which made it worse than irrelevant because it was a distraction from the intercepts that did provide actionable intelligence. But it still had to be read and translated and assessed, and that took time, of which Eva and her team had precious little.

That said, several days of trial and error—mostly before Eva had been released from detention—had helped the translators pinpoint the frequencies of some of the specific phones being used by the Mahdi himself and by Ayatollah Hosseini and President Darazi. Every time a transcript of a call was made, across the top of the page was printed the time the call was made, the time the call ended, the precise frequency of the phone making the call, and the precise frequency of the phone receiving the call—if the receiving phone was a satphone. One call early on, for example, that had been positively identified as occurring between the Mahdi and Ayatollah Hosseini had helped the translators identify which phones had been assigned to the two men by the frequencies printed at the top of the transcripts. The translators had then asked the NSA computer geeks to route calls with those specific frequencies to a special computer database that they could prioritize more highly than all the other calls.

But now a new problem had arisen: over the last forty-eight hours or so, the translators began noticing that other, lower-ranking officials were using those frequencies, rather than the Mahdi, Hosseini, and Darazi. The top brass at Langley were desperate to know why, but the translators couldn't provide a solid answer. Their best guess was that the Iranian leaders were being handed satphones by their subordinates when they needed to make or receive a call, but either the subordinates were being rotated, or the phones they were using were being rotated, possibly to recharge them every few hours due to heavy usage.

Whatever the reason, neither Zalinsky nor Fischer—the architects of the intercept strategy—had planned or prepared for such contingencies. Their plans had been built around stopping an Israeli-Iranian war from happening, not around processing the Niagara Falls of intelligence that was pouring in in the midst of such a war. They didn't have the manpower to manage the deluge, and they were now drowning in their good fortune.

Eva knew she didn't have the time to translate every single printed transcript of every single intercept in the stack that was already in her office, especially not when new batches of intercepts were being dropped off on her desk every fifteen to twenty minutes. Her only hope was to quickly skim each transcript, mark any interesting tidbits with a red pen, and put them in different baskets on her desk. Basket one was top-priority material—any call that seemed like it might be from or to the Mahdi or a senior Iranian official that also contained specific points of interest (i.e., references to specific operations, flights, meetings, or war plans of any kind) that might be actionable, especially if compared with similar transcripts that other translators might be working on. Basket two was top-priority material from unidentified callers—callers that specifically were not the Mahdi, the Ayatollah, or the president—but contained actionable or potentially actionable intelligence. And so forth.

Eva was working as hard and fast as she could, but after the way she had been treated, she was not doing any of it for the NSA nor for the CIA. She certainly was not busting her tail for President Jackson or Roger Allen or Tom Murray or Jack Zalinsky. Everything she was doing now was for David Shirazi—to save his life and get him out of Iran and back to Washington in one piece. She had no idea what motivated everyone else around her to work such grueling hours for such minuscule pay. But at the moment, she didn't really care. She had gotten David into this mess, and she was determined to get him out of it. If it were up to her, she'd be on a plane to Incirlik, Turkey, and then HALO dropping into Iran to help David in person. But that, clearly, was not in the cards. This was what she had been assigned to do, and she wanted to do it well, fearing if she didn't, she might never see David again at all.

After scanning another thirty or forty transcripts without hitting pay dirt, Eva suddenly sat bolt upright in her chair. Her red pen started marking furiously. She opened a file on her computer and began typing up an English translation. When she was done, she went back to the top and double-checked her work, then checked it again. *How had this been missed?* she wondered. She had to get it to Murray immediately . . . unless there was more. On a hunch, she began leafing through her stack of transcripts, looking for any others that had time stamps similar to this one. After about a minute, she found one. A moment later, she found another. Then a third and a fourth. She carefully translated these, too, typed up her work, triple-checked, and then e-mailed everything by secure server to Murray. Then she picked up the phone and speed-dialed the Global Ops Center at Langley.

"Tom, stop what you're doing," she said when she got him. "You need to open the e-mail I just sent you, and we need to talk."

ROUTE 21, WESTERN IRAN

Jazini's convoy raced along Route 21, heading southwest to Mamaghan. From there they continued along the same route to the town of Miandoab. Jalal Zandi was already fast asleep in the backseat, so the general felt comfortable unlocking his briefcase, pulling out his laptop, and powering it up. He had no intention of watching the increasingly lush Persian countryside, green with grassy hillsides and valleys and speckled with the colors of a hundred kinds of flowers, whiz by. This was not a family vacation. This was war. He had plans to make and refine—and precious little time to finish them.

No sooner had Jazini entered his password and opened his to-do file, however, than a call came in on his driver's satphone.

"Yes, hello?" the driver asked in Farsi. "Who's calling? Oh yes, my Lord. Thank you, my Lord. He is right here. Please, one moment."

The driver quickly handed the phone to Jazini, who recognized immediately that it was the Mahdi and braced himself for whatever was coming next.

"General?"

"Yes, my Lord?"

"Are you in motion?"

"We are."

"Any problems?"

"None," Jazini said. "Everything is going very smoothly."

"Good," said the Mahdi. "Now, you wrote about another matter in your proposal. Do you remember?"

"Yes, my Lord."

"Your idea is an excellent one, but we must move up the timetable. Tomorrow midday will be too late. It must be tonight."

Jazini was stunned. "Tonight, Your Excellency? With all due respect, my Lord, I don't know if we can arrange matters so quickly."

"You must," the Mahdi said. "Set it for midnight, and set into motion all the plans you laid out in the memo."

"Yes, Your Excellency, I will—"

But before Jazini could finish his answer or ask another question—as was characteristic of a call with the Twelfth Imam—the signal went dead.

TEHRAN, IRAN

David pulled Marco Torres aside and complimented the paramilitary commander on his choice of their temporary safe house. The Tooska Park Inn, located in the southeast quadrant of Tehran, just off the Tehran South Highway, was a seedy-looking joint typically used by pimps and prostitutes. But now, with the war in full swing, the parking lot was empty. The place was completely deserted.

Not surprisingly, the owner was a "don't ask, don't tell" kind of guy who desperately needed the cash Torres had given him. And it wasn't like he could have called the police anyway. The landlines connected to the motel weren't working any more than the owner's mobile phone was, a fact Torres had double-checked before directing Mays at the very last moment to take them there. The police had not been on regular patrols since the beginning of the war, so there should be no interruptions.

David instructed Mays and Crenshaw to ditch their bullet-ridden van and steal two alternate vehicles, quickly. They couldn't afford to be stranded. "Also, ask Nick to look at Javad's phone," David said to Torres. "See if he's got a contact list. Who's in it? Who is he calling? Who is he getting calls from? You know the drill."

"Will do, boss."

"And one more thing," David added.

"An extraction plan," Torres said, seeming to read his mind.

"Right," David said. "Make one. Fast."

David had to get started, and he really didn't know how to break Javad Nouri, how to get a zealot like him to talk. On the entire drive from the gun battle at the hospital, the question had been foremost on his mind. He didn't have a lot of time to warm Nouri up, and the normal inducements of money and freedom and a new life in the United States weren't likely to work on a top personal aide to the Twelfth Imam. What would work? Fear, perhaps, but fear of what? David had no answers.

Pondering all that, and saying a silent prayer for wisdom, David opened the door to room 9 and stepped inside, Torres right behind him. As Torres closed and locked the door, David surveyed the room. It stank of stale cigarettes. A queen-size bed with a lumpy mattress and a thin blue quilt took up the center of the room. Along the right wall was a beat-up wooden dresser, on top of which sat an old television set covered in dust and looking like it hadn't been used in twenty or thirty years, if that. He doubted it even worked. If it did, it looked like it might actually be black-and-white. Along the far wall was a small closet and a door, presumably leading to a bathroom. On the left side of the room was a battered wooden desk and a crooked lamp. The walls were painted a light blue but were dingy and smudged.

Fox had taken up a position by the desk, occasionally peering through the threadbare plaid curtains, looking for signs of trouble, his weapon at the ready.

As David had instructed, Javad Nouri was blindfolded and gagged, strapped to a wooden chair, his hands and feet tightly bound. Fox nodded when David glanced at him, letting him know Fox had, as directed, given Nouri an injection to wake him up but leave him in a somewhat foggy state of mind. David's voice would be the first Nouri would hear in captivity, and a plan began to come to him. It wasn't foolproof by any means, but it just might work, and in the absence of an alternative, David decided to go with his gut.

He walked behind Nouri's chair and motioned for Fox to hand him a pistol. Fox gave him a black Sig Sauer P226 Navy, a 9mm handgun built specifically for the SEALs. David stared at it for a moment, weighing it in his hand. It felt colder than he'd expected and heavier. He walked over to Nouri, pulled back and released the slide, chambering a round, and held the 9mm to the man's temple.

"Javad, I know you can hear me, so I'm going to make this very simple," David began. "I'm going to ask you questions. You're going to give me answers—truthful answers. Got that?"

Nouri didn't move, didn't nod, didn't say a word, so David pressed the pistol harder against his temple. Nouri nodded ever so slightly.

"You recognize my voice, don't you, Javad?" David continued.

Nouri nodded again.

"That's right, Javad. My name is Reza Tabrizi, and I work for the Central Intelligence Agency."

27

"The Twelfth Imam has cut a deal with the Pakistanis," Eva told Murray.

"What kind of deal?" Murray asked.

"Tom, he's going to get full operational control of 170-plus nuclear missiles by midnight on Monday."

Murray said nothing for a moment. Then, "He'll be unstoppable. Are you sure it's all finalized?"

"As you can see from the transcripts I sent you, everything's done but the handshake," Eva said. "It looks like the Iranian ambassador in Islamabad has been the middleman. He's been doing most of the negotiating, and I'm guessing he's been communicating with the Mahdi and with General Jazini mostly by secure e-mail. So the calls—at least the ones I've seen so far—don't give chapter and verse. But one thing is clear: the Paks are going to publicly announce they are joining the Caliphate in the next twenty-four hours. The Mahdi and his team are trying to arrange a face-to-face meeting with Iskander Farooq. The logistics, as you can imagine, are challenging, to say the least. The Mahdi doesn't have the time or interest to go to Islamabad, and he doesn't have a lot of working airports left from which to depart, either. By the same token, it's really not feasible for Farooq to get to Tehran. But Farooq won't hand over the launch codes to the Pak nuclear missiles unless he gets an in-person meeting."

"So it's not entirely a done deal," Murray said.

"Seems like a formality at this point. Farooq is a Sunni. He rules a predominantly Sunni country. Yet he's about to give the Twelfth Imam the keys to the kingdom."

"But he hasn't yet, right?" Murray pressed.

"Not technically, but it's just a matter of hours," Eva said.

"Don't we have intel that the Mahdi was supposed to meet with Farooq in Dubai last Thursday?"

"We did, and we know that the Mahdi even sent his aide . . ."

"Javad Nouri?"

"Right, right—Nouri—to Dubai for a quick trip to scout out a location."

"It was only a few hours, right?"

"I think so, but then again, I'm just catching up on that by reading the intercepts," Eva said. "You'll recall I was locked up at the time."

"I know, and I'm sorry, but listen—my point is, the meeting between the Mahdi and Farooq was scrubbed, right?"

"Yes. The war started Thursday, and everything changed," Eva confirmed. "Why? What are you saying?"

"I don't know," said Murray. "I'm just thinking."

"What are you going to do, suggest the president order U.S. special forces invade Pakistan and secure every missile?" Eva asked, incredulous. "For crying out loud, Tom, the man didn't even want to hit Iran."

"Careful, Eva," Murray cautioned. "That's the president of the United States—your commander in chief—you're talking about."

"I'm just saying that—"

"I know what you're saying," Murray said, cutting her off. "And you might be right. But *I'm* saying this deal could have been done Thursday, and it wasn't. So it's not done until it's done. But don't you worry about that. You just keep translating. Let me worry about whether we can stop this or not. You're doing good work, Eva. Thank you. Really. Thanks."

"Don't thank me yet."

"Why not?"

"Because there's more."

TEHRAN, IRAN

Nouri's entire body stiffened involuntarily as if David had just nailed him with a high-voltage cattle prod. But Torres's eyes widened as well.

Even Fox turned his head away from the window as if to see what in the world David was doing.

Admitting to being a spy for the CIA on enemy soil during a hot war in the enemy's capital while interrogating a top advisor to the enemy himself was an unconventional strategy, to say the least. They certainly didn't teach it in the Agency training program at the Farm, nor had David ever seen or heard of Murray or Zalinsky using it. If Eva were here, David knew she'd go ballistic. But this was the course he'd chosen, and he was determined to see it through.

"That's right, Javad. Every single phone I gave you, every single phone you gave the Mahdi and his army, each and every one of them was supplied by the American government, by the CIA and the NSA, and all of them are being carefully monitored."

David paused for a moment to let his words sink in and let Javad's mind—foggy though it was—contemplate the full import of what he had just heard. He noticed Torres nervously tapping his fingers on his weapon and Fox forcing himself to look away and keep his eyes peeled out the window.

"The CIA is listening to every phone conversation the Mahdi is having, Javad. We're listening to every call the Ayatollah is having. We're listening to every call President Darazi is having, and all the rest of them," David continued. "But we also know there are things you're saying to each other that you're not saying on the phone. So here's the deal. You're going to talk to me. You're going to answer my questions, and as a reward I'm not only going to let you live, I'm going to get you out of this country, get you to a safe place where the Mahdi can't torture you once he learns that you work for me."

Nouri's body language made it clear David had his full attention now.

"It's a simple proposition, Javad. Cooperate, and live. Don't cooperate, and die. But let's be clear: just between you and me, I'm not going to put a bullet through your temple. That would be the easy way out for you. If you don't help me, I'm going to make certain the Mahdi kills you, but only after he makes you suffer in ways that are too terrible for me to even want to think about."

David pulled the Sig Sauer away from Nouri's head and pressed it into the top of his knee.

"But I'll tell you one thing: if you don't talk, I am going to blow your kneecap off. Now, I've never experienced that level of pain myself, but I've seen people go through it. You might be interested to know that I shot Tariq Khan in the knee just three days ago. He didn't die, but he sure wanted to. The crazy thing is, Javad, the human body can actually endure an enormous amount of suffering. I'm not sure how. I'm not a doctor. I'm not a mullah. I'm not Allah. All I know is I've seen people suffer for days in wrenching, mind-blowing amounts of pain, begging for someone—anyone—to kill them once and for all and put them out of their misery. Khan did. But even blowing your kneecap off would actually be the least of your troubles. Because I'm going to make you the same deal I made Khan. He made the right choice—he talked. And you'd better do the same. Because if you don't talk, after I shoot you, my team and I are going to leave you in this room for the Mahdi and his men to find you. They'll find you right here in this CIA safe house. I know you can't see it right now. But I'm assuming you can imagine how it looks. Computers and satellite phones and maps and the like. And on your laptop, which will be open when the secret police arrive, there are all kinds of interesting files. Transcripts of the Mahdi's phone calls. Transcripts of Hosseni's calls and Darazi's. Files with code names for Najjar Malik and for Khan. Detailed plans to assassinate Dr. Saddaji in Hamadan. Lists of dead drops. Locations of other safe houses. Bank account numbers in Switzerland with millions of American dollars parked in your name. And the crazy thing is, it won't be fake. It's all real. Your fingerprints will be all over this operation. You know how angry the Mahdi is that this war isn't going like he'd hoped, like he'd planned, like he'd predicted? Imagine how he'll feel when he learns that you've been selling him out—his own personal Judas, betraying him with a kiss."

Nouri was perspiring profusely now, but David was not yet done.

"But I suspect that won't be the worst of it," he continued. "My guess—and it's just a hunch, I admit—is that what will really enrage the Mahdi is the pictures of you at the Buddha-Bar in Dubai."

Nouri's knuckles went white as he gripped the arms of the chair.

"You were being followed, Javad. We watched you arrive in Dubai last Wednesday. We know the Mahdi sent you to prep for the meeting with President Farooq. We have copies of all your receipts. We have pictures of every place you went. We have pictures of every person you met with, including the—how shall I put it?—scantily clad women. We have pictures of you holding those Smirnoff and Absolut bottles and video of you pouring those young ladies drink after expensive drink. And it will all be here, on your hard drive. Then VEVAK will get a discreet call with an anonymous tip about your whereabouts, and thugs from the secret police will descend upon this place and report everything they find to Imam al-Mahdi. Oh, you'll deny everything, of course. You'll profess your loyalty to the Mahdi and to Allah. And all these files I'm talking about won't be obvious at first. Asgari's men will have to do some digging into your computer. But they'll find it. I guarantee you they will find it all. And given all the evidence, do you really think they're going to believe you? Especially when they find an e-mail from you to me, warning me that the Mahdi has two more nuclear warheads that he's preparing to use?"

At that, Nouri's grip on the armrests actually began to loosen. The more David said, the more the life seemed to drain out of the young man.

"Now, listen carefully," said David, careful to stay behind and to the right of Nouri. "I'm going to take this gag off your mouth. You scream, you call for help, you make any sudden moves, and I blow your kneecap off. Got it?"

Nouri took a deep breath, then exhaled and nodded.

"And yes, the pistol is equipped with a silencer, just in case you were wondering."

LANGLEY, VIRGINIA

"What else?" Murray asked Eva, not sure he really wanted to know but having no other choice.

"A few more things," she replied. "First, Mohsen Jazini is now the acting defense minister and commander in chief of all Caliphate armed forces."

"Says who?"

"The Mahdi personally, in a phone call to Jazini," Eva said. "I'm forwarding you the transcript."

"What about Faridzadeh?" Murray asked.

"He's out."

"Why?"

"The Mahdi didn't say. Just told Jazini he was, quote, 'impressed by your memo and want you to start executing the first section immediately.'"

"That's odd."

"It is, but there's more."

"What?"

"Okay, second, I've got a strange set of intercepts here that I don't quite know what to make of, but they're . . . I don't know exactly. They're giving me the willies."

"What do they say?"

"One is of the Twelfth Imam talking to President Mustafa in Syria," Eva said. "He tells Mustafa to start killing all the Jews and Christians in the country."

"Why?" Murray asked. "The man has already slaughtered more than thirty-two thousand people over the past eighteen months."

"I know, but that's what he said," Eva replied. "And when Mustafa said Syria wanted to join the Caliphate, the Mahdi told him Syria could join the Islamic empire but couldn't yet join the war against Israel."

"Why not?"

"He didn't say exactly, but he did say he was sending Mustafa some special guests and that they should be well cared for."

"Who?"

"Again, he didn't say. Not on that call. But there were several other calls that didn't seem so important at first but might be. It seems the Mahdi is in touch—indirectly, mind you, but in touch nonetheless—with the IRGC hit team that took out President Ramzy in New York. He told Darazi to order the hit team to travel from Venezuela through Cyprus and Beirut to Damascus and await instructions there."

"You think the Mahdi is planning to assassinate Mustafa?" Murray asked.

"No."

"But you think this hit team are the ones the Mahdi told Mustafa to prepare for?"

"Mmm, no, I don't think so," Eva replied.

"Then what?"

"I don't know," Eva admitted. "I really don't. The 'special friends' the Mahdi referred to seemed like people at a higher level, at least to me, but I can't tell you why. It's just . . . it was the adjective he used in Farsi for the word *special*. It means, you know, very special, like a VIP or a high-ranking official or someone very close to you, someone in the family. I'm not sure. I'm going on instinct here, Tom, but something's going on in Syria. I wish I could tell you what, but I can't. But I think we should start putting more attention on trying to figure it out."

Murray shook his head. "Look, Eva, we'll do what we can, but we can only do so much at this point. Our top priority is finding those two warheads. Right now I'd say our second-highest priority is trying to thwart this deal between the Mahdi and the Pakistanis. I need to brief the director on that ASAP and make sure he briefs the president and the National Security Council. That could shift the entire balance of power in the next twenty-four hours. That's an awful lot to do in a very short period of time. Don't get distracted by Syria. They're not in the war. The Mahdi told them not to get into the war. We need to keep our eye on the ball."

"But, Tom, what if—?"

"No," Murray said, cutting her off. "It's a rabbit trail. We can't afford any diversions right now. Please, Eva. I need you to stay focused. And I need you to rally the other translators and keep them focused as well. This thing's coming to a head, and I'm counting on you."

TEHRAN, IRAN

Torres and Fox readied their weapons as David began to remove the gag from Nouri's mouth, leaving the blindfold on. Nouri made no sudden moves.

"Would you like some water?" David asked his prisoner.

"Yes, thank you," Nouri replied.

But David wasn't ready to give Javad Nouri anything just yet. "How about you answer my questions first?" he said.

"Please, Reza, I haven't had anything to drink since the hospital," Nouri replied.

"No, I want you to talk first," said David, taking a long drink of cold bottled water in front of Nouri and making sure the man could hear him enjoy every refreshing drop. "Where are the warheads?"

"I thought you and your people were listening in on everything we've been saying," Nouri said. "Why bother even asking me?"

"Because we know the warheads exist. We know the Israeli attacks destroyed six of the warheads but somehow missed two. We know your boss is planning to use them. But we don't know where they are currently."

"I don't know either."

"You're making a mistake, Javad."

"No, really, I don't," Nouri replied. "Why would they tell me?"

"Because you are the Mahdi's most trusted advisor."

"That's the Ayatollah, not me."

"Hardly," David said.

"Well, believe what you like, but I don't know where they are."

"Are they still in Iran?"

"I don't know."

"Have they been moved out of the country?"

"How many ways must I say it?" Nouri asked. "I . . . don't . . . know."

"Then how are they going to be used?"

"The Mahdi is going to fire them both at the Zionists."

"Both of them?"

"Yes."

"At Israel."

"That's what I said."

"Not at the United States?"

"No."

"Why not?"

"Because the Mahdi's focus is on the Zionists."

"The Little Satan?"

"If you say so," Nouri said.

"It's not my line; it's the Mahdi's," David said.

Nouri remained silent.

"So you're going to fire both of these warheads at Israel."

"Yes."

"For what purpose?"

"Why do you think? To wipe the Jews off the map."

"So Darazi was serious when he said that?" David asked.

"Of course he was serious. Why would you think otherwise?"

"Because Darazi also said he was enriching uranium for peaceful purposes."

"He lied," Nouri said matter-of-factly and without any hint of irony or guilt.

"So you're an admitted liar," David said, taking the tone of a Manhattan prosecutor more than an interrogator.

"Not me," Nouri replied. "But Darazi, yes."

"And the Mahdi."

"Never."

"The Mahdi never lied?" David asked.

"No, Imam al-Mahdi never lied," Nouri said, indignant. "He came to establish the Caliphate. He came to establish peace in the Middle East and around the world. He warned everyone—he explicitly warned your president and the Zionists, for that matter—that if the Caliphate were attacked, this would trigger the War of Annihilation. But none of you would listen. We didn't attack first in this war. The Zionists did."

"But you were about to launch a strike on the Israelis," David argued.

"Says who?" Nouri asked. "Your president asked for a meeting with the Mahdi to discuss peace terms. The Mahdi agreed. How is that preparing for a first strike?"

"You're actually going to sit here and deny that the Mahdi was preparing to launch a first strike against Israel?"

"Yes."

"But you just admitted that Darazi was lying about the reason for enriching uranium," David noted.

"Yes."

"Well?"

"Well, what?"

"You just admitted that Iran was building nuclear weapons when Darazi said they weren't, and the reason was to wipe Israel off the map."

"No," said Nouri, "I said Iran built nuclear weapons. I didn't say they were intended for offensive purposes."

"Of course you did."

"No, we built them for defensive purposes—just in case a scenario like this developed," Nouri insisted. "If the Jews hadn't attacked us, we would not have attacked the Jews. But now it is clear; the Zionists are the aggressors. And in attacking us, they have triggered a fully justified, fully legal jihad, and this was a very foolish mistake. For now we are waging a holy war with holy weapons, and that cancerous tumor known as Israel will be wiped off the map, just as our Iranian president prophesied it would be."

"You don't really believe all that crap," David said with disgust.

"I am speaking the truth," Nouri said. "It is you who is bothered by it, not me."

David was incensed, but mostly with himself. He had lost control of the conversation. Nouri's fear was turning to defiance. He was talking in circles, but he had gotten inside David's head, and David knew he had to turn the tables, to regain the initiative. But how?

28

"You're absolutely certain?" Ayatollah Hosseini asked, unable to believe what he was hearing.

He pushed for more information. *How long ago did it happen? How many were involved? Who was responsible? Were there any leads, any clues whatsoever?* Hosseini asked a dozen more questions, but Ibrahim Asgari, commander of VEVAK, Iran's secret police force, simply had no answers as of yet.

"Call me as soon as you know more, Commander," Hosseini ordered and then hung up the phone, nervously looking about the war room. His hands trembled. All color had drained from his face.

"Where is the president?" he asked a young aide.

"I believe he stepped out to get something to eat," the aide said.

"Get him, and bring him to me immediately," the Ayatollah said. "I must speak to him on an urgent matter."

"Yes, sir—right away, sir." The aide scurried off.

The room began to grow blurry. Hosseini blinked several times and reached for a glass of water and drank it down quickly. This couldn't be happening. Was it the Israelis? The Americans? Either way, they were getting far too close.

Moments later, Darazi rushed into the war room. "What is it? What happened?"

"Come in here," Hosseini said, motioning his colleague to follow him into the recently cleaned conference room where Faridzadeh had been killed earlier. "Now, shut the door and have a seat."

Darazi did as he was told. "What is it?" he asked again. "You look like you've seen a ghost."

"Javad Nouri has been kidnapped," said Hosseini.

"That's not possible," Darazi countered.

"Nevertheless, it happened," Hosseini replied. "So far Commander Asgari is reporting twelve dead, nine wounded."

"How many attackers?"

"Best we can tell, it was a team of five commandos. But they had air support as well. They took out a police helicopter over the city, killing all three men on board."

"Is that beyond the casualty numbers you just gave me?"

"No, that's everybody that we know of right now."

"Any leads?"

"None."

"Asgari has absolutely no idea who is responsible?"

"He thinks it's the Israelis."

"He's probably right," said Darazi.

"Maybe yes, or maybe the Americans are here too," Hosseini said.

"I thought the Americans were staying neutral in this war."

"The fact is we have no idea. We're flying blind here. But I'll tell you one thing: whoever it is, they're getting dangerously close to us. Think about it: if they have Javad and Javad starts talking, then they know where we are right now."

"We need to move everything to the new facility at the mosque—tonight."

"That's my thought too," Hosseini said. "But first, we need to talk to the Mahdi. Is he still up on the roof?"

"I'm afraid so."

"What's he doing?"

"Praying."

"We need to get him down from there. It's too dangerous to stay outside."

"You want me to ask him?" Darazi asked.

"No," Hosseini said. "I'd better go myself."

★ ★ ★ ★ ★

David tried to seize control of the conversation once again.

"Listen, Javad, I'm only going to say it one more time. You're making a mistake. Your sins are going to be exposed to the Mahdi within the hour unless you start cooperating."

Nouri sat up straight in the chair, puffing out his chest and lifting his head.

"I am not afraid of you, Reza," he replied.

"Maybe not," David said. "But you are afraid of Imam al-Mahdi. You care what he thinks about you. And now you're about to be exposed for the man you really are. We haven't manufactured these photos and this video of you in Dubai at that bar with the women and the alcohol, Javad. That's not cooked up. Those are decisions you made. And knowledge of those sins alone is going to infuriate the Mahdi. But as I told you, we're going to throw fuel on the fire by implicating you as the mole in this operation, with a direct, working relationship with the CIA."

"But that's a lie," Nouri shot back. "I never worked with you or for you."

"Really?" David asked. "Were you not my main contact within the Mahdi's inner circle? Didn't you and I speak on a regular basis? Didn't I provide you with the satellite phones the Mahdi and his war council are using now? And aren't those all CIA phones? And didn't you literally hand those phones to the Mahdi?"

"The Mahdi will never believe it," Nouri insisted. "He will never believe I betrayed him—and certainly not to a man like you."

"I wouldn't be so sure, Javad," David said, pulling out his own sat-phone, dialing a dedicated line back at Langley, entering his code number, and then—putting the call on speakerphone—playing for Nouri a phone call from just a few days earlier.

"Reza?"

"Yes, this is he."

"This is Javad Nouri. I just got back to Tehran and got your message."

"Hey, good to hear from you."

"I hope it's not too late to call you, but whatever you've got, we could use."

"It's no problem. Thanks for getting back to me. I expect to have a hundred of what we were discussing by late in the afternoon tomorrow—er, I guess today. They're being shipped to me in Qom. That's where I'm heading now to meet some of my tech team later this morning at some switching station that's having a problem. Are you guys going to be in Qom by any chance?"

"No, we're not. But I have a better idea. Could you bring them directly to us? Our mutual friend has heard many good things about you and would like to meet you in person. Would that be acceptable?"

"Of course. That would be a great honor; thank you."

"Wonderful. Our friend is deeply grateful for your help, and he personally asked me to apologize for the vetting process you were subjected to. He hopes you understand that we cannot be too careful at this stage."

"I understand. Abdol Esfahani explained everything. I'll survive."

"Good. Be in Tehran tonight at eight o'clock at the restaurant where we met before. Come by cab. Don't bring anyone or anything else with you, just the gifts. I'll have someone meet you there and bring you to us. Okay?"

"Yes, of course. I'm looking forward to it."

"So are we. I've got to go now. Good-bye."

"I have done nothing wrong," Nouri insisted, his voice more defiant than ever.

"Is that how it's going to look?" David asked.

The question hung in the air, but David wasn't certain it was working.

"Why would the CIA come and kidnap me from my hospital room

and then leave me for dead in this safe house if I really worked for them?" Nouri finally said. "It isn't logical, and the Mahdi won't buy it."

Now it was David whose body stiffened. Nouri had a point. Why, indeed?

The Ayatollah took three bodyguards with him and headed for the roof. When he got there, sure enough, he found the Twelfth Imam on his knees, bowing toward Mecca, and evidently in no mood to be trifled with. He also found the sun beginning to sink in the west and heavy storm clouds rolling in over the city. Several strikes of lightning flashed in the distance, but as of yet he could hear no thunder. What struck him most, as it had struck Darazi earlier, was the stench of death and the magnitude of the destruction of the airfield all around them and the Mahdi's seeming imperviousness to it all. *Was that faith,* Hosseini wondered, *or foolishness?*

"Hamid Hosseini, what a surprise," said the Mahdi.

The Ayatollah was immediately caught off guard. The Mahdi's back was to him, and Hosseini hadn't announced himself or made any sound.

"Here to coax me down off the ledge, are you, Hamid?" the Mahdi sneered.

How did he know? Hosseini wondered. *Could this man read his mind?*

"Well, my Lord, I . . . uh . . ."

"Save your breath, and don't waste my time," the Mahdi replied. "Do you think I am like all of you? Do you think I am a mere mortal? How do you think I knew it was you?"

"I . . . I don't—"

"Go ahead, Hamid," the Mahdi said, his back still toward the Ayatollah. "Take a pistol from one of your three bodyguards and shoot me in the back."

Hosseini was aghast. "Never, my Lord, I would never—"

"It's all right; go ahead," the Mahdi pressed. "Then you'll see if I'm a mortal or truly from above."

Hosseini didn't know what to say. He certainly couldn't bring himself to even contemplate testing the Mahdi's ability to withstand a gunshot from point-blank range.

"Are you a coward, Hamid?" the Mahdi asked.

"No, my Lord. . . . I—I'm your servant," he replied and dropped to his knees in worship.

"You are a coward," the Mahdi said, his voice dripping with disgust. "Your last truly courageous act was shooting your wife when she defied you for sending your sons off to be martyrs in the Great War with Iraq. Everything else has been easy for you. It has all been given to you, by Allah, to be sure, but it has made you a weak, sniveling little man. But that is why I have come, Hamid: to give the Muslim people what they want—true Islamic leadership—and to give the world what they need—a Caliphate governed from above, not from below."

Hosseini continued to bow toward Mecca, his forehead pressed to the ground, not sure what to say or do at the moment.

"You have come to bring me dark news," the Mahdi said after a brief pause. "In the last few hours, the battle has intensified dramatically. I feel it, and that is why I am on my knees in prayer. You should give yourself to prayer as well, Hamid, lest temptation overtake you and you succumb to the forces of evil."

"Yes, my Lord," Hosseini replied. "I am ready to commit myself to a night of prayer—indeed, to a new Ramadan of prayer and fasting, beginning this very night, if this will please you. But first I must tell you the disturbing news."

The Mahdi said nothing. Instead, he rose from his knees and wrapped his black robe around him tightly.

"What is your news?" he asked.

Hosseini didn't dare look up. But he did allow this one fleeting thought to cross the transom of his mind. If the Mahdi was omniscient, wouldn't he already know the news? *Maybe he* couldn't *read minds,* Hosseini thought, unsure if that was more reassuring or less so.

"Your Excellency, please know how it pains my heart to bring you this news, but I'm afraid it falls upon me to convey to you that your dear friend and trusted advisor, Javad Nouri, has been captured by forces of the enemy," Hosseini said, forehead still pressed to the ground. "Details are sketchy. Commander Asgari does not yet know who is responsible, but I am concerned that whether it's the Israelis or the Americans, if they truly have Javad, then they may now know—or soon know—this very location. I believe you are in grave danger, my Lord. So yes, it is my recommendation that you allow us to move you off this roof and get you to the new operations center, the one in the basement of the Imam Khomeini Mosque downtown."

"No," said the Mahdi. "I'm not going to the mosque. I am heading to Kabul to meet Iskander Farooq, and I leave in ten minutes."

David and his team were startled by the knock at the motel door. Abruptly halting the interrogation, David put the gag back in Nouri's mouth and told the man in no uncertain terms not to make a sound. "I'm not finished with you yet," he whispered as he readied the Sig Sauer and watched Torres cautiously move to the door, check the peephole, and then give the all-clear.

David checked his watch. It was 5:44 p.m. He was stunned that Mays and Crenshaw were back so soon—unless, of course, there was a problem. Leaving Fox in charge of the prisoner, David uncocked the pistol, reengaged the safety, and tucked the weapon in the back of his trousers, hidden under his shirt. Then he and Torres slipped out the door to huddle with their men.

"That was fast," David said, looking at a black 2005 Mercedes ML350 SUV and a silver 2009 Hyundai Entourage. "Any trouble?"

"Piece of cake, boss," said Mays.

"And you're positive you weren't followed?" Torres asked.

"We're good," said Crenshaw. "How's it going here?"

"Not good," David admitted. "He's confirmed the Mahdi has two warheads, and he's saying both are going to target Israel, not the U.S., but honestly he might just be saying what he thinks we want to hear."

"So what's the plan?" Mays asked.

"We can't stay here," Torres said. "Not for long. We need to keep moving. And first, boss, you need to decide whether you can break him.

If so, we can go a little longer. No more than an hour. If not, I say we send Matty here back to the safe house with Javad, ship Javad out of the country, and then have Matt hook up with us again ASAP. So, can you break him?"

"I honestly don't know," David said. "There's nothing I'd like more than to extract actionable intelligence out of this guy. We've already risked so much to get him; it can't be for nothing. But the fact is, Javad is too devout to be conned or bluffed into giving us anything real, anything valuable."

The room, obviously, wasn't really a CIA safe house. They didn't really have with them the computers and files here to make it look like one. That had all been a bluff, and while it had rattled Nouri, it hadn't broken him. The photos of Nouri in Dubai were real, the result of a brilliant sting operation Zalinsky had put together without even hinting about it to David or Torres. Indeed, until David had woken up in Karaj that morning and seen some of the photos in e-mails Zalinsky had sent, he hadn't even known about the op. But little good it did them here in Tehran. The notion of the Mahdi seeing the pictures and the video had scared Nouri—seriously scared the man in this case—but it hadn't broken him either.

That said, there was the safe house in Karaj. It was the real deal, and it had everything they needed—the computers, the files, the audio, the maps, the passcodes, the weapons. Maybe all they needed was for Mays to take Nouri there for a few hours and get Nouri's fingerprints all over everything. David smiled at the genius of it. If he really wanted to spread panic inside the Mahdi's operation, that was how to do it. First he had to persuade Zalinsky to let him tip off the local police about Safe House Six. Once the place was raided and the Iranians figured out what it was, the panic virus would spread up the chain of command with breakneck speed. As soon as the Mahdi found out that Reza Tabrizi was a CIA spy and came to believe that Javad Nouri was a CIA mole and that the satphones were a CIA operation from the beginning, the phones would become toxic. No one would be allowed to use them, virtually shutting down the Mahdi's ability to communicate with his high command in these critical days of the war. It was high risk, but what else did they have?

David turned to Crenshaw. "Any luck with Javad's phone?" he asked.

"I looked it over, but there's not much there, at least that I could see. I uploaded everything to Langley to have them cross-check it against their computers and see if anything popped, but I haven't heard back yet."

"Where is it now?"

"In the glove compartment."

"Which one?"

"The Hyundai."

"Well, it was worth a shot," David said.

Crenshaw nodded.

"So what's the plan?" Torres pressed. "We still have one more shot to make Javad talk, right?"

"You want me to really take his kneecap off?"

"That definitely got him thinking, boss," Torres noted. "I really thought he was going to give us everything. But when you shifted to talking about the Mahdi, I think he decided you were bluffing. That's when he got all self-righteous and defiant."

"Most people don't talk when they're missing half their leg," David reminded him. "Most people can't talk at that point."

"Javad Nouri isn't most people."

"You really think he'll talk if I do it?" David asked, skeptical of the notion but respectful of Torres's years in the field.

"I do."

"If I weren't here, would you do it?"

"If you weren't here, I'd have done it already," said Torres. "Look—this is it. We've got two nukes in the field. We don't know where they are. We've got the one person we're likely to bag who probably knows. And if he doesn't know where the nukes are, he sure as I'm standing here knows where the Mahdi is. Make him talk. Do it now. And then get Langley to use a Predator to blow the Twelfth Imam and his cronies to kingdom come. That's the deal, boss. You want to stop a nuclear war? You do it right here, right now. Simple as that."

Torres made a compelling case, David had to admit. He didn't believe in torture per se. The information extracted from a torture victim wasn't always reliable. Often the victim told you whatever he thought you wanted to hear. But this was clearly a moment that called for extreme measures. They were on the brink of nuclear war, and they did, after all, have a presidential directive to use all means necessary to hunt down these two warheads and destroy them.

That said, the risk was enormous. Was there another way to break Nouri? Any other way? He probably didn't actually know the current location of the warheads, David decided. Even if he had known twenty-four hours ago, or twelve or six or even two hours ago, the warheads had to have been moved by now. Especially now that the Iranian high command knew that Nouri had been captured.

But Torres was also probably right that Nouri knew where the Mahdi was, and if that was the case, the Mahdi and his entire team would soon be packing up and moving somewhere else. Indeed, they could already be on the move. But if they weren't, this was the CIA's best chance to take out the Mahdi and destroy the Caliphate once and for all. To hold Nouri and not to inflict any bodily harm against him certainly seemed the humane thing to do, and it meant they would be able to interrogate him over days and weeks and extract precious information about the Mahdi, about the Ayatollah, about the president, and about other high-ranking officials that was perhaps unknowable any other way. But ultimately that wasn't the mission, was it? The mission was finding and destroying the warheads or finding and destroying the man who controlled them. The humane thing, therefore, meant using all means necessary to protect millions of innocent souls from nuclear genocide.

"All right, you sold me," David said. "You guys go back inside. I'll be right in."

29

Dr. Birjandi, Ali, and Ibrahim were preparing to take a break from their intensive studies of the prophecies about the future of Iran when the phone rang. Eager to talk to David again, Birjandi didn't hesitate to take the call this time. But he was stunned by the voice he heard on the other end. It was not David Shirazi.

"Dr. Birjandi, please hold for the Grand Ayatollah."

Birjandi instinctively rose to his feet as he simultaneously snapped his fingers and signaled the men to remain quiet. There was a short pause, and then Hamid Hosseini picked up.

"Alireza," he said, "is that you?"

"Why yes, it is."

"What a joy to hear your voice, my friend."

"Uh, yes, well, thank you—that is very kind," Birjandi stammered, trying to regain his composure.

"I'm calling first and foremost to see if you are safe and well."

"I cannot complain," said the old man.

"You have not been affected by the Zionists' attacks?"

"Well, as you know, I live quite a ways from the city center and not close to anything anyone would want to bomb."

"So you're okay?"

"I am saddened events have come to this, but physically, yes, by the grace of God I am fine."

"Good, good," Hosseini said. "I am glad to hear this. For I have a request for you. It comes from the top."

"How can I be of service, Supreme Leader?" Birjandi asked, putting his hands together as if to pray and hoping Ibrahim and Ali would see the anxiety on his face and commit themselves to intercessory prayer.

"Please, Alireza, how many times must I insist that you call me Hamid?" Hosseini asked.

"At least once more," Birjandi replied, not wanting to be—or appear to be—too chummy with a man who was plotting to annihilate God's chosen people.

"Very well, I insist again," Hosseini chuckled. "Now listen, are you at home?"

"Yes, of course. Why?"

"Very good. I am sending a helicopter to fetch you."

Birjandi tensed. "A helicopter? Whatever for?"

Birjandi knew precisely what it was for, but that was precisely the problem. The Mahdi was requesting his presence, yet it was an encounter Birjandi wanted to avoid at all costs.

"The Mahdi wants you at an emergency meeting," Hosseini explained. "I cannot say where, of course. But needless to say, it is of the utmost importance."

"Who else will be there?" Birjandi asked, trying to stall for time and think of a way out.

"I'm sorry, old friend. I am not at liberty to say. But don't worry about the details. They have all been arranged. Everything will be taken care of. Just pack a bag with some clothes and personal effects and be ready in ten minutes."

"A bag?"

"Just in case."

"In case what?"

"You may be away for a few days."

"Why?"

"All will be revealed in due time, Alireza."

"No, no," Birjandi protested, his mind racing to find a plausible excuse. "This is a mistake. I am a foolish old man, old and very tired. You are in the midst of a very serious war. There's nothing I could say or do to help. I should not be wasting the time of any of our nation's leaders—not at a time such as this. Let me just stay home and pray. I am about to begin a forty-day fast. For this I need to be alone and quiet and undisturbed. Believe me, Supreme Leader, this is my best service to the country."

"Ever the humble man of God, Alireza," Hosseini said. "This is why the president and I consider you a national treasure. And this is why the Promised One has asked for you. But relax, my friend. You have been given a great honor. You are about to be ushered into the presence of the messiah for whom we have long been waiting, the messiah for whose coming you taught us so carefully to prepare. You are about to meet your savior and be honored by the same. And while I'm not really supposed to say anything more, let me encourage you: you will want to hear what Imam al-Mahdi has to say, especially when you learn how close we are to wiping the Zionist entity off the map forever. Now get yourself ready. You have five minutes."

"Only five?" Birjandi asked. "But Tehran is more than—"

But the line was already dead.

LANGLEY, VIRGINIA

"Are you freaking crazy?" Zalinsky yelled as a hush settled over everyone around him. *"Absolutely not! It's out of the question!"*

"Jack, listen to me; Torres is right," David pushed back.

"No, Torres is *not* right," Zalinsky fumed.

"Yes, he is," David argued. "If we don't force Javad to talk now— right now—anything he knows, any value he could give us, is going to evaporate. The warheads are going to be moved, if they haven't been already. The Mahdi is going to move too, as will all the senior team. Whatever he knows, we need to get it out of him now."

"Enough," Zalinsky shouted, not caring that every eye in the Global Ops Center—including Murray's—was on him and his tirade against his top NOC in Iran. "Enough. Now shut up and listen to me. That's right; shut your mouth and just listen to me, Zephyr. I'm running this op, not you. I want this information as bad as you, maybe more so. But you need to take a deep breath and start listening to me. I recruited

you into this Agency. You didn't even want to work for the CIA. It was my idea to send you into Iran. You wanted to stay in Pakistan. You've done some great work, but now you're tired, you're stressed, and you're about to destroy your one chance to get real intel out of Nouri and compromise our safe house in Karaj at the same time. So knock it off and start listening to me."

TEHRAN, IRAN

David was fuming, pacing the parking lot of the motel and doing everything in his power not to hang up this phone and smash it into the pavement.

"Are you listening?" Zalinsky asked.

David took a deep breath, forced himself against all his instincts not to retaliate, and said, "Yes. What is it?"

"Javad's phone," said Zalinsky.

"What about it?"

"Do you have it?"

"It's in the Hyundai."

"Get it."

David held his tongue and walked over to the van, opened the passenger door, and took Javad's satphone out of the glove compartment and powered it up.

"Okay, I've got it."

"Is it on?"

"Yes."

"Go to the contact list."

David found the contact list and opened it.

"Okay, I'm there."

"Good. Now look up Omid Jazini."

"Who's that?" David asked.

"Just look him up."

So David did. He found the man's home address and work phone number, along with his mobile number.

"Got it," he said after a moment.

"Good," said Zalinsky. "That's your new target."

"What are you talking about?"

"Omid Jazini is the twenty-eight-year-old son of Mohsen Jazini."

"General Mohsen Jazini?"

"The very same."

"The commander of the Revolutionary Guard Corps?"

"Well, he was, until today."

"And now?"

"He's the Caliphate's new defense minister and commander in chief."

"What about Faridzadeh?" David asked.

"He's out," said Zalinsky. "And don't ask—we don't know why. But we do know that General Jazini wrote a strategy memo that caught the Mahdi's eye. He called the general this morning, gave him the promotion, and told him to start putting the 'first section' into motion immediately."

"What's in the first section?" David asked.

"I don't know, but Omid might," Zalinsky said. "Omid is part of his father's security detail. But he was injured on the first day of the bombing campaign, nearly crushed under a collapsing wall. Was in the hospital for two days. Got sent home this morning. And guess what?"

"What?"

"He lives in an apartment complex nine blocks from the motel you're at right now. I want you guys to move—fast. Grab him and interrogate him and find out where his father is and what that memo says."

"What makes you think he'll talk any more than Javad?" David asked.

"Because I don't think Omid is a zealot," Zalinsky said. "A Muslim? Yes. A Shia? Yes. A Persian nationalist like his father? Yes. But a Twelver? No."

"How can you be so sure?"

"I'm not," Zalinsky admitted. "It's a hunch. Call it a gut instinct. But Omid's mother, Shirin, isn't a Muslim. She's Zoroastrian. Eva actually met her at an embassy party in Berlin a few years ago when General Jazini was assigned as the defense attaché to Germany. In fact, she tracked her for several months, and there was a point at which Eva thought she might actually be able to recruit Shirin, but suddenly they moved back to Tehran when Mohsen was promoted to commander of the IRGC. But Eva says Shirin wasn't religious and certainly not an ideologue. She never went to a mosque, even though her husband did. She didn't like to talk about religion. She preferred shopping and socializing."

"So how do we know Omid isn't more like his father?"

"We don't," said Zalinsky. "But that's the plan. And it's an order."

"What am I supposed to do with Javad Nouri?"

"Have Mays drop him at the safe house and secure him. We'll have someone pick him up, probably even before Mays rejoins the rest of you at Omid's apartment. Now get moving."

President Ahmed Darazi stood at the conference room door for a moment, making certain he was in full control of his composure. He reminded himself that at least the Mahdi had agreed to come down into the blastproof underground bunker. Then he knocked twice.

"Come," said the Mahdi.

Darazi opened the door, entered quickly, closed it behind him, and bowed low.

"Yes?" the Mahdi asked, an edge of exasperation in his voice.

"My Lord, I'm not sure why, but Daryush Rashidi, the head of Iran Telecom, is upstairs in the lobby and says he is here to see you," Darazi began. "He says you summoned him and that everything you asked for is ready. The security team told him there must be a mistake, that we would certainly have known if you requested any nonmilitary or nonpolitical personnel to come to the command center to meet with you. But he absolutely insisted, and eventually they requested that I intervene because Daryush and I have known each other such a long time. Anyway, I went up to see him, and—"

"Yes, yes, I know all this," the Mahdi said. "I did summon him here, and he is right on time. Did he give you a password?"

"Well, uh, he—"

"Did he or did he not give you a password?" the Mahdi repeated.

"He did have something he wanted me to say to you, but I—"

"Then don't stand there blabbering like a fool, Ahmed. Say it."

"Yes, Your Excellency, of course. He . . . uh . . . he told me to say, 'The fire has begun.'"

At that the Twelfth Imam arose instantly. "Excellent. Did he bring a trunk?"

"Uh, well, yes—several, actually."

"Good. Bring him—and them—down here immediately," said the Mahdi. "We don't have a moment to spare."

"But I don't understand," Darazi said. "What is this all—?"

"Just do what I have commanded you, Ahmed," the Mahdi bellowed, his countenance darkening. "And do it well and quickly."

"Yes, my Lord," Darazi sputtered, bowing again. "As you wish."

ISLAMABAD, PAKISTAN

"I have come to reestablish the Caliphate."

The haunting words of Muhammad Ibn Hasan Ibn Ali spoken during a phone call just a few days before still echoed in Iskander Farooq's ears as he stood beside the landing pad in the immense dust storm created by the descending military chopper that had come to whisk him away on a last-minute, unplanned, ill-timed trip to certain disaster.

"I have come to bring peace and justice and to rule the earth with a rod of iron," the Mahdi had said that day. "This is why Allah sent me. He will reward those who submit. He will punish those who resist. But make no mistake, Iskander; in the end, every knee shall bow, and every tongue shall confess that I am the Lord of the Age."

It was hard to believe, but it had only been a week since the so-called Promised One had threatened Farooq, his family, and his government, demanding that he acquiesce. Farooq remembered waking up that Sunday, the sixth of March, dreaming up many interesting projects to discuss with his advisors. Then, in an instant, everything had changed.

Every fiber of his being told him to resist. But more than a quarter of a million Pakistanis were demonstrating outside the gates of the palace. *"Give praise to Imam al-Mahdi!"* they had shouted again and again. *"Give praise to Imam al-Mahdi!"* He had feared they would overrun the place. And there was the Mahdi, pushing, pushing.

"What say you?" the Mahdi had asked. "You owe me an answer."

What was he supposed to have done? He was horrified that Tehran had suddenly become the seat of a new Caliphate. Neither he nor his father nor his father's father had ever trusted the Iranians. The Persian Empire had ruled his ancestors, stretching in its day from India in the east to Sudan and Ethiopia in the west. Now the Persians wanted to subjugate them all over again.

Everyone he knew, it seemed—everyone but him—had been bewitched. They all believed this Mahdi was the messiah, the savior of the world.

The chopper landed, and several members of the Pakistani Air Force helped the president inside and into his seat. As Farooq put on his seat belt and prepared to take off for the short hop to New Islamabad International Airport in Fateh Jang, west of the palace, he stared out the window, unable to believe this was really happening. The world had gone mad. The crowds had grown daily. Now his palace guard estimated upwards of half a million Pakistanis surrounded the presidential compound, clogging traffic for miles in every direction. They were still chanting, *"Blessed be Imam al-Mahdi,"* and *"Join the Caliphate now."* They were even threatening to burn the palace to the ground if he didn't move fast to form an alliance with the Mahdi. His Sunni-dominated Cabinet, meanwhile, had actually threatened to have him arrested and tried for treason if he didn't immediately join the Caliphate and hand Pakistan's launch codes over to this Shia "messiah."

Farooq had resisted, argued, and delayed as long as he could, but to no avail. Even his wife and children had begged him to make the deal and get it over with before they all met their grisly deaths. What more could he do? He was set to meet the Twelfth Imam face-to-face at half past midnight tonight.

The day of reckoning was at hand.

★ ★ ★ ★ ★

HAMADAN, IRAN

". . . so, Father, we pray for our dear friend and brother Dr. Birjandi, that you would protect him and that you would fill him with your Holy Spirit and that you would use him to say whatever you want him to say and do whatever you want him to do, no matter what the cost. We pray these things in the name of our Lord and Savior Jesus Christ, who was and is and is to come. Amen."

Dr. Birjandi, packed and dressed in the black robes and black turban he used to wear when he taught at the seminary in Qom, reluctantly lifted his head as Ali and Ibrahim finished praying with him. Even now he could hear the faint echo of a helicopter approaching in the distance. He loved these men so much. He didn't want to leave them and certainly not for an "emergency meeting" with the Twelfth Imam. But despite all his protestations that he would never go to such a meeting, the die now seemed to be cast. He had pleaded with the Lord to let this cup pass from him, but short of a miracle, in the next few minutes he would be picked up by Revolutionary Guards with orders to take him to some secure, undisclosed location for a face-to-face meeting with the personification of evil.

And yet now, strangely, after so much prayer and angst, Birjandi actually did not feel anxious. Rather, he felt a peace that surprised him. He knew the Lord had a good and perfect plan for his life, and maybe these boys were right. Maybe the Lord was about to give him the opportunity to share the gospel with Hosseini and Darazi.

"Thank you so much, boys," he told them. "I am forever grateful. But now you must go, before they get here. Please, there is not much time."

"But we want to stay with you," Ibrahim said. "We are not afraid."

"I know, and I am so grateful, my son, but you must not be connected to me. Not now, not today," Birjandi said. "Your courage is admirable, and it is from the Lord. But use it to share the gospel with your families and friends. Use it to start house churches and teach the Word throughout this nation. Use it to advance the Kingdom of Jesus, and I will see you in heaven, when all is well. Now go. Both of you. If you love me, you must leave right now."

Birjandi could hear the chopper approaching from the northeast. By God's grace, it was coming a little later than he had expected—later, at least, than Hosseini had said. The delay, whatever the reason, had given him a few minutes to put some clothes and a toothbrush and toothpaste in a small suitcase and to get the satellite phone David had given him and hide it under his robes. It had also given the three of them a few moments to pray together one last time, and for this he was grateful.

They stood, and Birjandi took his cane and walked them to the door. "Now, quickly, both of you, give me a kiss good-bye."

Ali turned and gave the old man a bear hug and then kissed him on both cheeks. Ibrahim did the same, though he held on longer, despite the fact that the chopper was less than a quarter mile away and coming in fast. They said nothing. There was nothing more to say. But Birjandi could feel the tears running down their cheeks. They knew this was the last time they would see him. He knew it as well.

30

Levi Shimon and Zvi Dayan arrived in unmarked, bulletproof cars with heavy security. They were immediately ushered into the prime minister's spacious, wood-paneled office, where Naphtali was finishing up a call with the U.N. secretary-general.

"Absolutely not," said Naphtali, pacing the room and red in the face. "That is completely inaccurate. . . . No, that's simply not true. . . . I . . . Mr. Secretary-General, I can assure you that at no time have Israeli forces purposefully attacked unarmed civilians either in Iran, Syria, Lebanon, or Gaza. . . . No, to the contrary, we are hitting legitimate military targets in self-defense. . . . How can you say that? . . . No, that's—sir, we are under attack from missiles and rockets and mortars that are being fired indiscriminately at our innocent civilian populations, and yet you have not issued a condemnation of our enemies but rather persist in portraying us as the aggressors. Well, I reject that characterization. . . . Mr. Secretary-General, again I direct your attention to the illegal testing by Iran of a nuclear warhead a few weeks ago in direct violation of a dozen U.N. Security Council resolutions, combined with the repeated illegal statements by Iranian leaders and by the Mahdi inciting the forces of their Caliphate to genocide against my people. . . . No, that is precisely the point—this is cold, hard, international law—the Convention on the Prevention and Punishment of the Crime of Genocide, which went into force on January 12, 1951, in which incitement to genocide is specifically outlawed in Article 25(3)(e) of the Rome Statute."

254 ★ DAMASCUS COUNTDOWN

The sixty-three-year-old Shimon was antsy. He took a seat when Naphtali motioned for him and Dayan to do so, but he was in no mood to sit quietly. Too much was happening and much too fast for his liking. He already hated being away from the IDF war room in Tel Aviv to come all the way to Jerusalem for a face-to-face meeting, but it couldn't be helped. The situation was as sensitive as any in his forty-five years in public life since joining the army at the age of eighteen. He needed the prime minister's ear, and he needed it right now, and it was all he could do to not stand up, walk over to the PM's phone, and hang up on the secretary-general.

"You are certainly entitled to your opinion, Mr. Secretary-General," Naphtali replied, "but you are not entitled to your own facts. We . . . No, again, that is not accurate. Look, that's just . . . Good sir, let me make this as plain as I possibly can. My country is facing annihilation from an apocalyptic, genocidal death cult. We will defend ourselves as we see fit, as we have a right to do under the U.N. charter. Need I remind you of chapter VII, article 51? Let me quote it for you, as you have obviously forgotten either its words or its meaning. 'Nothing in the present Charter shall impair the inherent right of individual or collective self-defense if an armed attack occurs against a Member of the United Nations, until the Security Council has taken measures necessary to maintain international peace and security.' . . . What do you mean we weren't attacked first? What do you call Iran's attack on my life in New York City last Sunday, an attack that killed President Ramzy of Egypt and nearly killed President Jackson and did kill several dozen others? . . . Okay, look, this isn't going anywhere. Let me simply restate my objection to where the Security Council is headed on this and ask you, humbly, to reconsider. . . . Very well. I look forward to hearing from you then. Good day, sir."

The moment the prime minister hung up the phone, Shimon could see he and Dayan were about to get an earful, but there simply wasn't time. He stood and stepped toward the PM's desk.

"Asher, you need to listen to me," he said as firmly as he could. "As much as I'd like to let you vent about that call, I need you to listen to me very carefully."

Naphtali was clearly taken aback by his defense minister's forceful manner, but as far as Shimon could tell, he didn't seem offended. Shimon wouldn't really have cared if he was. Not now.

"Of course. How can I help you, gentlemen?" Naphtali replied, a bit sarcastically.

"Zvi, tell him," Shimon said.

The Mossad director stood as well. "Mr. Prime Minister, for the last several days, my men and I were pretty confident we knew where the Twelfth Imam was," he began. "Somewhere on the Mehrabad Air Base, just outside Tehran. That's why we strongly recommended you authorize repeated air strikes and cruise missile strikes on the military portions of the facility, not the civilian airport."

"Yes, of course," said Naphtali. "I've read your reports. And I've authorized everything you've asked for."

"Yes, sir, and it's had a real impact on neutralizing the Iranian Air Force," Dayan continued. "But I can now report to you that my men and I have pinpointed the Mahdi's precise location."

"Where?"

"He's on the grounds of the air base, but not on the military side," Dayan said. "It turns out that he and his senior team are actually working from a facility on the civilian side of the airfield. We've learned that the war room for the Revolutionary Guards is located beneath a three-story administrative building connected to the main terminal at Imam Khomeini Airport."

"You're sure?" the PM asked.

"One hundred percent," said the Mossad chief.

"Don't tell me you want to hit it?"

The defense minister took that one. "Absolutely, and now, sir. We've got an armed drone keeping surveillance on the location. We've got a squadron of fighter jets racing to Tehran right now, each carrying bunker-buster bombs. They should be in range in the next thirty minutes."

"You want me to bomb Iran's civilian airport?" Naphtali asked incredulously. "Were you not listening to that call with the secretary-general? We're already being accused of war crimes. We're being accused of attacking innocent civilians. We've got radioactive clouds spreading across Iran into civilian areas because of the strikes we've already made on their nuclear facilities. We can't just hit their airport, Levi. The whole world will turn against us."

"Sir, I understand, but I'm telling you we have a once-in-a-lifetime chance to decapitate the enemy and end this war in the next thirty minutes," Shimon said. "We have to take it. History won't forgive us if we don't. And I must add that we have an unconfirmed but credible report that the Mahdi may be relocating and soon."

"To the Imam Khomeini Mosque?"

"Perhaps, but the report says he might go to Tabriz."

"Why Tabriz?"

"We don't know, sir. We're still tracking that down."

Naphtali stared at both men, but Shimon couldn't quite read him. The prime minister obviously didn't want to take more international condemnation. It could, after all, lead to U.N. sanctions on Israel for the first time in history. But Naphtali, Shimon knew, was also a patriot and a pragmatist. He might still say yes, and for this Shimon silently prayed to a God he wasn't sure really existed.

"Where's Mordecai in all this?" the PM said at last, abruptly changing the subject to the Mossad's top mole inside Iran's nuclear program—a mole who had gone dark in the last several days, much to the anxiety of everyone in Naphtali's War Cabinet. "Have we heard from him?"

"No, sir, we haven't," Dayan said.

"So we don't know if he's alive?"

"No—the last communiqué was on Thursday morning. He did say that was going to be his last report, but of course we've been hoping he would reestablish contact."

"We have no contact information for him?"

"The protocol was always for him to call us," the Mossad chief explained.

"And we still don't know where the warheads are?"

"No, sir, not yet."

★ ★ ★ ★ ★

TEHRAN, IRAN

Darazi went upstairs to the main floor and cleared Rashidi and his mysterious trunks through security. Then he strolled around the lobby for a few minutes, staring out once again at the destruction and misery all around him. He was careful to keep his emotions off his face, but internally he was seething. Hour after hour, day after day, the Twelfth Imam was belittling his existence. The Mahdi's contempt for Darazi's presence was palpable—and infuriating.

Searching his soul, Darazi tried to see what engendered such hostility. Wasn't he doing everything he possibly could to serve the Mahdi? Wasn't he risking his own life and the lives of his family to help destroy the Little Satan and eventually the Great Satan as well? He wasn't a perfect man. He conceded that right up front. But who was? What sin could he possibly have committed to make the Lord of the Age so agitated whenever they were together?

What bothered Darazi most, however, was not that the Twelfth Imam seemed to despise him so, though that did weigh heavily on his heart and mind. Far more egregious was a thought that Darazi dared not speak aloud and had resisted for days even letting himself actively consider. They were two thoughts, really, and he feared both were heresy. But he couldn't help himself. They were beginning to dominate his thinking whether he wanted them to or not.

The first was this: Why was Iran losing this war to the Jews? Hosseini and Jazini and the rest of the high command could spin it all they wanted, but that was the truth, wasn't it? They were losing. Naphtali had fired first and knocked out most of Iran's nuclear forces. They still had two warheads, to be sure, but they couldn't even fire them from Persian soil. Why not? Didn't the Mahdi carry the full weight and force of Allah himself? Wasn't he a direct descendant and messenger of the Prophet, peace be upon him? Then why was Iran's air force a smoldering wreckage? Why was Iran's mobile phone system almost completely down? Why were they cowering in an underground bunker, no better than Osama bin Laden, in his day, cowering in a cave in the

Kandahar mountains? The Jews should have been obliterated by now. The Caliphate should be triumphant. That was what the Mahdi had promised, yet thus far it was all talk, all empty promises and mounting casualties.

The second revolved around a deeply troubling conversation that he and Hosseini had had with Dr. Alireza Birjandi over lunch on Wednesday, less than twenty-four hours before the start of the war. Birjandi had not seemed himself, and when they had pressed him to talk about what was on his mind, he was reluctant, at best. But as Darazi thought back on Birjandi's words, he was increasingly concerned his old friend was onto something he and Hosseini were missing.

"I just find myself wondering, where is Jesus, peace be upon him?" Birjandi had said.

Darazi remembered there was dead silence. It wasn't a name that often got mentioned in the presence of the Grand Ayatollah and the president of the Islamic Republic of Iran. Yet the old man had a point. Darazi himself had given sermons from the ancient Islamic prophecies stating that Jesus would appear and serve as the Mahdi's lieutenant. So had Hosseini and Birjandi. Yet Jesus had not come, as far as any of them knew.

As though he were now hovering over the conversation, Darazi could see himself shifting uncomfortably in his seat and asking, "What exactly are you implying, Ali?"

"I am not implying anything," Birjandi had replied calmly. "I am simply asking where I went wrong. You preached that one of the signs preceding the Mahdi's return would be the coming of Jesus to require all infidels to convert to Islam or die by the sword. You did that because I taught you that. I taught you that because of a lifetime of studying the ancient texts and so many commentaries on the same. Yet Jesus is nowhere to be found."

Nor was that all. Birjandi had gone on to list five distinct signs that his lifetime of research suggested should precede the arrival or the appearance of the Hidden Imam. The first was the rise of a fighter from Yemen called the Yamani, who would attack the enemies of Islam. Darazi thought it was possible this had actually happened; certainly there had been any number of violent attacks against Christians in Yemen in recent years. But the second sign, the rise of an anti-Mahdi militant leader named Osman Ben Anbase, also known as Sofiani, had not occurred.

The third sign, voices from the sky gathering the faithful around the Mahdi, hadn't happened either. Yes, there were reports of some kind of angelic voice speaking in Beirut after the failed attack on the Mahdi the week before, but that hardly qualified as a host of angels.

The fourth sign was the destruction of Sofiani's army. But since Sofiani had never appeared, much less raised an army, the fulfillment of this sign didn't even seem possible. Then there was the fifth sign, the death of a holy man named Muhammad bin Hassan, which Darazi didn't think had happened either.

"I feel a great sense of responsibility," Birjandi had said. "I have been studying the Last Things most of my adult life. I have been preaching and teaching these things for as long as you have been gracious enough to give me the freedom to do so. But something isn't adding up. Something's wrong. And I keep asking: what?"

Birjandi was right, Darazi thought. Something was wrong. If the prophecies were all from Allah, why weren't they being fulfilled in their totality? If the Mahdi had truly come, why were there so many discrepancies between the ancient writings and current events? If the Twelfth Imam had truly come, how could he—and the entire Muslim world that was following him—be losing to the Jews?

And then another heretical thought flitted at the edge of Darazi's mind, if only for a moment before he banished it with all the vigor he could muster: what if the Mahdi had not really come and they were actually being deceived?

31

David glanced at his watch. It was precisely 6:45 p.m. The round trip to the safe house in Karaj to drop off Javad Nouri—sedated but with both kneecaps intact—had taken Matt Mays just over an hour, and he was back by the time Zalinsky called to report that Predator surveillance indicated Omid Jazini was home and that they were a go for the hastily conceived operation.

Now Mays circled the block once so everyone could get the lay of the land; then—not seeing any immediate threats—he drove into the parking lot at the rear of the building and stopped in front of the loading dock. David put a fresh mag into his silencer-equipped pistol, double-checked his MP5 and the rest of his equipment, then pulled on his ski mask and led his team into the back of the apartment complex.

Once inside, Fox found the mechanical room and disabled the building's alarm system and the video surveillance system. At the same time, Crenshaw found the telephone switch box and cut the main line, rendering inoperative all landline calls out of the building while Zalinsky used the Predator drone above them to jam the ability to make cell phone calls in the building, at least for the next few minutes. Fox then followed David up the north stairwell, while Crenshaw followed Torres up the south stairwell, headed for the twelfth floor.

Less than a minute after the team entered the building, Mays watched a police cruiser drive up the street, slow down for a moment—Mays wasn't exactly sure why—and then continue on its way. Not liking the feel of that, Mays decided he wasn't comfortable idling in the parking lot. Instead, he took the van down a tree-lined side street nearby, turned around, and then found a spot on the side of the road, not far from the intersection. This actually gave him a better view of who was coming in and out of the front of Omid's building as well as of any car that might pull into the rear parking lot.

"Bravo One, are you in position?" Mays heard David ask over the radio.

"Negative, Alpha One," Torres replied. "We're passing the ninth floor. Need another minute."

"Roger that," said David. "We're in position. Let us know when you're ready."

As Mays monitored the radio traffic, he saw a medium-size white truck pull up to the front of the apartment building and park in a fire lane. As two men got out, Mays's instincts went on alert. Both men were about six feet tall, muscular, dressed in suits, and near Omid's age. Mays grabbed a digital camera off the seat next to him, pointed it at the men, zoomed in, and snapped several pictures, but not in time. He had gotten their profiles and backs, not their faces, but he instantly transmitted the images to the Predator, which relayed them to a satellite, which sent the digital pictures to Langley for analysis. Ten seconds later, Zalinsky was on the radio.

"Home Plate to Alpha One and team—you've got company on the way, and they may be trouble," Zalinsky told them. "Bravo Three just snapped a photo of two men entering the building. Thermal imaging shows they're entering the lobby elevator."

"Roger that, Home Plate," said David, crouched in the stairwell just outside the exit door to the twelfth floor and slipping the fiber-optic camera snake under the door. "Who are they?"

"Not sure," Zalinsky said. "We're running the images through facial-recognition software, but they're not clear photos. They're not head-on shots, and we're not getting anything."

"They look like Revolutionary Guards to me," said Mays. "Probably colleagues of the target."

"Got it; thanks," David replied. "Bravo One, you ready to move?"

"Ready to move on your command, Alpha One," Torres replied.

"Good—now hold your position and let's see what these two do."

David didn't want trouble. He wanted to isolate Omid and get him talking. This was a complication he did not need. If these two men really were colleagues of Omid, that meant they were armed and dangerous. David knew they couldn't afford a repeat of the firefight at the hospital. He didn't want to risk a bloodbath in the hallway. This op had to be fast and quiet and could not get the whole building involved or the entire Tehran police force responding. If these guys were really going to Omid Jazini's room, David figured the best thing to do was let them get inside and then wait till they left. Then again, what if they were just friends of Omid's? What if they were coming to hang out for the evening, to cook dinner and watch a movie? It could be hours before they moved on, and David didn't have hours to spare.

Movement caught David's eye on the small monitor Fox was holding. He glanced at it. The elevator doors were opening. The two men got off the elevator and, sure enough, approached Omid's room. David's instinct was to move quickly and take these two out, but the fear of accidentally killing two potentially unarmed civilians made him hesitate.

"Alpha One, we need to move now, before they get inside," Torres said over the radio.

"No, not yet," David replied. "We don't know if they're armed, and I don't want any prisoners beyond Omid."

"Bravo One is right," Zalinsky chimed in. "You need to move now."

"Negative. Everyone hold your positions," David insisted, furious that Torres and Zalinsky would question his judgment in the middle of an operation when they should be maintaining radio silence.

But just then, David watched in horror as both men drew silencer-equipped pistols from underneath their jackets, kicked in Omid's door, and went in, guns blazing. For a moment, David was too stunned to speak. So were Zalinsky and Torres, who gasped but didn't say a word. But then David's anger began to burn.

"Let's move—now!" he ordered.

Bolting into the hallway ahead of his team, he sprinted toward Omid's door with Fox close on his heels. He pivoted into the room, holding his pistol out front, and found both men staring down at the bloody corpse of Omid Jazini.

"Put 'em down," he shouted in Farsi. *"Both of you—guns down—now!"*

Clearly startled, one of the men began to turn, his pistol in hand. David shot him twice in the chest.

"Don't do it!" David shouted again. *"Don't turn around. Don't make any fast moves. Don't even think about it. Just put the gun down now or you die like your friend."*

The second man slowly set the gun down and put his hands in the air just as Torres and Crenshaw reached the room.

"We need to get inside," Torres said in English. "Before someone sees us out here."

David nodded for his team to enter and close the door, which they did, but he kept his pistol aimed at the second man's back and told him to lie facedown on the floor. The man slowly, carefully, cautiously complied, but then he stunned them all.

"You speak English?" the man asked in English, with an accent that wasn't Persian. David couldn't quite place it. "You're not Iranian?"

"Shut up and stay still!" David replied in Farsi, ordering Torres to cuff and search the man.

Torres did but found no wallet, no ID, no keys, nor any other personal possessions on the man.

"Who are you guys?" the man asked, again in English, pushing his luck.

Maybe it was the circumstances. Maybe it was all the adrenaline coursing through his system. David wasn't sure. But he knew that accent, and he was kicking himself for not thinking clearly enough to place it. He glanced at Torres, who shrugged. He glanced at Crenshaw, who was guarding the door, and Fox, who was guarding the window. They didn't know either.

"Are they dead?" David asked Torres in Farsi.

Torres felt the pulses of the two bodies on the floor. "Omid is," he said, but then, to everyone's surprise, he said the other one wasn't.

"Search and cuff them both," David ordered.

Torres complied, dealing with the conscious gunman first and discovering he was wearing a bulletproof vest.

"Professionals?" said David.

Torres nodded.

"Turn them both over," David now directed. "I want to see their faces."

Alive, sure, but the first one was in severe pain.

"I think you broke my ribs," the man groaned.

"You're lucky I didn't double-tap you to the head," David replied. "Actually, I still might. Now who are you two and why are you here?"

"We could ask the same of you," the second man said in English.

"You could, but we're holding the guns, so you'll be the ones answering the questions just now," said David.

"Well, we've got nothing to say," the first man groaned.

David was about to respond when Zalinsky came over the radio and told him to stop talking, take a snapshot of both men on his satphone, and upload the photo to Langley. David did, and as he waited for the results, he told Fox to search Omid's room for phones, computers, and files of any kind.

David heard Zalinsky curse. "What is it?" he asked.

"You're not going to believe this."

"Try me."

"They're Israelis," Zalinsky replied. "They're Mossad."

Four fire trucks—two pumpers, a hook and ladder, and a hazmat response unit—pulled off the tarmac and drove up to the administrative building, lights flashing and sirens blaring. Nearly twenty firefighters, fully suited up and ready to do battle, jumped out of the trucks and rushed inside. There they were met by Revolutionary Guards who immediately welcomed them, despite no evidence of smoke or flames or any other emergency. The fire chief checked the alarm control panel in the lobby but found none of the warning lights lit up. To the contrary, all the evidence suggested systems were normal and under control. Nevertheless, with the permission of the Mahdi's head of security, the chief directed his men to rush up to the second and third floors to make sure everything was okay.

On the third floor, six of the firemen went into a large, windowless supply room on the west side of the building. Moments later, six different men came out of that supply room.

Following the plan laid out in General Mohsen Jazini's memo, an elaborate ruse was being set into motion. Daryush Rashidi was the first to exit the room, dressed in a fire helmet, Nomex fire coat, pants, gloves, and rubber boots, an air tank on his back and an air mask over his face. Rashidi was followed by the Mahdi and four members of the Mahdi's security detail, all similarly dressed and all but the Mahdi helping to carry several trunks that looked like they held firefighting equipment. They met the rest of the emergency crews in the lobby, and when the chief gave the all-clear signal, they all headed back to the trucks. Rashidi led the way for the other five, heading directly for the hazmat truck, a large, heavy-duty vehicle built by the Scania company in Sweden and painted a bright, almost-fluorescent yellow. He opened the back doors, let the five members of the team climb in, then shut the doors again and climbed into the front passenger seat and told the driver—another undercover IRGC commando—to follow the other fire trucks departing the airport grounds.

JERUSALEM, ISRAEL

Mossad chief Zvi Dayan scanned the incoming note on his secure PDA as Defense Minister Shimon informed Naphtali that the strike package was just a few minutes away from the Imam Khomeini International Airport in Tehran and pressed him for the authorization to launch their missiles.

"Excuse me, Mr. Prime Minister—we may have a change in plans," Dayan said.

"What do you mean?" Naphtali asked.

"You may not have to bomb the airport after all," Dayan said.

"Why not?"

"Something's happening at the facility in question," said the Mossad chief, now turning to an aide and ordering him to see if they could get the live images from the drone over the airport uploaded to the prime minister's communications center.

"What is it?" Naphtali asked.

"We have reports that a group of fire trucks have arrived at the scene and almost two dozen firefighters have rushed inside," Dayan reported.

"Into the facility where you think the Mahdi is?" Naphtali clarified.

"Where we know he is, sir," Dayan noted. "It houses the central war room for the entire Revolutionary Guard system, and we have growing evidence the whole war is being run out of that building. What's strange is that all these fire trucks have arrived when there's no evidence of a fire. I mean, there are fires raging on the other side of the airfield—the military side—but as we've said, the civilian side has been untouched. And yet here are all these trucks and firefighters right at the moment we're about to bomb the place to kingdom come."

"I haven't given my authorization yet," Naphtali reminded the Mossad chief.

"Yes, of course, sir, I realize that. I'm just saying . . ."

"You think the Iranians know we're coming right now."

"No, not necessarily—not right this minute—but as I said before, we believe the IRGC is going to move the Mahdi, and this might be how they're doing it."

One of the PM's aides knocked, entered the PM's office, and explained the video feed was now ready in the communications center. The three men quickly moved down the hall and found aerial images from the Israeli drone of the firefighters exiting the administrative building and getting back into their trucks.

"You think the Mahdi is in one of these groups?" Shimon asked.

"I do," Dayan said.

"Which one?"

"The hazmat team."

"Why?"

"Look at how they're walking. They're not walking like firemen. They've set up a perimeter around this one here—the one in the center. And look, they're not taking their equipment off while coming out of the building. They're getting into the back of the hazmat truck with their masks and air tanks on. That's not normal."

"You're saying that's the Mahdi?" said Naphtali, pointing to the screen.

"Yes, sir," Dayan said. "If it were the Supreme Leader, the Ayatollah, we would have seen him walking more slowly. Hosseini is seventysomething."

Naphtali watched the trucks head away from the airport complex, depart the grounds of the airfield, and pull onto Me'raj Boulevard, heading northeast toward Azadi Square. But all eyes were on the bright-yellow hazmat response vehicle, on whose roof was painted *Unit 19* in large black letters.

"Where's the fire station?" the PM asked.

"It's right by the Azadi subway station," Dayan said.

"And what are you recommending?"

"A missile strike on the hazmat vehicle, sir."

"Now?"

"Yes, sir."

"Where, in Azadi Square?"

"Absolutely, sir—but to minimize collateral damage I would definitely recommend a strike before the truck gets back to the firehouse."

Naphtali was running out of time. The hook and ladder and the two pumpers were already in the traffic circle that went around Azadi Square, just minutes away from the firehouse. The hazmat truck, however, was just entering the traffic circle.

"This is it, sir," Dayan said. "It's now or never. If the Mahdi gets to the fire station and slips away in another vehicle or via some other escape route we don't know about, we may never get another chance."

Naphtali knew Dayan was right in principle, but was he right in fact? Was the Twelfth Imam really in that yellow truck? If he was, then it would be a crime against the Jewish people, he calculated, not to take the shot and try to decapitate the Caliphate right here and now. But if

Dayan was wrong and Israel killed six innocent, unarmed firemen in downtown Tehran, the international diplomatic community—which was already dead set against Israel and this war—would go ballistic. The U.N. Security Council condemnation of Israel would pass for certain. Not even the U.S. would veto it, certainly not under the leadership of President Jackson. The ramifications of that were serious indeed. Israel could be subject to economic sanctions, trade embargoes, and International Criminal Court proceedings, and those were just for starters.

"Please, Asher, for heaven's sake, we have to strike now," Shimon insisted.

32

"You're Israeli?" David asked, incredulous but realizing that was the accent he'd been detecting—the sound of a native Hebrew speaker talking in English. He just couldn't believe he was hearing it in the heart of Iran.

"And you, are you the one they call Zephyr?"

Now David's eyes widened. How could they know that? No one outside the top echelons of the U.S. government knew he existed, much less his code name.

David hoped the ski mask was covering the stunned expression on his face, on all his team's faces. "We're asking the questions. Who are you? Are you two Mossad?"

The man said nothing, and David wasn't sure if he was following security protocols at that moment or simply too surprised to answer his question.

"I'll take that as a yes," David said. "Are you the guys who took out Mohammed Saddaji?"

"We don't know what you're talking about," said one.

"Sure you do," David replied. "You—or your colleague—put a car bomb in his Mercedes. It was a nice piece of work."

The two men said nothing.

"Look, I don't have time to play games," David said. "You've got three seconds to let me know who you are, or we'll end this now." He chambered a round and aimed his pistol. "One . . ."

Nothing but silence.

"Two . . ."

Still more silence, so David put the muzzle directly on the second man's forehead, right between his eyes.

"Three."

"You can call me Tolik," one said.

"Why are you here?" David asked.

"Same as you," said Tolik. "To shut down this war."

"But why here, why the apartment of Omid Jazini?" David pressed. "You didn't come here to find him, to interrogate him, to shake him down and squeeze him for information. You came here to kill him."

"Omid is part of his father's security detail," said Tolik. "And his father was just promoted to commander in chief of the Caliphate's military."

"We know."

"So our orders were to assassinate him."

"Why?"

"To send a message to his father."

"What message?"

"That we're onto him," Tolik said. "That we're closing in. That they've got moles in their ranks who are talking to the outside world and that they can't ever know whom to trust. We did our job. And believe me, word will spread fast through the top ranks of the Mahdi's inner circle. Key men are being picked off left and right. We're guessing you're the ones who kidnapped Javad Nouri today."

David didn't respond.

"I'll take that as a yes."

Suddenly Fox called from the master bedroom. "Boss, there's something here you need to see."

Rashidi hated having the Mahdi out in the open. There were too many risks, too many threats. What if there was a sniper out there? What if there was a team of assassins? This wasn't a bulletproof truck. The agents in the back had machine guns, but they didn't have RPGs or heavy firepower. And to minimize the risk of a leak, almost no one—including most of the security detail back at the war room—even knew the Mahdi was in this vehicle. But as General Jazini had explained, they had to take a risk if they were going to get the Mahdi to Kabul in time to meet President Farooq. The key wasn't avoiding all risks, Jazini's memo insisted; the key was doing everything possible to minimize the risks and then being ready for any threat you couldn't rule out.

They were nearly three-quarters of the way around the traffic circle, with Azadi Square on their left and Jenah Highway coming up fast on their right. In a few seconds, they would be on Lashkari Highway, taking a quick exit to the firehouse. That's certainly where the driver thought they were going. But it was Rashidi's job to make sure they never got to the firehouse.

"Turn here—right now!" Rashidi shouted. *"Yes, right here, onto Jenah Highway. That's an order from the Mahdi!"*

The driver was completely confused, but he was a man trained to follow orders, so he turned the wheel hard to the right and exited onto Jenah Highway.

JERUSALEM, ISRAEL

Naphtali had just given the order to fire at the hazmat truck when he saw the vehicle make a sudden turn.

"What's going on?" Naphtali shouted. *"Belay that order, Zvi. Belay that order."*

"Abort, abort!" Dayan screamed into the phone in his hand.

Shimon began cursing. The entire communications center erupted in confusion.

"Why are you aborting the mission?" Shimon demanded to know.

"Why is that truck turning?" Naphtali asked.

"How should I know?" Shimon shot back. "We've got a clean shot. Let's take it."

"No, not until I'm sure," Naphtali said.

"Sure of what?"

"Sure the Mahdi is in there."

"Sir, with all due respect, we can be even more certain the Mahdi is in that truck now," Shimon said.

"Why?"

"Because whoever is driving doesn't want to take him to the firehouse."

"Why not?"

"Because he's not a firefighter. They don't want him mingling with real firefighters. They're taking him someplace else."

"Where?" Naphtali pressed.

"I don't know, sir," Shimon conceded. "But once he gets there, I can't guarantee we'll ever have a shot like this again."

Naphtali stared at Shimon, then at the screen as the hazmat truck zigzagged down a series of side streets at breakneck speed, heading east. With the roads essentially devoid of rush-hour traffic since no one in Tehran wanted to be driving around during a war, the chance of collateral damage was minimal. Maybe Shimon was right. The PM now looked to Dayan for counsel.

"Sir, I'm with Levi," said Dayan. "I think the truck is heading for the Tohid Tunnel. You should take him out now, before he reaches it."

TEHRAN, IRAN

"Okay, take another right at the next intersection and then head west," Rashidi ordered, checking his BlackBerry to make sure he had the directions right.

The driver had no idea what was going on, but he complied. Rashidi checked his watch. They were doing well. They were actually a few minutes ahead of schedule. But they were not out of the woods yet.

The driver slowed down ever so slightly and then made a hard right turn.

"Good," said Rashidi. "Now race for the tunnel entrance at Fatemi Street—and step on it."

By Rashidi's reckoning, they were less than a quarter of a mile away now from the ramp into the Tohid Tunnel, a three-kilometer, six-lane highway that ran underneath the heart of the capital. It had cost nearly half a billion dollars but had been completed in just thirty-one months, setting a world record for the fastest construction of a tunnel this size. Rashidi couldn't be sure the entire plan would work, but his job was to make sure they got underground, at least, and he was determined to impress the Lord of the Age with his ability to manage in a crisis.

JERUSALEM, ISRAEL

"They're almost there, sir—they're almost to the tunnel," Shimon said, pleading with the prime minister to authorize the drone attack now and get it over with.

"No," Naphtali said. "They're making too many twists and turns. I don't want to run the risk of missing."

"Don't worry, sir. The missile will lock onto the heat signature of the truck. I guarantee you we will hit the truck and nothing else."

"We will hit them," Naphtali finally agreed, "but we'll do it on the other side of the tunnel—that will be the cleanest shot, on the straightaway as they're coming out of the tunnel."

TEHRAN, IRAN

The second they entered the Tohid Tunnel, Rashidi let out a whoop and said a prayer of thanks to Allah. He had no idea they were being tracked by an Israeli drone, no idea a heat-seeking Hellfire missile was waiting for them three kilometers away. He just prayed the next phase of the plan worked as well as the first.

Halfway through the tunnel, Rashidi suddenly yelled at the driver to stay in the right lane and then to slam on the brakes and stop the truck. Several hundred yards later, the air filled with the smell of burning rubber, they were safely stopped at the tunnel's midpoint. The four elite IRGC bodyguards—all changed into suits and ties again—burst out of the back of the hazmat track, brandishing automatic weapons. They checked to see if there was any traffic behind them, but no one was around.

Rashidi, meanwhile, jumped out of the front seat and took a look for himself. Confident the coast was clear, he walked about thirty yards behind the truck. There he found a door marked Authorized Personnel Only. As per the plan, it was unlocked, and when he opened the door, he found five young schoolgirls waiting for him. They ranged in age, he guessed, from about nine years old to maybe fifteen or sixteen. All wore chadors covering their heads. Their faces, what he could see of them, were ashen, and their eyes were full of fear. They had no coats and they were trembling, but perhaps more from the situation than the cool March temperatures.

Rashidi gave the all-clear sign to the security detail and then ordered the girls to head for the truck. The agents, meanwhile, helped the Mahdi out of the hazmat truck and directed the girls to take his place in the back. Rashidi noticed the Mahdi did not even acknowledge the girls. He did not greet them or even make eye contact with them. He treated them as though they were . . . what? Impure? Unworthy? He was not entirely sure. But the Mahdi did not pray for them or bless them or even speak a word to them. Rather, he moved quickly and without emotion toward Rashidi.

The security men grabbed their own equipment and closed the rear door of the truck, locking the girls inside. Then they ordered the driver to continue on, which meant continuing south through the tunnel before driving back to the fire station near Azadi Square. The driver did as he was told, and now, with the hazmat truck gone, the agents hustled the Mahdi through the door Rashidi was holding for them.

They raced through a narrow hallway that opened to the tunnel on the other side, where three lanes of highway took traffic in the opposite direction from the section of the tunnel they'd just come from. Today, of course, there was no traffic. This section of tunnel was completely devoid of vehicles except for a yellow school bus waiting for them. The bus was empty but for the driver, who was idling the engine. Rashidi, the

Mahdi, and the others quickly piled inside, and then Rashidi ordered the driver—in this case the Ayatollah's personal driver—to race north through the tunnel and out of Tehran as rapidly as possible.

JERUSALEM, ISRAEL

The prime minister stood and stared at the screen transmitting the live video image from the Israeli drone hovering over the southbound exit of the Tohid Tunnel as his defense minister and the director of the Mossad stood at his side, similarly transfixed. A vehicle suddenly came racing out of the tunnel and into view. Naphtali's pulse quickened, but it was not the hazmat truck. It was a military truck of some sort, and as quickly as it entered their field of vision, it was gone.

"Can you zoom that image out a bit?" the PM asked. "Can we get a wider shot?"

Dayan was holding a phone to his ear, a hotline connecting him directly to the Mossad operations center in Netanya, which was responsible for controlling the drone. He relayed the order, and within moments the shot widened. Another vehicle came into view, but this was not their truck either. This was an ambulance, its lights flashing, clearly racing to the scene of another emergency.

"What's going on?" Naphtali asked. "Why's it taking so long?"

"Patience, sir," said Shimon. "We'll see the truck at any moment."

But they waited a few moments more, and no more vehicles came through.

"Something's wrong," said Dayan.

"No, Zvi—quiet—everything is fine," Shimon insisted. "Please, everyone, we must—"

But before he could finish his sentence, the bright-yellow hazmat truck came barreling out of the tunnel.

"There!" Shimon shouted. *"That's it—that's our target!"*

Sure enough, it had *Unit 19* painted on the roof in large black letters. All eyes turned to Naphtali, who didn't hesitate.

"Take them out," the prime minister ordered.

Dayan immediately relayed the order to the Mossad's director of operations, who instantly relayed it to the drone controller.

Naphtali could see what looked like a bolt of lightning flash from the bottom of the screen. That was the missile with the Mahdi's name on it, and Naphtali watched it streak downward toward the hazmat truck, and suddenly the truck was no more. The screen erupted with fire and smoke. Through the haze, he could see tires go flying and large chunks of the engine and the chassis soaring in all directions. He could also make out the outlines of five burning and motionless bodies. And then he saw a sixth figure trying to crawl through the raging inferno, trying to make it to safety, but in less than a minute, that one stopped moving as well.

But Naphtali could not cheer. He was grateful to have taken out the Mahdi, but he was by no means certain this war was really over. Then something in him tensed. His body grew strangely cold, and at first he had no idea why. He stared at the screen while others slapped each other's backs in congratulations. He took a step closer to the screen, increasingly oblivious to the celebration going on around him. Naphtali turned his head and looked closer at the flickering images on the monitors, and then he turned to Dayan and asked him to order the controller to zoom in further.

"Why?" the Mossad chief asked. "What's wrong?"

"Just have them zoom in," Naphtali said, praying he wasn't seeing what he thought he was seeing.

Dayan relayed the order, and a moment later the controller got the word and the image began to zoom in.

"What's going on?" Shimon asked, noticing Naphtali's rapidly rising discomfort.

"That one," Naphtali said finally, pointing to the body of the figure that had been crawling. "Zoom in on that one."

Dayan passed his order along and then stepped closer to the monitor as well.

"There, in the left hand," said the prime minister. "What is that?"

The room was growing quiet now as everyone noticed Naphtali

wasn't reacting as they were and as everyone's eyes focused on the screen where he was focused.

And then Naphtali gasped. "That's a toy," he said. "That's a little girl, holding a toy—a doll. Look, none of them are men, except for the driver. They're all children. They're all little girls."

Zvi Dayan paled and sank into a chair. "What have we done?"

33

David ordered the two Israelis to stay quiet and directed his men to keep their weapons trained on them. Then he headed down the hall to the bedroom.

"What've you got?" he asked as he reached Fox.

"Boss, we've hit the mother lode," Fox replied, hunched over Omid's laptop.

Keeping his voice low so the Israelis wouldn't overhear them, Fox explained that he had already bypassed the computer's multiple layers of security and was now downloading the entire hard drive. Then he pointed to the text on the screen, whispering that this was the file on which Omid had most recently been working.

David was stunned. Before him was a detailed security plan to quietly move Omid's father, General Mohsen Jazini, from the IRGC command center in Tehran to the Tabriz Air Base. When David scrolled down a few pages, he found that the plan then involved moving the general from Tabriz to a Syrian military base on the outskirts of Damascus. The plan included maps, routes of travel, backup routes, the types of vehicles they were using (including a brief explanation of why it would be better to use Red Crescent ambulances than military vehicles), license plate numbers, names of all the security men that would be assigned to Jazini, and satphone numbers of the key people involved in the operation.

When David had finished skimming this document, Fox opened another recently updated file, revealing a memo written by Jazini to his security team explaining that they were to work closely with a Syrian general named Hamdi to set up an operations center capable of coordinating IRGC actions and directing the launch of short-range ballistic missiles.

As David kept reading, his mouth grew dry. The memo explained that at least one of the two remaining nuclear warheads would be taken to this new operations center, attached to a ballistic missile, and then fired at Israel from Syria. Toward the end, there was a cryptic reference to a "special guest" that would be arriving at the Syrian base shortly and that everything must be done to be ready for that guest, though Jazini didn't explain who or what the guest was. Was he referring to an actual person, David wondered, or to the warhead itself? He glanced at his colleague, but Fox just shrugged.

"How fast can you upload all this to Langley?" David whispered.

"I can't do it from here," Fox replied. "I mean, I could, but it wouldn't be secure. We really need to take this back to the safe house and send it from there."

"Then let's get moving," David said.

HIGHWAY 77, NORTHERN IRAN

In his heart, Daryush Rashidi was stunned and relieved by how effective their plan had been so far.

With the help of Allah, Rashidi had gotten the Twelfth Imam safely out of Tehran. They were now heading north on a highway that was nearly deserted of all traffic. They were far from any military bases or places of interest to Israeli or American satellites or spies. If everything worked as planned and they didn't encounter any significant delays, he would have the Mahdi out of the country and sitting with the Pakistani president in the next few hours. Yet suddenly the Mahdi became enraged.

"How could this have happened?" he fumed. "How could the filthy Jews have known where I was?"

Rashidi was about to respond, but the Mahdi continued his rant, his face flushed with anger.

"This is a major breach of security. I was told my departure would be secret. I was told all of my travel plans would be kept secret. Only a handful of people knew what was happening. But the Zionists knew. And if they knew I was leaving the airport command post in that fire truck, what else do they know? Who is leaking this information? Who is the mole in our operation? There is a traitor in our midst, and when I find him, he will burn in the fires of hell for all eternity."

Rashidi was aghast. He wanted to remind the Mahdi that General Jazini's plan had anticipated the possibility of an Israeli drone picking up the Mahdi's trail at the airport and following the fire trucks into the city. That was precisely why Jazini had planned for the switch in the Tohid Tunnel. That was precisely why the school bus had been waiting for them. Jazini's plan had accounted for everything, and it had worked brilliantly. The Mahdi's life had been spared. The Israelis had killed the five schoolgirls instead. The international media was going to have a field day with that. Israel was about to pay dearly in the court of public opinion. How could the Mahdi be angry with any of that? Yet he was. He was raging at both Rashidi and the head of his security detail, but neither man dared answer any of the Mahdi's questions. Answering any of them, Rashidi realized, was a fool's errand and possibly a death sentence. So they endured the ferocious tongue-lashing the Mahdi was spewing forth and tried their best not to make eye contact.

In the end, one practical decision actually emerged from the Mahdi's rant, but even that made little sense to Rashidi. The Mahdi was suddenly intensely suspicious that the Israelis might somehow be intercepting their supposedly secure satphone calls. Thus, the Mahdi said, he would no longer be using any of the phones they had with them. Instead, he said Rashidi would now communicate the Mahdi's instructions to his key lieutenants and then carefully pass their messages back to him. The Mahdi was adamant on the point, but why? If the satphones had really been compromised as the Mahdi suggested, why should any of them be used? Shouldn't all the satphones be discarded? How would it really help to have Rashidi tell people that he was giving direct instructions from the Mahdi? Why would people believe him? And if the Israelis were listening, they weren't really going to be fooled, were they?

Still, Rashidi was as certain the satphones were *not* compromised as the Mahdi now seemed certain that they were. The problem, Rashidi believed, was that the Mahdi had never met Reza Tabrizi. He didn't know what a fine and devout Twelver Reza was, how committed he was to their cause, and how trustworthy Reza was as a result. Rashidi was sure that if the Mahdi met Reza and began to get to know this faithful Muslim foot soldier the way he did, the Mahdi's fears would be relieved.

TEHRAN, IRAN

David ordered Torres and Crenshaw to get the Israelis downstairs and into the van while Fox finished downloading the hard drive. Meanwhile, he filled a duffel bag with Omid's mobile phone, wallet, ID badge, calendar, and various files. Then he photographed every room in the apartment and soon found himself in Omid's walk-in closet. Hanging there were a half-dozen IRGC uniforms, all freshly laundered and neatly pressed. On the floor lay three pairs of freshly polished black boots. David pondered that for a moment. These could come in handy, he decided, and he quickly found a suitcase to load them all into.

Five minutes later, they were ready to go. David radioed Zalinsky and gave him a quick update on what they'd found and why they were heading back to the safe house. Zalinsky agreed and urged David to get back to Karaj as fast as possible while he worked with the Global Ops Center staff to figure out what to do with the Israelis and also tried to come up with a way to get David and his team to Damascus.

NORTHWESTERN IRAN

Birjandi was still trying to imagine why on earth the Twelfth Imam wanted to see him at all, much less now, in the middle of a war the Iranians seemed to be losing. Did the Mahdi and the others at the top know about his conversion to Christianity? Were they watching his house? Were they listening to his conversations? Did they know of the young men he was discipling and their decision to renounce Islam and follow Jesus? Were Ibrahim, Ali, and the others about to be rounded up and martyred?

Birjandi was ready to suffer and die for Christ. Indeed, he was old and tired and eager to leave this corrupt world behind. He longed to enter eternity and be in the presence of his Lord and Savior, to be healed of his blindness, to really see Jesus face-to-face, to really hear his voice and worship at his feet. The truth was, Birjandi dreamed about it more and more. He couldn't wait to get home to glory, where he not only would be with the Lord but would finally be reunited with his beloved wife, Souri, who had already been called home to heaven and was waiting for him there. What had she experienced already? He longed to see her face and hear her voice and walk with her hand in hand. He yearned to worship Jesus at her side and to find out everything she had learned about the Lord in the time that they had been apart.

But as ready as he was, he couldn't help but wonder if these young men he'd been investing in were really ready to be tortured and executed for their faith in Christ. Would they hold up under such pressure, or would one—or all—crack and deny Christ rather than face execution? He loved them dearly, and he was deeply impressed by their hunger for the Word of God and their passion to share their faith. They had already taken bold, daring risks for the sake of the gospel. But were they truly ready for martyrdom? They said they were, but Birjandi was not yet certain.

As the pressure in his ears began to lessen, Birjandi could feel the helicopter start its long, slow descent. Eventually, he felt the aircraft touch down, the engines shut off, and the whirring rotors slow to a halt. Then he heard the side door slide open and soon felt someone taking his hands and helping him down onto the tarmac.

"Where are we?" he asked the Revolutionary Guard officer assigned to him.

"I'm sorry, Dr. Birjandi. I'm afraid I'm not authorized to say," the officer replied.

"You think this blind old man is going to run off?" Birjandi asked.

"No, I guess not," said the young man, carefully guiding Birjandi across the tarmac to a waiting truck. "But I have my orders."

"To maintain strict operational security."

"Yes, sir."

"But you do understand who I am, right, son?"

"Yes, of course, Dr. Birjandi. I know everything about you."

"So you know that the Ayatollah and the president and I are very close friends."

"Of course, sir. Everyone knows that."

"And you understand that I have been invited to this meeting at the Mahdi's personal request, right?"

"Yes."

"You understand all that?"

"Yes, sir."

"Then let me ask you, son," Birjandi said, folding up his white cane. "If the Mahdi trusts me, shouldn't you?"

"It's not that I don't trust you; it's just that . . ."

"It's just that what?" Birjandi asked.

"Well, I . . . It's . . ."

"Believe me, young man, I understand the need for operational security. But even if I were inclined to tell someone, whom would I tell? You took away my suitcase. You can see I am not holding a satellite phone. The only people with me are you and your fellow guards and the pilot. Presumably they already know. And besides, how would I even know you're telling me the truth?"

"I guess that's true."

"Of course it's true," Birjandi said. "Listen, son, I hope you never have the misfortune of going blind. But if you do, it is a very lonely existence. And somewhat unnerving, disorienting. Unless you're home in your own house, in your own bed or your own chair, eating food you've prepared for yourself, you never quite feel secure. You never really know where you are, who is with you, or what is happening around you. You do your best, mind you; you do your best. But it's nice every now and then to have some idea of what's happening. It can't completely give you peace, but it takes away some of the loneliness, some of the anxiety—for me, anyhow. But then again, I'm just an old man."

The young officer was quiet for a moment as he mulled the obvious logic of Birjandi's point. "Very well," the officer, whom Birjandi guessed was no older than thirty, finally said. "We have just landed on a small military base near Piranshahr."

"Near the Iraqi border?" Birjandi asked.

"Yes, you know of it?"

"Of course," Birjandi replied.

"But how?" the officer asked.

"My wife had an aunt who lived here once, but that was many years ago," Birjandi said. "I remember stories of Piranshahr from the war with Iraq back in the eighties. But I don't understand. What are we doing here? I thought we were going to Tehran."

"No, it's too dangerous to take you to Tehran," the officer said. "The Israelis are bombing the daylights out of Tehran."

"Not every neighborhood," Birjandi protested. "Surely there are secret centers from which the leadership is running the war."

"True, but my orders were to bring you here, transfer you to a vegetable truck, and drive you across the border to Erbil."

"Erbil?"

"Yes."

"The Erbil in Kurdistan?"

"Yes."

"Iraqi Kurdistan?"

"Exactly."

"But why?"

"I'm just following orders from General Jazini."

"Mohsen Jazini?"

"Yes, and I assume you know him, too?"

"We've met a few times, but no, I wouldn't really say I know him. But he's the one who developed this plan?"

"As far as I know," the officer said. "Anyway, from Erbil we'll fly you in a medical transport plane to a military base outside the city of Homs in Syria, and from there, you'll be driven to a military base in or near Damascus."

"Damascus?" asked Birjandi, genuinely perplexed. "What on earth for? I thought—"

But Birjandi stopped himself in midsentence. The beginning of an idea had just come to him, and he wondered why it hadn't occurred to him earlier.

"That's all I can tell you, Dr. Birjandi," the officer said, not noticing the old man was now deep in thought. "Actually, that's much more than I'm supposed to tell you. But you'll receive more information when you get to Damascus; that I can assure you. Now come, take my hand, and stay close to me. We need to get on the road."

JERUSALEM, ISRAEL

"I need to get out in front of this story," the prime minister said firmly, but Levi Shimon pushed back hard.

"Absolutely not," the defense minister said. "We are in the heat of battle. The Iranians just hit our nuclear reactor. That's the big story at the moment—the fear that the Iranians have tried to destroy us with our own peaceful nuclear power plant. That's all the world is talking about right now. We'd be fools to change the narrative."

"It was our mistake," Naphtali countered. "It was *my* mistake. And I must take responsibility for it."

"But not right now, sir," Shimon insisted. "Right now you and I need to stay focused on the hunt for two loose Iranian nuclear warheads . . . and a new and equally dangerous threat that is rising as well."

"What's that?"

"Sir, I think we have to consider the possibility that Iran is keeping the Syrians in the bull pen until our missile defenses are depleted, at which point they may launch a massive strike with chemical weapons."

"Do we have any intelligence the Syrians are considering such a move?"

"No," said Shimon, "nothing concrete."

"Then why do you bring this up now?"

"Instinct, sir. When this war began, the Syrians immediately launched three missiles at us. We had anticipated that, and we shot all three of them down. But then they went dark. No more rockets. No more missiles. It doesn't make sense. Hezbollah has unleashed on us. So has Hamas. Why hasn't Damascus?"

"That's what I keep asking you."

"And until now I haven't had an answer."

"But now you do?"

"Yes."

"You think Syria's about to unleash everything they have at us, but you have no proof."

"Sir, it's the only move that makes sense," Shimon insisted. "Tehran and Damascus have a mutual defense pact. The moment we attacked the Iranians, the Syrians began to retaliate. Then they stopped abruptly. Why? Because Gamal Mustafa got cold feet?"

"Mustafa doesn't get cold feet."

"Of course not," Shimon agreed. "The man is a ruthless killer. The only reason he stopped shooting was because Tehran told him to stop shooting. And who is the only man in Tehran with the authority to give such an order at the moment?"

"The Twelfth Imam."

"Precisely."

"You think the Mahdi is reining Mustafa in?"

"I do."

"For how long?" Naphtali asked.

"Not much longer, sir," Shimon replied. "I think we need to consider a massive preemptive strike against Syria's chemical weapons facilities and missile bases."

"Do you have a plan ready to go?"

"I do, sir."

"Then let me see it."

34

It had taken a little more than two hours, but just before 9 p.m. local time, the school bus carrying the Twelfth Imam along with Daryush Rashidi and their security team finally rolled into the Iranian city of Sari. Nestled between the Alborz Mountains and the southern shores of the Caspian Sea, Sari was the capital of the Mazandaran province. With a population of only about 250,000 people, it was a small, economically insignificant, and militarily unimportant city, which was exactly what they needed. It meant the place wasn't likely to be closely monitored by either the Israelis or the Americans. But it did have a decent general aviation airfield, and that was why General Jazini had chosen it.

As the bus pulled onto the airport grounds, Rashidi was struck by just how quiet and sleepy the place seemed. Night had fallen, and the runway lights were on, but not a single plane was taking off or landing, and few cars were in the parking lot. The guard station wasn't even manned, and Rashidi guessed they didn't have the budget for any serious security measures. The bus pulled onto the tarmac and drove over to a Dassault Falcon 20 business jet parked outside a hangar on the far end of the field. The plane had been freshly painted to look like a Red Crescent medical transport craft. Rashidi and the lead security officer jumped off the bus first and shook hands with the pilot, who was waiting for them, then waved the Mahdi and the rest of the security team aboard.

"How far are we from Kabul?" the Mahdi asked Rashidi once they were seated and buckled in on the plush, French-built plane.

"It's about 1,500 kilometers from here," Rashidi said. "If everything goes as we hope, we should be on the ground by midnight."

"Very well," the Mahdi said. "Wake me up when we're there."

"Yes, Your Excellency. Can I get you anything before we lift off?"

"Just dim the cabin lights and keep everyone quiet," the Mahdi said. "I don't want to be disturbed."

CAPE MAY, NEW JERSEY

The waves of the Atlantic lapped rhythmically upon the shore as bitter March winds continued to rattle the house. These were the only constants while everything else in Najjar Malik's life seemed to change minute by minute.

The country of his birth was at war, taken over by a madman, a false messiah who was preaching lies and hatred and cruelly leading the people Najjar loved into death and destruction. Syria, meanwhile, seemed about to plunge into the war as well. A madman was running that country too, slaughtering tens of thousands and sending many of them into a Christless eternity. And then there was Israel, whose civilian nuclear reactor in Dimona had just been hit by Iranian missiles and whose prime minister was surely preparing to unleash the nation's fury back upon Iran. There was no good news anywhere he looked. He knew he personally was in the care of the Good Shepherd, who would not leave him or forsake him, and he continued to urge all who would listen to give their lives to Jesus Christ before it was too late. But the intensity of the battle was taking its toll, and Najjar desperately needed to rest.

He rubbed his bloodshot eyes and checked his watch. It was 12:30 in the afternoon. He'd been scanning the web for the latest news from Iran, Israel, and Syria for the last four and a half hours. He'd also been tweeting and retweeting the stories he found most important to the 923,178 people who were following him on Twitter. From time to time, he'd send out a Bible verse that he felt was relevant for the moment, and occasionally he answered questions people were sending to him.

JOEL C. ROSENBERG ★ 293

There wasn't much he could really communicate in 140 characters, and he continued to be stunned that anyone was listening to anything he had to say, but mostly he was grateful that the Lord had given him the chance to speak the truth to those in the Islamic world who were living in utter darkness.

At this point Najjar was completely exhausted, not to mention freezing cold. He already had two T-shirts on and a sweater and a hoodie over those, but he still couldn't get warm, and he couldn't seem to figure out how to work the house's central heating system. What he really wanted to do was go upstairs and curl up in bed under lots of blankets and comforters for the next few hours and get some serious sleep, but his stomach was growling, and he decided his first priority was to eat something.

Stepping into the kitchen, he opened the refrigerator and stared into the empty void. The milk was gone. The orange juice was gone. The fruit was gone, and so was the bread. He went to the pantry but didn't find much else. He'd finished all the tea in the house, all the pasta, and all the rice, and as he looked at the dishes piling up in the sink and the empty jars of peanut butter and jelly and empty boxes and containers of myriad other kinds of food heaped up in the trash, he realized how obsessive he had been for the past few days. He'd been spending most of his time reading the Bible or praying for Sheyda and the rest of his family and for the people of Iran and the Middle East or tracking the war on TV and on the computer, and he hadn't made much time for anything else.

Najjar was embarrassed how messy he'd allowed this gorgeous beach house to become, and he wondered what the owners would say if they popped in unexpectedly to see how he was doing. He had never met the couple, friends of the producer at the Persian Christian Satellite Network. Their goal in having him stay here was to keep Najjar out of the hands of the FBI and CIA and to keep him communicating the gospel and the latest war news to the Iranian people via Twitter for as long as possible. Meanwhile, the folks back at PCSN were going to keep replaying his riveting television interview explaining how he, a Shia Twelver and the highest-ranking nuclear scientist in Iran, had come to renounce Islam, become a follower of Jesus Christ, and seek political asylum in the United States.

When he'd first been told by the producer that they had a place for him to hide away, Najjar had expected a couch in someone's basement or a little apartment or maybe a condo someplace on the outskirts of Washington, D.C., not far from the TV studio. He certainly hadn't expected to be put up in a multimillion-dollar beach house all by himself on the Jersey Shore. Yes, it was off-season, and yes, it was bitterly cold in a town largely depopulated, but it was, Najjar knew, a very gracious gift from his Father in heaven, and though flabbergasted, he was deeply grateful.

He scanned the disaster in the kitchen and made a quick plan. For now, he'd take out the trash and go get some groceries. Then he'd come back, check the headlines, and load the dishwasher. A few loads of laundry couldn't hurt either, he told himself, and suddenly he missed his precious Sheyda all the more. What was she doing right now? How were the baby and his wife, Farah? Was the CIA taking good care of them? Or were they punishing them for Najjar's escape? He felt fairly certain that the American government was nothing like his own. Indeed, the mullahs would have hanged or shot his family by now had he left them in their hands. No, he knew the Americans would never do such a thing. Yet he had to admit to himself that he didn't really know how the Agency handled such situations, and a wave of guilt began to wash over him. How could he have been so selfish? They needed him now more than ever, and in a sense he had just abandoned them. Not literally, of course. It was his CIA handlers who had separated him from his family and locked him up in a safe house. But maybe if he had cooperated more, they would have been reunited by now. Najjar began to wonder again if he should turn himself in.

Yet with his stomach grumbling more loudly now, he decided it was a bad idea to even consider such a major decision on so little food and even less sleep. So he sent one more tweet, then picked the car keys off the counter, settled behind the wheel of the black Honda Accord parked in the driveway, and carefully backed onto Beach Avenue before heading toward the grocery store he'd seen about a half kilometer away on Ocean Street.

★ ★ ★ ★ ★

SYRACUSE, NEW YORK

Marseille was startled by the unexpected ring of her iPhone. She had just finished saying good-bye to Mr. and Mrs. Walsh. She had given them both long hugs and had gotten into her rental car to head to the airport for her flight back to Portland. The identification of the caller was blocked, but Marseille answered it anyway, and every muscle in her body seemed to tense.

"Hello?" she asked, desperate for any scrap of news about Lexi and Chris, and even more desperate for news about David, yet fearful what any of that news might be.

"This is the operations center at Langley looking for a Marseille Harper."

"Yes, this is she."

"Very well, please hold for Deputy Director Murray."

Marseille held her breath. A moment later, Murray came on the line.

"Miss Harper?"

"Yes?"

"This is Tom Murray."

"Oh yes, hi, Mr. Murray," Marseille replied. "Thank you so much for calling. Honestly, I didn't really expect a call back from you personally. I know you have a lot on your plate right now."

"Well, that's true, and normally I don't return calls made at 3 a.m. to my office by people I barely know," Murray said. "But you seem to be proving an exception to that rule. As I mentioned when we met the other day, your father was a dear friend, as was your mom. So that's why I wanted to return your call myself once I had some news."

Marseille looked at Mrs. Walsh, who clung to her husband while whispering to Marseille, "What's he saying?" But Marseille motioned for her to wait.

"That's very kind of you, Mr. Murray," she said. "I'm actually here with Lexi's parents. We've been up all night watching the TV coverage, but they haven't really been talking about what's happening in Tiberias. It all seems to be about the missile attack on Dimona."

"Yes, the situation in Dimona is dominating everything right now, and I'm sorry about that," Murray said. "But I'm calling because I have some good news for you."

"Good news, really?" Marseille asked, surprised but encouraged.

She turned off the engine and got out of the car to be closer to the Walshes.

"A little," Murray said. "It's regarding our mutual friend, the one you came in here the other day to talk about."

"David?" she asked.

"Well, yes," Murray said, "but I was trying to avoid using his name over an open line."

"Oh, right, I'm so sorry. I wasn't thinking."

"It's okay. But between the two of us, I wanted you to know that our people just talked with him. He's still in harm's way, but for the moment, at least, he's alive and well and . . . Let's just say, I think you'd be proud of him. He's serving his country and his family with great distinction."

"Really, he's okay? He's safe?" Marseille replied, her eyes filling with tears.

"Well, he is okay," Murray corrected. "I can't say for certain that he's safe. But he's doing what he was trained to do, and he's doing it very well. I really can't say more than that, but I thought you'd like an update, however brief."

"Oh yes, Mr. Murray, thank you so much—*thank you.* I can't tell you how happy I am to hear you say that," she replied, burying her face in her free hand and trying not to dissolve into tears of joy or risk not being able to hear the rest of the call.

"You're very welcome, Miss Harper," Murray said.

Then Marseille looked up and saw Mr. and Mrs. Walsh waiting eagerly for the news.

CAPE MAY, NEW JERSEY

Najjar was just about to pull into the Acme supermarket on Ocean Street, only a few blocks from the shore, when he spotted a Cape May

Police Department squad car. His pulse began to quicken as thoughts of being captured flooded his mind. But just as quickly he chastised himself for becoming paranoid. There was no scenario in which anyone was looking for him in New Jersey, much less in this quaint, seaside, tourist community in the off-season. He was about as far off the grid as he could get. He didn't know anyone in Cape May. He hadn't talked to anyone in the area. He wasn't making mobile phone calls. He wasn't driving a stolen car. He was being as careful as possible, and he had no reason to worry, he told himself.

Forcing himself to take several deep breaths, Najjar double-checked his rear and side mirrors, made sure his right turn signal was on, then cautiously steered the Honda into the parking lot. The last thing he wanted to do was make a wrong turn or stumble into a moving violation, however minor, that could draw the attention of the local police and require him to produce an American driver's license, which he didn't have, or the car's registration or insurance, which he didn't have either, though he hoped paperwork for both were in the glove compartment.

Najjar breathed easier when the squad car drove past him without stopping, but he still felt the urge to move quickly. He didn't like being out of the house. He was uncomfortable being away from what he knew, exposed to the prospect, however remote, of even getting noticed by the local authorities, much less caught. So he proceeded to find a parking space not far from the grocery store's front doors, turned off the engine, locked the doors of the sedan behind him, and headed into the store to get some basics and get back as rapidly as he could.

SYRACUSE, NEW YORK

The Walshes could see Marseille's obvious sense of relief, and their faces brightened as they began to relax a bit, especially Lexi's mom, who came over and gave her a hug. Wiping her own eyes, Marseille asked Murray directly about Chris and Lexi Vandermark. But to her shock, there was a long, awkward silence on the other end of the line.

"Miss Harper, there's really no easy way to say this," Murray finally began.

"Oh no," Marseille said, her hands beginning to shake. "Please, no, no . . ."

"I'm so sorry to have to be the one to inform you, Miss Harper."

"No, no, no . . ."

"I'm afraid both of your friends were pulled from the wreckage of the hotel collapse about an hour ago. They were taken to a nearby hospital in Tiberias, but both were pronounced dead on arrival. An official from our embassy in Tel Aviv is on scene. He made a positive identification based on the passport photos we have on file for them. I'm truly sorry for your loss. Indeed, I wish there was something else I could say. Anyway, I am very sorry."

All of Marseille's joy turned to shock. She turned to Lexi's parents and shook her head. But before Marseille could say a word to them or ask Murray any more questions, Mrs. Walsh collapsed to the ground, wailing in a manner Marseille had never heard before and would never forget.

CAPE MAY, NEW JERSEY

Najjar was rolling his half-full grocery cart toward the dairy section to pick up a few gallons of milk when he first realized that there was hardly anyone in the store. There had been at least a dozen shoppers, maybe a few more, when he'd first entered, but now he couldn't find a soul. Not even a clerk or a stock boy.

His heart began to pound. Beads of perspiration formed on his brow. His palms felt sweaty, and he forgot about the milk. Something was very wrong. He wanted to tell himself that he was imagining it, that he was becoming paranoid, but he knew his instincts were not misleading him. Without making any sudden movements, he cautiously maneuvered his cart down an aisle that gave him a peek out the main windows in the front of the store, and it was then that he saw the flashing lights and heard the screeching tires as more and more police cars arrived on the scene.

Just then, milliseconds after his brain began to consider if not truly comprehend what might be happening, members of the SWAT team rushed into the store from all directions. Clad in black jumpsuits and black helmets, they had automatic weapons trained on his head.

"Najjar Malik, put your hands in the air!" their commander shouted. *"Put your hands in the air where we can see them, or you will be fired upon!"*

Trembling, Najjar did as he was told. He had no idea how they had found him, but found him they had, and he feared for what was coming next.

35

Back at the safe house, David pulled out his phone and noticed three new tweets from Dr. Najjar Malik, the most wanted Iranian in the world. The first was in Farsi. The second was in Arabic. The third was in English. All three said the same thing.

> I'm not ashamed of #gospel, cause it's the pwr of God
> that brings salvation 2 all who believe: 1st 2 the Jew,
> then 2 the Gentile /Rmns 1:16

David continued to be amazed by how radically Christ had changed Najjar in such a short period of time from a devout Twelver committed to the return of the Twelfth Imam to an even more devoted follower of Jesus doing everything he could to share the gospel with the Islamic world. He said a quick prayer for Najjar and his family—for their safety and for the Lord to use them to reach millions—and then he forced himself to refocus on the priorities at hand.

He made a quick call to Zalinsky to coordinate his next moves and learned that Langley had now positively identified the two Mossad agents in their custody as Tolik Shalev, twenty-six, and Gal Rinat, twenty-five. David directed Fox and Mays to take both Israelis to the holding room, where they could neither escape nor witness any of the team's sensitive discussions. He also directed Crenshaw to provide Rinat, the wounded Israeli, whatever additional medical attention he required.

"Whatever you do, don't let him die," David ordered.

"Wait a minute," said Shalev. "You're making a mistake."

"You mean we should let your man die?"

Shalev ignored the crack and argued that they should evacuate Rinat out of the country. He would likely need surgery and soon. "But you should take me with you," Shalev added. "I can help you."

"Don't be ridiculous," David snapped and turned back to Fox and Mays. "Get him out of here."

"No, wait, really," Shalev insisted. "Look, yes, we're both with the Mossad. There's no point pretending we're not. You know our names, our ages, and I'm sure you know a lot more. You also know our mission, and it's the same as yours—to hunt down these two last warheads and neutralize them before the Mahdi can fire them at our country. Now I think you know exactly where these weapons are—or at least where they're heading and how they're getting there. I think you pulled a treasure trove off Omid's computer, information that could save millions of Israelis' lives. So I'm pleading with you. Don't lock me up. Let me help you stop these madmen before it's too late."

"The answer is no, Tolik," David replied. "I have my orders. Now let's move."

"I can help you."

"Right now you're just slowing us down."

"Wait, wait—what if I told you we have a double agent deep inside the Iranian nuclear program?" Shalev asked as Mays began to lead him toward the doorway.

His colleague's eyes grew wide. "No, don't listen to him," Rinat insisted. "He doesn't know what he's talking about."

"*Sheket,* Gal," Shalev shot back, ordering his deputy in Hebrew to be silent.

"You have no authorization to do this," Rinat argued.

But Shalev wouldn't hear of it. He lowered his voice and rattled off a few heated lines in Hebrew before turning back to David and returning to English. "Listen to me. Please. Listen to reason. How do you think my country pulled off such a precise preemptive strike against the Iranian warheads?"

"If it was so precise, then why did you miss two?" David asked.

"You know exactly what I mean," Shalev said. "We knew where those warheads were because someone told us. Someone inside. Deep inside. A mole. A mole who reports directly to us. Obviously someone moved the other two warheads before our fighter jets could get there. But at the time our man inside called in the locations, they were accurate. How else could Prime Minister Naphtali have ordered those strikes? He couldn't afford to guess. He had to know. And he did know."

"So what are you saying?" David pressed. "Cut to the chase."

"I'm saying Gal and I aren't really hunting the warheads," Shalev replied. "We're hunting for our mole. If we can find him, we can find the warheads. If we can't, then there is no reasonable hope for my country. Now America is our best ally. You've always been there for us. And I don't believe it's a coincidence that we are together now, you and I—the men in this room. This is not a mistake. This is a sign from God. Please, let us work together. Let me help you. There's no more time to work apart."

SYRACUSE, NEW YORK

Marseille helped the Walshes back inside. She wondered if she should call 911. Lexi's mom was hysterical and had locked herself in her room, wailing uncontrollably and refusing to come out. Lexi's father sat at the kitchen table unable or unwilling to speak. He was so pale and so shaky that Marseille feared he might suffer a heart attack from the stress and grief. Yet he would not let Marseille do anything to console him, nor was he doing anything to console his wife.

She glanced at her watch. It was now clear that if she didn't leave for the airport immediately, she was going to miss her flight back to Portland. But how could she possibly leave these two alone right now? Either or both of them were capable of doing harm to themselves or to each other, and given the recent trauma of finding her own father after he had committed suicide, Marseille knew she had to stay. She riffled through several kitchen drawers and soon found a notebook that seemed to have doubled as a wedding planner. Inside, she found a directory of addresses and phone numbers of family members and close friends, all of whom had been invited to the wedding. Marseille scrolled to the end and found the number for Jan Walsh—Mr. Walsh's older sister—who lived in DeWitt, a town not far away. She dialed the number, got Jan on the line, and relayed the tragic news about Lexi and Chris as gently as she could. Then she explained how much trouble Sharon and Richard were in.

"I'll be there in ten minutes," Jan assured her. "And here's my cell number if you need to reach me on the way."

Marseille thanked her, hung up, and tried to assess the situation. She asked Mr. Walsh if he wanted some coffee. He didn't answer. She offered him tea, but again he didn't answer. Then she asked him if he'd like a glass of water, and still he couldn't seem to hear her, much less respond. He just stared blankly out the window, his hands trembling. She poured him a glass anyway and set it on the table in front of him. Then she pulled out her iPhone and dialed her principal back in Portland.

The conversation did not go well. Her boss tried to be sympathetic, to be sure, but he also had to remind her that she had used up all of her vacation time and personal days. What's more, she had a class of children that hadn't seen her face in two weeks and expected to see her bright and early the following morning.

"I know, I know," she said. "But, Mr. Martin, I simply can't leave."

"You have a contract, Marseille."

"I realize that, sir, but I also have an obligation to my friend's family."

"Didn't you say Lexi's aunt is on the way over there right now?"

"Yes, sir, but I can't bolt out the minute she gets here. And even if I did, I still might not make the flight, and it's the last one out there tonight."

The principal sighed and was silent for a moment. "Look, stay there tonight, and I'll get another sub for your class tomorrow," he finally said. "But you need to get back here tomorrow and be in your class ready to go first thing Tuesday morning, or I can't promise you'll have a job when you return. Is that understood?"

Marseille assured him it was and thanked him for his understanding, and the two hung up. She covered her face with her hands and did her best not to cry. She was grateful for the reprieve, but she wondered whether twenty-four hours would be enough. It wasn't just a matter of comforting the Walshes and helping them stabilize. There was a funeral for Lexi and Chris to organize. People to invite. A wake to be arranged, and all that went with that. Was Richard's sister going to do all that? Maybe yes, maybe no. But it was going to be an enormous task, and even if Jan was emotionally up for it all, she was going to need help.

Plus, Marseille realized, she had an obligation to Lexi to try to lead her parents to the Lord. At least Lexi and Chris were now in heaven with Christ. They were safe and free, and a part of Marseille envied them for it. But she knew she'd never forgive herself if she didn't do everything she possibly could to lead Lexi's parents to a saving knowledge of Jesus Christ as well. She hoped that wouldn't mean losing her job. She couldn't imagine not going back to those precious children in Portland. But the truth was, someone else could teach them as well as or better than she could. Right now, she was needed here. How long? She had no idea. But in her heart she resolved to stay as long as necessary.

She bowed her head and began to pray for wisdom, then heard a car pull up out front. Assuming it was Jan, she prayed for the Lord to comfort these two grieving parents. She prayed that she and Jan would have the strength and the wisdom to do the right thing and for the Lord to give her the opportunity to share the gospel with them in the right time and the right way and that each of them would be saved. And then she said a prayer for David, too, that wherever he was, Christ would give him the strength and courage to do the right thing as well.

KARAJ, IRAN

David walked over to Shalev and looked him straight in the eye.

"You want to help me?" he asked.

"I want to save my country," the Israeli replied.

"You want to help me?" David repeated.

Shalev paused and then nodded.

306 ★ DAMASCUS COUNTDOWN

"Then start spilling your guts. Tell my man here everything you know. He'll relay it to me on the road. If it checks out, fine. If not, God help you."

With that, David turned to Mays and Fox and ordered them to get the prisoners secured immediately. They complied without hesitation and despite Shalev's angry protests.

Once they were all out of the room, David and Torres huddled together to review their options, which both knew were scant at best.

"You think he's telling us the truth?" Torres asked. "I mean, you think they really have a mole inside the program?"

"I don't know," said David. "Why wouldn't Najjar have told us?"

"Maybe Najjar didn't know. Najjar was the son-in-law to the director of the entire nuclear program. If you were a mole, would you have confided in Najjar?"

"No."

"Maybe we really should take this guy with us," said Torres. "Maybe you should talk to Jack again."

"Absolutely not," David shot back, unlocking the gun cabinet and stuffing more boxes of ammo into his backpack. "This Tolik guy is a loose cannon. It's too much of a risk. Besides, the order to keep the Israelis here until Langley can extract them came from the top, not from Jack."

"Director Allen?"

"No, the president."

"The president knows that much detail about what we're doing?"

"He's requested updates every half hour. In fact, Jack didn't come right out and say it, but I get the feeling the president is trying to micromanage this op from the Oval Office."

"He could end this whole thing with a massive air strike on Al-Mazzah once the warheads get there," Torres said.

"You're right," David said.

"But he's not going to, is he?"

"No, he's not."

"Why not?"

"Do I really need to say it?"

"No, you don't."

"We've got to find those warheads ourselves, before the Iranians fire them."

"Of course, but how?"

"I don't know."

"And even if by some miracle we can find them, how do we destroy them?"

"I don't know that either."

"And how do we get into Syria in the first place?" Torres pressed.

"That I do know," David said, smiling, and quickly laid out his plan.

They would follow the protocols they'd found in the memos on Omid's computer. They had the maps Omid had prepared for his father's security team to drive from Iran to Syria, including detailed directions to get to the Al-Mazzah air base. They had radios and the precise frequencies and encryption codes the Revolutionary Guards would be using. And they would all wear the Iranian Revolutionary Guard Corps uniforms David had taken from Omid's closet. In short, they had everything they needed but time.

The warheads, they had to assume, were en route and might already be at the base. There, too, was the Iranian team capable of fitting the warheads on Syrian Scud-Cs, though none of the specific names of that team were mentioned in the memos. Circumstantial evidence suggested the Mahdi was headed to Al-Mazzah as well. At David's request, Zalinsky and his team at CIA headquarters were already retasking a satellite and several Predator drones to provide 24-7 surveillance of the base. But with the Mahdi expected at the base by noon local time, David feared the missiles could be ready to launch shortly after his arrival.

"We need to get on the road—now," he told Torres. "Matty will stay and guard the Israelis and try to get more information out of them."

"But we'll need Matt with us."

"We'll have to make do without him."

"Just four of us going into Syria to take out two nuclear warheads?"

"I get it, Marco," David replied. "The odds aren't exactly promising. But you really think a fifth guy is going to make all the difference?"

"I think we need all the manpower and firepower we can get."

"This is all we can get," David concluded. "Matty stays. Tell the guys to suit up in the Iranian uniforms and gear up fast. The rest of us roll out in ten minutes. We've already burned too much time as it is."

★ ★ ★ ★ ★

MONDAY
MARCH 14

36

At precisely 12:07 a.m. on Monday morning, March 14, the Falcon business jet carrying the Twelfth Imam, Rashidi, and their small but well-armed security team touched down in Kabul. No one was there to greet them. Almost no one knew they were coming. There was no pomp and circumstance. This was not a state visit. This was a hastily arranged and highly secretive meeting.

Pakistani president Iskander Farooq hadn't even been told the meeting would be in Kabul. All he was told by a representative of the Mahdi was to get to Kabul quietly and discreetly by 11:30 p.m. on an unmarked jet and accompanied by no more than five bodyguards. At that point, he would learn where to go and what to do next. Farooq had assumed he would be told to fly into an Iranian border town. Instead, upon touching down in Kabul, he and his team had been directed to a large but unassuming compound on the south side of the city. Farooq didn't know the compound was owned by the largest drug dealer in Afghanistan, the father of Iraq's speaker of the parliament and a devout Twelver who was an old friend and seminary classmate of Ayatollah Hosseini. Nor was that piece of information necessarily relevant to this meeting. The owner of the home was not there. Nor were any of his family members or servants. Twenty members of the Iranian Revolutionary Guard Corps had taken over the compound. Most of them had arrived earlier that day and were providing security, while the remainder of the team was there to handle communications, hospitality, and other logistics.

Stepping off the plane, the Mahdi immediately got into a black, bulletproof Nissan SUV with several members of his security detail. Rashidi boarded a second black SUV with the remaining members of the detail. Less than two minutes after their feet had touched the Afghan airport pavement, they were rolling.

Rashidi had never been to the Islamic Republic of Afghanistan, much less its troubled, war-torn capital. He would never have chosen it for a meeting of this import—or a meeting of any import. Indeed, he had never seen a city more devastated by war or terrorism or poverty than Kabul. Every building he saw looked more devastated than the one before it. They were poorly built to begin with, and almost all were now riddled with holes from machine-gun fire. The roofs of many were partially or completely caved in, some from aerial bombings, and some, the driver told him, from sheer neglect. Dust and filth covered everything, and though many of the buildings looked utterly uninhabitable, people seemed to live and work in all of them.

Normally, the driver said, the streets would be teeming with the wretched refuse of the Afghan tribes. Over the years, Rashidi had seen news reports from Kabul. To him, the men pictured on the streets always looked old, with long, scraggly beards and grimy, dusty clothing. Their eyes seemed sad and weary, though *haunted* was the word that described them best. The Afghan women he'd seen on television were even more traumatized. They walked around in blue burqas that covered them head to foot, even when it was ghastly hot.

But Kabul was a ghost town at this hour. The streets were dark and empty of people and largely empty of cars and motorcycles, scooters and bicycles, sheep and goats, as well. An armored personnel carrier drove by from time to time, and Rashidi noticed several Afghan military units patrolling various neighborhoods. But mostly all was quiet and unseasonably hot. Even this late at night, the temperature was still in the high nineties, and Rashidi found himself grateful for air-conditioning. He couldn't imagine how unbearable it must be for the women shopping in the marketplaces during daylight hours, women whose entire faces, noses, and mouths were covered by the blue cloth that looked, at least on television, like some kind of burlap. Rashidi thought of himself as a deeply devout Muslim. He believed strongly in Islamic women being modest in every possible way. But though he'd heard of the burqa culture, he had never seen it for himself, and something inwardly chafed against the notion that a woman who was properly submitting to Allah should have to go this far, especially in a place as brutally scorching as Kabul.

Rashidi glanced at his watch and wondered what the Mahdi was thinking. They were on a very tight schedule and needed to proceed with the utmost haste. But they were running a bit behind, and Rashidi feared another outburst. He was sure the Mahdi was boiling.

At 12:48 a.m., a full eighteen minutes behind schedule, the SUVs carrying the Twelfth Imam and his team finally pulled into the compound, and at precisely one o'clock in the morning, the meeting was under way.

The group gathered in a large and somewhat-ornate dining room complete with an impressive crystal chandelier and a massive rectangular mahogany table. President Farooq had been briefed ahead of time on the proper protocol, and he dutifully got down on his knees and touched his forehead to the ground when the Mahdi entered the room, as did his security men, all of whom had had their weapons and radios taken from them by the Mahdi's team upon arriving at the compound. The Mahdi did not greet Farooq or shake his hand. Indeed, Rashidi noted with a degree of curiosity and even a touch of disappointment he couldn't quite understand, the Mahdi barely acknowledged the Pakistani leader at all.

Muhammad Ibn Hasan Ibn Ali took his seat at the far end of the table. Rashidi quietly slipped into the dining room and took a seat along the wall, just behind the Mahdi and off to his left.

"Get up," said the Mahdi abruptly, and Farooq complied, though he did not immediately make eye contact.

"Now sit, and let us begin," the Mahdi added.

Farooq again did as he was told, taking a seat in the chair at the far end of the table, directly opposite the Mahdi. Rashidi couldn't imagine the Pakistani had ever been treated like this or spoken to so brusquely in the nine years he had been ruling the Islamic world's only nuclear-armed power.

"Are you ready to join the Caliphate?" the Mahdi asked, seething as far as Rashidi could tell and evidently ready to explode at the slightest provocation. "Your dithering thus far has been noted."

"Pakistan is ready," Farooq replied. "Indeed, we are honored to join the Caliphate, and we look forward to your enlightened leadership."

Rashidi could have sworn he detected an ever-so-slight edge of sarcasm in Farooq's reply, but he privately rebuked himself for being cynical and then felt a flash of fear when he considered the possibility that the Mahdi knew all that he was thinking. Nevertheless, the Mahdi seemed to welcome Farooq's support and did not question the man's sincerity, at least not directly.

"What token do you bring of Pakistan's desire to be part of the Islamic kingdom?" the Mahdi asked.

Farooq did not hesitate. "We offer you the keys to the kingdom."

Rashidi quietly gasped. He knew this was what they had come for, but it was hard to believe it was really happening right before his very eyes. There were many in the Iranian high command who privately doubted the Sunni Muslim leaders of Pakistan would ever willingly hand over outright control of their nuclear missiles to a Shia, even if it was the Islamic messiah. The Pakistanis were not Persians. They were not Arabs. Theirs was a rich and proud and complicated history, vastly different from his own.

"You have brought the launch codes?" the Mahdi asked.

"I have, Your Excellency."

"Have you done so willingly?"

"I have, Your Excellency, with the unanimous vote of the Pakistani Security Cabinet and the full support of all my senior generals. It pleases me to inform you that I am now prepared to turn over to you full control of all 273 of Pakistan's most advanced ballistic missiles, each of which possesses a nuclear warhead developed by our own A. Q. Khan."

Transfixed by the unfolding developments, Rashidi looked to the Mahdi, who suddenly seemed more surprised than pleased.

"273?" he asked. "Why was I under the impression there were only 173?"

"Well, it would not do for our enemies to know the full scope of our offensive capabilities," Farooq noted. "Perhaps we have allowed the misperception to develop that there are fewer missiles in our arsenal than there actually are."

"Perhaps," the Mahdi said with a slight smile. "Continue."

"May I?" Farooq asked, signaling his desire to come closer.

The Mahdi waved him forward, so Farooq got up from his seat and walked across the dining room, pulling up a chair beside the Twelfth Imam. Then he lowered his voice, though Rashidi wasn't sure why. Was it so all the security men couldn't hear him? Rashidi discreetly leaned in and tried to catch as much of the conversation as he could.

"Your Excellency, in the twentieth century, the main threat to Pakistan was, of course, from India," Farooq began. "But we now live in a new age, do we not? Your arrival on the international stage has been a game changer. Your ability to persuade the Saudis to join the Caliphate, along with the Egyptians and the Lebanese and so many others, is rapidly changing the geopolitical equation. The Islamic kingdom is rising fast, and the world is doing nothing serious or decisive to stop you. I believe you now have the opportunity not only to annihilate the Jews—a goal that my government and I fully support—but also to humble the arrogant Americans and the feckless Europeans, along with all the world's powers. You have the opportunity to build not just an Islamic empire but a global empire, something no other Islamic leader has ever been able to accomplish before. I have come to tell you that the government of Pakistan stands ready to serve you. We believe with all our hearts that Islam is the answer. Jihad is the way. The Qur'an is our guide. The Prophet is our model. But now you are our caliph and king. And so you must know the full extent of the arsenal—the power—now at your fingertips."

"You have all the documentation, the authorization codes, and launch instructions?"

"I do," said Farooq. "Let us begin."

EN ROUTE TO WASHINGTON, D.C.

The FBI had moved quickly to assume custody of Najjar Malik from the Cape May Police Department and had put Najjar on a Bureau jet back to the nation's capital. The CIA and the White House were immediately notified of the arrest, and the president insisted the story not be leaked to the press under any circumstances. Rather, he wanted Najjar to be interrogated thoroughly and then given an hour with his family before being placed in solitary confinement at the FBI building in Washington until further notice.

All this was explained to Najjar before he was handcuffed, shackled around the feet, blindfolded, and gagged for the thirty-seven-minute flight to Andrews Air Force Base, where he arrived under secure conditions with no possibility of the media catching wind of it. The cuffs were terribly uncomfortable as they dug into his wrists, but Najjar didn't mind. He wasn't anxious at all but felt very much at peace with himself and what he had accomplished.

He was willing to pay the price for his escape, and though as of yet he had not expressed remorse for breaking into the house in Oakton, Virginia, and "borrowing" the owners' cell phone and their red Toyota Corolla, he did feel terrible about it. Indeed, he silently vowed to repay the owners for all the trouble he had caused them, including the broken window in their basement.

But now, he concluded, was not the time to say such things. Rather, he told himself, now was the time to rest, the time to sleep, perchance to dream about reuniting with Sheyda and sharing with her all the adventures he had had.

DAMASCUS, SYRIA

"Dr. Birjandi, wake up," said the young Iranian officer. "We're here."

Birjandi rubbed his eyes more out of habit than necessity as he sat up in the backseat of the luxury sedan.

"What time is it?" he asked, emerging from a very deep slumber.

"It's getting late. Come, we need to get you into your quarters, and then I must return to Iran."

"But I don't understand," Birjandi said, trying to get his bearings. "Where are we now? What is this place?"

"Damascus."

"Yes, yes, of course, but where?"

"An air base."

"Which one?" Birjandi asked.

There was a long pause.

"Which one?" he pressed.

There was another long pause, and Birjandi could hear some whispering.

"We have just entered the Al-Mazzah Air Force Base," the young officer finally replied. "They have a private room ready for you in the officers' quarters. I'll lead you up there and bring your personal effects. I will explain to you the facilities and help you get acclimated to the room, and then I must go."

"Perhaps you should stay," said Birjandi, yawning. "I could use your help."

"I have my orders," the officer said.

"So do I," Birjandi replied.

"Please, Dr. Birjandi, you'll be fine," the officer assured him. "You need a good night's rest. You have a big day ahead of you. And I've been told that when the higher-ups are ready for you, they will send someone to your room to summon you."

"And breakfast?"

"It will be at 8 a.m. sharp. I've already informed them how you like your tea and toast. Don't worry about anything."

Birjandi turned away. The last line would have been laugh-out-loud funny if the situation weren't so dangerous. *Don't worry about anything?* Did this young man have any idea how close the Middle East was to full-scale, all-out nuclear war? Yet somehow the import of the moment appeared to be lost on the young Iranian soldier, and Birjandi saw no point in trying to educate him at this late hour.

"Very well," the old man said at last. "Let's get on with it."

As he was helped out of the Mercedes and up to the guest room, Birjandi couldn't care less when breakfast was or what they were serving. He wasn't listening as the young officer talked him through where the light switches and the toilet and shower were. He paid little attention as the man explained what drawers he was putting Birjandi's clothes into or any of the other myriad details pouring from his mouth. Rather, Birjandi was playing catch-up, desperately trying to analyze what was happening and why. He hadn't intended to fall asleep on the long journey. To the contrary, he had intended on praying without ceasing, urgently seeking the Lord's wisdom at this fateful hour. But he was old, and he was increasingly frail, and the rigors of the trip had overwhelmed him. He had slept, and slept soundly, and in so doing he had lost precious time.

While the young officer droned on, Birjandi tried to clear the fog from his thoughts and make sense of what few facts he knew. Apparently he was now at Al-Mazzah, one of the most important military bases in all of Syria, though not the largest. The base previously had been the home of the Damascus International Airport until a new, more modern facility was built in another part of town. Now Al-Mazzah was the home of the Syrian strategic air command.

Over the years, Birjandi had heard from sources as reliable as Hosseini and Darazi that the Syrians kept the bulk of their chemical weapons nearby, in deep underground caverns. And the entire base, allegedly, was ringed by the world's most sophisticated air defense system, the S-300, designed and built by the Russians. If that was true, and he had little doubt it was, that meant Al-Mazzah was among the most effectively guarded bases in the entire Arab Republic. It would, therefore, be a reasonably safe place to quietly bring the Mahdi.

Then again, why bring the Mahdi here at all? Why would the Twelfth Imam want to be in Syria? And why would he want to meet with an old man like Birjandi here, of all places? Such questions had been bothering him all day, but it wasn't until the young officer said good-bye, clicked off the lights, and left the room—locking the door behind him—that the answer finally came.

Birjandi was in the bathroom washing his face when the truth he had been nibbling at all evening suddenly dawned on him so plainly he wondered why it hadn't been this obvious before. He turned off the faucet and stood ramrod straight, water dripping from his face and hands. *The Mahdi was going to launch the last jihad against Israel from right here in Damascus.* He was sure of it. And now it dawned on him, too, that the Mahdi and his forces had pre-positioned the remaining two nuclear warheads here at Al-Mazzah. They were planning to fire both warheads—most likely with a massive salvo of chemical weapons—at the Zionists to destroy the Jews once and for all. Then, presumably, when the evil act was complete, the Mahdi planned to go on worldwide television and declare victory.

And what a victory it would be. To destroy Israel after Israel had launched a devastating preemptive strike would be even more unexpected and dramatic than if the Mahdi had ordered a sneak attack against the Jews in the first place. Few in the West now believed the Caliphate could prevail. Indeed, Iran and her allies appeared to be on the ropes. Many in the Muslim world were questioning the power of the Twelfth Imam. They had been rattled by the effectiveness of the Israeli first strike and had been left unsure as to the Mahdi's ability to counterpunch. The Mahdi was playing the expectations game more shrewdly than even Birjandi had anticipated.

Birjandi dried his face with a hand towel and proceeded to change into his pajamas, climb into bed, and slip under the sheets. A gust of wind began blowing across the base, stirring up dust and rattling it against the windows. But the old man barely heard any of it. All he could think about were these questions: How was the Lord going to stop the Mahdi, and what role did he want Birjandi to play? God had clearly brought him to the forefront of the drama for a reason. But what reason was that?

37

Rashidi couldn't believe it. The deal was done. Now the Mahdi and President Farooq were recording a joint "press conference" that would be aired in a few hours on Pakistan's state television network as if it were a live event. The rationale was that the Islamic world would wake up to what they believed to be a major news event happening in Kabul in real time, but by taping the event, the Mahdi and Farooq would have plenty of time to get to other, safer locations, lest the Israelis or the Americans try to attack the site of the press conference while it was under way.

"Good morning. I would like to begin by making a brief statement," said Farooq, standing behind a large wooden podium before a bank of microphones and sporting a charcoal-black suit with a crisp white shirt and a red power tie. He looked directly into the cameras in the back of the room. "The Islamic Republic of Pakistan today formally announces that we are joining the Caliphate and following the wise and courageous leadership of Imam al-Mahdi."

At this, the Mahdi's security staff took dozens of flash pictures with cameras they had brought for the occasion, helping to further create the appearance of a room full of reporters.

"In keeping with the spirit of unity and true partnership of this important new alliance, we are putting full control of Pakistan's 345 nuclear-tipped, long-range ballistic missiles into the hands of the Lord of the Age."

This statement brought another burst of flash photography, and Rashidi found it clever that Farooq—no doubt at the direction of the

Mahdi—had this time significantly inflated the number of Pakistani warheads to once more keep the world, and especially the Zionists, off balance.

"On behalf of my Cabinet and the Pakistani legislature," Farooq continued, "I can say that I have full confidence Allah will give Imam al-Mahdi divine wisdom to use these missiles and these powerful warheads to further build the Caliphate and bring forth justice and peace here in this region and around the world."

More flash photography.

"And let me add that the government of Pakistan wishes no harm to the people of India or their government," Farooq said. "We seek no hostilities with India, and we do not believe that our joining the Caliphate warrants any concern on the part of New Delhi. The only ones who should shudder in fear because of this dramatic and powerful new alliance are the filthy ones who currently occupy the Holy Land of Palestine but will soon be eradicated from the face of the earth, *inshallah*."

After more pictures, the Pakistani president stepped aside. Then a broadly smiling and apparently very contented Twelfth Imam strode to the podium in his black robes and addressed the handful of security and technical staff in the nearly empty room, none of whom, of course, would be shown on television.

"Ladies and gentlemen, it is a joy and an honor to be here in Kabul this morning," the Mahdi began. "I am grateful to Afghan president Zardawi for welcoming us to his capital and providing us a secure and quite lovely location to hold these vital discussions. And I want to say that I warmly welcome the Islamic Republic of Pakistan into the Caliphate, and I accept the gift of the nation's nuclear arsenal. This is a historic day in the long journey of the Islamic kingdom and one that will not be forgotten. As all of you know, we are engaged in a holy jihad against the infidels who currently occupy Palestine. We have been attacked by those infidels, and we are fighting back with the courage of our forefathers. With Allah's help, we would prevail over the Zionists anyway. But we accept this nuclear arsenal because we believe it is, in fact, a gift from Allah to help us finish the task at hand."

The security men in the room had been given slips of paper with questions they were supposed to shout at the end of the press conference, and they dutifully did their jobs. But the Mahdi and Farooq abruptly left the room as an aide to the Pakistani president stepped in to inform the alleged press corps that the event was over and the leaders "will not be taking questions at this time."

Rashidi quickly grabbed his briefcase and raced to catch up with the Mahdi, who was already saying good-bye to Farooq and climbing back into his bulletproof SUV. Rashidi waited for the all-clear from the security team and then climbed into the SUV as well and pulled the door shut behind him. He glanced at the Twelfth Imam, whose smile was nowhere to be seen.

"Get me to Damascus," snapped the Mahdi, and with that the motorcade began to roll.

DAMASCUS, SYRIA

It was just after four in the morning when the convoy of ambulances carrying General Jazini and Jalal Zandi finally arrived at the Al-Mazzah air base on the outskirts of the Syrian capital. As the convoy cleared security, Jazini and Zandi were immediately greeted by a large man in a ribbon-bedecked uniform. The military man sported a square jaw and piercing green eyes and was flanked by Abdol Esfahani.

"General Jazini, greetings in the name of Allah," said the man. "I am General Youssef Hamdi. Welcome to Damascus."

"It's an honor to be here, General," Jazini replied, saluting the man smartly.

"Please, please, it is my honor," Hamdi responded. "And of course you know Mr. Esfahani. He has been hard at work setting up secure communications for you between here and your new command center in Tehran."

"Yes, thank you," Jazini said. "How is everything coming along, Abdol?"

"I think you and Imam al-Mahdi will be very pleased."

"Just what I wanted to hear," said Jazini, who then turned back to the Syrian. "And this is the man I was telling you about: Dr. Jalal Zandi, the jewel of the Iranian atomic program."

"What a pleasure to have you here, Doctor," said the Syrian general, vigorously shaking his hand. "Have you been to Damascus before?"

"No, never," Zandi said.

"Then you're in for a real treat. You've come to the oldest continuously inhabited city on the planet."

"And here I thought Jericho held that honor."

"The Palestinians would love to have you believe that, wouldn't they?" Hamdi said. "But that's mere propaganda—and lame propaganda at that. Jericho is no great city. It's not a capital. It's not the epicenter of a great empire. Jericho is a mere village—small and dusty and old, to be sure, but hardly continuously inhabited. Damascus is the oldest and greatest city in the long history of the earth. And from what I surmise, we're about to make history once again, aren't we?"

Zandi said nothing.

"Yes, we are," General Jazini said. "And we'd best be getting started. Events are moving quickly now, and we have no time to spare. I trust all of the accommodations we requested are prepared."

"They are indeed," said the Syrian general. "But I have a recommendation."

"What's that?"

"For the sake of security, I recommend we move one warhead to one of our premier missile bases, just outside Aleppo," General Hamdi said. "In the event that the Zionists—Allah forbid—launch a surprise attack on us, it would be wise to have an insurance policy, don't you think?"

Zandi certainly did not think so. "General Jazini, with all due respect, I must weigh in against that idea," said Zandi, knowing he was stepping beyond his jurisdiction.

"And why is that?" Jazini asked.

"Yes, why is that?" the Syrian echoed.

"As you know, General, the Mahdi personally put me in charge of making sure these two warheads are properly attached to the nose cones of two Scud-C ballistic missiles, and I intend to do just that," said Zandi, doing his best to maintain his composure. "It will be difficult enough to attach one of the warheads in the severely limited time the Mahdi has given me. I certainly cannot attach the second one if it is not even on the premises but rather hundreds of kilometers away. And believe me, there is no one in Syria who knows how to do my job, and even if there were, they could not do it half as well—or half as fast—as me."

Before Jazini could respond, General Hamdi interjected.

"General Jazini, the doctor has a point," said Hamdi. "But with regard to the threat of a Zionist first strike, I know whereof I speak. And you have seen it firsthand for yourselves. Take my word for it, if the Zionists get even a whiff of the fact that you have moved nuclear warheads onto Syrian soil, they are going to unleash a devastating first strike against us unlike any in history, and you can rest assured this base will be one of the first to come under withering attack."

Zandi sensed the Syrian was about to prevail, but he took one last shot.

"General Jazini, please, let me do my job," Zandi pleaded. "I can have the first warhead fitted on a Scud-C by dinner, if I start right now and if I have the proper team and tools. As soon as I'm finished, you can move the missile wherever you want, and I'll start on the next one. But the Mahdi is supposed to be here by noon, and what am I to say— what are you to say—if one of the warheads has been moved without his permission and without being attached to a missile?"

"Are you a lunatic?" Hamdi pushed back. "Dr. Zandi, surely you must be joking! If we do what you say, if we try to move a ballistic missile off this base—especially one equipped with a nuclear warhead— every intelligence agency in the world is going to see it, starting with the Americans and the Zionists! And you'll have lost the element of surprise and lost the war for sure. Please tell me you are not the chief strategist for the Mahdi's war effort!"

Esfahani looked stricken. He had never been involved in the upper echelons of military strategy and certainly not in wartime, and his inexperience was showing.

"Fine," Zandi said. "Then let me attach the warhead to the Scud by sundown, and you can put it on the launchpad. Then you can transport the second warhead to Aleppo and I will go with it and attach it to another missile there. The point is—"

"*Enough!*" Jazini cried. "*Enough!* This is not a democracy. I will run this operation, not the two of you. Dr. Zandi, you have until three o'clock this afternoon to have one warhead fitted on a missile and ready to be fired, and not a minute more. General Hamdi, you will provide everything Dr. Zandi needs, and you will keep me updated every half hour. Understood?"

Both men nodded.

"Very well, then get started, and show me to my office, Abdol. We have much work to do."

HIGHWAY 48, WESTERN IRAN

Dressed as Revolutionary Guards, their SUV packed with every weapon and all the ammo and comm gear they had stashed at the safe house, David Shirazi and his team (minus Matt Mays) raced for Damascus. According to Zalinsky, the journey to Al-Mazzah was roughly 1,800 kilometers, or just over 1,000 miles. Assuming they could maintain an average speed of eighty miles an hour, and assuming no traffic—and no mechanical breakdowns and no other stops or interruptions, not even for food or bathrooms—it would take them thirteen and a half hours to reach their destination. They had no idea what they'd do when they got there, but they had plenty of time to think about it on the way.

David had already been driving for nearly seven hours. It was now 6:14 in the morning, and the sun was just coming up behind them. They had begun by taking Route 2 northwest from Karaj to the Iranian town of Qazvin, then had turned southwest toward Hamadan. Now they were on Highway 48, heading west to Qasr Shirin, the last town before the Iraqi border. Torres, Fox, and Crenshaw were all exhausted, and when David had urged them to get some sleep while he drove in order to be ready for whatever was ahead, none of them had pushed back. They were snoring away now, and thus for all practical purposes

David was alone, but for the Predator drone flying high and silent far above them.

The Predator, interestingly, had been Zalinsky's idea, and he'd promised not to tell Director Allen or the president for as long as possible. But it would give him and the rest of his team at Langley an eye in the sky, the ability to track David's progress and keep watch for trouble.

The first major challenge, David knew, was going to be crossing the border into Iraq. The techies at CIA headquarters had quickly whipped up fake Revolutionary Guard IDs for all four men, based on the design of Omid Jazini's ID, which Torres had digitally photographed and uploaded to Langley. Once the design had been downloaded back to them, Torres had printed out the IDs and laminated them using equipment at the safe house. They certainly looked like the real thing to David, but they didn't have the proper magnetic code on the back, just a facsimile of one. Could they bluff their way through? He had no idea, and even if they could, they still had to cross the Iraqi border into Syria a few hours later.

FORT MEADE, MARYLAND

Eva Fischer picked up the phone on her desk and speed-dialed Zalinsky.

"You're calling me directly," he said when he answered. "This must be bad."

"It is, Jack."

"How bad?"

"This one needs to go to the president."

She explained the flurry of satphone calls the NSA had intercepted over the past few hours and that she and her colleagues were feverishly trying to translate. There was very little news about the location of the Mahdi or any of his current war plans, but there was growing evidence that an Israeli missile attack had accidentally killed five Iranian children in downtown Tehran. One report said they were all girls, but Eva said several other calls indicated the gender of all the deceased was not yet clear. Police reports that were being called up the chain of command to the staff of Ayatollah Hosseini and President Darazi said the dead children ranged in age from nine to fifteen years old.

"The calls indicate the state-run satellite networks have some very grisly video," she told him. "The Ayatollah has authorized the stations to begin airing the footage within the hour. This one's about to hit the fan, Jack. If what the people on these calls are saying is true, international opinion is going to turn against Israel any moment."

"E-mail me the call transcripts right away, Eva," Zalinsky said. "You're right. I need to get this upstairs right away."

38

It was just after 10 p.m. on Sunday when Roger Allen and Tom Murray arrived at the West Wing and were immediately ushered into the Oval Office, where President Jackson and his chief of staff were waiting for them.

"I was told to brace myself for the worst," the president sighed, motioning them to take a seat on the couches while he got up from behind the *Resolute* desk and came over to sit with them.

"I'm afraid that's right, sir," Allen began. "We have a serious situation, Mr. President."

"Go ahead; lay it out for me."

"Well, sir, we have evidence that an Israeli air strike accidentally hit a school bus or some similar vehicle in downtown Tehran."

"Accidentally? What does that mean? And are there casualties?"

"I'm afraid there are, sir. Five children are dead."

Tom Murray picked up the story from there. He briefed the president on the details they had so far. He said they couldn't be 100 percent certain whether this was a strike from a fighter jet or a drone, but from looking at satellite images, the initial damage assessment suggested it was a drone attack. That's what was leading him and his colleagues to surmise that this was an accident.

Murray then pulled out a portable DVD player he'd brought with him and showed the president and chief of staff a two-minute clip of gruesome news footage from the scene, complete with the charred bodies of several little girls, their chadors nearly completely burned away, one of them holding the remains of what appeared to be a small stuffed animal.

Jackson winced and could look no further.

"How could this have happened?" the president fumed. "Don't the Israelis know better than to do something so stupid, so foolish? How could they put us in such an awkward situation? It's unconscionable!"

"The Israelis have very strict protocols, Mr. President," Director Allen explained calmly. "They've learned the hard way over the years, mostly through mistaken drone attacks in Gaza that killed innocents and created bad headlines. The only way the IDF would have authorized that drone to fire a missile at a vehicle—especially in the middle of Tehran during such an internationally condemned war—is if they thought they had ironclad evidence that the people in that vehicle were high-value targets."

"But these weren't high-value targets, for heaven's sake. Those charred bodies on the screen are innocent, defenseless children."

"That's why it's clearly a mistake," Allen repeated. "It's obviously not Israeli policy to kill civilians. Indeed, they take every precaution to prevent such tragedies from happening. But mistakes do happen, sir. We make them too. Our enemies try to hang us with our mistakes, and they're going to try to hang the Israelis. With your permission, I'd like to call Zvi Dayan, the director of the Mossad. I want to talk to him off the record and get the real story. I'm sure they're mortified by all of this, and I'm sure they'll be honest with us about what happened and why. And while I'm on a secure line with Zvi, I think we'd better tell him we've got two of his men in custody inside Iran."

"No," the president said firmly. "Not yet. Don't talk to the Israelis. They should be calling us to give us a heads-up on this. But they haven't, and it's going to cost them. I'm sick and tired of Asher Naphtali driving the agenda in the Middle East. I warned him not to strike Iran first, but he wouldn't listen. Now the whole world is against him, and he's going to start losing public opinion here in the U.S., too."

Surprised by how vehement the president was, Allen tried a different angle to get permission to call Dayan and open a back-channel dialogue. But Jackson wouldn't hear of it. His relationship with Naphtali had always been strained, but this, Allen feared, could prove a very troubling turning point. "Sir, at the very least I need to let them know we've got two of their Mossad agents in custody," Allen pressed.

"Why?" the president shot back. "They were interfering in one of our operations. They're lucky they're not dead. I'll tell the Israelis when I'm good and ready, but I'm certainly not going to tell them now."

"Mr. President, it's not just about these two agents," Allen noted as tactfully as he could. "It's about the information we've recovered from Omid Jazini's apartment. We now know the warheads are being moved to the Al-Mazzah air base in Damascus. We know, or at least we strongly believe, that the Mahdi is headed to the same base. We can surmise, therefore, that the Iranians and the Syrians are getting ready to attach those two warheads to missiles, probably to some Scud-Cs. The probability that they will be fired at Israel in the next twenty-four hours is very, very high."

"What are you saying?" the president asked.

"I'm asking what you want us to do to stop it, sir," Allen replied. "I can brief the defense secretary and the joint chiefs. I'm certain we can provide all the intel they'd need to launch a decisive air strike against the Al-Mazzah base in the next few hours. But it seems only fair that we at least let the Israelis in on what we know so they can be on full alert."

"Roger, you're out of line," said the president. "Your job is to give me information and analysis. But the CIA doesn't make policy. I make policy."

"I understand, sir," Allen replied, "but I'm just trying to—"

The president cut him off. "I know what you're trying to do, and I'm telling you it's not your place. You want me to launch an attack against Damascus and the Mahdi? You want us to start a whole new war? That's not what the American people want from me. I was elected to prevent wars in the Middle East, not start new ones or pour fuel on fires already burning."

Then the president turned to Murray and asked, "Where did you get this footage? Has it been broadcast to the world yet?"

"No, sir," Murray said. "We intercepted it from a state-run news crew on the scene. They were uploading it to the main studio. We have intercepted phone calls from the Ayatollah's office authorizing this footage to be shown at 7 a.m. to lead the morning news."

"How long from now is that?"

"About twenty minutes, sir."

The president suddenly stood, catching the others off guard and forcing them to stand as well.

"We need to drive this story," said the president. "We need to leak it, and then we need to manage it."

He turned to his chief of staff and told him to provide everything they knew—including the video footage—to the Associated Press, *New York Times*, and CNN.

"Actually, start with CNN, but make certain there are no White House or CIA fingerprints on this," the president insisted. "Give it to these reporters on deep background, but make sure the story begins to break quickly, before the Iranians break it. That's why I'd recommend you go with CNN first. Then, once the news does break, we'll be asked to comment. At that point, call the White House press corps in immediately. I want to make a statement and take questions. This war has to stop. The Israelis have to stand down. And right now I'm the only one who can make that happen. You gentlemen are dismissed. Good night."

DAMASCUS, SYRIA

While it was still late Sunday evening in Washington, it was dawn in Damascus. The warmth of the rising sun was beginning to creep through the windows of the guest room to which Birjandi had been assigned, but he hadn't slept. He remained now where he had been all night, on his knees at the foot of the bed, earnestly pleading for the Lord to end this war and protect the people of Israel and protect all the people of this region from the genocidal plans of the Twelfth Imam. Birjandi had long warned the men he discipled that "the most dangerous corridor on the planet is the corridor between Tehran and Tel Aviv," and tragically his instincts were being proved correct.

The more he prayed for God's grace, the more the Twenty-Third

Psalm burned in his heart. Throughout the night, he had found himself repeating it from memory every few hours, meditating on its meaning, chewing on it again and again, savoring every word and every nuance, and now he did so again.

"'The Lord is my shepherd; I shall not want,'" Birjandi said to himself, not wanting even to whisper lest he be overheard by agents of the Mukhabarat. *"'He makes me to lie down in green pastures; He leads me beside the still waters. He restores my soul; He leads me in the paths of righteousness for His name's sake. Yea, though I walk through the valley of the shadow of death, I will fear no evil; for You are with me; Your rod and Your staff, they comfort me. You prepare a table before me in the presence of my enemies; You anoint my head with oil; my cup runs over. Surely goodness and mercy shall follow me all the days of my life; and I will dwell in the house of the Lord forever.'"*

What weighed most heavily on his heart and soul was the fact that in just a matter of hours, the Mahdi would arrive and summon him for their first face-to-face meeting. The Mahdi would be expecting to meet a true disciple, a faithful servant and supplicant, not just a Twelver but Shia's leading authority on the Twelfth Imam and Islamic eschatology. Birjandi desperately needed Christ's wisdom. He didn't want to go to such a meeting with a demon-possessed tyrant at all, but he was beginning to resign himself to the fact that the Lord might be in this, that the Lord might actually be preparing a table before him in the presence of his enemies. If that was really the case, then he certainly didn't want to enter such a meeting in his own strength. He wanted to truly be able to say, "I will fear no evil; for you are with me."

As he repeated his favorite psalm for the umpteenth time, another passage came to mind, a piece of Scripture he had not thought of even once in recent months. The verse was John 12:49, where Jesus said, "The Father who sent me has commanded me what to say and how to say it." At first, it struck Birjandi as odd. Why had that passage occurred to him, and why now? He knew that Jesus loved the Father and did only what the Father wanted him to do. There was nothing new in that truth. But then it struck him that he had never really applied the verse to himself. He was not, after all, a public speaker, or at least he had not been for many years since retiring from the seminary and since the passing of Souri and his decision to live a more reclusive life. But as he reconsidered the verse and its meaning for the moment, Birjandi realized that he had literally no idea what to say to the Mahdi, nor how to say it. He certainly didn't want to guess. He wanted—or more precisely, he desperately needed—the Father to command him what words to speak, to fill him with the Holy Spirit and give him the power and authority to say what needed to be said.

The forty-ninth verse in the twelfth chapter of John suddenly became very precious to Birjandi in a way that it never had before. For Birjandi had no illusions. The simple truth was that he could not reasonably expect to come out of that meeting alive if he were to maintain his testimony for Jesus. To profess his love for and allegiance to Christ in the presence of the Mahdi meant his head would surely be separated from his shoulders. He thought he was ready. He wanted to be ready. But he prayed more earnestly than ever before that the Lord would make him readier still by giving him supernatural grace and courage to remain faithful to his Lord and Savior Jesus Christ to the very end.

And then, after hours on his knees in prayer, Birjandi felt the fog beginning to lift from his thoughts. As the rays of fresh, sparkling sunlight began to warm his face, he could feel the Spirit of God speaking directly to his heart, explaining what was happening and why and some of what was about to happen next.

WASHINGTON, D.C.

"This is CNN breaking news. Live from London, here's senior international correspondent Karan Singh."

President Jackson and several senior aides huddled in the Situation Room, watching a bank of television monitors and working on a statement the president would make to the White House press corps in a few minutes. But the report on CNN was not playing out anything like they had anticipated.

"Good evening to our CNN viewers in North America, and good

day to the rest of our viewers around the world," Singh began. "We have breaking news this hour out of Kabul, Afghanistan. CNN has learned that the Twelfth Imam and the president of Pakistan have been engaged in high-level talks there throughout the night, and . . . Hold on. . . . My producer tells me the two leaders are about to make a joint statement. There is an unconfirmed report moving on the wires right now that Pakistan has decided to join the Caliphate, but again, this is an unconfirmed report. Let's go now to a live feed of a press event now under way in the Afghan capital of Kabul."

No one in the Situation Room was paying any attention to the draft of the president's statement. Every eye was riveted on President Farooq as he appeared on all the American cable and broadcast TV news networks and many overseas networks as well. Farooq proceeded to announce Pakistan's decision to turn over full control of its immense nuclear arsenal to the Twelfth Imam. It took a moment for the horrifying truth to register, but as it did, the president demanded to be connected to Roger Allen at the CIA immediately.

"Are you watching this?" Jackson asked.

"Tom and I just pulled into Langley," Allen said. "We're not near a TV yet, but Tom's got Jack Zalinsky on the other line. He's translating Farooq for us right now."

"It's a doomsday scenario."

"I'd have to agree, sir."

"What are our options?" the president asked.

"For that you need the SecDef and the joint chiefs, sir."

"Roger, I'm asking you. Privately. Man to man. What would you recommend right now?"

"Honestly?"

"Honestly. Give it to me straight."

"Mr. President, if it were me, I'd direct the SecDef to contact Carrier Strike Group Nine. They're currently operating in the Indian Ocean. I'd order the launch of two F/A-18 fighter jets off the USS *Abraham Lincoln* to race for Kabul. In the meantime, I'd direct my guys to find out exactly where that live press conference is happening and take out the Mahdi and Farooq right now before they can do any harm. I'd guess we have about thirty minutes. Otherwise, we're about to go from a madman in the Middle East with two nuclear warheads to a madman running a nuclear superpower with more than 300 nuclear missiles, some of them long-range."

Jackson said nothing. He had no idea what to say or do. Part of him knew Allen was right. They had a very narrow window to take action, if they were going to take action at all. But how could he justify killing two leaders in one strike when neither had directly attacked the United States of America? Some in Washington believed in the doctrine of preemption, but Jackson had risen to political power opposing such a doctrine with every fiber of his being. His critics berated him for being "in over his head." If he didn't move decisively now, they would have a field day at his expense. The political price to him and his administration could be catastrophic. But if he ordered a military strike, wouldn't he be ceding the very principle over which he had taken Naphtali to the woodshed?

Even as he considered his rapidly shrinking set of options and weighed the costs of each, a news flash was scrolling across the bottom of the screen on CNN. *"EXCLUSIVE: CNN has learned that five Iranian children in Tehran have been killed in an Israeli missile strike. . . . Ayatollah Hosseini has denounced Israel for 'stepping over a line' and has vowed to 'accelerate the collapse of the Zionist entity' by turning Israel into a 'crematorium.' . . . Israeli leaders have not yet commented on the record, but one unnamed senior military official told CNN that it was possible there had been a 'mistake' and the IDF was 'taking a careful look at the accusation.'"*

Jackson's knuckles were white as they gripped the armrests of his chair. Events were rapidly spiraling out of control. It was not difficult to imagine the Mahdi launching nuclear missiles at Israel—possibly dozens of them—from Pakistan at any moment. His own press conference, therefore, was obviously off. Jackson couldn't possibly go out there now and denounce the Israelis and call for a cease-fire. He couldn't threaten to side with the Russians and the Chinese at the United Nations and support a U.N. Security Council resolution condemning Israel for its "targeting of civilians." That had been his plan. But in an instant the dynamic had changed, and Jackson felt paralyzed, entirely unsure what to do next and bitterly aware that time was not on his side.

39

Dr. Birjandi stopped praying, got off his knees, rose to his feet, and began pacing the guest room, trying to get his mind around the enormity of what the Lord had just revealed to him. The end of Damascus had come. Indeed, its utter destruction was imminent.

The Lord had spoken to him from two Old Testament passages—Isaiah 17 and Jeremiah 49. As Birjandi padded back and forth from one end of his little guest suite to the other, the old man chastised himself for being so focused on teaching his disciples about the prophetic future of Iran that he had failed to ponder the prophetic future of Syria. In his defense, of course, it was only in the last few hours that he had even considered the possibility that Syria was going to be a critical element in this war. So far President Mustafa had not launched an all-out offensive against the Israelis, and Birjandi's thoughts had thus far not been drawn to the Syrian leader or the Syrian capital. But now that he was here, and now that the Lord had opened his eyes and allowed him to see a glimpse of what was coming, it was all beginning to make sense, and Birjandi's fragile heart was racing.

"'The oracle concerning Damascus,'" Birjandi muttered to himself, reciting Isaiah 17:1. "Behold, Damascus is about to be removed from being a city and will become a fallen ruin," the Lord God Almighty had declared through his prophet. The next few verses then revealed that the "fortified city" and the "sovereignty" of Damascus would "disappear" and "fade."

Souri had once read to him another translation of the first few verses of Isaiah 17, and these were even more clear.

A Message concerning Damascus: "Watch this: Damascus undone as a city, a pile of dust and rubble! Her towns emptied of people. The sheep and goats will move in and take over the towns as if they owned them—which they will! . . . Not a trace of government left in Damascus."

As Birjandi then recalled the prophecies of Jeremiah 49:23-27 from memory, he found them just as chilling.

Concerning Damascus. "Hamath and Arpad are put to shame, for they have heard bad news; they are disheartened. There is anxiety by the sea, it cannot be calmed. Damascus has become helpless; she has turned away to flee, and panic has gripped her; distress and pangs have taken hold of her like a woman in childbirth. How the city of praise has not been deserted, the town of My joy! Therefore, her young men will fall in her streets, and all the men of war will be silenced in that day," declares the Lord of hosts. "I will set fire to the wall of Damascus, and it will devour the fortified towers of Ben-hadad."

Not once but twice in the Holy Scriptures, the Lord had foretold the utter and complete future destruction of Damascus. The second of the prophecies clearly indicated the destruction would come by fire. Yet neither prophecy had ever been fulfilled. Yes, Damascus had been attacked and conquered numerous times throughout history, but it had never been utterly destroyed and made uninhabitable. To the contrary, Birjandi knew that Damascus was one of the oldest continuously inhabited cities on the planet, if not the oldest.

As Birjandi considered both texts, he found it odd that neither passage gave a direct indication of when the prophecies would come to pass. The prophecies of Ezekiel 38 and 39, by contrast, said Iran's military (among others) would be judged by the God of Israel in "the last days" of history. Indeed, the prophecies of Jeremiah 49:34-39—also about the future judgment of Iran's leaders—were specifically described as happening in "the last days." Yet as Birjandi reviewed the prophecies regarding Damascus again and again, he found no specific time reference in either passage.

Still, what was important, Birjandi reminded himself, was the context of both prophecies. The thirteenth chapter of Isaiah through at least the nineteenth chapter were all End Times prophecies, as far as Birjandi could tell. Isaiah 13 was about the future destruction of Babylon, and at least twice in that chapter the Hebrew prophet made reference to "the day of the Lord," saying it was "near" and "coming," indicating that these events would occur near but prior to the literal, physical, actual second coming of Jesus Christ back to earth. Isaiah 19, meanwhile, was about the coming judgment of Egypt followed by a tremendous spiritual awakening in Egypt in the End Times. Indeed, one of Birjandi's favorite passages of Scripture, one that gave him hope for the future of the Middle East, was the last few verses of Isaiah 19, in which the Lord declared that after a time of tyranny in Egypt and subsequent judgment, "the Lord will strike Egypt, striking but healing; so they will return to the Lord, and He will respond to them and will heal them." What a blessed future that foretold.

The same was true about Jeremiah's prophecies. The forty-ninth chapter through the fifty-first chapter of Jeremiah all described events the Hebrew prophet indicated would occur in the "last days," from the judgment of the leaders of Damascus and Iran to the judgment of Babylon in the final days of history before the return of Jesus Christ.

Birjandi was well aware that not every prophecy scholar agreed about such things. Indeed, while his wife was still alive, Birjandi and Souri had read more commentaries about such prophecies than he could count and had found disagreements among many of the scholars. But Birjandi knew there was no mistaking the message the Lord had spoken to him; Isaiah and Jeremiah had both written about the same future event . . . and that future was now.

HIGHWAY 5, EASTERN IRAQ

David and his team had cleared through the border crossing more smoothly than expected and were racing across Iraq. Having taken Highway 5 to Muqdadiyah, referred to in classical literature as Sharaban, they had stopped briefly for fuel, topped off their tank, and were now on the road to Baghdad, the war-torn capital of Iraq. All the men were glued to the live press conference from Kabul being broadcast on local Iraqi radio, and they were sickened by what they heard. When it was over, they switched to BBC and heard the news out of Tehran of the five schoolgirls allegedly killed by an Israeli missile, though the BBC didn't use the word *allegedly*. Indeed, they reported it like an intentional attack and a war crime at that.

"Should we even keep going?" Crenshaw asked from the backseat. "I mean, if the Mahdi now has 350 or whatever nuclear missiles, what does it matter if he has two more? He's about to turn Israel into a mushroom cloud. What could we possibly do to stop him?"

The questions hung in the air for a few moments. No one wanted to touch them, not even David. They were logical questions, and the truth was, he didn't have an answer, just a lot more questions of his own.

"How do we know the Paks have really handed control over to the Mahdi?" David finally asked his team.

"What are you talking about, sir?" Fox asked. "Farooq just told the world he gave the Twelfth Imam all his nukes."

"But he's been agonizing about doing so for days, hasn't he?" David noted.

"Perhaps the Mahdi made Iskander an offer he couldn't refuse," Torres said.

"Maybe, but we know Farooq is a Sunni, while the Mahdi is a Shiite. Farooq is not Arab; the Mahdi is. The Pakistanis have always had a proud tradition of separation from the Arab world and of asserting themselves as leaders within the Islamic world. Why would they fold now to the Mahdi—whom they don't even really believe in?"

"What are you trying to say, sir?" Crenshaw asked. "You think Farooq is playing chicken with the Mahdi on worldwide TV and radio? You think he's lying to the Mahdi about giving him control of the nukes? How does that end well for him?"

"Maybe it buys him time," David said. "I don't know. I just know something seemed fishy about that press conference."

"Like what?" Torres asked.

"Where was the press? Where were the questions?"

"That's not unusual, sir," Fox said. "Jackson gives brief statements to the press all the time without taking questions."

"True, but why didn't the Mahdi at least take a question about the death of the schoolchildren in Tehran? Wasn't that an obvious opportunity for the Mahdi to score major propaganda points? Something doesn't add up."

No one said a word, and for the next hundred kilometers or so, they drove in silence, weighing their options and wondering if their mission really had become futile. David feverishly tried to come up with any scenarios in which his team, assuming they got into Syria, could actually penetrate the secure outer perimeter of the Al-Mazzah base and fight their way in to the warheads. But he couldn't come up with one plan that gave them a realistic shot of even getting to the warheads before they were cut down, much less neutralizing either or both of the weapons in a way in which they couldn't be repaired after David and his team were either captured or killed.

David was willing to die for his country. He was willing to die for this mission. But he needed a ray of optimism. He needed a strategy, a plausible one that gave them even a sliver of hope of accomplishing their objective. He didn't believe in suicide. But that's what this mission increasingly totaled up to. He had no confidence that President Jackson would authorize an attack on the Al-Mazzah base, which was the only certain way to destroy both the warheads and the Mahdi, once he arrived there. As for the president quietly informing the Israelis of the intelligence they had gathered and letting them get the job done, David privately put the chances of that as no better than one in ten thousand. It was unconscionable, to be sure. The Mahdi with nuclear warheads and ballistic missiles posed a clear and present danger to the national security of the United States and her allies, especially Israel. The Mahdi was the head of a genocidal, apocalyptic death cult. He had to be stopped before his actions caused the deaths of millions. Yet it was increasingly clear to David that this president was neither willing nor perhaps able to do what was necessary.

But he had pretty much known this from the start. What bothered him most was that it seemed he and his team were willing but apparently unable to do what was necessary. And when that painful thought flashed across his mind, David began to steel himself for the growing likelihood that he would never get home alive. He was driving himself and his team into a lethal dead end. He was doing so because Zalinsky had ordered him to, and he had willingly agreed. They all had. But it was time to face the cold and sober truth: this was a death trap, and there was no way out.

David wished he knew enough Scripture to calm his troubled heart at that moment. But as the road leading toward Damascus continued to speed by under the vehicle, only the words of Alfred, Lord Tennyson came to mind.

> *Half a league, half a league,*
> *Half a league onward,*
> *All in the valley of Death*
> *Rode the six hundred.*
> *"Forward, the Light Brigade!*
> *Charge for the guns!" he said:*
> *Into the valley of Death*
> *Rode the six hundred.*
>
> *"Forward, the Light Brigade!"*
> *Was there a man dismay'd?*
> *Not tho' the soldier knew*
> *Someone had blunder'd.*
> *Theirs not to make reply,*
> *Theirs not to reason why,*
> *Theirs but to do and die:*
> *Into the valley of Death*
> *Rode the six hundred.*

★ ★ ★ ★ ★

JERUSALEM, ISRAEL

Asher Naphtali had barely slept in the past four days. His staff was worried for him and begged him to go to bed and let them manage the war. Even the defense minister and the Mossad director urged him to get some desperately needed shut-eye. But Naphtali said a twenty-minute catnap here and there would suffice. He had a war to win and a nation to save, and he was not going to be caught sleeping on the job.

It was foolish and arrogant, his wife told him. He wasn't an eighteen-year-old. He was no longer the commander of "The Unit," the nation's most elite special operations force. "The people of Israel need you rested and healthy so you can make wise decisions when the time comes," she insisted. But she was having precious little effect.

Now came the most ominous news of all—the Mahdi in full control of 345 nuclear missiles, and just at a time when Israel's stockpile of Arrows and Patriots to shoot such missiles down was running dangerously low.

Naphtali asked an aide for another cup of café afouk, essentially an Israeli version of cappuccino, and then called Levi Shimon at the IDF war room in Tel Aviv.

"Levi, tell me we've heard from Mordecai," the prime minister began, referring to the code name of their mole inside the Iranian nuclear command.

"I'm afraid not, sir."

"What about Zvi's operation to take down Omid Jazini? That was supposed to happen hours ago. What happened?"

"The last I heard, Zvi's men hadn't checked in," Shimon said. "He fears something went wrong, but it's possible everything's fine and they just need to keep radio silence for longer than expected."

Naphtali paced in his private office. He was still in great pain from the wounds he'd sustained during the Iranian terrorist attack at the Waldorf-Astoria just eight days earlier. Indeed, it was a miracle he was alive. But at the moment he wondered if it would have been better if he hadn't survived the attack after all. Then all of this would be someone else's responsibility, not his own.

"Do you have any good news for me at all, Levi?"

"I wish I did," Shimon replied. "And actually I regret to inform you that I just learned two more of our fighter jets have been shot down over Iran."

Naphtali clenched his fists. He couldn't bear to hear any more heartbreak, but he asked the question anyway. "And the pilots?"

"Both KIA, Mr. Prime Minister."

"You're certain?" Naphtali pressed. "Those are both confirmed?"

"I'm afraid so, sir."

"What were their names?"

"They were brothers, sir. The first was Captain Avi Yaron. He was a squadron leader and highly decorated. His twin brother, Yossi, was a captain as well. Both first-rate pilots. Avi was shot down over Tabriz. We believe he died instantly. There was no indication of an ejection. Yossi's jet was hit by triple-A fire over Bushehr. He did eject but was captured and executed immediately."

"Has the family been notified yet?" the PM asked.

"Not yet, sir. I'm just getting the news now."

"Get me their parents' phone number," said Naphtali. "I will make the call myself."

"Yes, sir. Right away, sir."

"And get me some good news, Levi," the PM added. "Quickly."

40

DAMASCUS, SYRIA

General Jazini pulled Esfahani aside. "Have you heard from my son, Omid?"

"No, sir," Esfahani said. "Why do you ask?"

"I've called him twice," Jazini said. "He's not answering his mobile phone. Track him down. I must speak to him at once."

Esfahani agreed and immediately called Commander Asgari, head of the secret police in Tehran, to send agents to Omid's apartment and make sure everything was all right.

HIGHWAY 11, WESTERN IRAQ

Not long after skirting Baghdad, they passed through Fallujah and Ramadi and then turned northwest on Highway 12, paralleling the Euphrates River, toward the Syrian border.

As the hours passed during the trek across the desert, David's thoughts turned again and again to two people—his father and Marseille Harper. It was dawning on him now that it was increasingly certain he would never see either of them again—not in this world, at least—and he began seriously considering taking the risk of calling them before he reached Damascus. He desperately wanted to hear their voices one more time. He wanted to tell each of them that he loved them dearly, that he would give anything to be with them and embrace them. He would not hint to either of them the futility of his mission. He didn't want his last acts to violate his oath to the CIA and the American people. Nor did he want to give them reason to fear. He would need to sound strong. Indeed, he needed to *be* strong—for them and for himself.

He was most concerned about his father. The man had just lost his first love, his wife of four decades, and must be struggling emotionally and physically. What's more, David worried about his father's spiritual future. He didn't know Christ as his Savior. Though his father was no longer a practicing Muslim, David wasn't aware that he had ever heard the gospel before. Certainly, even if his father had heard some Christian teaching or had read some of the Bible, the man had never seriously considered whether Jesus was Savior and Lord. Now that David had made his own decision and was certain that Christ had forgiven him and saved him and that he was going to spend eternity in heaven, he was praying again and again for his father.

There was nothing David could do about his mother now. She was gone, and he couldn't imagine a scenario in which she had received Christ before slipping into eternity. That fact was a bitter pain he would take to his grave. But he himself hadn't known Christ personally when he had seen his mother last. He hadn't known the peril she was in, and in the end he had to leave her fate to a sovereign and loving God. He couldn't take the burden of her eternal destiny upon himself.

But his father was another matter entirely. Now David knew Jesus Christ was the Truth, and the Truth had set him free. He desperately wanted his father to know Christ as well and to receive Christ as his Messiah and King. David knew he had a solemn obligation to do everything he could to share the Good News of Christ's love with his father, though at the moment he couldn't see a way to make that happen.

And then there was Marseille. Just the thought of her made him choke up, and he realized in those moments how deeply and utterly he was in love with her. He had loved her as a boy, as a teenager, and now as a man. He would do anything to get back to her and profess his love to her. Honestly, he had no idea whether she shared that love for him. She certainly cared for him, but there were very few clues as to just how much he meant to her. But he wanted so much to tell her what she meant to him. He wanted to tell her how much he missed her.

The simple fact was, he wanted to propose to her. He wasn't sure if he could bear her rejection if he was wildly misreading her heart. But all he wanted now was to look into her eyes, take her by the hands, bend down on one knee, and ask her to spend her life with him. Maybe she would say yes. Maybe not. But he had to ask. He had to know. He had to try.

It was a pipe dream at this point, and he knew it. But somehow the very prospect of seeing her again and asking her to marry him—however slim, however unlikely, however ridiculous—gave him some inexplicable measure of hope to keep going, keep looking for a way to accomplish his mission and get back home against all odds.

TEHRAN, IRAN

From the IRGC's war room ten stories underneath the largest airport in Iran's capital city, President Ahmed Darazi was coordinating all aspects of the ongoing military and media war against the Zionists. He was working the phones with presidents and prime ministers around the world, urging them to issue strong statements condemning Israel for "murdering our five beloved daughters of Islam." He also urged them to back a United Nations Security Council resolution the Chinese had drafted and were circulating that would censure Israel and call for draconian economic sanctions to be imposed upon the Jewish State until they ended the war and agreed to pay reparations not only to the families of the five schoolgirls but to all the people of Iran who had suffered as a result of Israel's preemptive strike.

It was all theater, Darazi and his inner circle knew. By day's end, if everything went according to plan, the vast majority of Jews in Israel would be incinerated in a nuclear holocaust. But the U.N. resolution was the Mahdi's idea to keep the Israelis off balance and build international sympathy for the Islamic cause.

At precisely 9:30 a.m. local time in Tehran, Darazi finished a half-hour conference call with all of Iran's ambassadors around the world, instructing them to keep up the pressure against the Jews by holding press conferences in every capital showing video of the burned bodies of the five Iranian schoolgirls and calling for boycotts against Israeli goods and services. Then he was given a briefing by Commander Ibrahim Asgari of VEVAK on the status of the Mahdi and Ayatollah Hosseini. With General Mohsen Jazini now operating out of Damascus as the Mahdi's chief of staff, Darazi had brought the VEVAK commander into the inner circle to help coordinate intelligence and security matters and serve as a direct liaison to Jazini and his men.

"The Ayatollah is almost there," Asgari began. "We expect him to arrive in the next ten to fifteen minutes."

"He's almost at Al-Mazzah?" Darazi clarified, sifting through a binder of the latest classified cable traffic of reports from various IRGC intelligence officers around the world.

"That's affirmative, sir."

"Does anyone there know he's coming?"

"Only General Jazini, sir."

"Excellent," Darazi said. "And the Mahdi? What is his status?"

"We just heard from Mr. Rashidi, sir. He says they seem to be on track for a noon arrival."

"Very good. And the preparations at the Imam Khomeini Mosque? How are they coming along? We haven't much time."

"Actually, I just spoke to the watch commander on site," Asgari said. "The new war room there is now fully operational. We've been shifting personnel over there for the past hour, and they are ready for you as soon as you're ready to depart."

"You have a helicopter waiting?"

"It just landed upstairs."

"Then what are we waiting for, Commander? Let's move."

HIGHWAY 12, WESTERN IRAQ

David said a silent prayer for his father and for Marseille, then forced himself to stop thinking about them and return to the pressing matters at hand. He and his team began discussing how best to penetrate the Al-Mazzah air base, but it was soon clear they were getting nowhere.

Yet as David and his men kept considering various scenarios—all of which were built on the premise that the president of the United States was not going to authorize any additional help for them to accomplish their mission—David found himself thinking in an entirely new direction, though he said nothing as he continued to drive. Was there a way to make contact with the Israeli government? Was there a way to tell them that the two warheads were at Al-Mazzah and that the Mahdi would be there soon? At this late hour, the only way he could envision stopping the Mahdi from unleashing a second Holocaust was if the Israelis attacked the Syrian air base. If the Mahdi was dead, would any of his underlings really launch 345 nuclear missiles at Israel? Would the Pakistanis let them? It was a gamble, to be sure, but was there a better scenario? David couldn't think of any.

Going through with it—making contact with the Israelis and giving them top-secret intelligence—would be tantamount to treason. If by some miracle he lived through this nightmare, he could never marry Marseille and live happily ever after in Portland or wherever. He would be sent to a maximum-security prison for the rest of his natural life for breaking who knew how many laws.

But did any of that really matter? Didn't he have a moral obligation to help the Israelis save themselves from another Holocaust? There was no question in his mind that he did. The only question at this point was how he could contact them. The most logical answer was to use Tolik and Gal, the Mossad agents in custody back at the Karaj safe house. But that meant getting Mays involved. Indeed, his entire team would have to know, and David couldn't send them all to prison. They couldn't know. None of them. Not Mays. Not Torres. Not Fox or Crenshaw. If he did this, he'd have to go it alone and pay the consequences alone. That much was certain.

By the same token, he couldn't let Zalinsky or Murray or anyone in the chain of command at Langley know what he was doing. They'd never let him get away with it, and like his own team, he respected them too much to endanger their lives or careers. He didn't always agree with his superiors, but he respected them enormously.

Making his decision to help save the Israeli people felt almost as liberating as receiving Christ as his Savior. Indeed, he was certain that somehow the two decisions were related, though he had neither the time nor the training to understand quite how at the moment. He only knew that when he died and went to heaven and stood before the Jewish Messiah in heaven—probably today—he wanted Jesus to know he had done everything in his power to protect the Jewish people.

The critical question was how best to proceed. How could he make contact with the right people in the Israeli government? He didn't know a soul in Jerusalem or Tel Aviv. He'd never even been there, and he couldn't very well call 411 and ask some operator for the personal phone number of the Mossad chief or the prime minister. Still, as he continued to race through the deserts of western Iraq, David pored over every conversation he'd had with Zalinsky over the years, hoping to remember a name and number of someone he could connect with. Yet he was coming up blank. He thought back through his previous assignments, desperately looking for a scrap he could use in this present moment.

His first posting fresh out of CIA training at the Farm in rural Virginia had been as some assistant to the assistant to the deputy assistant of whatever for an entire year at the new American Embassy in Baghdad. That had been about as boring as he could imagine. Then he'd essentially been a fetcher of lattes for the economic attaché at the U.S. Embassy in Cairo. Lame. Then he'd been transferred to be a communications and intelligence liaison in Bahrain for a SEAL team assigned to protect U.S. Navy ships entering and exiting the Persian Gulf. It had sounded cool when he first heard about the job, but it hadn't been nearly as interesting as he'd hoped. Nor had it put him in contact with anyone in the Israeli military or intelligence services. The same was true of his work in Pakistan, hunting down al Qaeda operatives. Looking back, it seemed strange that he hadn't crossed paths with Israelis, but as best he could recall, he simply hadn't.

He began to wonder if he should have brought Tolik Shalev along for this mission, though he quickly ruled it out again. Still, if he could talk to Tolik in private . . .

Then David remembered something Tolik had said almost offhandedly before they'd set out for Syria. Tolik had alluded to the fact that Israel's mole inside the Iranian nuclear program had "called in" the precise locations of the warheads, allowing Naphtali to order precise air strikes. Was it possible, David wondered, that the mole could have had access to one of the satphones David himself had supplied to the Mahdi through Abdol Esfahani and Javad Nouri? Was it possible that the mole had used one of those satphones to make contact with his Mossad handlers? He would have had to, David concluded. How else could he have been certain the Iranians wouldn't be listening in on his call?

Still, if that were really true, that would mean the NSA had a recording of the call, wouldn't it? Did the team at Fort Meade actually have it buried in mountains of recordings they were ill-equipped to process fast enough and thoroughly enough? Had it been translated? Had it been analyzed? If not, could they find it?

The faster David processed the questions, the faster he seemed to drive. But he certainly wasn't worried about getting pulled over by an Iraqi police officer. They were miles from civilization and cruising across the desert at nearly a hundred miles an hour. In another hour or so, they would be at the Syrian border. But then what?

David's pulse quickened at the possibility of establishing contact with the Mossad, but first he had to carefully and delicately extract the right information from the NSA supercomputers. How? His only contact on the translation team was Eva Fischer. Did he dare bring her into his plan? He didn't want to harm her, either. Perhaps there was a way to get the information from her without making her privy to how he was going to use it.

He had to call her, he decided. He had to try, at least. But he could only make the call when the rest of his team wasn't listening. Which meant he had to make the call when he—or the others—were out of the car. Which meant he couldn't call Eva until they got to the next town and stopped again for fuel and bathrooms. Yet the next town wasn't for another eighty kilometers, and David wasn't sure he could wait until then.

41

The knock on the door came on time and as expected.

"Just a moment," Dr. Birjandi said, reaching for the satphone on the nightstand next to his bed and hiding it under his robes. He felt strongly that he needed to call David and let him know where he was and what was happening, but he was certain his room was bugged. His only chance to make the call, he concluded, was somewhere else on the base. The risk, of course, was that he could never be certain he was truly alone at any given moment, but if the Lord wanted him to make the call, Birjandi knew he would find a way where there was no way.

Birjandi walked slowly to the door of his room and felt for the handle.

"Please forgive an old man," he said, finally opening the door. "I'm not as spry as I once was."

He fully expected some young Syrian military aide to gather him for breakfast, but to his surprise it was actually someone he knew.

"Sabah al-khayr," said the familiar voice.

"Sabah al-noor," Birjandi replied, then added, "Abdol, is that you?"

"It is, indeed, Dr. Birjandi," Esfahani replied. "I'm impressed by your memory."

"At my age, me too," Birjandi quipped.

Esfahani chuckled. "Forgive me for not greeting you and talking to

354 ★ DAMASCUS COUNTDOWN

you more last night when you arrived, Alireza, but I assumed you would be fatigued from the journey."

"That is quite all right. There is nothing to forgive. And indeed I was fatigued."

"May I escort you down to breakfast?"

"Yes, of course," said Birjandi. "I have decided to fast today, if that is all right. But I would be honored to join you. Will it just be you?"

"No, there are several, actually, who are looking forward to spending time with you, including General Jazini and General Hamdi. They are eager to meet the world's leading expert on Shia eschatology."

"Whatever for?" Birjandi demurred. "The end has come. The words of the ancient prophets are coming true before our very eyes."

He meant the words of the Bible, of course, not the words of the Qur'an or other Islamic writings, but for the moment the ambiguity helped him maintain his cover. The question was, how much longer should he wait before revealing himself as a true follower of Jesus Christ, not the Twelfth Imam? As he walked, Birjandi silently prayed John 12:49, that the Father would command him "what to say and how to say it," just as the Father had commanded Christ himself.

After a long night of prayer, Birjandi was at peace about what was coming. He was ready to see the Lord face-to-face and eager to share the gospel with everyone on this base before he departed. He had no idea whether he could persuade anyone to renounce Islam and follow Jesus as he had done, but he was determined to try.

As they made their way down the hallway and onto an elevator, Birjandi looked for a way to begin a spiritual conversation, but once Esfahani had started talking, he would not stop. He went on and on about how thrilled he was to have been chosen for this assignment, to be on the advance team for the Mahdi's visit, and to actually be on the front lines when history was made.

"The world will remember this day forever," Esfahani said proudly.

"It will, indeed," Birjandi replied, though his heart grieved for this young man, for how blind he was and how close he was to perishing forever.

Lord, may I share the Good News of your Son with him right now, on this elevator? Birjandi prayed, but the answer he received was no, he must wait; the time was not yet right.

HIGHWAY 12, WESTERN IRAQ

David and his team were coming up on a medium-size town called Al Qa'im, at the far edge of which they planned to cross the border into Syria. Noticing a small shop selling fruit, snacks, water, soda, cigarettes, newspapers, and the like, David pulled in and told his team they had five minutes and no more. He was going to find a toilet. He'd be right back.

While his men bought some provisions and were glad to stretch their legs, David did track down a toilet room so filthy he couldn't bear to enter it. He found some bushes and relieved himself, then powered up his satphone and speed-dialed Eva.

"Fischer."

"Eva, hey, it's me—but don't say my name out loud."

"It's okay, David; I'm by myself."

"Fine, listen; I need a favor, and I need it fast."

"Sure, what's up? Are you okay? Where are you right now?"

"Yeah, I'm fine, but I can't really say anything else," David replied. "Listen, I need you to hunt down a phone call that would have been made last week, probably Wednesday or Thursday."

He quickly explained precisely what he was looking for. "Can you do that for me?" he asked.

"Yes," Eva said. "But why do you need it?"

"I'm working on a hunch," David explained. "But I don't want Jack or Tom or anyone else there to know about it until I can verify it."

"Why not?"

"I don't think they'll get it," he said. "Not at first."

"Won't get it, or won't approve it?" Eva asked.

"No comment," he said.

"So you're going rogue."

David sighed. She was onto him. "Will you help me?"

"Of course," she said. "What are friends for?"

"You're a great friend, Eva; thank you. Now one more question," David said. "Can you tell me how many other NOC teams are out here in the field with us, and do you know if there's a way I can link up with any of them?"

There was an awkward silence.

"Eva?"

"Yes?"

"Did you hear my question?"

"Yeah, I heard it."

"Well?"

"You want the official answer or the real answer?"

"Both."

"The official answer is, 'The administration is doing everything we can to bring peace to the Middle East and protect the U.S. and our allies from any threat of an Iranian nuclear arsenal,'" Eva said.

"And the real answer?"

"The real answer is you're on your own, my friend."

David was startled.

"There's *no one* out here with us?"

"They pulled everyone out."

"Except us."

"Right."

"Then why keep us in the field?"

"So the president can tell the Israelis with a straight face that he's got men risking their lives to stop Iran."

"But in reality he's cutting us loose."

"Your words," Eva said. "Not mine."

"Thanks for the brutal honesty."

"My pleasure," Eva quipped. "Now listen, don't get yourself killed. You owe me big-time, and if you're dead, I won't be able to collect."

"I'll do my best," he promised.

"You'd better."

They hung up quickly, and sixty seconds later David was back in the driver's seat, leading his team to the Syrian border.

★ ★ ★ ★ ★

JERUSALEM, ISRAEL

Prime Minister Naphtali was infuriated by the Iranian propaganda offensive. But two could play this game, and he decided to turn the tables. He called in the foreign minister, his communications director, and his chief spokesman and told them to immediately release all the details of the grisly deaths of the young American couple honeymooning in Tiberias who had been killed by an Iranian missile.

"What were their names again?" he asked.

"Christopher and Lexi Vandermark," said the communications director.

"Do you have all the details of their itinerary?" the PM asked.

"Yes, sir."

"Their passport photos from when they entered the country?"

"Yes."

"Can you edit together some of the videos you retrieved from security cameras close to the hotel, showing the hotel being hit by the missile and then collapsing?"

"My men are working on it now."

"How soon will it be ready?"

"Twenty minutes. Half hour tops."

"Good, and is there footage of the Vandermarks being pulled from the rubble?"

"There is."

"Use that, too," Naphtali said. "Just don't use any explicit footage of their faces or any close-ups. We don't want to offend the American people. We want to infuriate them with the actions of the Iranians. We want to make this war real and personal to them. But it's late in the States now. Everyone is in bed. Give this material to the Jerusalem bureau chiefs of the major American networks and the *New York Times* and *Washington Post* and *L.A. Times.* Embargo the video until tomorrow morning. But make sure it's the major story every American sees and hears about and reads when they first wake up. And draft a statement for me to release to the press, expressing my condolences to the families of the couple and to the American people and expressing my determination to bring the killers of the Vandermarks to justice."

DAMASCUS, SYRIA

The Iranian and Syrian generals warmly welcomed Dr. Birjandi and asked him and Esfahani to join them for breakfast. They explained what an impressive spread of food had been laid out for such a close friend of the Ayatollah and a special guest of the Mahdi. Birjandi, however, declined to partake of the lavish buffet, saying he was grateful for all the trouble they and their staff had gone to but that he wanted to fast that day to be close to God and most attentive to his will. He did not intend to impress them or draw undue attention to himself or his piety, but his words had that effect anyway. Jazini and Hamdi decided to fast for the day as well, and when they did, Esfahani eagerly followed suit.

"We just checked on the good Dr. Zandi," Jazini said, shifting gears. "He and his team have been working since well before dawn. They seem to be ahead of schedule. At this point, it looks like the first warhead could be attached by as early as one o'clock this afternoon, perhaps two at the latest. Then, *inshallah*, they will begin working on the second warhead. Zandi believes that one could be done by dinnertime."

"But he remains insistent that the two warheads stay together," General Hamdi said. "I still recommend you move the second warhead to Aleppo the moment the first one is attached to the Scud and send Zandi and his team to attach it to another Scud up there. We cannot be too careful."

"I fully agree," Jazini said. "In fact, I've already ordered the transport of the second warhead, Dr. Zandi's reservations notwithstanding. It is currently en route to its launch location. Zandi will go there as soon as the first warhead is attached. I will update Imam al-Mahdi on our progress when he arrives around noon."

Then Jazini turned back to the octogenarian professor. "In the meantime, I have so many questions for you, Dr. Birjandi. Do you mind?"

Birjandi was burning to call David. The time remaining before these warheads were ready to fire was shrinking rapidly, and David was the only person he knew who could do anything to stop the Mahdi and his forces before it was too late. But there was nothing he could do now, Birjandi realized, except answer these men's questions and try to win their trust.

"I would be delighted to answer your questions," he said as cheerfully as he could under the circumstances. "Where would you like to begin?"

AL QA'IM, IRAQ

David asked Torres to give the team one final briefing on the details of Omid Jazini's memo so they would all be ready when they got to the Syrian border. Besides showing their IDs to the border guards, Omid's instructions to all of the Revolutionary Guards entering Syria included a series of authentication codes they would need to recite from memory and answers to a number of challenge questions they could be asked by the Syrian officials standing post. Given how slim their chances of succeeding in their mission were anyway, the last thing David wanted was to be detained or arrested at the border. They had to be ready for any eventuality, but the goal—first and foremost—was to get in without incident. They had already memorized the codes and protocols, and now they reviewed everything as Torres walked them through the procedures for the last time.

David's satphone rang. He apologized to the team for the interruption and encouraged them to keep working. Then he put on a Bluetooth headset rather than hit speakerphone and answered on the fifth ring.

To his shock, it was not Eva.

"David, is that you?" came a completely unexpected voice—and in a whisper, at that.

"Dr. Birjandi?"

"Yes, yes, it's me, but I only have a moment."

David motioned for his team to be silent as he turned up the volume and pressed the Bluetooth receiver closer to his ear.

"Can you speak up, Dr. B.? I can barely hear you."

"I have to whisper, David. I am in grave danger. But you must listen to everything I say because I may not get another chance to call you."

"Where are you? You don't sound like you're at home."

"I'm not," Birjandi said. "I'm in Syria, at the Al-Mazzah air base. Do you know it?"

David couldn't believe what he was hearing.

"Of course, on the edge of Damascus."

"Yes, that's the one," Birjandi said. "The Mahdi summoned me here. He sent a helicopter to get me. I arrived last night, and now I'm at a breakfast with General Jazini and a Syrian general named Hamdi."

"How close are they to you?"

"I am alone for the moment and near a window, which is how I have the satellite connection. The others are just outside the room. That's why I must whisper, and I must be quick. Now listen carefully. There is much I must tell you."

TEHRAN, IRAN

Three military choppers shot low and fast across the skyline of the capital, hoping to make it unclear which one carried President Darazi and confuse any enemy planning to take down his helicopter. As the three approached the Imam Khomeini Mosque near the heart of the city, however, the two decoy choppers peeled off and flew in circles around the mosque, their doors open and sharpshooters looking for any suspicious movement on the ground. Darazi's helicopter hovered for a few minutes over the mosque's enormous courtyard before slowly touching down.

A moment later, despite the fact that the engines were still running and the rotors spinning, the side door of the chopper opened, and a set of steps was lowered to the pavement. Two IRGC security men stepped off first, followed by a military aide to the president and the official government spokesman. Only then did Darazi himself appear in the doorway, and that's when the Mossad's man fired.

The rocket-propelled grenade exploded from the shoulder-mounted tube and sliced across the morning sky, its contrail creating a damning route back to the window of the high-rise apartment building from which it came. But the RPG found its mark. In a millisecond, it ripped off the head of the Iranian president, then detonated inside the helicopter. The result was a monstrous fireball that incinerated everyone within five hundred meters and took the Revolutionary Guards in the other two helicopters completely by surprise.

Both Mossad agents—the spotter and the shooter—grabbed their equipment, including the video camera that had captured the entire event, and bolted out of the apartment as a burst of .50-caliber bullets sprayed into the apartment and shredded everything in sight. The two men raced down the stairwell. When they reached the ground floor, they sprinted out the back door, jumped on separate motorcycles, threw on their helmets, and tore off in opposite directions. Neither one was convinced he would actually make it to safety, but both were already speed-dialing the Mossad ops center in Israel to report the success of their operation.

42

David hung up the phone but said nothing.

"What was that all about?" Torres asked. "Is Dr. Birjandi all right?"

Every man in the SUV was on pins and needles, but David remained quiet for another long moment.

"Hey, man, is everything okay?" Torres pressed. "Talk to us. What's going on?"

David took a deep breath and nodded at a road sign. They were finally entering the area of Al Qa'im that was adjacent to the Syrian border, now just a kilometer or so ahead. That meant they had only a minute to talk, but David was still trying to make sense of what he had just heard.

"You're not going to believe this," he began, "but President Darazi has just been assassinated."

"What? How?" Torres asked.

"A few minutes ago, in Tehran," David said. "Apparently a Mossad team in Tehran fired an RPG at Darazi's helicopter. It exploded on impact and killed everyone on board."

"How does Birjandi know this?"

"General Jazini just got the news from Tehran and told Birjandi. Everyone's in shock."

"Birjandi is in Syria?" Fox asked.

"Yeah, he's at Al-Mazzah."

"What on earth for?"

"The Mahdi summoned him."

"I thought Birjandi had refused," Crenshaw said.

"That's what I thought too," David confessed. "I guess the Mahdi wouldn't take no for an answer this time. He sent a chopper for Birjandi last night. The old man was having breakfast with Jazini and some senior staff at Al-Mazzah when they got the news that the Israelis had taken Darazi out. But there's more."

"What?"

"The Mahdi is due to arrive there at noon."

"That's barely two hours from now," Torres said.

"Right," David agreed. "Both warheads were definitely there on the base this morning, but one is already moving. An Iranian nuclear scientist named Zandi is overseeing a Syrian team that is presently attaching one of the warheads to a Syrian Scud-C missile. Birjandi says the original plan was that by no later than three this afternoon, Damascus time, the unattached warhead was going to be moved, along with Zandi and his team, to Aleppo, where it, too, would be attached to a Scud-C. But Jazini is terrified the Israelis are about to attack Damascus and Aleppo, especially now that they've taken out Darazi. So he started the transport early—but I don't think he ever planned to send the warhead to Aleppo anyway."

"Why do you say that?" Torres asked.

"Because now it's headed to a small air force base outside Dayr az-Zawr. The Syrians have several dozen Scud missiles positioned there, but generally it's not a base that attracts much attention."

"Dayr az-Zawr?" Torres repeated.

"Right."

"That's not far from us," Torres said. "We're actually headed right through there. How are they sending it, by air or by ground?"

"Jazini thought it was too risky to move it by air," David replied. "He's convinced that any aircraft that takes off from a Syrian military base, especially one in Damascus, would be shot down. So they've got it on a Red Crescent ambulance."

"The same way they got Jazini to Damascus," Fox said.

"You got it," David said. "Now look, we're coming to the border crossing. I'll take the lead. The rest of you start thinking through how we're going to intercept this ambulance."

"How long did Birjandi say it would take to transfer the warhead to the other base?" Crenshaw asked.

"An hour and a half," David said. "How soon can we be to Dayr az-Zawr?"

"Maybe a little less than that," said Torres. "It all depends on how fast we get through this checkpoint."

"Okay, boys, look sharp," David said. "This is it."

David didn't say any more, but he knew everyone on his team was thinking the same thing he was. Had Omid's body been found? Did the Mahdi's forces know his computer had been hacked and his IRGC uniforms had been stolen? Had the Syrian border guards been alerted?

JERUSALEM, ISRAEL

Naphtali was just about to dash outside his residence and board an IDF helicopter to make the short hop to the war room in Tel Aviv when an emergency call came in from Zvi Dayan.

"Mr. Prime Minister, don't get on that chopper," Dayan shouted, already hearing the roar of the rotors.

"Don't worry, Zvi," Naphtali shouted back. *"I'll be there in a few minutes. Whatever you have can wait till then."*

"No, it can't, sir. We heard from one of our teams in Tehran. They just took out Ahmed Darazi."

"Did you say Darazi is dead?" Naphtali replied, wondering if he had heard his Mossad chief clearly.

"Yes, sir, not ten minutes ago."

"How? What happened?"

"My team took out his helicopter, Mr. Prime Minister," Dayan said. *"I'll e-mail you the details in a few minutes. But that's why I suggest you stay out of the air—at least for now."*

★ ★ ★ ★ ★

IRAQI-SYRIAN BORDER

This wasn't going as planned. There was an enormous traffic jam at the border crossing. Ahead of their SUV were at least thirty or forty 18-wheel cargo trucks, and for whatever reason, the Syrian border guards were subjecting each to a thorough inspection—and taking their sweet time.

David looked at his watch. It was just after 10 a.m. By the looks of things, they weren't likely to cross the border for at least another hour. And they were at least a good hour away from the air base. That meant if things didn't change quickly, they were going to miss their only opportunity to intercept the warhead before it entered the base and was too secure to be reached.

Suddenly the phone rang. Frustrated but hoping it was Birjandi with more news, David turned on his Bluetooth headset again. But it wasn't Birjandi; it was Eva.

"Hey, it's me," she said. "Can you talk?"

"For a moment."

"Good. I found it."

"Really?" he asked. "You're sure?"

"Hundred percent. You want me to read it to you?"

"Absolutely."

"Now?"

"Yes, go."

"Okay," she said. "Here goes."

First, Eva gave David the phone number that the mole had used to call the Mossad headquarters. David scribbled it down on a sheet of paper while waiting in this horrendously long line. Next she gave him the number of the satphone from which the mole had called, and he wrote that down too. Then she gave him the exact coordinates in longitude and latitude from which the satphone call originated and the precise coordinates of where the call was received.

"Why would I need any of that?" he asked.

"I have no idea," she conceded. "I'm just giving you everything I have."

"Fine. Keep going."

Eva read the short transcript, translated from Farsi.

RECEIVER: Code in.

CALLER: Zero, five, zero, six, six, alpha, two, delta, zero.

RECEIVER: Password?

CALLER: Mercury.

RECEIVER: Authentication?

CALLER: Yes, uh, this is Mordecai. I have very important information to pass on, and I have only a few minutes.

RECEIVER: Go ahead. I'm recording.

CALLER: Eight nuclear warheads being prepared for imminent launch. Repeat: eight nuclear warheads being attached to missiles for imminent launch. Stop. The following are the precise GPS coordinates for each of the warheads. Stop. Can only guarantee these locations as of this call. Stop. Warheads could be moved at any time. Repeat. Time-sensitive information. Stop. Will change soon, and I won't have access to their locations once they are moved. Stop.

Eva asked if he needed her to read the locations of the warheads at the time.

"No, skip that part. Does he say anything else?"

"A little bit, yes. Here it is."

CALLER: Please, I'm imploring you—don't kill me like you killed Dr. Saddaji and like you've killed Dr. Khan. I don't want to end up like the others. That's not what I signed up for. I'm trying to help my country and help you. I've done everything that you have asked. I have risked my life and that of my family. Now I'm begging you to show mercy to us.

RECEIVER: Calm down, Mordecai. Relax. Take a deep breath. We're not going to kill you. Just the opposite. We told you if you helped us we would spare your life and your family's, and we will keep our word.

CALLER: Then what about Saddaji and Khan?

RECEIVER: I cannot give specifics. But I can tell you this: both of those men were working to destroy us. You, on the other hand, offered to help us. We told you if you worked against us that your life could be measured in days, not years. But you have helped us, and we have helped you. Now, I need you to call again in one hour and give us an update on the locations.

CALLER: No. I have done all that I can. I can guarantee you the warheads are where I say they are as I speak. But I can make no guarantees where they will be even a few hours from now. Events are moving rapidly here. I fear I will soon be exposed. This will be my last communiqué. I have done all that I promised, but I cannot do more.

Eva paused.

"And then?" David asked.

"That's it," Eva said. "The call ends. The guy sounds terrified."

"Wouldn't you be?"

"Absolutely."

"The question is, who is this guy, and is he still alive?"

"I just listened to your call with Dr. Birjandi," Eva said. "Didn't he say he was at Al-Mazzah with an Iranian scientist who is going to transfer to the military base where the second warhead was moved?"

"That's right; he did," David said. "What was his name?"

Eva rechecked the transcript. "Zandi."

"That has to be Jalal Zandi," David said. "He and Tariq Khan were deputies to Dr. Saddaji before the Mossad took out Saddaji in the car bombing a few weeks ago."

"Do you think Zandi is Mordecai?"

"I don't know," David confessed. "It's a good question."

"Who else could it be?" Eva asked.

"I'm sure there are several candidates."

"But think about it," Eva pressed. "With Saddaji, Najjar Malik, and Khan out of the picture, Zandi's got to be the most senior nuclear scientist the Iranians have."

"That doesn't prove Zandi is Mordecai," David pushed back. "Dr. Saddaji wasn't a double agent. Neither were Najjar or Tariq. In fact, Najjar only had a change of heart when he had a vision of Christ. Do you think Zandi had a vision too?"

"I don't think you need a vision of Jesus to become a double agent against the Iranians."

"But these men were chosen for their supreme loyalty to the regime and to the Mahdi," David noted. "No, I think it's unlikely Zandi is the mole. It's probably someone a bit lower on the food chain."

"Why else would Zandi be with Jazini working on the final two bombs?"

"Precisely because he's most trusted."

"But wouldn't the most trusted people be the only ones with access to the precise locations of the warheads?" Eva asked. "How many people do you think knew the exact locations of each and every warhead on that Thursday? I'd bet the Mahdi himself didn't know. I'm telling you— it has to be Zandi."

Eva made a compelling case, but David remained skeptical. Two other questions puzzled him at the moment. How had the Mossad found Mordecai, whoever he was? And how had they recruited him?

DAMASCUS, SYRIA

"Dr. Birjandi, you must come with me right away."

The voice was that of Abdol Esfahani. It was stern and dark, and Birjandi's stomach tightened. Esfahani was in charge of all the on-site communications for Jazini, the Mahdi, and the rest of the Iranian team. Was he also assisting the Revolutionary Guards with counterintelligence? Had he intercepted Birjandi's call to David? Birjandi knew the risks and was prepared to suffer the consequences, but he was praying that at the very least he would have the opportunity to speak the Word of God directly to the Twelfth Imam before they executed him.

Esfahani took Birjandi by the arm and began moving him swiftly down a long corridor. In the wake of the news of Darazi's assassination, the entire dynamic on the base had changed. The tenor of every conversation was anxious and edgy now in a way that had not been the case only minutes earlier. Birjandi, constrained by the need for his cane, could barely keep up with Esfahani's pace, but eventually, after numerous twists and turns, various corridors, elevators, and stairs, they entered a room that Birjandi sensed immediately was a power center. He had no idea how many people were in the room or who they were, but he wondered if the Mahdi had arrived early, and if so, whether that meant the launch against Israel was being sped up, as was his own death sentence.

"Alireza, it is good to see a friend amid such sorrow."

To Birjandi's surprise, it was an old and very familiar voice, that of the Grand Ayatollah of Iran, Hamid Hosseini.

"Hamid, is that you?" Birjandi replied, using the Supreme Leader's first name—a rare occurrence since Hosseini had been elevated by the Assembly of Experts to such a lofty position.

"It is, indeed," Hosseini replied, coming across the room, embracing Birjandi, and giving him a Persian kiss on each cheek.

"This is a surprise," said Birjandi. "I understood I was summoned by Imam al-Mahdi, but I had no idea that you would be here as well."

"Forgive me for the secrecy, but obviously we cannot be too careful about broadcasting our movements these days, even to friends."

"Obviously."

"You must be horrified by this news about our friend Ahmed," Hosseini said.

"It is a very dark day," Birjandi said, choosing his words ever so carefully.

"But not for long," said Hosseini. "The Zionists will pay dearly for stooping so low. May Allah rain fire from heaven on these descendants of apes and pigs before the sun goes down."

"Surely divine judgment is coming," Birjandi replied.

"Indeed," the Ayatollah agreed. "I trust you have met Dr. Zandi and are familiar with all he is doing to prepare these two warheads for delivery."

"He and his entire team have been in my prayers all night."

"Mine as well. In fact, I have asked him to take a five-minute break to come up and sit with us and have some Turkish coffee and allow us to pray for him."

"An excellent idea, Hamid, though with your permission I will forgo the coffee, as I am fasting today."

"Of course," Hosseini said. "You have always been the pious one among us, Alireza. Forgive me for not having thought of that myself. I will fast today as well."

"Please, Hamid," Birjandi replied, "do not let my actions influence you. I am not a pious man. I am a sinner in desperate need of God's forgiveness. Today is no day for me to be proud, but humble. Indeed, I seek only to be a humble servant, not a leader of men and certainly not of you. I would never presume such a role."

"All the more reason I should listen to you and heed your example," Hosseini responded.

Just then a military aide announced the arrival of Dr. Jalal Zandi. The Ayatollah helped Birjandi into a large, comfortable, overstuffed chair that Birjandi sensed was in the middle of the large hall. Then Hosseini greeted Zandi and offered him coffee and baklava. Zandi begged the Ayatollah's indulgence and said he was fasting and would prefer not to drink, if this was acceptable to the Supreme Leader.

"We have a room full of men devoted to submitting to Allah and Imam al-Mahdi," Hosseini said with great excitement and even a trace of pride in his voice. "How can the Zionists possibly stand against such servants of the Lord of the Age?"

Hosseini bid Zandi take a seat on the floor in front of him, and Zandi submitted. Then the Supreme Leader asked for an update on Zandi's work. "Is the first warhead attached?"

"Not yet, Your Excellency, but my team and I have found some ways to accelerate the work."

"Will you be done by 2 p.m. as expected?"

"Sooner, I think. I believe we will be finished by noon, when the Mahdi arrives."

"Excellent, and the second warhead?"

"Well, Your Excellency, as you know, it has been loaded into an ambulance and is being driven to that base in the north."

372 ★ DAMASCUS COUNTDOWN

"Yes, I have been briefed on all that."

"Of course, yes, I'm sorry. I just mean to say that it is about 10:20 now, and the warhead should reach the base within the hour. And as soon as my team and I finish our work on this first warhead and present it to the Mahdi, we will race up to the base in the north and start work on that one. I suspect we could have that one attached to a Scud no later than midnight, hopefully much sooner."

"That's the best that you can do?" the Ayatollah pressed.

"Yes, sir, I'm afraid it is. If my colleague Tariq Khan were still with us—or Dr. Saddaji, of course—we could have been finished much sooner. Their deaths have really slowed down this effort, but what can be done?"

"Yes, most unfortunate have been these deaths. But today is the day of reckoning, is it not?"

"Yes, Your Excellency, I believe it will be," Zandi said, his voice quivering somewhat, at least in Birjandi's judgment.

"One more question, Dr. Zandi," said the Supreme Leader.

"Yes, of course, whatever you want to ask. I am here to serve you."

"How powerful are these warheads?" Hosseini asked.

"I beg your pardon?"

"How powerful are they really, Dr. Zandi?" Hosseini repeated. "Will they really kill everyone in Tel Aviv and everyone in Jerusalem as Dr. Saddaji used to promise us?"

"They are among the most powerful weapons man has ever created," Zandi replied. "And yes, each is capable of taking out an entire city."

Birjandi felt a shiver run down his spine. Inwardly he implored the Lord not to allow this madness to go on. He silently pleaded for the peace of Jerusalem, as the Holy Scriptures commanded, and he pleaded for the souls of the men in this room. He continuously asked the Lord to command him what to say and when, where, and how to say it. Time was running dangerously short. Didn't he have to speak out soon?

Just then, General Hamdi came and summoned the Supreme Leader to an emergency meeting with General Jazini. Birjandi and the scientist, however, were told to remain here for the next few minutes until they were notified it was safe for them to return to what they had previously been doing. At that point, dozens of others seemed to clear out of the room; Birjandi presumed they were Revolutionary Guards assigned to protect Hosseini.

"Dr. Zandi?" he asked quietly.

"Yes, sir."

"Who is left with us?"

"No one," Zandi replied. "There are two guards posted in the hallway, outside the doors. But other than that, we seem to be alone."

43

"We're never going to intercept that warhead if we don't get through this line in the next few minutes," Torres said.

David knew Torres was right. The commander of the CIA paramilitary unit had become a good friend and a trusted ally in recent days. But the fact was that getting through this checkpoint, as urgent and important as it was, wasn't David's only objective at the moment.

"Marco, switch spots with me," David ordered, rapidly deciding his course of action.

"What?"

"Get out of the car and come over to this side and get in the driver's seat," David explained. "I'll be right back."

Torres began to comply but asked, "Where are you going?"

"To clear a path for us," David replied. "Just be ready to bolt around these guys when I wave you forward."

David grabbed his satphone and one of Omid's handheld two-way radios, jumped out of the driver's seat, and ran toward the checkpoint. When he had passed twelve or fifteen semis and was out of view of Torres and his team, he ducked between two of the 18-wheelers in line and made the most dangerous call of his life.

To call the Israeli Mossad in a situation like this meant breaking multiple American laws. He knew that—and the risks that came with it—all too well. He knew the call was going to be intercepted by the NSA, recorded, and archived. Eventually Zalinsky, Murray, and Allen were going to know what he had done. So, too, would the president of the United States, the director of the FBI, and the attorney general. In the near term, his best hope was that Eva would be able to run interference for him and bury the call in the mass of so many other intercepted calls from Iran that were neither transcribed nor analyzed. He knew in the long term, however—if there was a "long term" for him—he would likely be arrested, tried, convicted, and sent to prison. But he had made his peace with this. He knew he was doing the right thing. Since he wasn't likely to live through this day anyway, why not let his final acts be in defense of the Jewish people, those so beloved by the Messiah he now worshiped?

David carefully dialed the number Eva had given him. The call went through. It rang once, twice, three times, and then a fourth. On the fifth ring, someone picked up the line and breathlessly said, "Code in." With his heart racing and pulse pounding, David meticulously followed the protocol the Israeli mole code-named Mordecai had used. And then, to his shock, an Israeli accent at the other end said, "Mordecai, thank God you're all right. We thought we'd never hear from you again."

This was it. David had someone from the Mossad on the line. He knew the call was being recorded. He knew it would be analyzed at the highest level of the Israeli government, up to and most likely including Zvi Dayan, the Mossad chief, and Prime Minister Naphtali himself. He had only a moment. He had one shot. He had to get this right, clear, and concise.

"One nuclear warhead is at Al-Mazzah Air Force Base in Damascus. Stop," David began. "The other is being transported in a Red Crescent ambulance to the air base at Dayr az-Zawr. Stop. Both will be fired at Israel within hours. Stop. Urge immediate air strikes on—"

But David never got to finish the sentence. Suddenly he heard a computerized voice say, "Voice match—negative," and the line was cut.

David was stunned. Had the Israelis really hung up on him? Or had the call been intercepted somehow by Iranian intelligence? The former seemed more logical than the latter, but why wouldn't the Israelis have wanted to hear him out? Why wouldn't they have wanted to find out who he was and how he'd gotten all of Mordecai's information?

Frustrated and confused, wondering if he had broken U.S.

national-security laws for nothing, David knew he had to shake it off and stay focused. It didn't matter now. All that mattered was getting across the border. He shoved the satphone in his back pocket, tried to smooth the wrinkles out of his IRGC uniform, then ran to the border, yelling at the top of his lungs.

"I demand to know who is in charge here!" David bellowed. *"What kind of moron is running this operation? He should be shot! This is treasonous!"*

Six heavily armed Syrian border guards stepped out of the shadows and surrounded him, their AK-47s pointed at his head.

"Who is in charge here?" David shouted again, then pointed at a twenty-three- or twenty-four-year-old who appeared to be the unit commander. *"You? Is it you? Come here. I demand to talk to you."*

The commander cursed at him and told him to get down on his face, spread-eagle, and prepare to be searched. David ignored him and kept shouting, his face beet-red and veins bulging from his forehead.

"Search me? Do you have any idea who you're talking to? General Hamdi and General Jazini are waiting for me and my men. They're waiting for us at Al-Mazzah right now. But where am I? Stuck in a traffic jam nearly a kilometer long. In case you didn't notice, we're in the middle of a war here. Now clear out this traffic, and get me and my men across this border, or heads are going to roll, soldier, starting with yours."

Out of the corner of his eye, David could see another half-dozen heavily armed border guards emerging from a nearby but previously unnoticed bunker and taking up positions around him. He was not exactly following Omid Jazini's script. But there was hardly time for business as usual.

The commander began screaming back at him to get down on the ground and prepare to be searched. But David marched toward him, telling him to pull out his daily operations sheet and verify this number—941996656. David stopped only when a soldier to his left looked like he was getting a little twitchy in his trigger finger. But David didn't stop shouting.

"That's right! That's the number. Now you want the authorization code? You want me to answer the challenge questions? Then put the guns down and start showing some respect to agents of Imam al-Mahdi."

Suddenly everything grew quiet. Those last words seemed to defuse the hostility in a way that stunned all of them, including David. The commander stopped screaming at him and put up his hand, telling his men to remain silent.

"You are servants of Imam al-Mahdi?" the commander asked quietly and with respect, even reverence for the name.

"Of course," David insisted, maintaining his arrogant swagger. "We work directly for General Jazini, and we are on a mission for Imam al-Mahdi. That is what I've been trying to tell you fools. Now clear out this traffic, and let us get moving."

The commander told his men to lower their weapons, then walked over to David and asked if he had a letter of directive from General Jazini. David pulled a piece of paper from his pocket and handed it over in disgust. In this case, it wasn't a replica. It was an actual letter that had been sitting on Omid's desk, bearing the authentic signature of Omid's father. Not surprisingly, then, the letter was convincing. The commander asked David a few more questions, which David answered from memory according to the protocol in Omid's memo, and then the commander got down on his knees and bowed his head to the ground.

"Forgive me, sir," he pleaded. "My men and I meant no disrespect to you, your father, or Imam al-Mahdi."

"Make your men clear a path for my car," David ordered, seizing control of the moment.

"Yes, of course," the young commander replied, furiously motioning his men to comply.

Was it a trap? David wondered. How could things go this smoothly? Had the Mahdi's forces really not yet discovered Omid's body and realized what had happened?

David didn't have time to mull such imponderables. If they died, they died, but he couldn't afford to delay. He pulled out Omid's walkie-talkie and radioed Torres to move quickly and come to the head of the line. Less than a minute later, Torres pulled up to the front. David was pleased to see that Fox was now sitting in the front passenger seat and that his men had made a seat available in the rear of the SUV for David. That was certainly the proper protocol for any VIP clearing an international border, and David was grateful for his men's careful attention to detail.

With the commander and his men still in the dust groveling for forgiveness, David got into the backseat and was about to order Torres to get them out of there as quickly as possible when he had an idea. He turned back to the commander and ordered him to make available a van and a tractor trailer truck to "assist with a mission related to the Mahdi." Not surprisingly, the young commander looked startled, but he didn't question the order and ran off to get the necessary vehicles.

"Now, which one of you is best at driving a semi?" David asked his men.

"I am," Crenshaw said.

"Fine," said David. "Go get in the one they give you and follow us." Then he turned to Fox. "Steve, you get in the van and follow Nick," David explained. "Marco and I will hash out a plan of attack, and we'll let you know. Now let's move it. We're pushing our luck as it is."

DAMASCUS, SYRIA

"You're certain that we're alone?"

It was a risk, Birjandi knew, but he felt oddly compelled to take it anyway.

"Yes," Zandi said. "It doesn't happen often in my line of work. But yes, we're actually alone for a moment."

"Good," said Birjandi. "Then I have a question for you."

"Of course, Dr. Birjandi. It is a great honor to speak with you."

"I am not the man you think I am," Birjandi replied.

"What do you mean?" Zandi asked.

Birjandi had no idea how long they would be alone, so he wasted no time getting to his point.

"I have renounced Islam," he told the young nuclear scientist. "I was enslaved by it for many years, but I am free now. Jesus Christ set me free. Christ opened my eyes to the truth that he, not the Mahdi, is the Messiah. Jesus said, 'I am the way, and the truth, and the life; no one comes to the Father but through Me.' Jesus said, 'I am the resurrection and the life; he who believes in Me will live even if he dies.' It was Jesus who said, 'For God so loved the world, that He gave His only begotten Son, that whoever believes in Him shall not perish, but have eternal life.'"

"Why are you telling me this?" Zandi asked nervously. "You're going to get us both killed."

"I realize I'm taking a great risk to tell you this, Jalal, but Christ told me to speak to you," Birjandi replied. "Jesus told me to tell you that he loves you. He wants to forgive you of all your sins. He wants you to spend eternity with him in heaven, not burning in the lake of fire forever with no way of escape. You don't realize this, my young friend. But your life and mine are measured in hours, not days or years. God is going to bring a terrible judgment upon this city, Damascus, and upon these leaders. None of us will survive. And the minute we breathe our last breath on this earth, each of us will go either to heaven or to hell, forever. And Jesus wants me to tell you that he wants you to come to heaven. But you can only do so if you cry out to him and repent of your sins."

"You're a crazy, blind old fool," Zandi answered, backing his chair away. "Don't say anything else. I'm warning you."

"Actually, it is I who warn you," Birjandi replied in a calm and gentle manner that surprised even him, given the peril he was putting them both in. "The prophets of the Bible spoke of a day when Damascus would be utterly destroyed. They wrote of a day when Damascus would be judged by the God of Israel. That day is today. I can't tell you exactly how or when this judgment will come, but personally I suspect the Israelis know what we are doing here and are going to attack us with everything they have. We shall see, but one thing I know for certain: every minute judgment draws closer. And I can tell you with absolute assurance that neither of us will make it through the day. So please, my young friend, I am pleading with you, imploring you—give your life to Christ before it is too late. The Scriptures promise that 'if you declare with your mouth, "Jesus is Lord," and believe in your heart that God raised him from the dead, you will be saved. For it is with your heart that you believe and are justified, and it is with your mouth that you profess your faith and are saved. . . . "Everyone who calls on the name of the Lord will be saved.""

Yet Zandi would not listen. He got up, bolted out the door, and demanded to be taken back to the production line. He had a nuclear missile to finish building, he insisted to the guards, and he was running out of time.

HIGHWAY 4, EASTERN SYRIA

Torres hit the gas, and they were flying along the border between the desert wilderness of eastern Syria and the fertile Euphrates River valley. In the backseat, David reviewed the maps again and explained what was ahead. They were heading northwest on Highway 4. Shortly they would come to the town of Al Ashara and then Al Mayadin. After that, another thirty miles would take them to Dayr az-Zawr.

David explained his plan of attack to Torres, his rationale for sending Crenshaw and Fox to follow them in a semi and a van, and what he saw as the most serious risks facing them once they made contact with the enemy. Torres liked the operational concept but made several suggestions that David recognized as significant improvements. Minutes later, when they were satisfied they had the best plan possible under the circumstances, David was about to call Zalinsky when his satphone rang first.

"We're tracking the ambulance with a Predator," Zalinsky told him. "They're about twenty-five minutes from the base. We're tracking you guys, too. You're about twenty minutes out. But why the convoy?"

David quickly explained, and Zalinsky liked what he heard.

"How many other vehicles are with the warhead?" David asked.

"It's a package of three," Zalinsky said. "A police car out front, two ambulances following. The warhead is in the first ambulance."

"How many men in the package?"

"Fourteen—four in the lead car, four in the car with the warhead, and six in the tail car."

"That's it?" David asked, perplexed. "Why so few?"

"I'm guessing they felt more cars and more men would draw too much attention," Zalinsky replied.

"Do they have air support?"

"No, none," Zalinsky said.

"Do we?" David asked.

Zalinsky didn't respond.

"Jack, are you there?"

"Yeah, I'm here."

"Do we have air support?" David asked again.

Zalinsky paused, then said quietly, "I can't promise you anything. Just do your best without it, and I'll see what I can do."

"What kind of answer is that?" David shot back. "The president's national-security directive was clear. We're authorized 'to use all means necessary to disrupt and, if necessary, destroy Iranian nuclear weapons capabilities in order to prevent the eruption of another cataclysmic war in the Middle East.'"

"I think we've passed that point," Zalinsky said. "The cataclysmic war is already under way."

"Meaning what, that now we're now supposed to use *less* force?"

"Look, Zephyr," Zalinsky replied, "that directive was designed for operations inside Iran. Now you're operating inside Syria. Everything's changed."

"No, no, I memorized that document. Every word. Every comma. The president's authorization for covert action wasn't limited to inside Iran."

"You're out of line, Zephyr."

"I'm risking my life here and the lives of my men, and for what?" David asked. "Is there authorization for this mission or isn't there?"

Zalinsky took a deep breath. "There is."

"Under the same NSD that we're talking about?" David pressed.

Zalinsky hesitated for a moment, then said yes.

"Does the president want us to be here? Does he want us to move forward or not?"

"He does," Zalinsky replied, "and so do I. So does the director. But you've got to admit—the entire dynamic has changed. The Mahdi now has control of more than three hundred Pakistani nukes."

"Maybe yes, maybe no," David said. "But these are the two he's trying to launch today. All I'm asking for is some help here. Just give us the tools. Give us the air support we need, and I promise we'll do everything we possibly can to stop them."

"I know, and your country is grateful, Zephyr. Like I said, I'll do my best. Really. I promise."

David was furious. It wasn't enough. But he realized he was no longer doing this mission for Zalinsky or Murray or Allen or the president or even for his country anymore. He was responding to a higher calling, and he'd have to leave his fate in the hands of a higher power than the bureaucrats at Langley or the politicians in the White House.

44

DAMASCUS, SYRIA

"He's here!"

General Hamdi burst into the hall where Dr. Birjandi was now all alone.

"Who is here?" Birjandi asked.

"Imam al-Mahdi," Hamdi replied breathlessly. "He just arrived a few minutes ago, and he ordered me to summon you to his chambers."

"What time is it?"

"About 11:20," Hamdi said.

"I thought he wasn't arriving until noon. Wasn't that what they told us?"

"Yes, they did," the Syrian general confirmed. "But let's just say that was a bit of misinformation for security purposes. Believe me, Dr. Birjandi, he is here now, and he is calling for you to come to him immediately."

TEL AVIV, ISRAEL

Zvi Dayan entered the command center of the Israel Defense Forces looking ashen.

It was not because Israeli cities were still being pummeled by a seemingly never-ending shower of rockets, missiles, and mortars fired by Hezbollah, Hamas, and Iranian forces. Nor was it because IDF mechanized units and ground forces were encountering heavy resistance in southern Lebanon and Gaza. Nor was it because three more Israeli fighter jets and an Israeli reconnaissance plane had just been shot down—one over Tehran, one over the Persian Gulf, and two near the Iranian-Turkish-Iraqi border. All of these weighed heavily on his heart and mind, of course. This war was far from over, and international pressure on Israel to commit to a cease-fire was mounting by the hour. Yet Dayan had something far more urgent in his hands when he strode through the main war room and knocked on the door of Defense Minister Levi Shimon, operating out of a side conference room.

"Come in," said Shimon, looking up from his laptop, where he was reading the latest dispatches of his commanders in the field.

"Levi, we have a serious situation."

Shimon took off his trifocals. "What is it, Zvi?" he asked. "You look like you've seen a ghost."

"We just got a call on the line dedicated to Mordecai," said the Mossad chief.

Shimon instinctively stood. "What did he say?"

"It wasn't him."

"What do you mean it wasn't him?"

"Someone called the number. Someone had the authorization code and password. Someone got all the way through our security, but it wasn't Mordecai. He started talking, but after a few moments the voice-recognition software determined it wasn't our man and cut off the call."

"Then who was it?"

"We have no idea."

"How did he penetrate your security?"

"I cannot tell you that either."

"What did he say?" Shimon pressed.

Dayan set a portable digital sound recorder on the desk and pressed Play.

"One nuclear warhead is at Al-Mazzah Air Force Base in Damascus. Stop," said the voice in flawless Farsi. "The other is being transported in a Red Crescent ambulance to the air base at Dayr az-Zawr. Stop. Both will be fired at Israel within hours. Stop. Urge immediate air strikes on—"

Then Shimon heard a computerized voice say, "Voice match—negative," and the call was abruptly cut off. Dayan shut off the recorder.

"We're running that voice against everything we have in our system," Dayan explained. "But so far, we've got nothing."

"It has to have been someone close to Mordecai," Shimon said.

"Not necessarily," Dayan said. "If Iranian intelligence has captured Mordecai, perhaps they were able to force him to talk. Perhaps they are trying to get us to strike the Syrians to provoke them into the war."

"Or maybe the Iranians are already planning to launch a nuclear attack from Syrian soil." Shimon let out a string of curses. "Your people should never have cut off the call," he bellowed. "They should have engaged that guy, kept him talking, and learned everything they possibly could."

"Fair enough," Dayan said. "But the real question is whether anything he said was accurate."

"And?"

"And nothing. I've put my best men on it. We're turning over every leaf. We're in the process of redeploying drones to Al-Mazzah and Dayr az-Zawr, but that's going to take time, Levi. Most of our assets, as you know, are tied up over Iran, not over Syria."

"What's your best guess, Zvi?" Shimon pressed.

"If I had to guess—and I hate to guess; I want to know—but if I had to guess, under these circumstances, I'd say Mordecai has been compromised, so he's found another ally. He's using this ally to get us this information, and it's legit. I can't prove it. But Mordecai has always told us the truth."

"This wasn't Mordecai," Shimon reminded his colleague.

"You asked for my best guess, Levi," Dayan replied. "That's it."

Shimon lit a cigarette and paced the room. He cursed again and then said, "I think you're right. We need to take this to the prime minister immediately."

DAMASCUS, SYRIA

This was it, thought Birjandi.

He had dreaded and resisted this moment for weeks, but now it had come. He was being led down a series of hallways and secret chambers and antechambers, and soon he would be ushered into the presence of the Twelfth Imam.

The Bible specifically forbade followers of Jesus Christ from willingly going to meet with a false messiah, but somehow Birjandi did not feel as anxious at this moment as he had expected. He was not, after all, going willingly. He had been forced to come to Syria against his will, and he was being forced into this meeting as well. Birjandi could think of plenty of examples in Scripture of men of God being dragged before evil authorities as a result of God's sovereignty, not their own human will. Moses was sent by God, against his will, to confront Pharaoh. Elijah was sent to confront King Ahab and the false prophets of Baal. Jesus was dragged before Pontius Pilate. The apostles Peter and Paul were brought to Rome by cruel tyrants.

Birjandi said nothing as General Hamdi led him to the Mahdi. Silently, however, he kept meditating on a passage from the Gospel of Matthew. "You will even be brought before governors and kings for My sake, as a testimony to them and to the Gentiles," Jesus told his disciples. "But when they hand you over, do not worry about how or what you are to say; for it will be given you in that hour what you are to say. For it is not you who speak, but it is the Spirit of your Father who speaks in you."

Again and again Birjandi repeated these words to himself as he thanked his Father in heaven for the opportunity to suffer for the name of Jesus.

HIGHWAY 4, EASTERN SYRIA

As Torres raced along Highway 4 in a northwesterly direction, David, still in the backseat, called Fox on his satphone to brief him on the plan, then called Crenshaw to do the same. By the time he was done explaining everything and answering their questions, Torres indicated they were nearing Dayr az-Zawr and were approximately six minutes from intercepting the convoy.

"Marco, I need to ask you a question before we get there."

"Sure thing, boss."

"I'm not asking as a boss," David said. "I'm asking as a friend."

"No problem," Torres replied. "What's up?"

"If we don't make it through this thing—and you know as well as I do there's a real chance that we won't—do you know where you're going?"

"What do you mean?"

"I'm saying when you die, whenever that is, do you know if you're going to heaven or hell?"

"Wow, gee; that's a little grim, isn't it?"

"Seriously, Marco. You're a good man and a good friend. But we've never had a spiritual conversation, and I really want to know."

"I . . . No . . . I don't really . . . I haven't given it much thought," Torres stammered, clearly caught off guard by the question.

"You know, it's actually kind of amazing—kind of crazy, really—that people who have jobs as dangerous as ours haven't given this topic much thought," David said. "I mean, you and I are willing to die for our country. That means we're willing to plunge headlong into eternity. Yet most of us have absolutely no clear idea of where we're going. It's not just you. Until a few days ago, I hadn't thought about it much either."

"And now?" Torres asked.

"A few days ago, I got down on my knees and gave my life to Jesus Christ," David replied, his heart racing. "Lately I've been reading the New Testament and really searching for the truth. And it finally became clear to me the other day how messed up I've been, how lost I've been, how much danger I've been in of going to hell forever, and it scared me, you know? I've never been a religious person. My parents were turned off by religion when they lived in Iran. And until recently I never thought much about God."

"What happened?" Torres asked.

"A lot of things," said David. "I found out my friend Marseille had become a follower of Christ. Then I found out Dr. Birjandi had become a Christian. Then I met Najjar Malik and heard his story of how he gave his heart and soul to Christ. And I've seen how much it's changed them, how much peace and joy and courage it's given them.

And I finally decided I wanted what they had. I wanted what Christ was offering. And honestly, I should have said something to you—to all of you guys—sooner, but I didn't. We were busy, and I wasn't sure how to explain it. But I couldn't forgive myself if I didn't ask you right now—do you believe that Jesus is the Christ, the Savior, the Messiah?"

"Well, sure," Torres said. "I mean, I grew up Catholic, but honestly I never really took it seriously as a kid."

"Do you believe Jesus is the Son of God?"

"Of course."

"Do you believe he died on the cross to pay the penalty for all your sins?"

"Yeah, I do."

"Do you believe that God the Father raised Jesus from the dead to prove to us that he really is the Messiah, the Savior, the Lord of the universe?"

"Sure, I think I've always believed those things," said Torres. "My mom and my grandmom used to teach me those things growing up."

"Then the question is: have you personally received Jesus Christ into your heart to save you?"

"What do you mean?"

"Dr. Birjandi taught me that it's not enough just to believe these things about Christ in your head," David explained. "We must consciously, intentionally choose to receive Christ into our hearts by faith. The Bible says, 'But as many as received Him, to them He gave the right to become children of God, even to those who believe in His name.' To receive Christ, we have to admit we're sinners, that we've fallen short of God's perfect standard. And we have to ask Christ to forgive us and adopt us into his family. Have you ever done that?"

"I never knew you had to."

"Would you like to?"

"Right here? Right now?"

"Before it's too late, my friend."

It *was* almost too late. They were only a few minutes away from the intercept. But to David's surprise, Torres said yes. He did want to receive Christ, but he didn't know how.

"I appreciate you saying something to me," Torres added. "No one has ever made it quite so clear to me."

"It's my honor," David said. "How about if I pray and you follow my lead? It's not so much about the precise wording as it is about whether you really mean it. But if you do, I'd love to help you accept Christ right now."

"I would," said Torres. "Let's do it."

"Great—now usually I pray with my eyes shut and on my knees, but under the circumstances I'd say let's keep our eyes open," David quipped.

Torres smiled and nodded.

"Okay, then," David said. "I'll lead you in a prayer similar to the one I prayed. Let's go. 'Dear Father in heaven, please have mercy on me. I am the worst of sinners. I have been resisting you for so long, yet you have not given up on me. Thank you. Please forgive me for the wrong things I have done. I know that the Bible is your Word. I know it alone contains the true words of life. And I know that Jesus Christ is your Son and the only true Messiah. I believe Jesus Christ died on the cross for me. I believe he rose for me. I want to know that I'm going to heaven when I die. I want to know that all my sins are forgiven. Lord Jesus, I love you, and I need you. I promise to follow you forever, so long as you will help me and lead me all the way. Thank you for saving me. Thank you for forgiving my sins and adopting me into your family. Give me the courage to follow you no matter where you lead me and no matter what the cost. I pray in the name of my new Savior and Lord, Jesus Christ. Amen."

To David's great amazement but great joy, Torres prayed right along with him, line by line, phrase by phrase. And Torres didn't just recite the lines; he prayed with passion, with a deep sense of conviction and hunger for God that both stunned and electrified David. And just in time, too, since Zalinsky was calling on the satphone. The convoy with the warhead was only three kilometers ahead of them.

45

Mossad chief Zvi Dayan began the hastily convened meeting of the War Cabinet via secure video teleconference. He explained the strange phone call to the line that had been set up expressly for Mordecai's use and the impossibility of someone penetrating the Mossad's multiple layers of security without, in his view, direct help from Mordecai himself.

"The three key questions in my mind," Dayan said, "are: One, did Mordecai provide the information to this mystery caller willfully or under duress? Two, is the information that we received regarding the two warheads accurate or not? And three, if the intel is legitimate, what do we do about it?"

The prime minister listened carefully to the brief. "Forget the first question," he said. "At this point, it's irrelevant. Zvi, you're the chief of Israeli intelligence. What's the answer to the second question? Is there a warhead at Al-Mazzah and one at Dayr az-Zawr, or are we being set up?"

Dayan shook his head. "I really cannot say, Mr. Prime Minister. Events are moving too rapidly. All my primary assets are focused on Iran, not Syria. But are there strange tidbits here and there that suggest something is going on in Syria? Yes. Are there reports of Iranian Revolutionary Guards arriving in Damascus from all points on the globe? Yes. Is it strange that President Mustafa hasn't already launched a full-scale war with us, and could it be that he's holding back until some key moment? Yes. Could that mean the Mahdi has chosen to launch the final two Iranian warheads from Syrian territory? It could, but I hate to speculate. I want to give you facts, not opinions. But I simply don't have enough facts to draw a firm conclusion nor the time to gather those facts."

Naphtali thanked the Mossad chief and turned to his trusted defense minister to get his assessment.

Levi Shimon took a deep breath and stared at a stack of reports on his desk. After a moment, he looked up and looked straight into the camera, straight into the eyes of the prime minister and his other colleagues on the video teleconference, ranging from the vice prime minister for strategic affairs and the IDF chief of staff to the head of military intelligence and the foreign minister, the head of Israeli internal security, and several others.

"I don't know the answers to questions one and two," he conceded. "But at this point, do they really matter? We know Mustafa has made an alliance with Iran and now the Twelfth Imam. We know Mustafa wants to obliterate us. We know Syria has massive stockpiles of chemical weapons. We know they could be minutes away from launching everything they have at us. I say we hit them now, while we still can. We can put as much firepower on the two air bases as you want. But I say it's time to go and go hard."

DAYR AZ-ZAWR, SYRIA

Still barreling up Highway 4, David and Torres now had to slow down significantly as they left a swath of farmland and villages and entered the outskirts of the city of Dayr az-Zawr with its population of about two hundred thousand residents. David played navigator while Torres kept his eyes on the road. Rather than turning north into the city proper and heading toward the Ali Bek Quarter, they bore left, still on Highway 4, through the Maysaloun Quarter.

"The convoy is on Highway 7, approaching the city from the southwest," Zalinsky said over the speakerphone.

"How far?" Torres asked.

"About half a klick," Zalinsky said, tracking their every movement via video feeds from two Predators in the heavens above them. "In a moment, they'll be turning onto Highway 4, heading straight toward you. Now listen, you've got to hit them before they make that turn and head for the air base. You need to get to the intersection where Highway 7 and 4 meet before they do," Zalinsky insisted, the anxiety in his voice palpable. "If they get past that point, you won't be able to stop them before they enter the base, and believe me, they have seriously ramped up security on that base in the past hour. Tanks, armored personnel carriers, sharpshooters on the roofs. They've even got helicopter gunships on the tarmacs warming up."

"They haven't put the gunships in the air?"

"Not yet."

"Why not?"

"Eva just intercepted a transmission from General Hamdi. He doesn't want any Syrian jets or choppers in the air, lest it make the Israelis nervous and they decide to launch a first strike. And of course, all civilian aircraft has been grounded since the war began."

Torres was making the best time he could, but traffic was building. What's more, he was also afraid of catching the attention of local police. Getting pulled over for speeding—or triggering a high-speed chase—was the last thing they needed. But Zalinsky was furious. Shouting through the satphone, Zalinsky unleashed a withering barrage of obscenities. He ordered them to blow through this city at all costs or miss the convoy, which was just minutes away from its intended destination.

David agreed, and Torres hit the gas again. He wove in and out of traffic, shifting from one lane to another, laying on the horn and flashing his lights as he went. David glanced behind them. Crenshaw was losing ground. He simply couldn't maneuver the semi through so much traffic, and David saw his plan unraveling before his eyes. He couldn't see Fox in the van at all because he was bringing up the rear.

Checking his map one more time, he noticed there was a huge stadium or sports complex of some kind coming up on their right. But now he tossed the map aside, rechecked his seat belt, grabbed his MP5, and made sure it was locked and loaded.

"They're almost at the junction!" Zalinsky shouted. *"They're about to turn onto Highway 4. Let's go, let's go, let's go! Move it! You're going to miss them!"*

Torres was gaining ground, but it wasn't enough. So without warning, he turned the wheel hard to the right and swerved the SUV onto the sidewalk. He laid on the horn nonstop and accelerated. Businessmen and couples and young children dove off the sidewalk, ducking into shops and jumping onto the hoods of cars. David was terrified of hitting a civilian, but he had no control at this point and one objective. If they didn't make it to that intersection, a million innocent civilians were going to be in grave danger.

David could see the stadium coming up fast on their right. Then suddenly he heard the horn of the tractor trailer blasting behind them. He turned and was stunned by what he saw. Crenshaw had crossed the median and was accelerating into oncoming traffic. *Brilliant,* David thought, wishing he'd had the idea himself. By heading into oncoming traffic, Crenshaw was forcing drivers coming toward him—drivers who could see this maniac coming at them—to veer off to the left or the right to avoid a head-on collision. And that's precisely what they were doing.

Fox, on the other hand, had chosen his own alternate route. He was literally driving on the grassy median between the eastbound and westbound lanes. He was occasionally having to weave in and out of the many trees that had been planted in the median, but to David's shock, Fox was rapidly gaining ground.

"Zephyr, do you still have Omid's walkie-talkies with you?" Zalinsky asked.

David turned and focused exclusively on what was ahead.

"Yes, sir, I've got one," David replied. "The other is in the semi."

"Good. Turn yours on and switch to channel six," Zalinsky ordered and then relayed the same information to Crenshaw in the 18-wheeler.

"I'm a little busy at the moment, sir," Crenshaw replied, still forcing his way up the wrong lane.

David turned on his radio and didn't like what he heard. Sure enough, they'd stirred up a hornet's nest. Local police in every part of the city were being alerted to the chaos ensuing along the southern edge of town, and they were being told to converge at the intersection of Highway 7 and Highway 4. The real question, though, was whether they had lost the element of surprise. Did the security forces in the convoy expect an attack, or did they just think a few drunk drivers were tearing up the town?

Sirens could be heard coming from all directions. And then—just as they were racing past the stadium—a pregnant woman pushing a stroller came around a corner. David screamed. So did Torres. Torres slammed on the brakes. He swerved back into the street, but it was too late. Not for the woman or her baby. By the grace of God, they were safe. But Torres plowed straight into a police cruiser that had just entered the intersection.

There were two Syrian officers in the patrol car. Both looked stunned, but they immediately jumped out, guns drawn.

"Get out!" one shouted at Torres. *"Get out of the car! Now!"*

"We are Revolutionary Guards," Torres replied as calmly as he could. "We are on a mission for Imam al-Mahdi."

"I don't care who you are," the officer shouted back, his pistol aimed at Torres's head. "Put your hands in the air and get out of the car slowly—don't make any quick movements."

LANGLEY, VIRGINIA

CIA director Roger Allen now joined Tom Murray and Jack Zalinsky and their team in the Global Operations Center.

"What in the world is Torres doing?" Allen asked as he looked up at one of the large-screen video monitors and saw Marco Torres, the head of their paramilitary unit, carefully exiting his SUV at gunpoint while a second officer pointed his weapon at the head of David Shirazi—aka Zephyr, the linchpin of their Iran strategy—who was now exiting the backseat of the SUV.

Zalinsky cringed. On the other screen he could see the Iranian-Syrian convoy rapidly approaching the intersection, and no American was there to stop them.

DAYR AZ-ZAWR, SYRIA

Suddenly Crenshaw found an opening. The traffic had cleared. He now had a straight shot at their objective. Laying on the horn, he blew past Torres and Shirazi and careened headlong into the intersection just seconds ahead of the convoy, with Fox in the van close on his heels.

Every head turned and every eye was riveted as Crenshaw finally slammed on the brakes and the 18-wheeler's rear wheels began fishtailing. At that very instant, the driver of the police cruiser leading the convoy hit his brakes as well, but not nearly in time. The police car hit the side of the semi going a hundred kilometers an hour. The force of the impact sliced off the entire roof of the car, instantly decapitating the Revolutionary Guards in the front seat, and then both the car and the semi erupted in flames that shot twenty and thirty feet into the air.

Behind them, the drivers of both ambulances slammed on their brakes as well, but there was no time to stop. They both crashed into the police cruiser and the semi and into each other. A fraction of a second later, Fox careened the van into the side of the rear ambulance at full speed, without ever braking, sending the ambulance rolling a dozen times or more into a rocky, barren field on the other side of the street.

For a moment, the Syrian police officers were transfixed—as was David—by the massive wreck in front of them. Fire and smoke. Burning rubber. Flying shards of glass and metal. And blood everywhere. But then one of the officers came to. Without warning, he swung back around, his pistol aimed at Torres, and Torres had no time to react. The officer pulled the trigger three times in rapid succession. One of the bullets went wide, shattering what was left of the front windshield of their SUV. But the other two hit Torres in the chest, sending him crashing to the pavement.

David couldn't believe what he was seeing. Nor could the officer beside him. David saw his chance. He ducked down and reached for the MP5 on the backseat. Then he popped up again and took out the officer closest to him. He pivoted quickly and fired two short bursts at the officer on the other side of the car—the officer who had shot Torres—killing him instantly. David now scrambled around the front of the car. He got to Torres's side, but it was already too late. His friend was dead, his eyes still open. Though he knew it was pointless, David checked for a pulse, but there was none to be found. This was it. He was gone. And David was enraged.

He began sprinting for the center ambulance, the one with the warhead. Several IRGC officers were beginning to crawl out of the mangled vehicle when they saw David coming at them. He was moving quickly and firing the MP5 in short bursts. Two of the Iranians—the two closest to him—went down. But the two on the other side of the ambulance got away, one breaking to the left, the other to the right.

David reached the ambulance. He could see a casket-like box in the back and wanted to confirm that was the warhead. But fires were raging all around him. The heat was unbearable, and the thick, acrid smoke made his eyes sting and water. He tried to wipe them clean, but doing so seemed to irritate them more. Then, out of the corner of his right eye, he saw one of the Iranian officers he'd shot reaching for his pistol and preparing to take aim. David unleashed another burst from the machine gun, and the man died instantly.

Suddenly David heard gunfire behind him. Ducking down, he scrambled for cover behind the ambulance. This was not the plan. This was not the operational concept that he and Torres had sketched out or that Zalinsky had approved. That plan had been much more subtle. They would jackknife the semi at the intersection, creating a roadblock. But the rest of the team would take up positions that would enable them to ambush the convoy when it arrived. Fox was supposed to have parked along Highway 4 in such a way that when the convoy arrived and was blocked by the semi, he could pull in behind them and cut off their exit route. At that point, they were going to open fire with machine guns, sniper rifles, and even an RPG. The objective was to kill or wound every Revolutionary Guard with the convoy, get to the warhead, and dismantle it, rendering it completely inoperative, no matter what it took. David had been clear with his men: destroying the warhead was the objective. Nothing else mattered. Nothing could distract. No matter who on the team was wounded or who was killed, the survivors—or survivor—had to keep to the objective. Whoever got to the warhead first, it was his responsibility. A million souls depended on their commitment to achieving their objective at all costs.

Now that plan was shot. The scene was absolutely chaotic. The semi was nearly completely consumed by flames. The lead police car was a molten shell. Torres was dead. David had no idea of the whereabouts or condition of Fox or Crenshaw. He desperately scanned in every direction, looking for them and for hostiles. At the moment, he saw no one he knew and no one threatening.

Just then there was an enormous explosion to his right. The van Fox had been driving was flying through the air amid a gigantic spray of flames and smoke. Had Fox escaped? Was he okay? Where was he? David was flooded with questions, but more shooting erupted. It was coming from the other side of the semi. His thoughts turned to Crenshaw. Was his teammate in trouble?

David agonized. He knew his orders. He knew what Zalinsky expected, and he knew everyone in the Global Ops Center and the White House Situation Room was watching. But as much as he needed to get into the ambulance, identify the warhead, and begin dismantling it, he couldn't help himself. He had to make sure Crenshaw was okay. The gunfire on the other side of the semi was rapidly intensifying. Was it a diversion? Was it a trap? David knew he shouldn't go. He had a job to do. He had a mission to accomplish, and he wasn't supposed to be diverted. The future of Israel hung in the balance. But at that moment, he could only think of saving the life of Nick Crenshaw.

David gripped the MP5 tightly. He could hear sirens coming from every direction and suddenly had the strongest sensation of déjà vu. He had a flashback of his escape from Tehran with Najjar Malik, but now the stakes were so much higher. He wasn't after a nuclear scientist. He was after a nuclear bomb. Indeed, he'd found it. It was right beside him. Why then was he moving away from it?

46

Esfahani's phone rang.

"Hello?"

"This is Commander Asgari. I need to speak to General Jazini."

"He is meeting with Imam al-Mahdi just now," Esfahani replied. "But I can have him call you back."

"No, I must talk to him immediately," Asgari demanded. "His son is dead. I believe an Israeli or American hit team is coming to assassinate the Mahdi at this very hour. And I believe they know about the warheads in Damascus."

DAYR AZ-ZAWR, SYRIA

David moved steadily to his right, aiming for the front of the semi but continually glancing from side to side and behind him lest he get caught off guard. For a moment, he brushed up against the truck's engine. It was blazing hot.

He looked up and saw dark black smoke pouring from the shattered window of the cab. Then he noticed a red streak on the cab, coming from the window. He looked down and saw blood on the ground, mixed with a thousand bits of glass. Crenshaw was alive. Or at least he had been when he jumped out of the truck. Was he still? Did he have a weapon with him?

A machine gun fired, and David heard pings of metal as bullets ricocheted off the truck next to him. Instinctively he dropped to a crouch and wheeled around, only to find a Revolutionary Guard officer racing toward him with an AK-47. David aimed his MP5 and pulled the trigger, cutting the officer down but emptying his magazine in the process. Scanning for other hostiles, he ejected one magazine and popped in another. Then he began moving toward the gravely wounded officer, who was squirming in his own blood.

The man was not dead. Indeed, a first glance suggested he could still live, but there was nothing David could do for him now. He had to find Crenshaw and Fox. So David took the officer's pistol, shoved it into his own belt, then slung the man's machine gun over his shoulder and moved quickly back to the front of the cab.

David reached for his satphone. He needed to call Zalinsky. He needed help. But he couldn't find it. He checked both front pockets and both back pockets. But the phone was gone. It must have fallen out somewhere between the SUV and here, David concluded. His stomach tightened as the sobering thought dawned on him that he had no way to contact either Langley or his men. He had no air support, and he had precious little time to disable the warhead.

LANGLEY, VIRGINIA

Zalinsky was screaming at the video monitors, shouting at David to get back to the ambulance and unable to fathom why his key operative on the ground was letting himself be drawn away from the warhead.

But now he saw new threats rapidly materializing. Two armored personnel carriers were coming up Highway 4 from the air base, no doubt filled with Syrian special forces. That wasn't all, however. Murray noted that a tactical unit from the local police department, the Syrian equivalent of a SWAT team, was approaching from the other direction. Zalinsky's heart sank. There was no way David, much less Fox or Crenshaw—if those two were still alive—were going to make it out of this in one piece, much less have time to disable that warhead, unless they got help from above and quickly.

Zalinsky knew the answer, and he knew it was going to be no. He knew because that was his answer when he'd had Eva Fischer arrested for doing the exact same thing. What's more, he knew just the act of asking was going to hammer the last nail in his coffin after this disastrous operation. Yet he did it anyway. He'd recruited David Shirazi for this mission. He'd trained him. He'd deployed him. And he'd been David's handler through it all. Zalinsky couldn't abandon his man now.

Turning to Roger Allen, he blurted out, "Sir, requesting permission to use all means necessary to defend my men on the ground."

You could hear a pin drop in the Global Operations Center. Most of the personnel present had been there the day Eva had used a Predator to save Zephyr's life. They had seen Zalinsky go ballistic, and they could only imagine how the CIA director was about to react. But Allen didn't hesitate.

"Permission granted," he said, his eyes glued to the screens.

Zalinsky was stunned. He wasn't the only one. All eyes were on Zalinsky as he just stood there for a moment, unable to react.

"Well?" said the director, growing impatient.

"Really?"

"Yes."

"What about the president?" Zalinsky asked.

"That's my problem," Allen responded. "Not yours. Now get moving before it's too late."

"Yes, sir," Zalinsky said, and he turned and began barking out orders to the Predator operators.

DAYR AZ-ZAWR, SYRIA

The only option was to move forward, David concluded. Aiming the MP5 ahead of him, he moved around the cab. Following the trail of blood, he hoped to find Crenshaw at the other end, but now he could hear a full-blown shoot-out under way on the other side of the semi.

David quickly glanced around the front end of the cab. To his relief, he saw Crenshaw. The man was covered in blood and clearly in great pain, but he was holding his own. He was crouched behind a pickup truck and using an AK-47 to try to hold back a half-dozen Syrian police officers moving toward him. Never surrender.

David's first instinct was to run to Crenshaw's side and fight it out with him to the bitter end. But just as he was about to sprint for the pickup truck, he had another thought. A better one. Rather than rush forward, he pivoted and began to work his way through the flames and searing heat and blinding smoke down the "safe" side of the semi—or what was left of it. Most of the truck had been consumed by the raging fire and had essentially melted in place. But for now, at least, the leaping, licking flames were creating a shield between him and the six Syrian officers.

Above the roar of the flames he could hear more sirens. He knew reinforcements were coming. But he had to save Crenshaw. If he could, then together they could get back to the warhead, and he could dismantle it while Crenshaw gave him covering fire. Otherwise, David would be completely exposed while working on the warhead and wouldn't last two minutes.

David looked down Rue Ash 'Sham It was a snarled traffic jam for a kilometer or more. He could see the flashing lights of police cars trying to weave their way through the mass of cars, trucks, motorcycles, and humanity. He could also see a helicopter gunship. It was about two kilometers out but coming in fast.

Once again he was forced to shift gears. As much as he needed to take out these Syrian officers, he couldn't leave his team—whatever was left of them—exposed to death from the air. There was no way he could take out the gunship with an MP5 or an AK-47. But seeing the doors of their SUV still open, he had an idea. He made a break for it.

As gunfire erupted all around him, David moved low and fast toward the SUV, zigzagging through the abandoned cars and realizing that this end of the street was completely deserted. Everyone had fled from the war zone it had become. Bullets whizzed over his head, smashing car and store windows and ripping into the brick walls of the apartments around him. Reaching the SUV, he opened the trunk and found the case he needed.

The Russian-built Mi-24 Hind helicopter gunship was closing fast.

He could hear the roar of the rotors and knew the Syrian pilot was going to open fire any moment. David ripped open the case with the RPG launcher and started to load it, but there wasn't time. The helicopter was approaching too quickly. Dropping his weapons, he also dropped to the pavement and did his best to crawl under the hood of the car next to him. And then he heard the gunship's twin 30mm cannons let loose as the pilot opened fire. The rounds destroyed one car after another as the chopper blazed up the street, barely clearing the rooftops at more than 250 miles an hour. All David could do was press himself to the pavement, cover his head and eyes, and pray.

With a rush of wind that felt and sounded like a tornado, the gunship passed immediately overhead, and in a moment it was gone. David began to breathe again, but he knew he had no time to waste. The pilot would circle around and come back through, and he wouldn't make the same mistake twice. Next time he wouldn't fire the 30mm cannons, David was certain. He would fire Russian-made antitank missiles, and David would be instantly incinerated.

Quickly scrambling to his feet, his heart pounding, sweat pouring down his face, David heard footsteps approaching fast. He raised the MP5 and was about to fire when he realized he was staring into the eyes of Steve Fox.

"Steve? You're alive."

David couldn't believe it. His colleague's head was bleeding. The man's hands were bloody and raw. His face was covered with soot. His IRGC uniform was ripped and covered in dirt. He had no machine gun with him. No pistol. No weapon of any kind. But Fox had fire in his eyes.

"I killed them, sir—all of them," Fox said without emotion.

"Hand to hand?" David asked.

"Eye to eye."

"You okay?"

"No, but I'm alive, and I need a gun."

"Good; take this one," David said, handing him his MP5. "There's a box of extra magazines in the backseat. But you'd better move fast. That gunship is coming back."

As they both looked up, they could see the Mi-24 banking hard to the right and preparing to roar back down Rue Ash 'Sham. Fox went for the extra ammo while David went again for the RPG launcher. He screwed a propelling charge on the end of one of the warheads, then began loading the assembled artillery onto the end of the launcher as Fox turned back to him and asked for new orders.

"I'm good—where do you need me?"

"Go help Nick," David said. "He's pinned down behind a pickup truck at two o'clock. Last I saw, there were six Syrian hostiles firing at him. Take them out, get Nick, then join me at the ambulance. We need to disable that warhead."

Though clearly in tremendous pain, Fox smiled and nodded. "Done, boss. See you soon."

"Good luck, Steve."

"You too."

As Fox ran off, David could see the gunship leveling and beginning its strafing run. He quickly mounted the rocket launcher on his shoulder, looked through the sights, and pulled the trigger. Instantly, the RPG exploded away and streaked into the sky. The Syrian pilot must have seen the flash because he suddenly jerked the chopper to the right, but it was too late. The RPG smashed through the glass of the cockpit and detonated. The chopper exploded in midair as David reloaded and raced to catch up with Fox.

As he came around the corner of a pharmacy at the end of the street, he saw a nightmare unfolding before him. Fox was sprawled out on the ground. He wasn't dead, but he was bleeding profusely, and the air had erupted in gunfire again. David wanted to stay with Fox and assess his wounds, but he was forced to dive behind the pharmacy for cover. The Syrians started shooting through the shop's plate-glass windows. David could see that Fox had killed two of them, but four remained. And two armored personnel carriers of additional Syrian troops were already pulling up to the scene.

David wasted no time. He hefted the launcher onto his shoulder again, pivoted around the corner, and squeezed the trigger. Once again the grenade exploded from the tube and streaked toward the Syrian police officers, who now dove for cover as well. But again it was too late. The grenade exploded, killing all of them.

That was it, though. David had no more RPGs. The back doors of the APCs were opening. Dozens of Syrian troops were about to emerge, and David had no way to stop them. Nevertheless, he ditched the rocket launcher, took the AK-47 off his shoulder, and raced forward to Fox's side.

"Go get Nick; I'll be fine," Fox groaned.

"Forget it," David replied. "Where are you hit?"

"My left leg," said Fox. "I think it's shattered."

"All right, listen," said David. "I'm going to pick you up, fireman's carry. It's going to hurt, but stay with me."

Fox nodded. David first slung both machine guns over his right shoulder. He was lifting Fox and putting him over his left shoulder when he heard an intense, high-pitched whistling sound. He looked up and saw two contrails streaking down from the sky. Assuming they were air-to-ground missiles from a Syrian MiG-29 or equivalent fighter jet, David began to run as fast as he could toward the ambulance and away from the pharmacy. He stumbled twice but finally got to the side of the bullet-strewn vehicle just as the missiles hit their marks. But they did not hit the pharmacy, nor the spot where he and Fox had just been. Instead, the missiles scored direct hits on the two armored personnel carriers, destroying both with a deafening roar and two searing fireballs.

David's heart leaped. Stunned, he looked up at the sky. The Americans had arrived. Zalinsky had come through. Langley was watching their backs after all, and David could hardly believe it. He wanted to smile. He wanted to laugh. But they weren't out of the woods yet. He propped Fox up against one side of the ambulance and gave him back the MP5.

"Shoot anyone you don't recognize—you got it?"

"Got it, boss."

"I'll be right back," David promised, then took his AK-47 and raced to find Crenshaw.

"Nick!" he shouted as he ran through the flames and smoke and toward the pickup. "Nick? It's me, David. Are you there?"

"Yeah, I'm here," Crenshaw shouted back. "Is that really you?"

"Yes, it's me, Nick," David replied. "Don't shoot. I'm coming around."

He was glad to hear Crenshaw's voice, but when he got to his colleague's side, all the color drained from his face. The man had been shot multiple times. David counted two bullet holes in his chest and several more to the legs.

David groaned and bit back a curse. "What happened?"

"I'm fine," Crenshaw lied. "I'll be fine."

"You're not fine," David replied. "We need to get you out of here."

"Did you see those missiles?" Crenshaw asked. "Those were Hellfires. I thought we were toast for sure when those reinforcements arrived. But somebody up there is taking care of us, eh?"

"They certainly are," David said, but he was worried his friend was slipping into shock. Crenshaw's voice was actually quite strong. But he was losing blood quickly and didn't seem to be focusing on the issue at hand: survival.

"I'm going to pick you up now," David said. "Steve is over by the ambulance. We need to get you over to him. Now hold on tight. Let's go."

As David picked up Crenshaw, the man began writhing in pain. For a moment, David doubted the wisdom of moving him at all, but he had no choice. His only shot at disabling the warhead was keeping the team together. He hoped Crenshaw could hold a weapon for a few more minutes and provide at least some covering fire, as more reinforcements were sure to arrive at any moment.

Despite Crenshaw's shrieks of pain, David heaved him over his shoulder and ran him to the ambulance as well, shouting ahead to Fox to let him know they were friendlies. Fortunately Fox heard them and held his fire.

David lowered Crenshaw down on the other side of the ambulance and gave both men orders to watch his back. This was it. He needed five minutes. No more, but no less either. Despite their severe injuries, both men gave their word.

47

Once again David and his team could hear the distinctive, high-pitched whine of an incoming Hellfire missile. All of them pressed themselves to the ground and covered their heads and faces and felt the ground shake violently as another massive explosion erupted a few hundred yards to the north. As David looked up, he could see that Zalinsky had struck again, this time taking out the Syrian special police unit that was just about to overrun them.

Still, there was no time to breathe easier. David asked Crenshaw and Fox if either of them still had their satphones with them. Fox had his and handed it over. David speed-dialed the Global Operations Center at Langley.

"Don't say thanks," Zalinsky said when he came on the line. "There isn't time."

"I know," David said. "But thanks anyway."

"You've got more special forces units rolling from the air base. You need to get this warhead disabled and then get your men out of there."

"I'm with you on that," David said.

He tried to open the back of the ambulance, but it was stuck. He tried to pry it open, but to no avail. Then he used the butt of his machine gun to smash what was left of the rear window and tried to jimmy the door open, but it still wouldn't work. Abandoning that approach, he entered through the front door and crawled into the back, opened the protective steel case, and found himself staring at an actual, viable, fully armed Iranian atomic warhead. He used a Swiss Army knife to carefully unscrew a plate on the side and within seconds was looking inside the heart of the weapon.

The problem, however, was that there was no angle by which the cameras on the Predator could see what he could see. Thus, Zalinsky and the nuclear weapons experts at his side back at Langley were at a severe disadvantage, unable to assess the weapon's precise design or possible security features.

Zalinsky ordered David to begin describing everything he saw. David shuddered. He'd broken out in a cold sweat and his hands were shaking.

"It looks a lot like a W88," David began, referring to the U.S.'s most advanced thermonuclear warhead.

"It can't—Khan's design wasn't that advanced," said Zalinsky, referring to the plans that A. Q. Khan, the father of the Pakistani nuclear weapons program, had sold to the Iranians several years earlier.

"Then Saddaji improved it," David insisted.

He described to Zalinsky the key components he saw one by one, beginning with the Primary at the top, the bomb's initial explosive trigger, designed to create an implosion that would begin to release the thermonuclear detonation.

"Is it spherical?" Zalinsky asked.

"No."

"Two-point?"

"Yes."

"Hollow-pit, fusion-boosted?"

"Yes, sir."

"What about the Secondary?" Zalinsky asked, referring to the weapon's additional explosive trigger, whose function was to accelerate and intensify the implosion and create a maximum thermonuclear blast. "Do you see that, too?"

"I do."

"Is that one spherical?"

"I'm afraid so."

"All-fissile, fusion-boosted?"

"Yes, sir."

"Uranium or plutonium pit?"

"Looks like the core is plutonium-239, sir," David replied. "But it's got a uranium-235 spark plug and a U-235 pusher as well."

"What about high-explosive lenses?"

"I see two of them."

"How about in the lower left corner, down near the base of the warhead?"

"There's a booster gas canister," David replied. "And there's a small metal pipe going from the canister into the heart of the Primary."

"And the metal casing around the whole device? What shape is it?"

"I don't know," David said. "It's kind of curved—like an hourglass or a peanut."

Zalinsky cursed. "They really did it," he sighed. "This thing could take out all of Tel Aviv."

"Or all of New York," David added, his heart pounding so hard he thought Zalinsky ought to be able to hear it.

"You can't let it ever get that far," Zalinsky ordered.

"I won't, sir," David replied. "I promise."

Suddenly fresh gunfire erupted.

"What is that?" Zalinsky asked.

David frantically looked around through the windows of the ambulance but couldn't see clearly.

"I don't know," he told Zalinsky. "I don't have a visual."

He called to Crenshaw, but Crenshaw said he didn't see a thing. Just then, however, another burst of automatic gunfire erupted, then a second and a third.

"Steve, man, you okay?" David shouted.

"No," Fox shouted back. *"I've got three hostiles approaching up Highway 7. And another dozen moving up the street—maybe more."*

"Can you hold them off?"

"Not for long," Fox shouted. *"Not without help."*

"Do your best, brother," David replied. *"I'll be right with you."*

David picked up the satphone and took it off speakerphone. "I need some more help down here, Jack. We're not going to make it more than a few minutes."

"I see it and I'm on it," Zalinsky replied. "You just stay focused. I'm going to walk you through this."

Fox opened fire once again. Then, to David's surprise, he lobbed two hand grenades at the Syrian forces coming up Rue Ash 'Sham. David hadn't realized Fox had any grenades with him, but the successive explosions shook the ambulance violently. Seconds later, the car shook harder as another Hellfire missile streaked down from a Predator and created an even more enormous explosion at the head of the street. It likely bought them a few more minutes, but David's hands were shaking badly now, and he wondered if any of this movement could set off the warhead.

"Steady, Zephyr, steady," Zalinsky ordered. "Take a deep breath. Wipe your brow. Wipe off your hands, and focus. The last thing you want is sweat dripping into the interior."

"Got it," David said and followed his orders. "Okay, I'm ready."

"Good. Now, you need to find the wires coming from the power source," Zalinsky said.

"There are all kinds of wires here, sir," David replied.

"Atom bomb makers use pure gold to make their wires because gold is most conducive for electricity," said Zalinsky. "My experts here say the Pakistanis typically insulate these wires with yellow plastic. Do you see any yellow wires?"

"Yes, one."

"Where does it lead?"

David carefully followed the yellow trail to a small metal cylinder in the lower right, directly across from the booster gas canister.

"It looks like a flux compression generator," he told Zalinsky.

"That's it," said Zalinsky. "Okay, now, you need to cut the yellow wire."

David wiped his brow again.

"Is there any chance this thing is rigged with security devices?" he asked.

"Like what?" Zalinsky asked.

"Like something to make the core detonate if it's tampered with?"

"Probably not."

"*Probably* not?"

"There would be no point to it," Zalinsky said. "The warhead is designed to be fired at Israel—or at us—not to accidentally detonate in Iran or Syria."

David's eyes were still watering from the heat and smoke. His fingers quivered as he lowered his Swiss Army knife into the warhead and prepared to snip the wires.

"One thing, though," Zalinsky suddenly added.

"What's that?"

"I wouldn't touch anything metal on or near the plutonium core."

"Why not?"

"I just wouldn't."

David tried to swallow, but his mouth was dry. He desperately needed a drink of water but realized he hadn't taken any of the water bottles they'd brought from the car.

"Fine, here goes," he said. "Wish me luck."

Zalinsky, however, didn't say a word. David said a silent prayer, then again lowered the knife into the warhead, said a second prayer, and snipped the yellow wire. Nothing happened. *That was good, wasn't it?* David wondered. They were still here. The bomb hadn't gone off. But they were not done.

"Finished?" Zalinsky asked.

Fox was shooting again. Now so was Crenshaw.

"Yes."

"Okay, you need to stuff the pit."

"What?"

"The pit," Zalinsky repeated. "The hollow sphere of plutonium—can you see it?"

"I can see where it is," David replied, hearing bullets beginning to whiz by the vehicle. "But I can't see it directly."

"That's fine. That's okay. Now, there should be a small, thin tube that goes into the center of that pit."

"To feed the tritium?"

"Exactly."

"Okay, I see the tube."

"Good," said Zalinsky. "You need to clip the near end of that tube and then feed in some steel wire through the tube and into the pit."

Bullets were now smashing into the side of the ambulance. Every muscle in David's body tensed. But he couldn't stop now. Fox and Crenshaw were firing short bursts in multiple directions, trying to keep their attackers at bay. They were sacrificing their own lives to protect David, so he could disable this warhead and make all that they'd been through worth it. If he failed, it would all be for naught.

He forced himself not to think about the other warhead, the one at Al-Mazzah. That one was already attached to a Scud-C ballistic missile. It was going to be fired soon, likely within the hour and maybe sooner once word got back to the Mahdi of the battle under way over this warhead. How were they going to get there in time? How were they possibly going to stop that missile from being fired? Doubt and fear kept pushing their way into David's thoughts, but he forced them out. He couldn't let himself get distracted. He had a job to do, and he had to finish.

Reaching into the core of the warhead once more, David tried to cut the tubing but couldn't get enough leverage. Careful not to touch the scissors to anything but the tiny tube, he leaned in farther and again tried to snip it clean. Glass started smashing around him. More bullets were flying. The gunfight was intensifying, and now Fox was shrieking in pain. He'd been hit. The next moment, another Hellfire missile rained down from above, brutally shaking the ambulance and knocking David onto his side.

Sparks flew inside the warhead. David pulled out his hand and with it the scissors, then held his breath for a few moments. Still, the warhead did not go off. They were still alive, but they wouldn't be for much longer. Wiping soot from his eyes, he reached back into the warhead with the knife. The scissors weren't working. They were too small. So using the knife, he began carefully but quickly trying to saw his way through the tube. To his surprise, it was working. He was making progress. And soon he had cut clean through.

"I got it!" he shouted to Zalinsky.

"You got the tube open?"

"Yeah, I'm in; I got it," David repeated.

"Good, now you need to find some steel wire."

"Where?"

"I have no clue."

The gunfire had erupted again. David frantically tried to imagine where he could find steel wire. He had no idea, and it angered him. If this was so important, why hadn't Zalinsky told them to bring it with them? Then again, maybe he had. The last few days were a blur. David had barely slept, barely eaten. He wasn't thinking sharply. And now he needed steel wire. He called out to Fox and Crenshaw. He told them what he needed, but not why. Neither had steel wire or any suggestion where to find some. He desperately looked around the ambulance but realized that all the medical supplies had been removed. He scrambled into the front passenger seat, wiping more sweat from his face and looking for anything he could possibly use. He found nothing.

He spotted the car's two-way radio system and quickly ripped it out of the dashboard and smashed it open. But there were no wires to be found. It was all solid-state electronic circuit boards. He looked up through the shattered front windshield to see who Fox and Crenshaw were shooting at now, and as he did, he noticed the Chinese-made radio antenna sticking up from the side of the front hood. It was a K-28 model for two-way CB radios. He grabbed the satphone and described the relatively thin antenna to Zalinsky.

"That's perfect," said Zalinsky. "That'll do. Just go quickly."

David kicked open the side door, grabbed the antenna, snapped it off its mount, and scrambled back into the rear of the ambulance. "Now what?" he asked.

"Okay, you need to feed the antenna through the tube," said Zalinsky.

David did as he was told.

"Done," he said.

"No," said Zalinsky. "You need to stuff it in. Cram as much of the antenna into that pit as you possibly can. Wiggle it around. It's flexible, right?"

"Yeah."

"Good. Then keep stuffing it in—again, as much as you can."

David complied.

"Okay, that's it. I did it."

"Good," said Zalinsky. "Now, take your scissors and snip off the end of the antenna."

"Done," David said when he was finished.

"Take the tip of your knife and push the last bit of the antenna into the pit so it can't be seen, can't be grabbed hold of, and can't be pulled out."

David did this as well. "Done," he said again.

"You're sure?" Zalinsky asked.

"I'm sure."

"Good," said Zalinsky. "Now the warhead is permanently disabled."

"Permanently?" David asked.

"Yes," Zalinsky confirmed. "At this point, even if someone could feed tritium into the pit, the implosion can't occur. With the steel wire in there, the pit can't be compressed enough, no matter how intense the explosives. And that's it. No implosion, no detonation. The only way someone can use that warhead now is to cut the entire thing open, take the pit out, take the steel wire out, completely overhaul and remanufacture the plutonium, and put the whole thing back together. It would take weeks if not months."

David couldn't believe it. He'd done it. He started to breathe again, then asked, "Now what?"

"Get your men out of there," Zalinsky ordered. "I'm firing two Hellfire missiles at that ambulance in ninety seconds. No one is touching that warhead. You hear me? No one."

"Got it," said David. "Just find me some wheels."

"Up the street, about forty yards, there's a white four-door Khodro Samand," Zalinsky said, referring to an Iranian-made sedan.

"Thanks," said David.

He cut the line to Langley, shoved the satphone in his pocket, crawled out of the ambulance, and raced up the street. Sure enough, the car was right where Zalinsky said it would be. It wasn't running, but the driver had fled too quickly to remember to take his keys. David jumped in, gunned the engine, and raced to the ambulance. He carefully loaded Fox into the front passenger seat and lowered it to about a forty-five-degree angle. Next, he picked up Crenshaw and laid him on the backseat. Then he gathered their weapons, made sure he wasn't leaving behind any ammo, and jumped in the driver's seat. Seconds later, as he sped along Highway 7 heading southwest, he both heard and felt the Hellfires obliterating the Red Crescent ambulance and what was left of the Iranian nuclear warhead.

"Now what, boss?" Fox asked as David pushed the pedal to the metal.

"Next stop, Damascus, gentlemen."

For David, there were just two questions remaining: Could they neutralize the second warhead? And could they rescue Birjandi? He knew the odds. He also knew his men desperately needed medical attention, but the brutal truth was there was no place to get it. Not yet. Not now. They had to press forward. They had to see this mission through to the bitter end.

48

General Youssef Hamdi raced down the hallway toward his large, plush corner office overlooking the flight line where two dozen MiG-29 fighter jets were parked, gleaming in the midday sunshine. Standing in the hallway were ten heavily armed Revolutionary Guards, along with two bodyguards from the Syrian presidential detail. Sitting there on a chair in the hallway was Dr. Birjandi, still waiting for his meeting with the Twelfth Imam. But the Mahdi was behind closed doors with Ayatollah Hosseini, Syrian president Gamal Mustafa, and General Jazini, along with the Mahdi's most senior aides, Daryush Rashidi and Abdol Esfahani.

"General Hamdi, is that you?" Birjandi asked. "Are you okay?"

"It is me, Dr. Birjandi, but I'm sorry; I cannot speak now," Hamdi replied, his voice agitated, almost panicky. "I must see the Mahdi."

"I'm afraid he is busy," Birjandi said calmly. "He summoned me, as you know, but I keep being told I must wait a little while longer. It's okay, of course; I'm not in a hurry."

"But I am," said Hamdi. "This cannot wait."

It felt strange to Hamdi, knocking on the door to his own office, but he had to remind himself that he was not in charge any longer. He took a deep breath, tried in vain to calm himself, to steady his nerves, then knocked twice.

"Who is it?" Jazini asked.

"Your humble servant," Hamdi replied.

"Come," said the Mahdi.

Cautiously the Syrian commander entered, knelt, and bowed to the ground.

"Is everything all right, General Hamdi?" Jazini asked. "You're breathless."

"I have terrible news, Your Excellency," Hamdi replied, his forehead still touching the Persian carpet.

"The convoy has been attacked by the Zionists outside of Dayr az-Zawr," said the Mahdi.

The general looked up, startled. He had no idea whether the attack had come from Israelis or Americans or some other force, but he was still reeling from the fact that the attack had happened at all. Who could possibly have known they were sending the warhead to the north? They hadn't told anyone. Jazini hadn't even allowed Hamdi to alert the commander of the air base in Dayr az-Zawr, a close personal friend for more than a quarter of a century. Strict operational security had been maintained.

"How did you know, Your Excellency?" Hamdi asked. "I just got the news from the commander of the air base there myself."

"My men called me from the scene a few minutes ago," Jazini explained.

"How could this have happened?" Daryush Rashidi now asked, taking the words out of Hamdi's own mouth.

"Ye of little faith," the Mahdi said. "The ruse worked just as I had suspected."

Perplexed, Hamdi asked, "How so, my Lord?"

"We have a mole," the Mahdi explained. "Someone on this base— indeed, likely someone in this very room—is working for the Zionists."

The room went deathly silent.

"And since I know and trust everyone in this room except you, General Hamdi," the Mahdi continued, "I'm going to have to conclude it is you."

Hamdi began shaking. He couldn't believe what he was hearing. He had been a loyal servant of the Syrian Arab Republic since he had been drafted into the air force at the age of eighteen. He was a devout Muslim, an Alawi, and a distantly related cousin of President Mustafa. He had numerous medals for bravery and was known, above all else, for his loyalty to the regime. In fact, he had personally overseen many of the massacres in recent weeks against Syrian Christians and Jews and even the stepped-up, targeted murders of high-ranking pastors and priests in just the past two days, a command that had come directly from the Mahdi. What's more, he had created the very infrastructure of ballistic-missile development and deployment that was making possible the Mahdi's goal of attacking the Zionists with a nuclear warhead from Syrian soil. How could anyone believe he had sold out his country or the Caliphate?

Both terrified and angry, Hamdi wanted to defend himself. He wanted to prove his faithfulness, but a deep chill suddenly descended upon the room or at least upon him. He felt paralyzed by a force that had come over him. He couldn't speak, couldn't move. Though he could not turn his head, he sensed a dark spirit moving close by, and then he sensed several. They were swirling about his feet and his chest and now his head, and then it was as though they had entered through his nostrils and his mouth, and he felt himself being choked to death, but it was as though he were being choked from within.

"Take him out," the Mahdi ordered. "Gather the senior staff in Hangar Five, where Dr. Zandi is making his final preparations for launch. We will execute him there."

Hamdi wanted to scream, wanted to cry, but he was immobilized, frozen solid inside his own body. He looked at Mustafa as if to appeal for his honor and for his life, but the Syrian president's eyes were cold and cruel and showed not the slightest bit of mercy. How was that possible? How had Hamdi's career of dedicated service come to this? And what would happen to his beloved wife and his three beautiful daughters? If he were executed, they would all be slaughtered by sundown. He wasn't sure of much at the moment, but of that he had not a shred of doubt.

Several Revolutionary Guards rushed in, handcuffed him, and dragged him away. No one spoke for him. No one came to rescue him, not even his own men whom he had trained, whom he had commanded. The last thing he saw and heard as he was being whisked away was Abdol Esfahani stepping out into the hallway and telling Dr. Birjandi, "I'm sorry, my friend; much is happening. It's still going to be a few more minutes."

★ ★ ★ ★

Birjandi heard the door to General Hamdi's office fly open and then slam closed. Then it opened again, and he could hear a commotion as someone was being dragged away, but of course he had no idea what was happening. He asked Esfahani, but the man wouldn't answer directly. Indeed, Esfahani seemed quite scared. He would only say that the Mahdi was not yet ready to see him. But just before the door to Hamdi's office slammed shut yet again, Birjandi heard the Mahdi say something to the effect that they needed to "launch the warhead immediately" and they could "not wait any longer" because it was now getting "too dangerous."

Men with heavy boots were coming down the hallway toward him. Birjandi sensed these were more Revolutionary Guards, come to beef up protection around the Mahdi. Something serious had happened. Birjandi wondered if David and his men were involved in whatever it was.

"Abdol, are you still there?" he asked.

"Yes, but I must go back in," Esfahani replied.

Birjandi reached out and found Esfahani's arm and took hold of it.

"May I use the restroom before this meeting starts?" he asked.

"Of course, but I cannot take you," said Esfahani. "The Mahdi needs me."

Esfahani directed one of the guards to escort Birjandi, and soon they were shuffling down the hallway to a men's room. When they got to the door, Birjandi asked the guard to check and make sure no one else was in there. The guard complied, and when Birjandi heard him open the door and click on the light, he knew immediately the facility was unoccupied. Still, the guard stepped back out a moment later to assure him that everything was safe and that Birjandi would be alone.

The old man thanked the young guard, stepped into the restroom, and locked the door. He felt around the walls to get the dimensions of the room, then stood still in the center of the room and listened carefully. It was quiet, save the buzz of the fluorescent lights above, none of which Birjandi needed, but he did notice a cool breeze coming from somewhere. He raised his right hand and felt a slight current of air moving along the top of the room. That meant there had to be a window.

Birjandi unlocked the door and stepped out for a moment.

"Young man," he said to the guard.

"Yes, sir?"

"I will need to wash my hands and face, but my legs are a bit shaky today," Birjandi said. "Would you mind bringing me a sturdy chair that I may sit on at the sink?"

"Why, of course, Dr. Birjandi," the soldier replied in a Farsi that belied a slight accent from southern Iran. Birjandi wondered if the young man might be from the city of Shiraz. There was no point in asking. There wasn't time to get personal at the moment. But it made him think again of David Shirazi and how urgently he needed to talk to his friend. Events were unfolding so rapidly now. This would, in fact, likely be the last time they could speak.

A moment later, the guard was back with the chair, and he set it in front of one of the bathroom sinks. Birjandi thanked the man, then closed the door behind him and locked it. He went over to the chair, picked it up, and set it against the far wall. Then slowly, carefully, he climbed up on the chair and felt along the wall until he found that, sure enough, there was a small window there. It was open slightly, but he cranked it all the way open. Then he reached under his robes, pulled out his satphone, powered it up, and stuck it out the window, praying for a connection. Birjandi felt along the keypad until he found the Redial key David had shown him, and he pressed it. Would it go through? If it did, would David answer? And if he did, could Birjandi tell him what he needed to tell him without being overheard by the guard?

M20 HIGHWAY, CENTRAL SYRIA

How was this ever going to work? How was he ever going to get there in time?

David was racing through the wastelands of central Syria at nearly a hundred miles an hour. Unfortunately the car wouldn't go any faster, and David berated himself for not stealing a Mercedes rather than this Iranian family sedan.

At this point, he was off Highway 7 and was flying down the M20 expressway. He had already blown through the town of As Sukhnah and would soon be passing the ancient ruins of Palmyra, known in Arabic as Tadmur. At that point, according to Fox, who was in charge of the map, they would exit onto Route 90 and later onto Route 53. Eventually they would shift onto Highway 2, which would take them directly into Damascus.

David glanced at his watch. It was 12:17 p.m. local time. The problem was, Damascus was over 200 kilometers from Palmyra. At this rate, it would take them more than an hour to get there, and David was certain they didn't have that much time.

Fox's satphone rang. David answered it immediately. He was sure it wasn't going to be Zalinsky. David had already talked to his handler for much of the past half hour, briefing him on Fox's and Crenshaw's conditions and war-gaming their next moves. And he was right. It was Eva.

"Hey, it's me—why aren't you answering your own phone?" she asked.

"I lost it in the gun battle," David replied.

Eva gasped. "What gun battle?"

"It's a long story, but I can't talk about it now," David said.

"Where are you?"

"Near Palmyra."

"And you're heading for Al-Mazzah?"

"Exactly."

"Well, you've got a friend looking for you," Eva said.

David immediately thought of Marseille, then his father. But how could it be either? Neither had his satphone number.

"Who?"

"Dr. Birjandi."

"Really?" David asked. "He called me?"

"Yes, about ten minutes ago."

"Why? What did he say?"

"He had three things to tell you," Eva replied. "First, he told you not to call him. He said it's too dangerous and that this would likely be his last communication with you 'in this life.'"

David swallowed hard. He tried to press harder on the accelerator, but it was already on the floor. The car simply wouldn't go any faster than it was, and David harbored doubts the vehicle could really make it all the way to Damascus at this speed. He couldn't imagine this engine ever having been pushed so hard, especially not in the dust and heat of the Syrian desert.

"Second, he said the warhead is attached to the Scud and on the launchpad, and he believes the Mahdi and President Mustafa are heading there any moment to watch it be launched."

David pounded his fist on the dashboard. He wasn't going to make it. He pleaded with the Lord to do something, to help him, to give him wisdom, but he couldn't find any possible way to stop this launch from happening.

"And third?" he asked impatiently.

"He said he was proud of you and loved you like the son he never had," Eva said. "He said he would see you on the other side and that he hoped Jesus would let him be the first one to welcome you into heaven."

At that David choked up. He had never had a friend in his eighties, nor had he ever imagined having—or wanting—a friend that old. But neither had he ever had a friend he'd loved and appreciated more than Dr. Birjandi, and just hearing these words made him miss the man and his gentle wisdom all the more.

"You okay?" Eva asked.

"Not really," David replied.

"He meant that much to you, huh?"

"He still does," said David. "He's not dead yet."

"What are you going to do?" Eva asked.

"For starters, I'm calling Jack."

Zalinsky answered David's call immediately.

"I just heard from Birjandi," David began, abandoning all protocol. "The missile is on the launchpad. The Mahdi and Mustafa are heading there now. They're about to launch, Jack, and I'm not going to get there in time. You've got to call the president. You've got to tell him to order an air strike—now, before it's too late."

"Hey, hey, settle down, Zephyr," Zalinsky replied. "We've got that air base covered—a satellite and three Predators are monitoring everything going on there. Believe me, they're not ready to launch."

"Just because you can't see it doesn't mean it isn't true, Jack," David insisted. "What have you always taught me? *'To misunderstand the nature and threat of evil is to risk being blindsided by it.'* Right? I'm telling you, Birjandi is there. He's inside, and he's telling us the Scud is on the launchpad. The warhead is attached. They're getting ready to launch—probably at Tel Aviv—at any moment. I've done my job. So has my team. We've done everything you've asked us to do. We found the warheads. We took one out, with your help. Now we're racing to the second one because you ordered us to. Right?"

"Of course it's true," Zalinsky replied, clearly annoyed but also somewhat—and uncharacteristically—restrained.

"Then listen to me," David continued. "Even if by some miracle we could get there before they launch, you don't have a realistic plan to get us into that base, and neither do we. This is it, Jack. We've done everything we possibly could. Now it's up to you. This is the moment. You need to get the president to order a strike now."

"Zephyr, listen to me," Zalinsky said. "The two Iranian terrorists responsible for the recent attacks at the Waldorf in New York have just arrived in Damascus. They're heading for the Al-Mazzah base as we speak. We've had two operatives tracking them the whole time, and now those operatives are in Damascus, awaiting instructions. I can link you and your team up with them."

"And then what?" David asked. "That's still not enough men, and there's still not enough time. You have to get the president to order a strike now."

The debate got more heated—a lot more heated—and went on several more minutes. It was time, David knew all too painfully, they couldn't afford. Still, he made an impassioned and nearly insubordinate case for a massive, lightning-fast attack by F/A-18s and cruise missiles launched from Carrier Strike Group Ten and the USS *Harry S. Truman*, currently steaming through the eastern Mediterranean. When Zalinsky refused to commit, David argued that at the very least the Agency had the moral obligation to inform the Israelis that they were about to be hit, but an even greater moral obligation to proactively and aggressively defend Israel, the United States's most faithful ally in the region, not to mention the Palestinians, who were completely defenseless and unprepared for what was coming.

David knew he was on speakerphone. He knew the entire Global Operations Center was listening in, including Tom Murray and Director Allen, and that's precisely why he was making the case so strenuously. Because he was being listened to. Because he was being recorded, and not just in the GOC but by the NSA as well. Because if somehow he lived through this day and stood trial for illegally informing the Israelis, he wanted evidence on the record that he had made the case, that he had done everything he could to push the Agency and the White House to do the right thing . . . and had failed.

Another few minutes passed. Zalinsky wasn't budging. It wasn't because Zalinsky didn't agree with him, David could tell from the conversation, but because he knew the president wouldn't act regardless. Nevertheless, David pleaded with his mentor and handler one more time to at least make the case to the president or have Allen do it. At least try.

"Just think of it, Jack," David concluded. "Not only could the president take out this warhead and save Israel in one shot, but it could be a decapitating strike. The president could take out the Mahdi, Hosseini, and Mustafa all at the same time. With Darazi dead too, that would effectively neutralize the threat of any of the Pakistani missiles being used by the Caliphate. Indeed, the Caliphate would likely unravel. Jackson would be a hero. With one strike, the United States might never have to go to war in the Middle East again."

David knew the last thought was a bit of an overreach, but only a bit. And then, to his surprise, Director Allen came on the line.

"You make a compelling case, Zephyr," Allen said calmly. "I'm convinced, and I'm calling the president right now."

49

"Do you believe him?" Crenshaw whispered, in excruciating pain but still conscious and apparently still paying attention.

"Who? Allen?" David clarified.

"Yeah."

"Do I believe he's going to make my case to the president?"

"Right."

"Yes, I do," David said.

"Will it matter?" Fox asked.

"You mean do I think the president will order an air strike to defend Israel?"

"Exactly."

"Do you?" David asked them both.

He glanced in the rearview mirror. Crenshaw shook his head. Then he looked at Fox, who also shook his head. Well, he thought, at least they were all on the same page.

"So what are we going to do?" Fox asked.

"There's nothing we can do, not together," David conceded. "But there's something I can do."

"What do you mean?" Crenshaw asked.

"I'm going to make a call," David said. "You're not part of it. You didn't support it. I'm doing it on my own, and I'm ready to pay the consequences. But as for me, I don't have a choice. This is something I have to do."

Fox and Crenshaw looked as bewildered as they must have felt, but David didn't have time to explain. He dialed the number to the Mossad from memory. It didn't go through. He dialed again. It still didn't go through. Speed-dialing Eva, he asked her to repeat the phone number to him, lest he'd dropped or added a digit. But he hadn't. The number she gave him was the number he'd just dialed not once but twice. *Had the Mossad shut it down, even with Mordecai still out there?* he wondered. It was an awfully big risk, one that might prove fatal.

DAMASCUS, SYRIA

The door of General Hamdi's office swung open. Esfahani watched as General Jazini led the way out of the office and down the hall with the Mahdi right behind him, followed by the Ayatollah, President Mustafa, and Rashidi, who was carrying the "nuclear football" of communications gear and Pakistani launch codes. They were surrounded by Iranian and Syrian bodyguards and they were moving quickly.

Once they were gone, Esfahani took a deep breath and stepped out of Hamdi's office as well. He asked Dr. Birjandi to take his arm and keep up with him. "We don't have much time," he explained.

"Why? Where are we going?" Birjandi asked.

"Hangar Five," said Esfahani.

"Is that where the warhead is?" Birjandi asked.

"Not for long."

At the end of the long hallway, they boarded an elevator and descended to ground level. There, a lone black sedan was waiting for them. The rest of the entourage, Esfahani noted, was already gone. He put Birjandi in the back, closed the door, and got into the front passenger seat.

"Move it," he ordered. "Hangar Five."

Birjandi was a hero of Esfahani's, but events were moving rapidly now, and Esfahani somewhat resented being the old man's babysitter. He didn't want to risk the possibility, however slim, of getting left out—or shut out—of witnessing the launch.

His slight frustration at his current task notwithstanding, Esfahani was trembling with excitement. This was the day they had prayed for so long, the day they had planned and worked for so long, and it was finally here. He had been a devoted Twelver all his life, but ever since first actually meeting the Mahdi in Hamadan on the day of the massive earthquake—what turned out to be the day of Iran's first underground nuclear test—Esfahani had been in something of a fever. He could barely sleep. He desperately wanted to be found faithful in the Mahdi's service, and now here he was, in the inner circle, on launch day, the day the War of Annihilation of the Zionists would finally be won.

It was turning into a nasty March day, threatening clouds moving in. Esfahani expected it to burst out raining at any moment. He wondered if that would delay the launch in any way and desperately hoped not.

"Faster," he ordered the driver. "You must move faster."

The driver accelerated, and they sped across the air base to the far side, to a remote corner, a good six or seven minutes away from the main facilities.

"Why is it taking so long?" Birjandi asked.

"You'll see," Esfahani said, then realized how ridiculous that was. "I'm sorry, Dr. Birjandi. Please forgive me. There are certain things I am not permitted to say."

"To me?" Birjandi asked. "Why?"

"Well—"

"You think a blind eschatology professor—personally summoned here by Imam al-Mahdi himself—is going to give secrets to the Zionists?" Birjandi charged.

"No, no, I'm just—"

"Then where are we going?" Birjandi asked again. "I don't have much in my life, my young friend, but I like to have some idea where I am. It gives me a sense of peace, of clarity, that I'm not sure I can adequately explain to you."

"You're right, and I'm very sorry," Esfahani replied. "I have been very rude. You are the father of the Twelver movement, Dr. Birjandi. Until Imam al-Mahdi revealed himself to mankind, no one had done more than you to explain who he was and why he mattered. My deepest apologies."

"You're stalling, Abdol."

Esfahani smiled. The old man was a shrewd judge of character.

The car stopped. They had arrived. He leaned over and whispered in Birjandi's ear. "Hangar Five is a secret. It's an underground hangar on the far edge of the base. It's out by the leach field, near where they burn all the refuse. Come, my friend; let's go see history be made."

PALMYRA, SYRIA

David and his team were now cruising past the ancient ruins of Palmyra.

"Do you see signs for Route 90?" Fox asked.

"The turn is just ahead," David said.

"Good," said Fox. "Take it, and then watch for Route 53 in about another seventy or eighty kilometers."

"Who were you calling?" Crenshaw asked from the backseat.

"No one," said David. "It's not important."

"It *is* important," Crenshaw responded. "You said so yourself. That's why you made such a big deal about making sure we had deniability."

"It didn't work anyway," said David. "The call didn't go through."

"Who were you calling?" Crenshaw pressed again.

"Look, it doesn't matter. Let it drop."

"You were calling the Israelis, weren't you?" said Fox.

David stared straight ahead and kept driving. "You guys need to rest."

"No, we need to stop these madmen from incinerating an American ally," said Fox. "You think we're not with you? That's our mission, David. That's what we're here to do—protect the American people and our allies from a nuclear holocaust. Isn't it?"

David was silent.

"How did you get that number?" Crenshaw asked.

"I'd rather not say."

"Get off it, David," Crenshaw shot back. "This is it, man. We're dying here. Fox and me might very well not make it. We get that. We're okay with that. But we're not okay with you holding back information that could save the lives of millions. Now start talking!"

David felt ashamed. Crenshaw was right. He didn't know why he hadn't brought them into this sooner. He'd been trying to protect them.

But maybe he should have at least given them the option of rejecting his plan rather than keeping it from them. He explained the call he had made earlier at the border and why he'd made it.

"And now that number won't work?" Fox asked.

"Right."

"They probably cut the line," Crenshaw said.

"Maybe," said David. "But that's it. I'm out of ideas."

"You don't have any other numbers to the Mossad?" Fox asked.

"No, do you?"

"As a matter of fact, I do."

David looked at him quizzically. "How?"

"Tolik," said Fox.

"What?"

"Call Matty," Fox continued. "Tell him the situation. Tell him to give that Tolik guy a satphone and have him call the Mossad. They'll listen to their own man a lot more than they'll listen to you. They've got to listen to him. And Naphtali will definitely order a strike. But you'd better move fast."

"You know we'll all go to prison," said David.

Fox shook his head and looked at David. "Just you, my friend," he said. "Nick and I . . . it's not going to matter. We're not going to make it back."

David winced. He refused to believe that. He didn't even want to think about it. But deep down, he feared Fox might be right.

"You're sure?" David asked. "Both of you?"

Fox and Crenshaw nodded, and David finally did as well.

"Then get Matty on the phone," he said.

He wasn't convinced they had time for one last ploy, but these guys were right. They had to try.

DAMASCUS, SYRIA

It was called a hangar, but it wasn't really, Esfahani realized, not in the classic sense. There were no fighter jets housed here. No bombers. No refueling tankers or trainers or any other jets or planes of any kind. This was a strategic missile base—and a clandestine one at that.

As they cleared through two heavy security checkpoints and he helped Dr. Birjandi off the elevator and onto the hangar floor, Esfahani was struck by what an enormous facility it really was. In one of their brief coffee breaks, Zandi had hinted to him that it was large, but Esfahani had had no idea. It stretched at least twenty soccer fields in both directions, maybe more. At this end, it was both an R & D center and an assembly line for state-of-the-art missiles. Several hundred yards down the range, it was a subterranean launch facility. So fascinated was he that he began to whisper to Birjandi details of what he was seeing, and Birjandi seemed to indicate he was grateful for Esfahani's play-by-play reporting and color commentary.

"What are you seeing now?" Birjandi asked.

"There's a group of technicians scurrying around," Esfahani replied. "They're all wearing white lab coats, and they seem to be making last-minute preparations."

"On the missile?"

"Actually, on six."

"Six what?" Birjandi asked.

"Six missiles," said Esfahani. "They all look like Scuds, but they seem to be an advanced model. I've never seen any quite like this."

"Meaning what?"

"Meaning they're taller and wider, and their rocket engines look larger," Esfahani said.

"But only one has the warhead, right?"

"Apparently, but they all look the same to me," Esfahani observed.

"Clever," Birjandi said. "I'm guessing they'll fire them all at once, and the Israelis won't know which one to shoot down."

"Perhaps you're right," said Esfahani. "That *would* be clever."

He then began describing other elements of the building, beginning with the six launchpads themselves. He described the enormous metal blast shields that were now being hydraulically raised from the floor, presumably to prevent the Mahdi and his guests from being incinerated upon launch. He also noted the unique ceiling of the facility, which had some kind of gigantic levers and pulleys and other devices he didn't quite know how to describe, all of which would evidently open on cue to allow the missiles to be fired into the afternoon sky.

Esfahani was marveling at it all when they heard General Jazini call for quiet and for all the guests to come forward to the missiles.

"Imam al-Mahdi is going to say a few words; then we have some business to attend to, and then the historic moment will commence."

ROUTE 90, CENTRAL SYRIA

David quickly briefed Matt Mays over Fox's satphone. Then he put Fox and Crenshaw each on the line to confirm they were all in agreement.

"You in?" David asked.

"Absolutely," Mays replied. "Maybe we can get sent to the same prison."

David smiled for what felt like the first time in days. "We should be so lucky, Matty."

David could hear Mays unlocking the makeshift holding cell and calling Tolik Shalev and Gal Rinat to come out and sit with him. A moment later, Mays turned on the speakerphone and David briefed the two Israelis as quickly and concisely as he possibly could, even explaining the call he had made several hours earlier to the Mossad.

"So will you do it?" he asked when he was done.

"Of course," said Tolik. "You really should have used us sooner."

DAMASCUS, SYRIA

Gathered together in front of the launchpad for Missile Four were Ayatollah Hosseini, Syrian president Gamal Mustafa, General Jazini, and Dr. Birjandi, with Esfahani and Rashidi standing nearby, along with Dr. Zandi, numerous armed Revolutionary Guards, Syrian bodyguards, various other military officers and technicians, and both an official videographer and a still photographer.

To Esfahani's shock, on the floor underneath the nozzle of this particular missile, both handcuffed and chained to the nozzle, lay a trembling and pale General Hamdi. The Twelfth Imam, meanwhile, stepped up on a small stand and began to speak.

"Gentlemen," he began, for there were no women to be seen, "we have a traitor in our midst. General Hamdi is a mole. He is a betrayer of the Caliphate, and he must now die for his crimes. But rather than behead him, I have decided that he should burn in the fires of this rocket before he burns for all eternity in the fires of hell."

Esfahani was glad they had caught the mole, but he had never imagined it would be Hamdi. He felt sorry for the man and shuddered to think of what his fate was going to be moments from now.

"That said, let us not allow the sins of General Hamdi here to distract us from this historic moment," the Mahdi continued. "I have gathered you all here to celebrate the dawn of a new era in human history, the rise of the Caliphate that is consolidating power throughout the Islamic world and will soon—with Allah's help—sweep across the planet. As I said in Mecca when I first revealed myself to the world, the age of arrogance and corruption and greed is over. A new age of justice and peace and brotherhood has come. It is time for Islam to unite. No longer do Muslims have the luxury of petty infighting and division. Sunnis and Shiites must come together. It is time to create one Islamic people, one Islamic nation, one Islamic government. It is time to show the world that Islam is ready to rule. We will not be confined to geographic borders, ethnic groups, or nations. Ours is a universal message that will lead the world to the unity and peace the nations have thus far found elusive."

Esfahani trembled with anticipation.

"No longer will the blasphemous powers of the West subjugate Muslims with their armies and their laws," the Mahdi boomed. "Nor will they defile our women and children with the toxic cultural pollution they pump into the air—their satanic movies and music and television programs and religious heresies. It is time for the peoples of the world to open their eyes and open their ears and open their hearts. It is time for mankind to see and hear and understand the power of Islam, the glory of Islam. For I have come to usher in a new kingdom. At the beginning, the governments of Iran, Saudi Arabia, and the Gulf States joined together as one nation. I noted at the time that these would form the core of the Caliphate. I promised then that in short order we would be announcing our expansion, and I have kept my word."

The Twelfth Imam pointed to the six missiles behind him.

"I told those who would oppose us that this Caliphate would control half the world's supply of oil and natural gas, as well as the Gulf and the shipping lanes through the Strait of Hormuz. I told our enemies that this Caliphate would have the world's most powerful military, led by the hand of Allah. Furthermore, I told them that this Caliphate would be covered by a nuclear umbrella that would protect the people from all evil. At the time, the Islamic Republic of Iran had just successfully conducted a nuclear weapons test, their weapons were finally operational, and—thanks to our dear friend Ayatollah Hosseini—they had just handed over command and control of these weapons to me. Now, thanks to our dear friend President Farooq, our arsenal has been expanded manyfold. I warned the Zionists and the Americans that any attack by any state on any portion of the Caliphate would unleash the fury of Allah and trigger a War of Annihilation, and so it has. Today, we will show the world who we really are. We will erase the stain of the State of Israel from the map of the earth. We will begin to eradicate this cancer of the Jewish people from the global body politic, and we will not rest until every Jew and every Christian and every infidel of every kind bows to me and gives his praise to Allah."

Esfahani was about to clap and cheer, but no one else was doing so. It was, he decided, too solemn and holy a moment.

"In a moment, we will pray and dedicate these weapons of life," the Mahdi continued. "But first I want to acknowledge a special guest. You all know Dr. Alireza Birjandi as the world's foremost expert on Islamic eschatology and the teacher whom Allah used to help people understand who the Twelfth Imam is, why I would return, how I would return, and why it would matter. I asked him to come here today to see the culmination of all his writings, to see the prophecies truly come to pass. I know he cannot literally see these things, but this is only because

Allah has taken away his physical sight in order to give him something more precious—a supernatural ability to see the spiritual world more clearly than anyone else but me. So I welcome you, Dr. Birjandi. I honor you for your service to Allah, for helping to prepare the way for me. And I look forward to making you a valued member of my kingdom in the days and weeks and years ahead."

At this, all the assembled VIPs and staff erupted in sustained applause. Esfahani was touched by how humble Birjandi was, how he shook his head and seemed genuinely uncomfortable with all the attention.

"Dr. Birjandi, we have only moments," the Mahdi added. "But would you say a few words before we begin?"

There was more applause that echoed through the cavernous facility, and Esfahani helped Birjandi walk over to the missile and step up on the small podium, while the Mahdi stepped aside several paces. The old man stood there for a moment, cleared his throat, but seemed to hesitate.

"Please, Dr. Birjandi, share what is on your heart," the Mahdi prompted.

Birjandi cleared his throat again and nodded. "Very well," he said, "I will share what is on my heart. I must say that I agree that God has taken away my physical sight to give me spiritual eyes, and for this I am most grateful. Sometimes the truth is right in front of us, and most men cannot see it. But God rewards those who walk by faith and not by sight. God rewards those who seek the truth with all their heart and soul and mind and strength. When we know the truth, that truth will set us free. And I am here to declare to all of you today that in all my years of studying the end of days, I finally found the One who is the Way, the Truth, and the Life, and his name is Jesus Christ. I have given my life wholly and completely to him, and I implore each of you today to do so as well."

Esfahani was aghast. What was Birjandi doing—and why now of all moments? The Twelfth Imam was not offended, however; he was enraged.

"Alireza, what are you saying?" the Mahdi demanded. "Do you dare renounce Islam and speak such blasphemies in my presence? Do you dare—?"

But Birjandi cut in and insisted that he was not speaking blasphemies, that he was not speaking lies but only speaking of each man's desperate need to receive Jesus Christ as Savior and Lord and renounce all others.

"Do not dare interrupt me, Alireza!" the Mahdi bellowed. *"You are here at my invitation, and I am grateful for your contributions to the Revolution. But you will bow before me and beg me for my pardon. No one interrupts me and certainly not today."*

"I will not bow to you, Ali," Birjandi retorted, using the Mahdi's never-used name. "I will bow only to the one true God, and that is not you. Ali, you are not the true Messiah. You are a false messiah, and today you and all who follow you will face the judgment of the living God, the God of Abraham, Isaac, and Jacob, the God of Israel, the God and Father of the Lord and Savior Jesus Christ, the one true Messiah."

Esfahani gasped. Horrified and perplexed all at once, he instinctively took several steps back, away from Birjandi, as did the others.

"General Hamdi is not guilty of betraying you, Ali," Birjandi continued. *"You* are guilty of betraying us all, of leading millions into evil with false teaching, witchcraft, and sorcery." Then Birjandi raised his blind gaze and seemed to address all those gathered in the hangar. "I am not a follower of the Mahdi. I am a follower of the Lord and Savior Jesus Christ, and in the name of Christ I bring the word of the Lord to you: Repent. Turn away from this wickedness. Judgment is coming. Damascus is about to be destroyed, as is your false kingdom built upon lies. You do not have much time. You must repent and turn to Christ for salvation. He will forgive you. He will save you from this devil. But you must repent now, before it is too late."

Esfahani was shifting from shock to rage. He couldn't believe what this beloved mentor was saying. Birjandi had gone crazy. He didn't know how or when, but all Esfahani could see was red. This was the mole. This was the betrayer. It was clear to him. It must be clear to all of them. But just as he decided to attack the old man and shut his mouth and beat him to death for daring to blaspheme here in the presence of the Mahdi, he saw General Jazini—eyes wild with rage—draw his pistol, lunge for the old man, and put a bullet between his eyes.

Birjandi snapped backward. The back of his head exploded. His body collapsed to the floor. Blood pooled. The old man was clearly dead, but Esfahani couldn't help himself. He, too, lunged forward and began beating the body like a man possessed.

50

David silently prayed for Birjandi. At least the old man was at Al-Mazzah. He was on the inside. He knew what was happening. Maybe there was some way he could stop the launch or at least stall it. It wasn't much to count on at this late hour, but it increasingly seemed all they had.

David and his team were fast approaching the junction with Route 53. That meant the outskirts of Damascus were less than an hour away. There was nothing more to do, David told himself, but wait and pray that the Israelis got the message and launched their attack. He also prayed for Marseille and his father and then for Torres's wife and two little daughters. He couldn't imagine the pain that would hit them when they heard the news of Marco's death. But he was so grateful to the Lord that at least he'd had the opportunity to share the gospel with Torres and that Torres's heart had been so open and that he'd said yes to Christ.

And then it dawned on David that not only was there more he *could* do, but there was something he *had* to do and thus far had failed to. He had to share the gospel with Fox and Crenshaw, too, and quickly. He realized he had no idea what their spiritual backgrounds were, but how could he forgive himself if he did not do all he could in the next few moments to share with them the Good News of forgiveness and eternal life through faith in Jesus Christ? God had given David a great gift, a great treasure, and David had offered it to Torres. Now he urgently needed to offer it to these two dear men as well.

"Gentlemen," he said, "it has been a great honor to go into battle with you. I couldn't have asked for a better team. And I need to say something to you both that I told Marco before he died. . . ."

TEL AVIV, ISRAEL

Zvi Dayan burst into Levi Shimon's office. The defense minister was on a call and put up his hand, motioning for Dayan to wait.

Shimon covered the phone's mouthpiece. "I'm on with London—MI6. I'll be with you in a moment."

"It can't wait," Dayan said.

"It'll have to."

Dayan reached over and depressed the disconnect button on the desktop console, severing the connection.

Shimon cursed and jumped to his feet. "What the—?"

"Levi, listen to me—I just heard from one of my men inside Iran."

"Mordecai?"

"No, Cyrus."

"This had better be good."

"It is—he confirmed both warheads are in Syria," Dayan breathlessly explained. "He says a CIA team took out a convoy carrying one nuke in northern Syria, not far from the Iraqi border. The other, Cyrus says, is at Al-Mazzah Air Force Base in Damascus. What's more, he says the Mahdi is there at the base, along with Ayatollah Hosseini, President Mustafa, and, presumably, all the Pakistani launch codes the Mahdi just got from Farooq in Kabul."

"Can he prove it?" the defense minister asked.

"Not in the time we have," Dayan said.

"Do you trust him?"

"Absolutely," said Dayan. "He's one of my best men."

"A mole?"

"No, an Israeli, a sabra—one of us."

Shimon closed his eyes for a moment. Launching a preemptive strike on Iran was one thing. Launching a preemptive strike on Syria was still another. But this did appear to be confirmation from a second source.

The prime minister was likely to order the attack any moment regardless. Now all signs were pointing to Al-Mazzah as the best target.

"Okay, get the PM on the line," the defense minister finally said. "If he's going to go, he's got to go now."

DAMASCUS, SYRIA

"Silence!" the Mahdi shouted. *"Silence.* Allah is the one true God, and you have no need to fear. Allah can see the traitors in our midst, and he will bring them to judgment. This is war, gentlemen. Our enemies are everywhere. Many are deceived. Few are chosen to know and follow the path to Allah. But you are. You know the truth. You know that Islam is the answer, jihad is the way, Muhammad is our prophet, and I am your savior. Stay focused. Do not let the enemy distract you. Not now. Not when we are so close to victory. You must pray for strength, for the courage to submit to the will of Allah, no matter what the cost. Come, I will lead you into his presence, and together we will dedicate these missiles to achieving Allah's will."

Several guards pulled Esfahani off Birjandi's body. Esfahani was covered in blood. He was shaking with rage. He could barely hear what the Mahdi was saying. But he followed suit as the others got down on their knees, faced Mecca, and prayed for victory in the War of Annihilation.

When they were finished, the Mahdi stepped down. General Jazini then directed his men to push the body of Dr. Birjandi next to General Hamdi, directly under the nozzle of the nuclear-armed Scud. The general desperately protested that he was not the traitor in their midst, that Birjandi was, but neither Jazini nor the others would listen. Then Jazini directed everyone to the rear of the facility, behind the blast shields, and into steel and concrete bunkers, where they would be able to watch the launch of all six missiles through specially treated and reinforced glass, as well as on multiple video monitors and radar tracking displays.

Just as everyone began to follow Jazini and the Mahdi, however, Dr. Zandi walked over to General Hamdi and called out to the others.

"These men were not traitors!" he shouted. *"I am the mole!"*

Once again, Esfahani and the others were stunned.

General Jazini drew his pistol again. A dozen Revolutionary Guards aimed their AK-47s at the Iranian scientist.

"Stop it, Dr. Zandi," Jazini ordered. "Be silent and step away from that missile."

"I will not be silent!" Zandi shouted, his trembling voice echoing throughout the huge facility. "I did not sign up to build nuclear weapons. That's not why I joined the Atomic Energy Organization of Iran. Dr. Saddaji recruited me to help him build peaceful nuclear reactors, to safeguard Iran's energy security. But he lied to me. He betrayed me. And now it will cost him."

Esfahani noticed two guards coming to his side, presumably to keep him from taking any rash actions. The last thing they needed was a shoot-out inside a nuclear missile facility. He tried to stay calm, but his mind was reeling. What was Zandi saying? Had he really turned against the Mahdi as well? What was happening? And why now?

"You will be silent, or you will be possessed by a legion of demons," the Mahdi bellowed, striding forward in his black robes and black turban to confront this new enemy of the Caliphate.

"I warn you," Zandi shouted. *"I warn you not to fire this missile."*

"Or what?" Jazini demanded to know.

"Or it will detonate above your heads, just seconds after liftoff."

"He's bluffing," said the Ayatollah.

"I am not bluffing," Zandi shot back. "How do you think the Israelis found Dr. Saddaji? I gave him to them. Why do you think the Israelis knew precisely where to strike last Thursday? Why do you think your nuclear program keeps failing? Because I'm opposed to it. I hate it. I hate it with every fiber of my being. This warhead will never destroy the Zionists. I programmed it to detonate two seconds after liftoff. I would have done the same with the warhead you sent to Dayr az-Zawr. If you launch this missile, you will destroy only yourselves. Not that it really matters. I have no doubt the Israelis are launching a massive air strike against Syria, and especially against this base, even as we speak."

"He's a liar!" Jazini shouted. *"He speaks lies from his father, the devil. Shall I behead him right now, my Lord?"*

"No," said the Mahdi. "I don't think he is lying about being a Zionist mole. I think he is telling the truth. Which means he is stalling for time. I think the Zionists are about to hit us. But Dr. Zandi here is trying to prevent us from using our trump card—trying, but failing. Tie him up, and chain him to the nozzle of Missile Four, along with Hamdi the betrayer. Let them both burn—now and forever."

JERUSALEM, ISRAEL

"Do it!" Naphtali ordered in an emergency conference call with the defense minister, Mossad chief, and IDF chief of staff. *"Do it now. Launch the attack. And may the God of our fathers have mercy on us all."*

"Yes, sir," Shimon said. "I am ordering our fighter jets into the air as we speak."

"And sound the rocket alarms all over Israel," Naphtali also ordered. "A firestorm is coming, and it cannot be stopped."

ROUTE 90, CENTRAL SYRIA

Fox was open to what David was sharing. Though he had been raised in northern California by two atheist parents, he said he'd always been curious about God and had read lots of books about religion over the years. He'd never been to a church except for a few weddings and funerals, but David was struck by his sincere heart. He was asking questions. He was trying to understand why Christ had to die on the cross and what it would mean in a practical way for him to "pick up his cross" and truly follow Jesus.

Crenshaw, on the other hand, not only didn't want to hear what David had to say, he was offended by the notion that he needed a savior. He insisted that they stay focused on their mission.

"You're not my priest," Crenshaw snapped. "Quit trying to be one."

"Nick, man, I'm not trying to be a pastor or priest," David replied. "I never went to a church either. My family isn't religious. I'm just saying, if we don't make it, I know beyond the shadow of a doubt where I'm going to be the moment I die. Do you?"

DAMASCUS, SYRIA

At Jazini's order, everyone raced into the fortified bunkers at the rear of the facility, far from the missiles and well out of danger. At the Mahdi's order, hundreds of missiles began to lift off all over Iran and Syria, screaming for Israel, all of them designed to create a blizzard of inbounds that would overwhelm the Israelis' ability to track them and shoot them all down.

All at once, the massive roof started retracting above them, and the countdown for these six missiles began.

"T minus ten . . . nine . . . eight . . ."

Esfahani held his breath as the moment of reckoning drew near.

ROUTE 90, CENTRAL SYRIA

David and his team were twisting and turning through mountain passes. They were steadily descending to the plains where the Syrian capital was nestled in the shadow of the Golan Heights. David slowed slightly to come around a particularly sharp curve. Then, as he cleared the rocky ridges and approached a straightaway along the top of a large hill, he accelerated again and passed a bus and an oil tanker, along with a large truck carrying crates of fruit.

DAMASCUS, SYRIA

". . . seven . . . six . . . five . . ."

The roof was completely open. Esfahani stared into the skies above and praised Allah for giving him the privilege of being part of this glorious rise of the Caliphate.

LANGLEY, VIRGINIA

Director Allen was still on the phone with the president when Tom Murray and Jack Zalinsky realized the Iranians and Syrians were launching a massive missile strike. At first count, the commander of the Global Ops Center counted 169 rockets and missiles lifting off or in the air, each and every one of them headed for Israel.

DAMASCUS, SYRIA

"... *four ... three ... two ... one ...*"

This was it. The missiles' engines roared to life. White-hot flames came rushing out of the nozzles below them, instantly incinerating all three men—one Syrian and two Iranians, all of whom Esfahani had once thought to be heroes.

The entire underground facility shuddered and quaked as the launchpads fell away and the Scuds began to lift off. Esfahani was beside himself with joy. The thought crossed his mind that he should turn and look at the faces of the Mahdi, the Ayatollah, and President Mustafa. Each was standing close beside him, and it would be fascinating, he thought, to see their reactions and compare them to his own. But he was mesmerized by the missiles beginning their launch. He simply couldn't pull his eyes off the sight of the fire and the smoke. It was such a beautiful, glorious sight, one he knew he would cherish forever.

"You see," said the Mahdi, "Zandi was a liar, and Allah hates liars—"

But then suddenly everything went white. The nuclear warhead in the nose cone of Missile Four detonated at an altitude of just five hundred yards. Temperatures surged into the millions of degrees. Everything and everyone on the Al-Mazzah base was instantly vaporized. The blast wave leveled all buildings and incinerated all life-forms for ten kilometers in every direction in a fraction of a second. Every bit of air and gas in the surrounding area was sucked into the center and erupted into a fireball as hot as the sun. The fireball roared across Damascus, scorching anything and everything that was not already dead, and as it shot into the air and expanded and cooled, the distinctive mushroom cloud of a nuclear detonation could be seen for hundreds of kilometers.

TEL AVIV, ISRAEL

Levi Shimon and Zvi Dayan sat in stunned horror. Every screen in the command center displaying satellite, drone, and radar feeds from the Syrian front suddenly went black. For a moment, Shimon feared that Tel Aviv had been hit with a nuclear weapon. But just as quickly the systems rebooted, and Shimon saw the sobering truth. It was Damascus, not Tel Aviv, that had just experienced a nuclear holocaust, but for the life of him Shimon's mind could not register how.

ROUTE 90, CENTRAL SYRIA

Without warning, the most intense white light David and his team had ever witnessed burst across the Syrian skyline. Instantly blinded and completely disoriented, David lost control of the car. He tried to slam on the brakes, but at the high speed at which they were racing, the car swerved violently, then ran off the left side of the road, careened down an embankment, and flipped six times before smashing upon the craggy rocks below.

LANGLEY, VIRGINIA

Jack Zalinsky was in shock. He stared at the screens in front of him. Both of the feeds from the Predators ended abruptly and did not come back. But from the Keyhole satellite feed, Zalinsky and his colleagues had watched the detonation in real time. They could see the mushroom cloud rising into the atmosphere. They were watching as the fireball annihilated the world's oldest continuously inhabited city. They just couldn't believe what they were witnessing.

There was no evidence that any Israeli missiles had reached Syria, much less Damascus. So Zalinsky was certain Naphtali hadn't yet ordered a nuclear strike against the Syrians. What then had happened? Had the Iranian nuke malfunctioned, and if so, how was that possible?

Behind him, he could hear President Jackson shouting at Director Allen over a speakerphone, *"What happened? What just happened?"* But Allen could not yet reply. He, too, was in shock.

For several minutes, Zalinsky and everyone else in the Global Operations Center just stared at the screens. They could see what was happening, but it still wasn't computing. None of it made any sense. And then Zalinsky thought of David and his team. He reached for one of the receivers on the bank of phones in front of him. He knew by now that David had lost his satphone during the gun battle at Dayr az-Zawr. So he speed-dialed Steve Fox's number. The phone rang once. Then five times. Then ten times and fifteen. But there was no answer.

He hung up and speed-dialed Nick Crenshaw's phone. He waited through five rings. Then ten, then fifteen and twenty. But no one answered that line either.

Panicked, he tried Fox's phone again. Then Crenshaw's. He called Eva and told her to stop everything and just keep redialing those two numbers every two minutes for the next hour. But no one answered.

The phones just rang and rang.

51

"Abort the strike order!" Naphtali ordered over his secure line to the IDF Operations Center. *"I repeat, abort the strike order."*

Dozens of Israeli missiles were already in the air, racing for Al-Mazzah and other key Syrian military bases, particularly those housing caches of chemical and biological weapons. Naphtali knew there was nothing he could do to bring those back. But he listened as Shimon immediately relayed the order to the chief of staff of the Israeli Air Force and the wave of fighter jets that were currently lifting off and en route to Syria were called back.

Naphtali couldn't fully conceive of what had just happened. He had confidence his team would eventually piece together the puzzle and figure it out. But for now his instincts told him to do everything in his power to avoid the charge by the international community that Israel had vaporized Damascus. Had he ordered a massive strike on Syria's military facilities? Absolutely. But he had not ordered the annihilation of an Arab capital, and he did not want the world to think he had. Israel was isolated enough. Neither he nor his people could afford to be charged with a crime such as this.

The Iranian and Syrian missiles were still inbound, however. Some of them were being shot down, but well over a hundred of them were hitting Israeli cities from Haifa to Beersheva. For some reason Jerusalem was being spared the deadly barrage, but at the moment that was little comfort. More than seven million Israelis were huddled in bomb shelters and wearing gas masks and riding out one of the most devastating attacks in the modern history of the Jewish State. Casualty projections from the latest strikes were expected to be high. Dayan feared more than 1,500 Jews and Arabs could die in these latest missile attacks. But Naphtali felt certain that an Israeli retaliation was out of the question. What more could they do to Syria than had already been done? The great and proud and ancient city of Damascus was no more. It had been wiped off the face of the map, never to rise again. More than two million Arab souls had perished in a matter of milliseconds. It was a tragedy of epic proportions, but it was a tragedy of Iran and Syria's own making. Naphtali had no reason to feel guilt, but he grieved nonetheless, and he wondered what all this would mean for the future of the Middle East.

To his astonishment, reports began to come in almost immediately from southern Lebanon and even from Gaza that the fighting had stopped. It wasn't clear whether the forces of Hezbollah and Hamas believed that Israel had just nuked Damascus, but Shimon had begun forwarding reports from IDF commanders in the field that as news of the destruction of Damascus spread, the Arab forces were going into shock. They weren't exactly laying down their arms, but they weren't using them either. They were disengaging from the Israelis and beginning to retreat.

"Our commanders want to know, should they continue to engage the enemy? Should they press the offense?" Shimon asked Naphtali.

The prime minister considered that for a moment, but in the end he said no. Iran and Syria had been dealt a death blow. The Twelfth Imam was now dead. The Ayatollah—Iran's Supreme Leader—was dead. So was Syrian president Mustafa and most of the Caliphate's top military leaders and political advisors. The heads of two snakes had been cut off.

Nothing in the region would ever be the same. Tehran, Naphtali believed, would never be in a position to fund and supply Hezbollah and Hamas again. Nor, clearly, would Damascus. The horror of what had just happened would take time to sink in fully, but Naphtali was willing to bet an enormous sum that as the flow of funds and weapons to these terrorist organizations dried up, so would their spirit and the threat they had once posed. Out of the fire and the smoke, a new world was being born, Naphtali realized, a world in which Israel's most dangerous enemies had just been dramatically neutralized in the blink of an eye.

OAKTON, VIRGINIA

It was cold and dark, and northern Virginia was being pounded by a torrential rainstorm. Najjar Malik had woken up several times throughout the night to immense claps of thunder that made the windows and the walls shake. But though the rain and the thunder would still not let up, now he woke to the sound of someone knocking on the bedroom door.

"Just a second," he said as he sat up, rubbed the sleep from his eyes, and tried to remember where he was and what time it was.

Najjar looked over at his beloved wife, Sheyda, snuggled up beside him, then at their baby nestled in the crib beside their bed. And then it all came back. He was once again in the custody of the CIA. He was back at the safe house from which he had escaped. There were more armed guards in the house now. There were bars on the bedroom windows and more surveillance cameras in the hallways and in the trees front and back, allowing the Agency to make certain none of them tried to slip out of their grasp again. It was a prison, basically, but at least he was finally back together with his family.

Najjar forced himself out of the warm bed, wearing only a pair of boxer shorts. He threw on some blue jeans and a T-shirt and opened the door. His mother-in-law, Farah, bundled in a thick blue bathrobe, was standing there looking quite anxious.

"What is it?" he asked. "What's wrong?"

"You have a visitor," she said. "Someone from the Agency. I think something is wrong."

Najjar suppressed a smile. Of course their visitor was from the Agency. All their visitors were from the Agency. No one else knew where they were, and some of the people who were looking for them wanted them dead. Najjar nodded to the armed guard in the hallway, then rubbed his eyes again and headed downstairs, saying good morning to the guard at the bottom of the stairs as well as the two in the kitchen.

To his astonishment, Eva Fischer was standing there, looking pale and stricken.

"Agent Fischer, what a surprise," he said. "Are you all right?"

"Not exactly," she said. "Can we sit down and talk?"

"Of course," he said, then turned to Farah. "Would you mind making us some coffee?"

"I already have a pot brewing," she replied. "I'll bring it over when it's done."

Najjar and Eva went into the family room. She took a seat on the couch. He sat down in a large, overstuffed chair.

"What is it?" he asked. "What's brought you all the way out here to see me?"

"There's been an explosion," Eva began. "A detonation, actually."

Najjar tensed, not wanting to hear what was coming next. But Eva told him anyway. She could not share classified details, of course, but she told him what was being reported on the news. The Agency had denied the Maliks access to television, radio, newspapers, magazines, and the Internet. Until his debriefings and the criminal investigation into his recent activities were completed by the Agency and the FBI, the U.S. government didn't want Najjar or his family to have contact with the outside world or much knowledge of it either. So this was the first Najjar had heard of the Damascus tragedy.

"The devastation is beyond anything you or I can comprehend," Eva said. "Damascus is no more."

Najjar sat for a moment without speaking, trying to process all that he was hearing.

"So," he said quietly at last, "the prophecies came true."

"What do you mean?"

"The prophecies—you know, in the Bible, the ones in Isaiah and Jeremiah that say in the last days Damascus will be obliterated as a city—they just came true."

Eva clearly had no idea what he was talking about, and she asked him to explain. He did so, but he had questions of his own. Having been one of Iran's top nuclear scientists for years, Najjar asked for more technical details about what the Agency had ascertained about the cause of the blast. Eva bent the rules a bit and told him what she knew. She made it clear that there was no evidence this was an Israeli nuclear strike. Rather, she said, it appeared that the warhead detonated moments after the Scud-C lifted off. She gave a few more details. It wasn't much, but it was enough for Najjar to posit a theory.

"This was deliberate," he told her.

"What do you mean?"

"Nuclear warheads don't detonate during launch unless the man who built them is either an idiot or a suicide bomber," Najjar said. "None of the scientists on Dr. Saddaji's team were idiots. They were brilliant, brilliant men. But none of them besides Tariq Khan had been recruited by Saddaji to be part of building bombs."

"So what are you saying?" Eva asked.

"I'm saying one of those men knew he had the chance to take out the entire Iranian and Syrian leadership in one shot and stop the Mahdi's nuclear weapons nightmare at the same time," Najjar said. "And he took it."

It was a radical theory—one Eva said the top officials at the CIA had not even considered in these early hours. She pursued it for several minutes, peppering Najjar with one question after another until Najjar abruptly changed the topic.

"So does this mean Reza Tabrizi will be coming home soon?" he asked. "The man saved my life and my family's lives. I would very much like to see him again. I would like to say thank you."

The question hung in the air for a while. Eva looked away and said nothing. Farah came into the room and set a tray before them with two mugs of hot black coffee, along with a small pitcher of creamer, a bowl of sugar, and some spoons.

"Is that not possible?" Najjar now asked. "Is that against the rules?"

"No, it's not that," Eva said finally. "It's just . . ."

She didn't finish the sentence.

"What?" Najjar asked. "If it's not against the rules, then what?"

Eva picked up one of the mugs and took several sips. "Najjar, I'm not sure how to say this the best way," she began. "So I'm just going to be straight with you. Reza is . . . I'm afraid Reza is missing, and . . ."

"And what?" Najjar pressed.

"And presumed dead."

Najjar gasped, as did his mother-in-law. She knew all the stories of what Reza Tabrizi had done for them. Indeed, she—like all of them— had been praying night and day for Reza's soul as well as his safety.

Just then Sheyda came downstairs, still wearing her pajamas but wrapped in a thick gray sweatshirt. "What happened to Reza?" she asked, coming around the corner and taking a seat next to Eva. "I don't understand. Where is he now?"

Eva greeted Sheyda and reminded them that there were some things she wasn't authorized to say. "What I can tell you is that he and his team were hunting two Iranian warheads that the Israelis missed in their initial air strikes," she said. "The hunt took them out of Iran and into Syria. They were headed right into Damascus when the missile lifted off and exploded. We were tracking his team with a drone. But when the explosion happened, we lost contact with the drone and with Reza."

"But he could still be alive, right?" Najjar asked.

"Anything's possible," Eva said. "But I . . ." She began to choke up.

Farah ran to get a box of tissues and gave several to Eva, who dabbed her eyes and apologized for her lack of professionalism.

"Anything's possible," she said again. "But I wouldn't hold your breath, Najjar. As I told you, the devastation is beyond belief. We've never seen anything like this in the history of the world. Believe me, you don't want to see the satellite photos. It's . . . well . . . I don't see how anyone could have survived."

The room was quiet for several minutes, and then Sheyda asked Eva a question. "You two were very close, weren't you?"

Eva was clearly caught off guard by the question, but she chose to answer it anyway. "We'd become good friends, yes," she said.

"Just friends?" Sheyda asked, but Najjar reprimanded her and quickly apologized.

"It's okay," Eva replied. "Your wife is a very perceptive woman. The truth is, I guess I was hoping for something to develop between us. But it never did. And even if he had lived, honestly, I don't think it ever would have happened."

"Why not?" Sheyda asked, more gently this time.

Eva sighed and dabbed her eyes with a tissue again. "He didn't love me," she said, her bottom lip quivering. "He loved someone else."

EPILOGUE

Looking out over the twenty young faces in her classroom, Marseille Harper knew she had done the right thing coming home to Portland. She needed some semblance of normalcy, needed a sweet routine to make it possible to keep breathing. Her heart and mind had taken so many turns, felt so many blows in the past two weeks. It was a miracle she wasn't under the covers of her bed, just weeping or numb. Of course, there had been several nights since her return to her responsibilities in the classroom when she had sobbed herself to sleep. She thought of the psalmist who wrote about his tears being his food, and she felt like a kindred spirit had written that especially for her.

The obliteration of the Syrian capital and the deaths of more than two million people, including the Twelfth Imam and the top leaders of both Syria and Iran, had dominated the news and everyone's conversations all week. The utter horror of it all had deeply penetrated the culture, Marseille had noticed. People talked about it constantly, always in hushed, somber tones. Conversations on completely unrelated topics seemed to be more subdued since the detonation as well. Even the children were asking questions about what had happened in the Middle East. *Where was Damascus? Where was Syria? What was a mushroom cloud? Why did Mommy and Daddy seem so quiet, so sad?*

In a way, being asked these questions helped Marseille feel needed, like at least she was helping her little friends process the world-shaking event in Damascus in a way that was simple and brief. The hugs of the children were like a balm.

On Monday morning, she had been waiting at Hancock Field in Syracuse, ready for the early-morning flight back to Portland. She had wanted to stay in Syracuse and help the Walshes as much as she could after the news of Lexi and Chris's deaths. But she had a job to do back home. She'd signed a contract. She'd given her word, and she had to keep it. At least Lexi's aunt lived nearby and seemed very capable of assisting the Walshes in their planning for the funeral arrangements. Lexi and Chris had a strong church community, and Marseille knew meals would be brought and friends would be there to listen and cry and pray.

She remembered reaching her gate at the airport and sitting down with a cup of coffee to read her Scripture passages for the day. She had just started to pray about the verses in front of her when a wave of gasps and shock moved through the atmosphere at the United gate. People were suddenly standing and staring at the television monitors and shaking their heads. They were making phone calls and looking wide-eyed at one another. Marseille had not been sitting where she could see any of the TVs, but when she walked to the nearest monitor, she found a CNN breaking news story and a single, horrifying image—a mushroom cloud over Damascus.

She had barely been able to believe what she was seeing. Her mind had been flooded with questions. *How had it happened? What did it mean? Was David safe, or had he been killed in the explosion?* Though Tom Murray had told her only the day before that David was alive and well and doing his job—a job she had assumed was in Iran—she wondered if he could have been in Syria when this happened. If so, had he died instantly and painlessly, near ground zero of the blast? Or was he burned and dying a slow death somewhere on the outskirts of Damascus?

Marseille tried to push such thoughts out of her head. She wanted to believe David was in Iran. But the doubts kept creeping in. Maybe he had been trying to stop this very thing from happening. If he was doing that, then maybe he had been right in the middle of it. She remembered one of the United reps calling her and her fellow passengers to board their flight at that moment, and she had forced herself to put one foot in front of the other. She told herself she would wait for Dr. Shirazi to call. No news was good news, right? Then she wondered if maybe she should call Mr. Murray again. Or maybe he would call her?

She desperately wanted to believe that David had been in Tehran or some secret location far away from the nuclear blast, but over the last few nights as she cried herself to sleep about Lexi and Chris, she had shed many tears over David, too. Where was he right now?

Thankfully, her class didn't know about Lexi and Chris and of course had no knowledge of David. She could mourn her friends in private, in prayer, and wait for God's comfort, if not his answers to why all this had happened. One thing was clear, at least. She'd been praying and study-ing and trying to understand for weeks if the Twelfth Imam was the Antichrist who would come and rule the world in the end of days as the Bible foretold. But he was gone now. He was not the Antichrist—not the final one, at least. Marseille wasn't sure if that made her feel better or worse. But at least she knew for certain.

Tomorrow, she would head back into sorrow, flying to Syracuse early in the morning for the Saturday-afternoon memorial service of the newlywed couple she still had trouble believing were really gone. Then she would fly straight back to the West Coast early Monday morning, missing only one more day of class and, hopefully, bringing this chapter of tragedy to an end. It would be an incredibly fast trip, one she wasn't sure she would handle well emotionally or physically, but she had to be there.

She was still trying to seek God's wisdom about whether she should visit Dr. Shirazi again while she was in Syracuse. She felt she should, but it would be so painful. And what right did she have to keep attaching herself to that family? She would already be involved in the Vandermarks' memorial—only weeks after she'd been in their wedding, only a week after she'd helped with Mrs. Shirazi's memorial, only months after her own father's memorial . . . No, she couldn't let herself start that line of thinking. It was all too much.

She looked out at the heads bent over their chapter books. She was so proud of them and satisfied to see their reading progress since the school year started. She prayed that each of them would someday read the greatest Book of all and learn about the character of the heavenly Father who loved each one of them. She knew they would need his wisdom to navigate a world that seemed to lack any sense these days.

The bell rang to bring the school day to a close, and the children packed up their backpacks and headed for their buses. Marseille hoped most, if not all, would be greeted by their moms at home with cookies and hugs. She hoped these little dear ones were still enjoying the simple innocent pleasures of childhood, despite the sad news that just kept on coming from the Middle East. Couldn't they be shielded from it for a while longer?

Getting into her pale-blue VW bug, she paused before heading to the homestead her father had bought on Sauvie Island, situated in the middle of the Columbia River about ten miles northwest of downtown Portland. She tried to thank God for the events of the last weeks. She thanked him that she had gotten to see David one last time after all those years, thanked him for the chance to make some things clear that had been left unsaid. She thanked him for the opportunity to serve the Shirazi family in a time of great sorrow and for the shared secret she now kept with David's dad. She thanked the Lord that Lexi had known love, had known Jesus, had enjoyed a beautiful wedding, and had seen her dream of visiting the Holy Land fulfilled. Now she was seeing Jesus face-to-face, and this was another reason to thank him.

Marseille started the VW and connected her iPhone to the car's stereo system.

She sang along for a few minutes and resonated with the lyrics, straight from Psalm 103: "Bless the Lord, O my soul." The song spoke of worshiping God from morning till evening, and as she sang, she offered her own sacrifice of praise, feeling it change everything in her heart, making it possible to hope, if not to smile. She was grateful that God was teaching her how to face the shock of searing losses by relying on him. She didn't know how people outside of Christ could keep going.

She drove onto the main street of her little town, contemplating dinner. Should she pick up Thai food or some Italian? But she quickly dismissed the thought. She'd been eating cereal for the past few nights and still had no stomach for much else.

The fog hugging the streets and lampposts made the shops seem snuggled in for the evening, and she looked forward to one more night in her own bed before she got on another plane. Coming around the corner to the quiet neighborhood where she'd lived with her dad and grandmother, she took in the front porches and the toys the kids had left along the sidewalk. It was a nice place to come home to. But her train of thought ended there as she saw a man sitting on the front porch of her house.

She almost lost control of the car and slammed into the garage door as she turned into the driveway. It wasn't possible—it wasn't possible at all. But there he was. David Shirazi was smiling at her from her front steps. He was bundled in a warm coat and hat. His arm looked like it was in a cast, and his face was covered in scars. But he was there, waiting for her. She wasn't sure she had the strength to open her door, but it was okay because he was walking over to her car to open it for her. She looked through the rapidly fogging window, and suddenly the door was open and she was in his arms. She buried her face in his shoulder and began to sob, and he held her as though his life depended on it.

She wasn't alone in her tears. David seemed only slightly embarrassed by his, and they steadied each other as they walked up the steps to the house quietly and got out of the cold and into the warmth of the old-fashioned front room. She didn't want to speak and break the moment, so she just sat down on the couch and expected him to sit beside her. But he didn't sit. He lowered himself to his knee, not without a slight wince of pain but with a big smile. He took a small, carved wooden box from his coat pocket and cleared his throat, thick with emotion.

"Marseille Harper, by God's grace—his amazing grace alone—I have survived all that has happened in the past few days and weeks. I believe I know why God gave me a second chance at life. To come here and be with you. And I am here now to tell you that I have loved you since I learned to love at all. I want you to know—I need you to know—that I can only love you because the love of Jesus Christ now lives in me. I am his child. I've given my life to him, and he's changing me day by day. And I believe he has given me the honor of serving you for the rest of our lives, if you will have me. I love you so much. Marseille, will you marry me?"

She couldn't believe her ears, and yet at the same time it seemed exactly right, as if her heavenly Father had written the most beautiful and miraculous story for her, and David was reading right from the script. And then she knew that was exactly what was happening. The author and perfecter of her faith had created a glorious scene, and this was her cue to walk onstage and answer with all her heart.

"Yes, David, yes—I love you, and I am yours."

The rest of the evening was like a dream. David told her about racing toward Damascus when the bomb detonated. He told her about losing control of the car in the blinding flash, though he thanked God they weren't close enough to be affected in any other way. He described crashing down the hillside and the death of one of his two teammates in the crash. He explained how he and his one surviving colleague had somehow made it back up the ridge to the highway, despite their many injuries. Eventually they had acquired a car and driven to a remote place where they could be picked up by American special forces and taken back to the United States.

As they talked, she made a pot of coffee while David built a roaring fire in the fireplace. Marseille kept asking questions, and David told as much of the story as he was able. She sat amazed to hear how Najjar Malik had come to Christ and how he'd wanted to defect from the Iranian regime. He briefly told her of his role in helping Najjar and his family get out of Iran and come to the U.S. She was delighted by the story of how Najjar had escaped the custody of his CIA handlers and how God had used him to preach the gospel to millions in Iran and the Muslim world. Now, David said, Najjar had been returned to the care of the Agency but also reunited with his family.

Then she marveled as David explained how an old, blind friend had opened David's eyes to the truth about Jesus.

David explained how he'd called his father immediately upon escaping from Syria and how Jack Zalinsky had helped him get to Syracuse to see his father within twenty-four hours of being extracted from the war zone before being treated for his injuries. He described what it meant to him to give his father a bear hug and to be in the warmth and safety of his own childhood home. Though he and his father had spoken first of David's mom, the memorial service, and the well-being of David's brothers, the conversation had quickly turned to Marseille. David was deeply moved by the sacrificial love that his father said she had shown the family, how she had stayed and served. He was stunned but thrilled that in God's providence he had allowed Marseille to know his secrets and to be proud of him. And when he had left Syracuse early Friday morning to fly to Portland, he had carried with him not only his father's joyful blessing but his mother's diamond engagement ring as well.

Though David's face had several deep gashes that had been stitched up, and though he suffered from multiple dark bruises and a compound fracture in one of his strong arms, he was sitting before her truly and completely alive. They now shared the greatest Love, and through him they could share a lifetime of loving each other.

Marseille had so many more questions. She wished she could hear every detail about his life since they had been together so briefly in Syracuse. She wondered what life lay before them, what would come next. But instead of asking questions, she simply laid her head on David's chest. She looked at the engagement ring on her finger and said right out loud, "Bless the Lord, O my soul."

ACKNOWLEDGMENTS

By God's grace, I continue to be blessed to work with such a great publisher. Very special thanks to all the team at Tyndale House, including Mark Taylor, Jeff Johnson, Ron Beers, Karen Watson, Jeremy Taylor, Jan Stob, Cheryl Kerwin, and Dean Renninger (for his continually wonderful cover designs).

Thanks to Scott Miller, my friend and literary agent at Trident Media Group.

Thanks to my loving family: my mom and dad, Len and Mary Jo Rosenberg; June "Bubbe" Meyers; the entire Meyers family; the Rebeizes; the Scomas; and the Urbanskis. Thanks, as well, to Edward and Kailea Hunt, Tim and Carolyn Lugbill, Steve and Barb Klemke, Fred and Sue Schwien, Tom and Sue Yancy, Jeremy and Angie Grafman, Nancy Pierce, Jeff and Naomi Cuozzo, Lance and Angie Emma, Lucas and Erin Edwards, Renae and Gordon Debever, William and Mary Agius, Chung and Farah Woo, Indira Koshy, Jay and Suzi Koshy, and all our teammates and allies who work with or for The Joshua Fund and November Communications, Inc.

Most of all, thanks to my sweet and wonderful wife, Lynn, and to our four wonderful sons and prayer warriors, Caleb, Jacob, Jonah, and Noah. Can't wait to see where this adventure leads next!